Lincoln Peirce

BiG NATE

WHAT COULD POSSIBLY GO WRONG?

WITHDRAWN

HARPER

An Imprint of HarperCollinsPublishers

MRS. GODFREY TO THE RESCUE

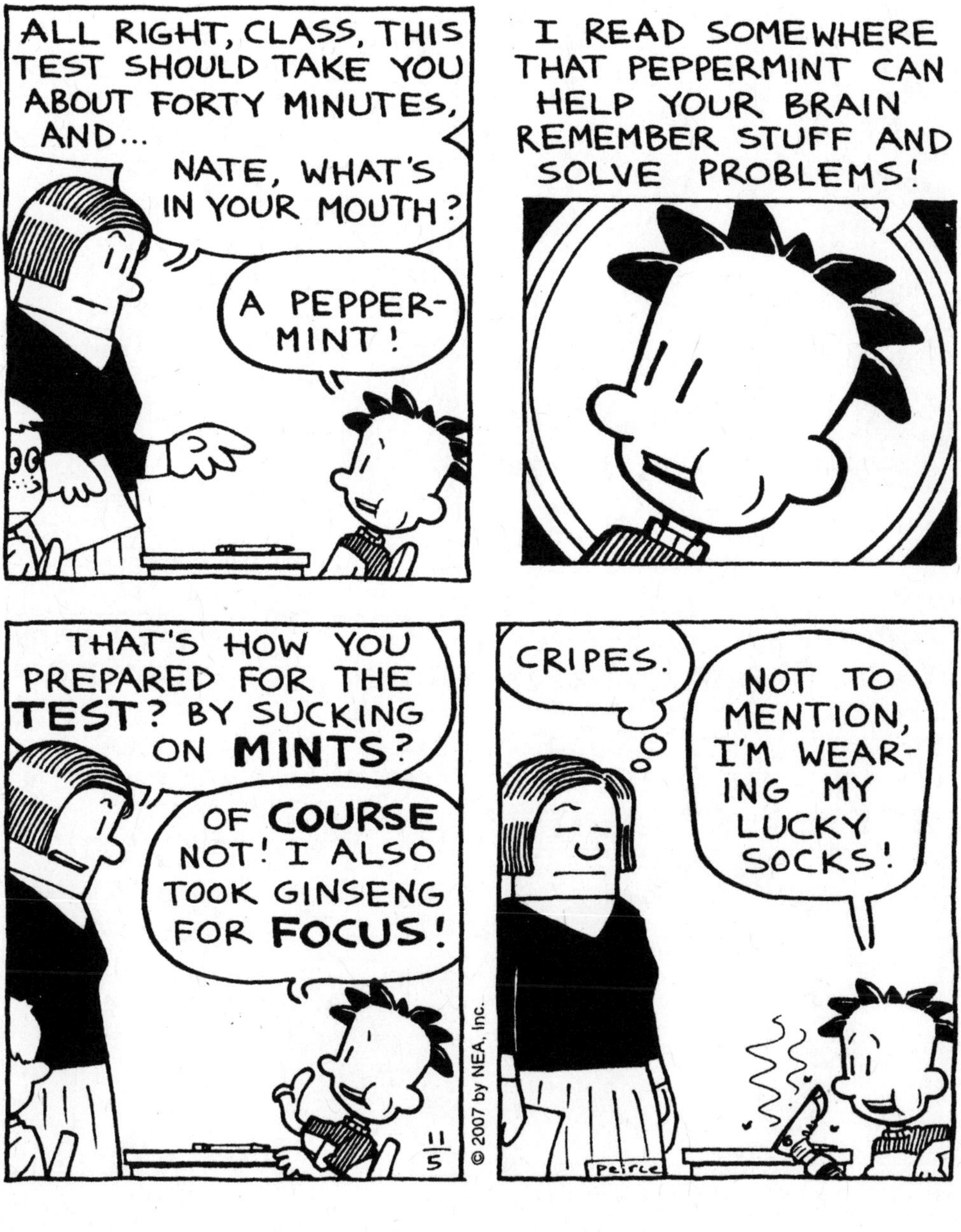
ALL RIGHT, CLASS, THIS TEST SHOULD TAKE YOU ABOUT FORTY MINUTES, AND...
NATE, WHAT'S IN YOUR MOUTH?
A PEPPERMINT!
I READ SOMEWHERE THAT PEPPERMINT CAN HELP YOUR BRAIN REMEMBER STUFF AND SOLVE PROBLEMS!
THAT'S HOW YOU PREPARED FOR THE TEST? BY SUCKING ON MINTS?
OF COURSE NOT! I ALSO TOOK GINSENG FOR FOCUS!
© 2007 by NEA, Inc.
11/5
CRIPES.
NOT TO MENTION, I'M WEARING MY LUCKY SOCKS!
Peirce

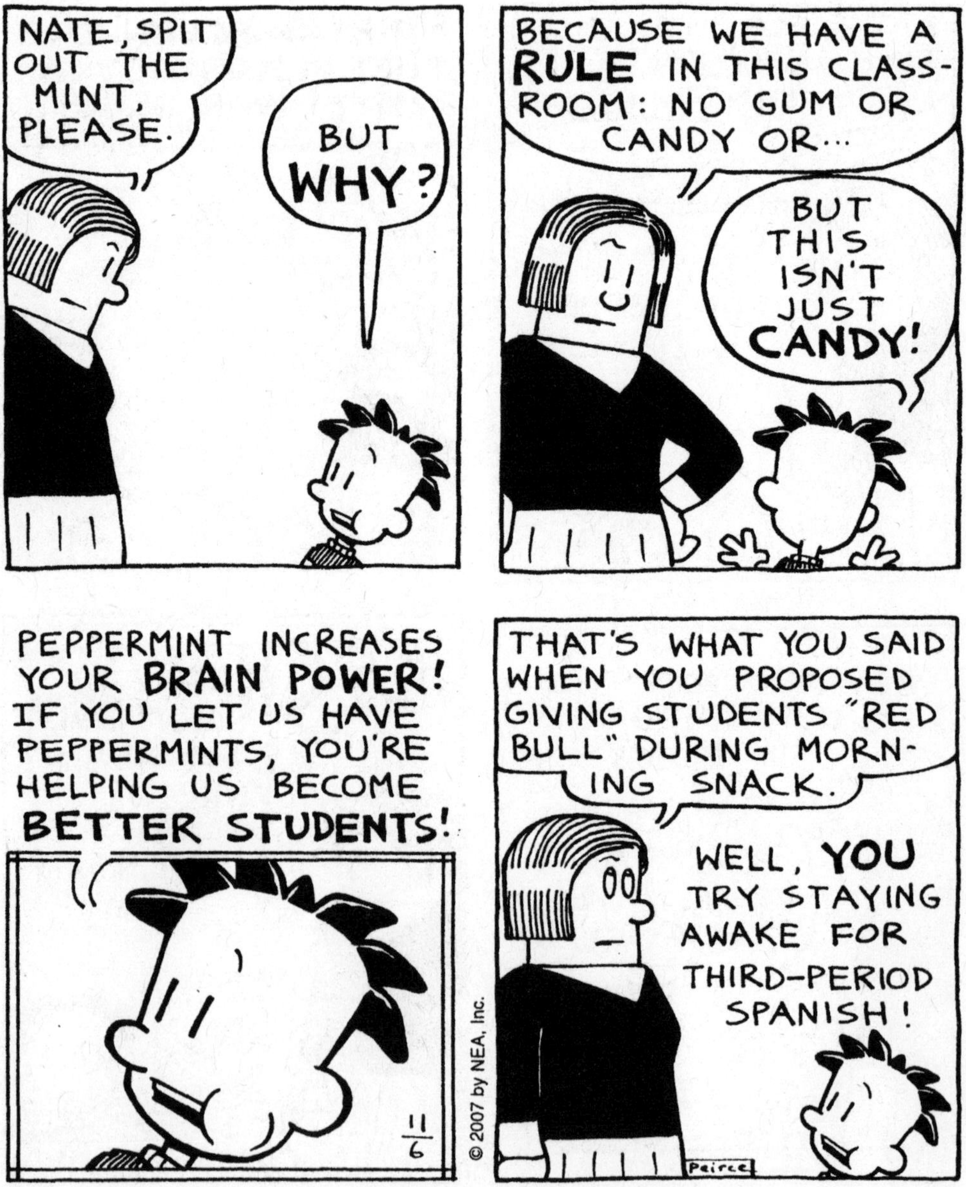
NATE, SPIT OUT THE MINT, PLEASE.
BUT **WHY**?
BECAUSE WE HAVE A **RULE** IN THIS CLASSROOM: NO GUM OR CANDY OR...
BUT THIS ISN'T JUST **CANDY**!
PEPPERMINT INCREASES YOUR **BRAIN POWER**! IF YOU LET US HAVE PEPPERMINTS, YOU'RE HELPING US BECOME **BETTER STUDENTS**!
11/6
© 2007 by NEA, Inc.
THAT'S WHAT YOU SAID WHEN YOU PROPOSED GIVING STUDENTS "RED BULL" DURING MORNING SNACK.
WELL, **YOU** TRY STAYING AWAKE FOR THIRD-PERIOD SPANISH!
Peirce

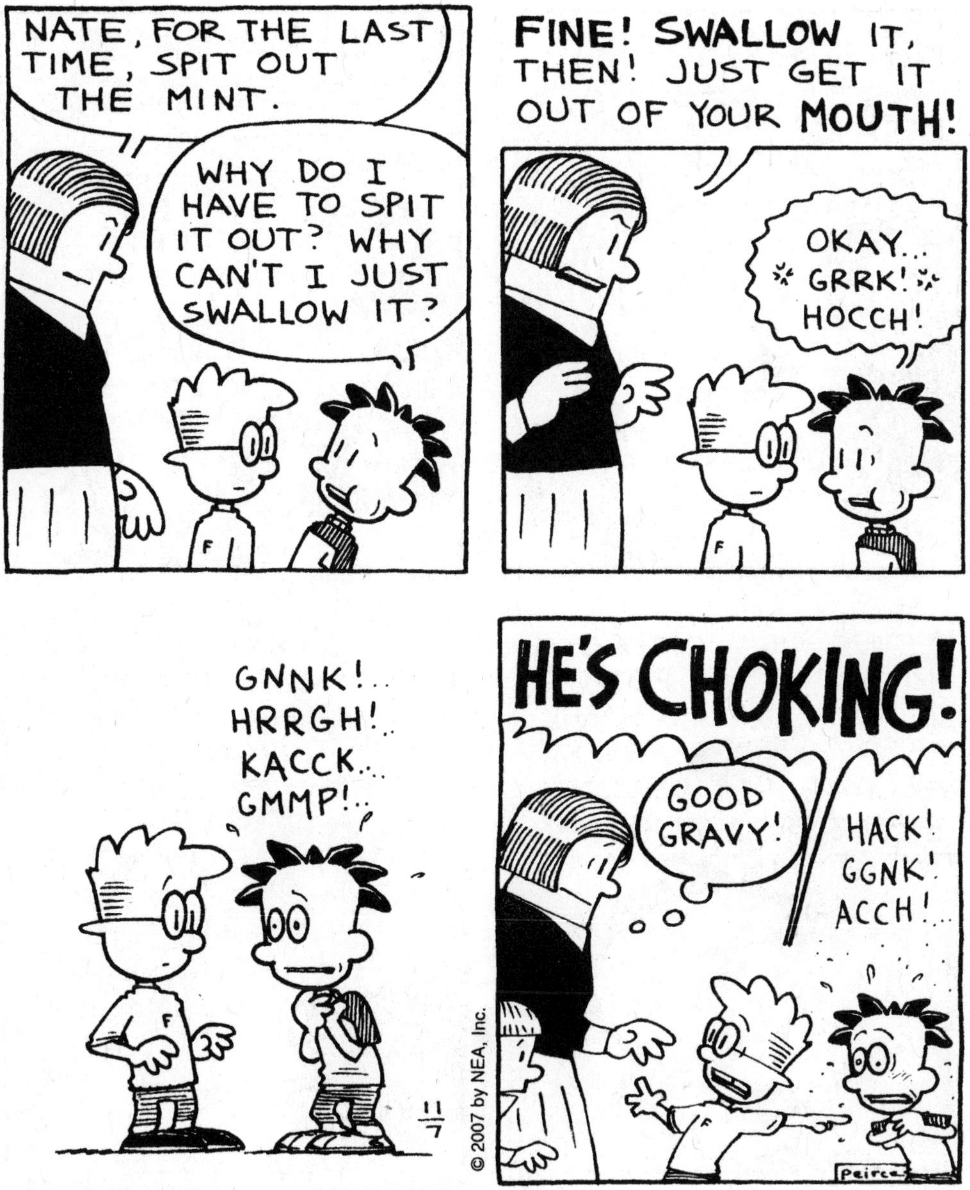
NATE, FOR THE LAST TIME, SPIT OUT THE MINT.
WHY DO I HAVE TO SPIT IT OUT? WHY CAN'T I JUST SWALLOW IT?
FINE! SWALLOW IT, THEN! JUST GET IT OUT OF YOUR MOUTH!
OKAY... GRRK! HOCCH!
GNNK!.. HRRGH!.. KACCK... GMMP!..
11/7
HE'S CHOKING!
GOOD GRAVY!
HACK! GGNK! ACCH!...
Peirce

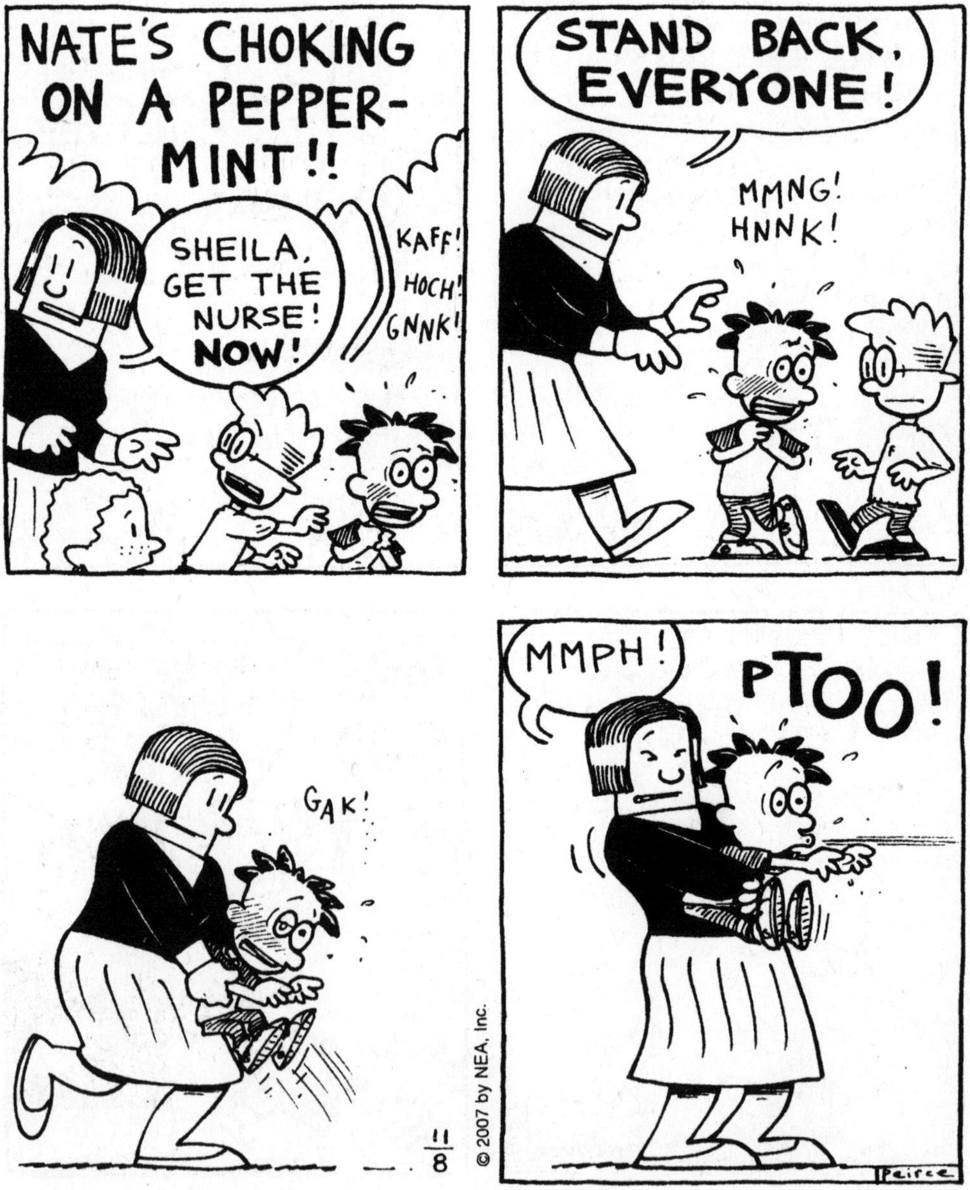
NATE'S CHOKING ON A PEPPER-MINT!!
SHEILA, GET THE NURSE! NOW!
KAFF! HOCH! GNNK!
STAND BACK, EVERYONE!
MMNG! HNNK!
GAK!
11/8
© 2007 by NEA, Inc.
MMPH!
PTOO!
Peirce

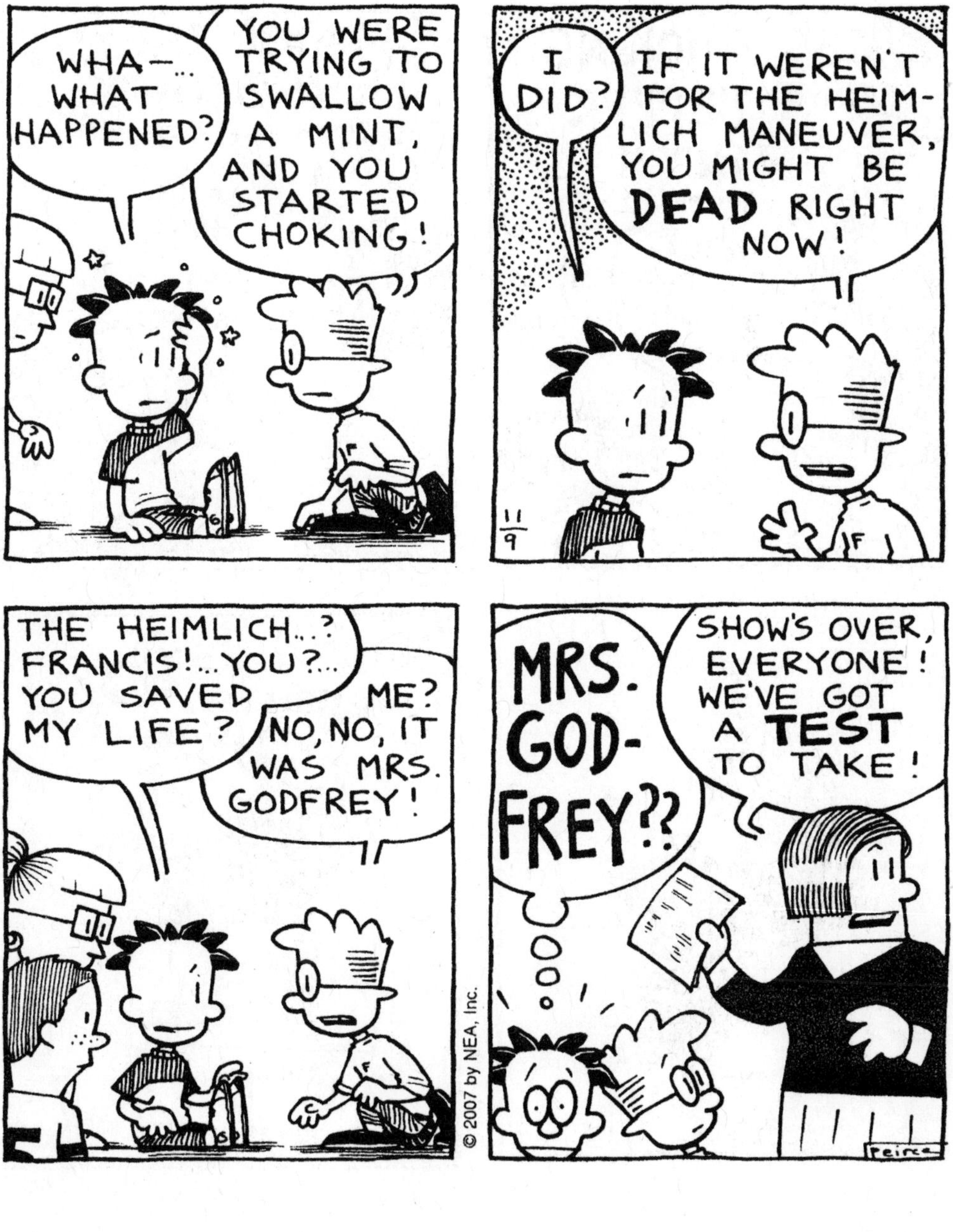
WHA—... WHAT HAPPENED?
YOU WERE TRYING TO SWALLOW A MINT, AND YOU STARTED CHOKING!
I DID?
IF IT WEREN'T FOR THE HEIM-LICH MANEUVER, YOU MIGHT BE DEAD RIGHT NOW!
11/9
THE HEIMLICH...? FRANCIS!...YOU?... YOU SAVED MY LIFE?
ME? NO, NO, IT WAS MRS. GODFREY!
MRS. GOD-FREY??
SHOW'S OVER, EVERYONE! WE'VE GOT A TEST TO TAKE!
peirce

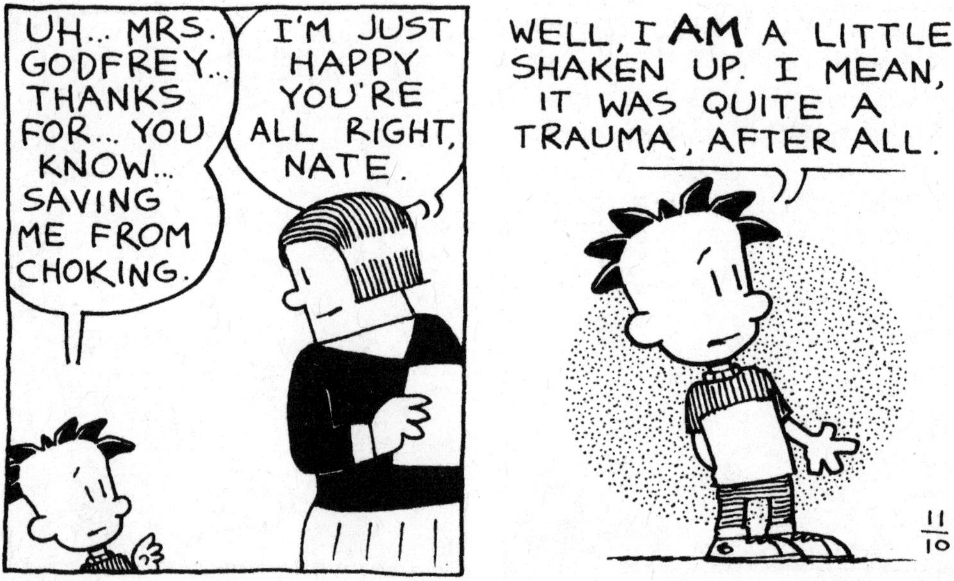
UH... MRS. GODFREY... THANKS FOR... YOU KNOW... SAVING ME FROM CHOKING.
I'M JUST HAPPY YOU'RE ALL RIGHT, NATE.
WELL, I AM A LITTLE SHAKEN UP. I MEAN, IT WAS QUITE A TRAUMA, AFTER ALL.
11/10

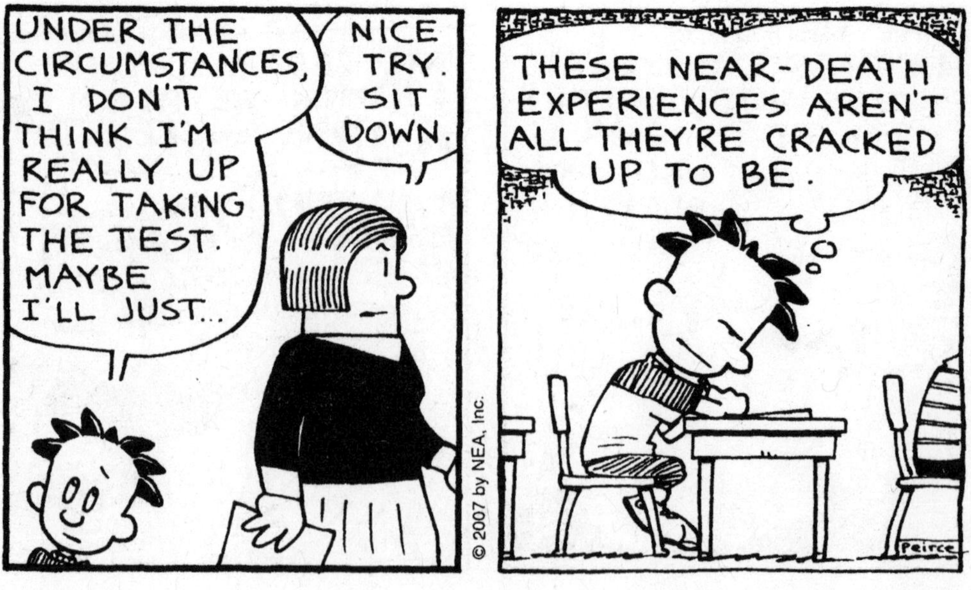
UNDER THE CIRCUMSTANCES, I DON'T THINK I'M REALLY UP FOR TAKING THE TEST. MAYBE I'LL JUST...
NICE TRY. SIT DOWN.
THESE NEAR-DEATH EXPERIENCES AREN'T ALL THEY'RE CRACKED UP TO BE.
Peirce

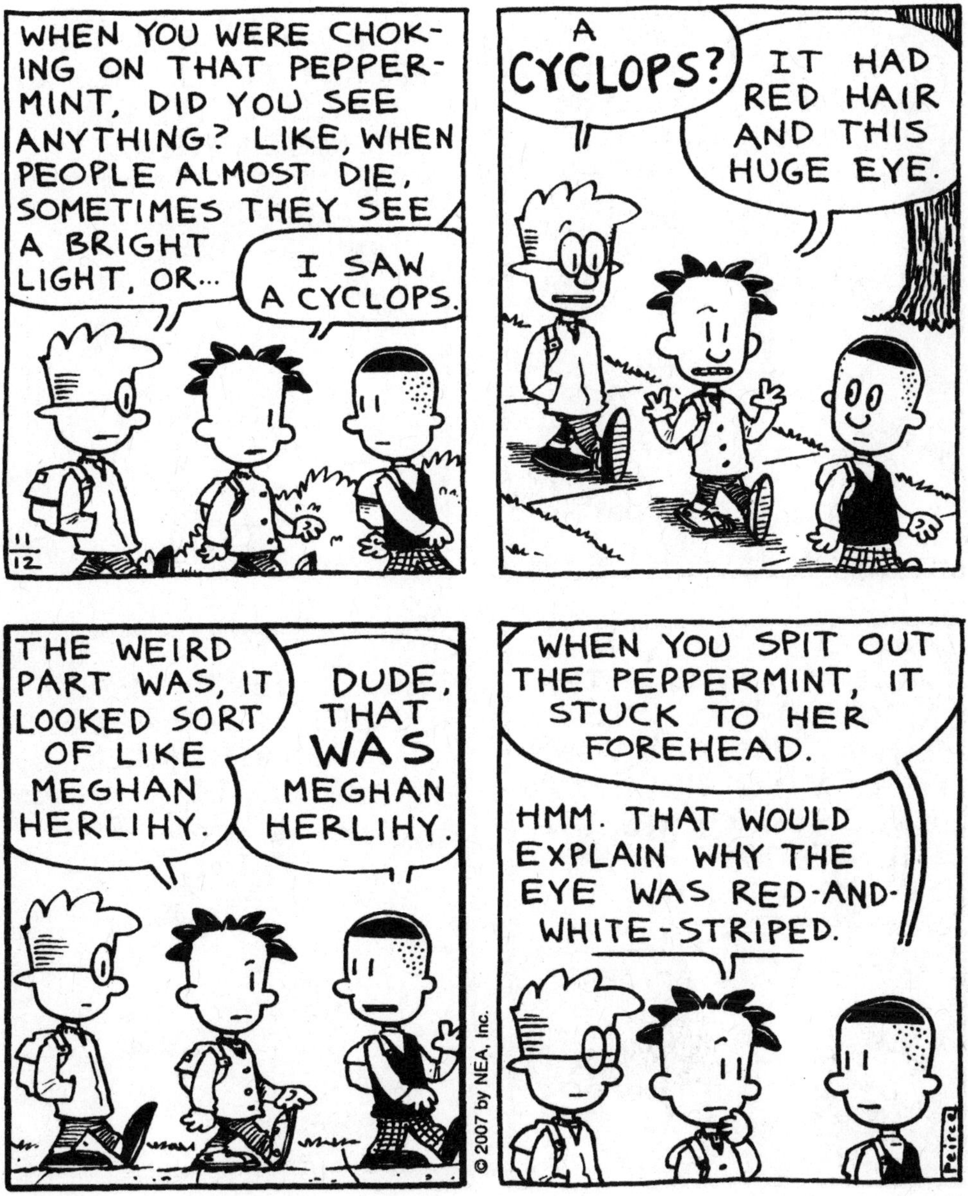
WHEN YOU WERE CHOKING ON THAT PEPPERMINT, DID YOU SEE ANYTHING? LIKE, WHEN PEOPLE ALMOST DIE, SOMETIMES THEY SEE A BRIGHT LIGHT, OR...
I SAW A CYCLOPS.
11/12
A CYCLOPS?
IT HAD RED HAIR AND THIS HUGE EYE.
THE WEIRD PART WAS, IT LOOKED SORT OF LIKE MEGHAN HERLIHY.
DUDE, THAT WAS MEGHAN HERLIHY.
© 2007 by NEA, Inc.
WHEN YOU SPIT OUT THE PEPPERMINT, IT STUCK TO HER FOREHEAD.
HMM. THAT WOULD EXPLAIN WHY THE EYE WAS RED-AND-WHITE-STRIPED.
Peirce

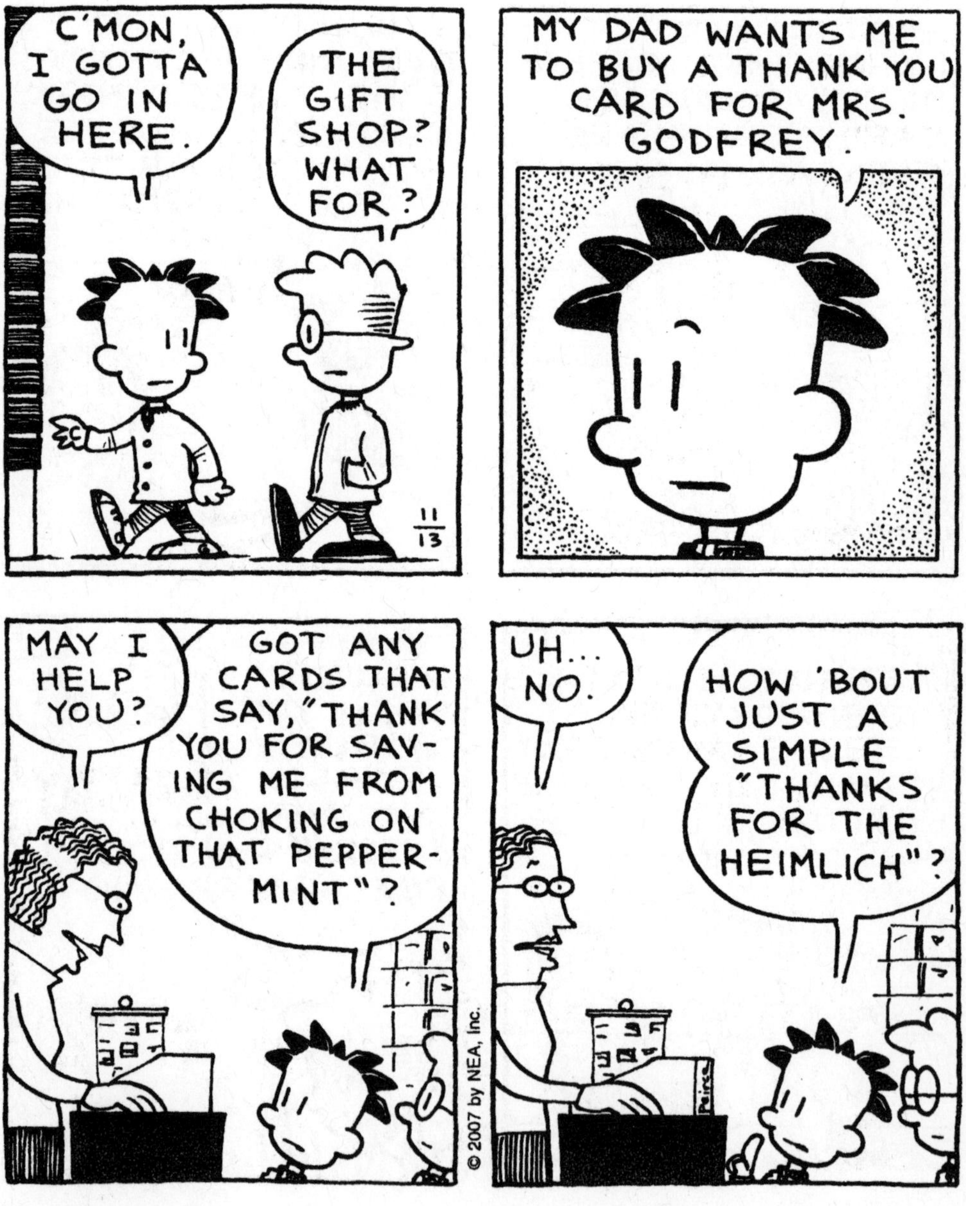
C'MON, I GOTTA GO IN HERE.
THE GIFT SHOP? WHAT FOR?
11/13
MY DAD WANTS ME TO BUY A THANK YOU CARD FOR MRS. GODFREY.
MAY I HELP YOU?
GOT ANY CARDS THAT SAY, "THANK YOU FOR SAVING ME FROM CHOKING ON THAT PEPPERMINT"?
© 2007 by NEA, Inc.
UH... NO.
HOW 'BOUT JUST A SIMPLE "THANKS FOR THE HEIMLICH"?
Peirce

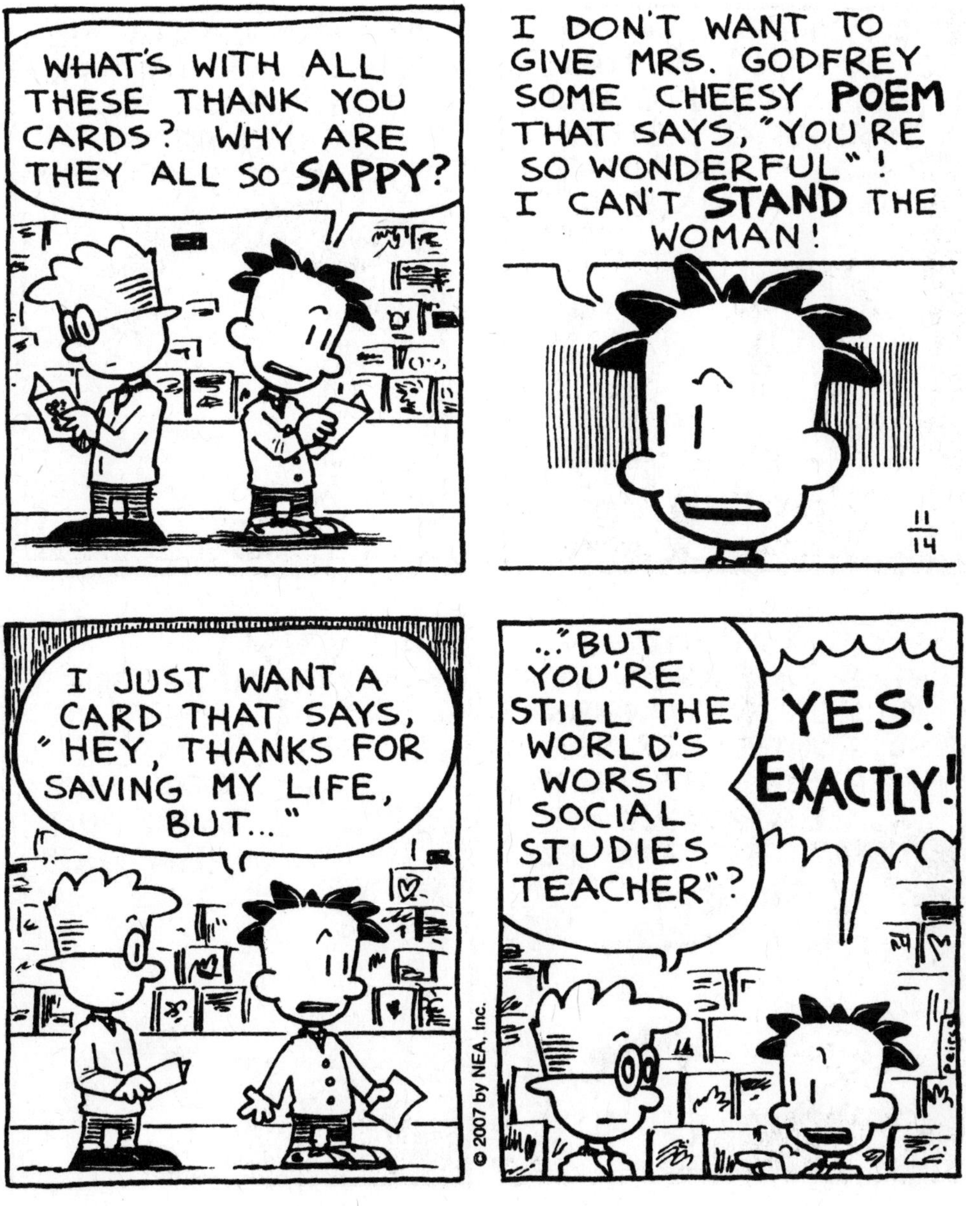
WHAT'S WITH ALL THESE THANK YOU CARDS? WHY ARE THEY ALL SO **SAPPY?**
I DON'T WANT TO GIVE MRS. GODFREY SOME CHEESY **POEM** THAT SAYS, "YOU'RE SO WONDERFUL"! I CAN'T **STAND** THE WOMAN!
11/14
I JUST WANT A CARD THAT SAYS, "HEY, THANKS FOR SAVING MY LIFE, BUT..."
...BUT YOU'RE STILL THE WORLD'S WORST SOCIAL STUDIES TEACHER"?
YES! EXACTLY!
Peirce
© 2007 by NEA, Inc.

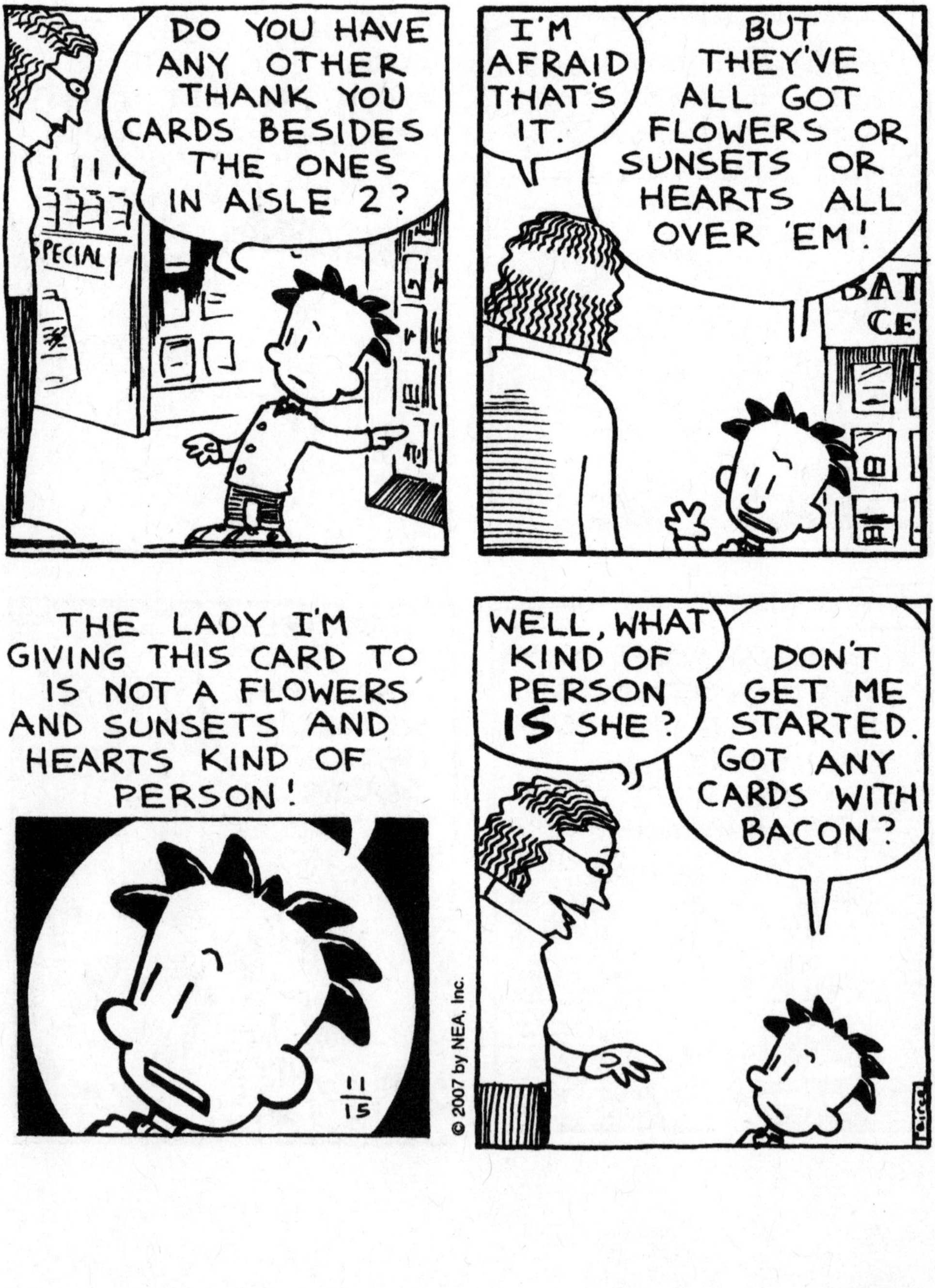
DO YOU HAVE ANY OTHER THANK YOU CARDS BESIDES THE ONES IN AISLE 2?
SPECIAL
I'M AFRAID THAT'S IT.
BUT THEY'VE ALL GOT FLOWERS OR SUNSETS OR HEARTS ALL OVER 'EM!
THE LADY I'M GIVING THIS CARD TO IS NOT A FLOWERS AND SUNSETS AND HEARTS KIND OF PERSON!
11/15
WELL, WHAT KIND OF PERSON IS SHE?
DON'T GET ME STARTED. GOT ANY CARDS WITH BACON?

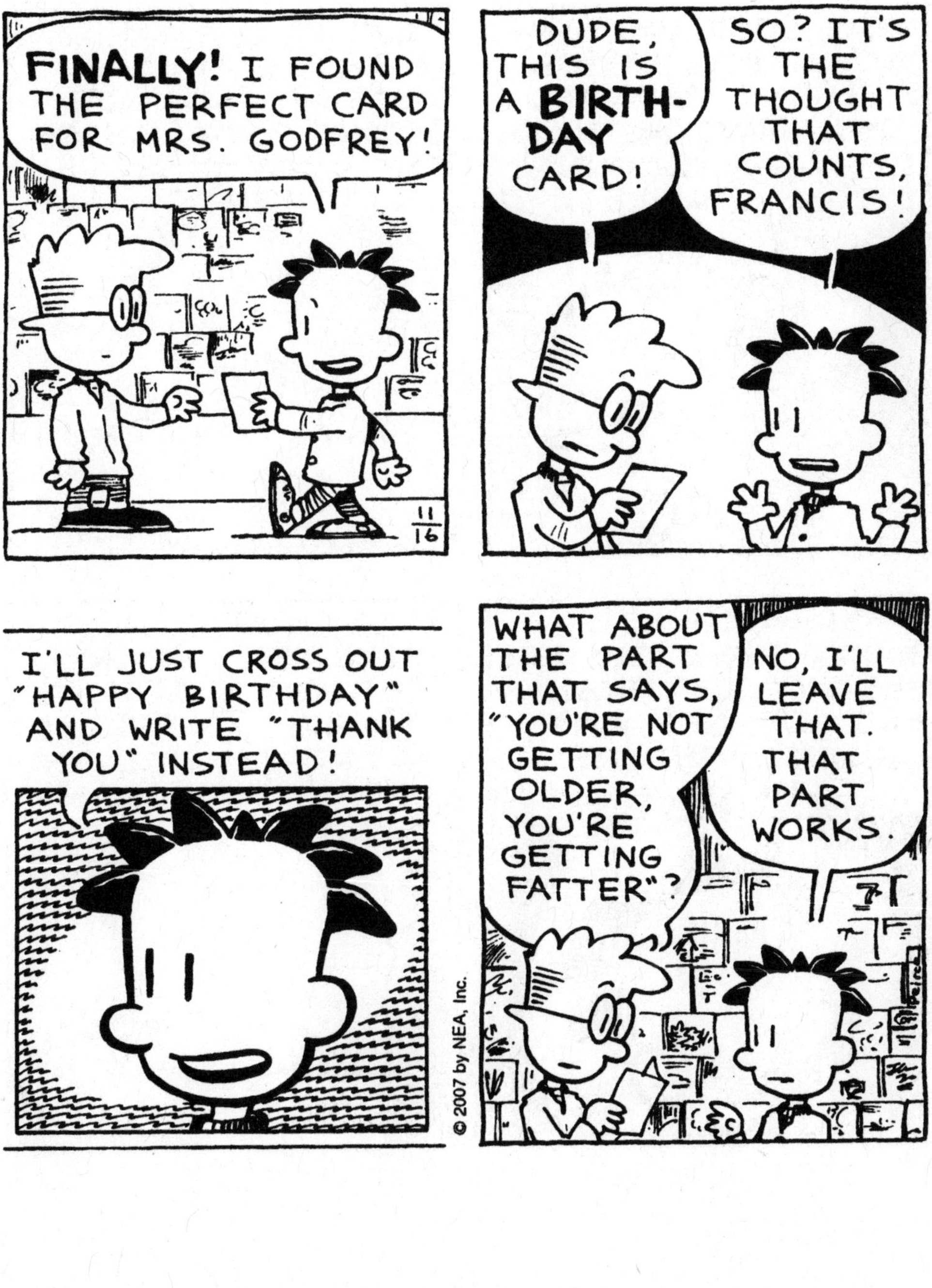
FINALLY! I FOUND THE PERFECT CARD FOR MRS. GODFREY!
11/16
DUDE, THIS IS A BIRTHDAY CARD!
SO? IT'S THE THOUGHT THAT COUNTS, FRANCIS!
I'LL JUST CROSS OUT "HAPPY BIRTHDAY" AND WRITE "THANK YOU" INSTEAD!
WHAT ABOUT THE PART THAT SAYS, "YOU'RE NOT GETTING OLDER, YOU'RE GETTING FATTER"?
NO, I'LL LEAVE THAT. THAT PART WORKS.
© 2007 by NEA, Inc.

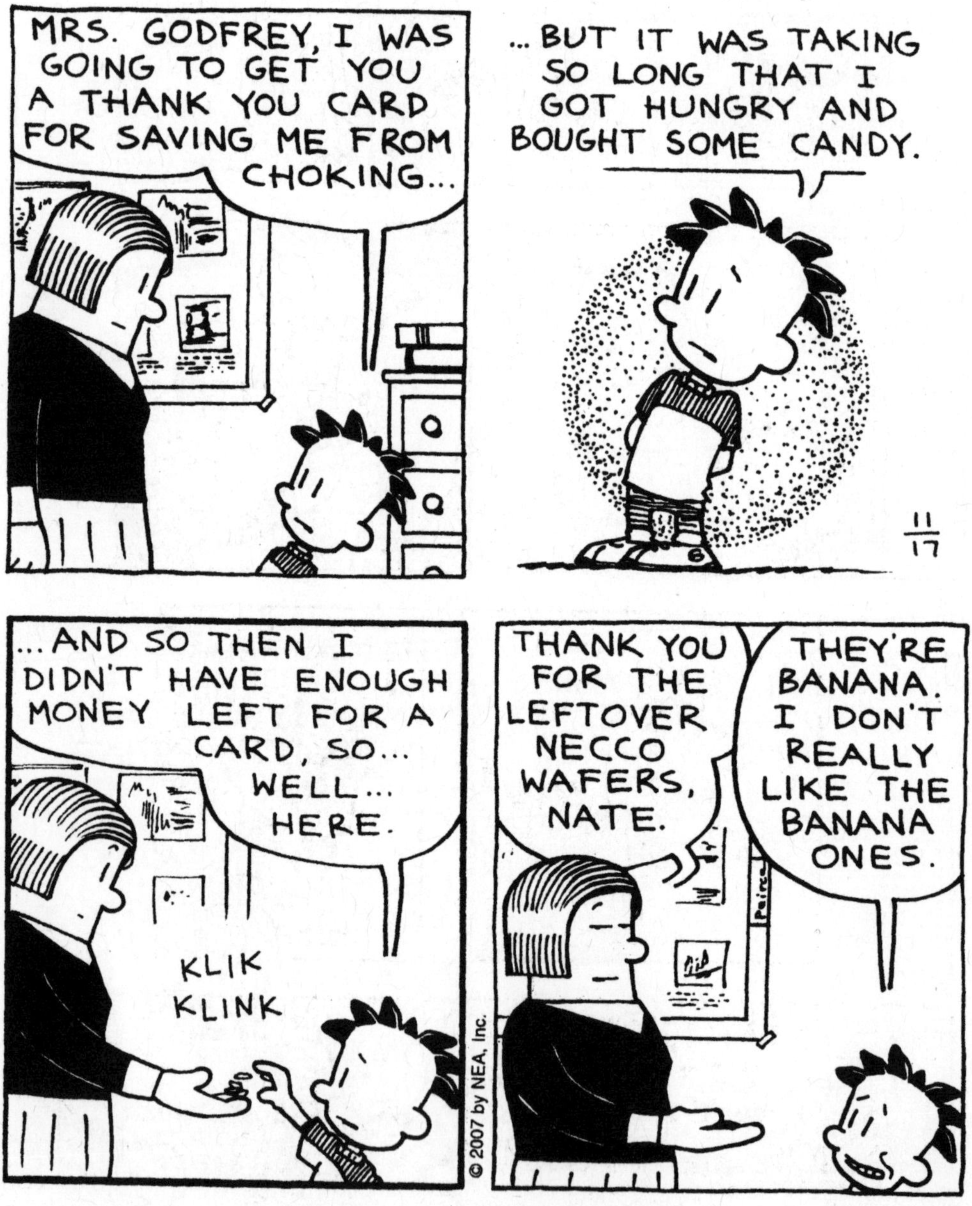
MRS. GODFREY, I WAS GOING TO GET YOU A THANK YOU CARD FOR SAVING ME FROM CHOKING...
...BUT IT WAS TAKING SO LONG THAT I GOT HUNGRY AND BOUGHT SOME CANDY.
11/17
...AND SO THEN I DIDN'T HAVE ENOUGH MONEY LEFT FOR A CARD, SO... WELL... HERE.
KLIK
KLINK
© 2007 by NEA, Inc.
THANK YOU FOR THE LEFTOVER NECCO WAFERS, NATE.
THEY'RE BANANA. I DON'T REALLY LIKE THE BANANA ONES.
Peirce

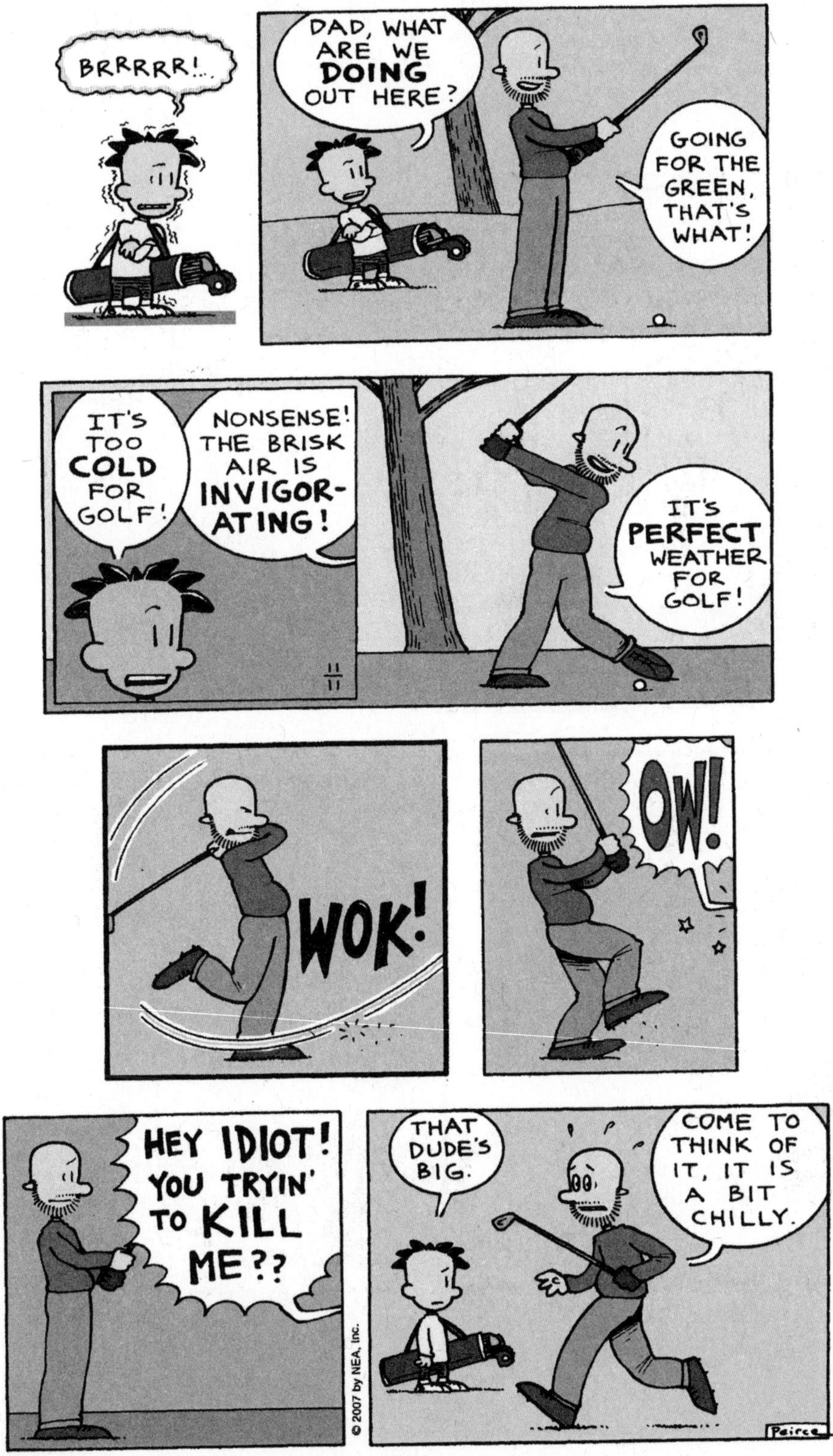
BRRRRR!...
DAD, WHAT ARE WE DOING OUT HERE?
GOING FOR THE GREEN, THAT'S WHAT!
IT'S TOO COLD FOR GOLF!
NONSENSE! THE BRISK AIR IS INVIGOR-ATING!
IT'S PERFECT WEATHER FOR GOLF!
WOK!
OW!
HEY IDIOT! YOU TRYIN' TO KILL ME??
© 2007 by NEA, Inc.
THAT DUDE'S BIG.
COME TO THINK OF IT, IT IS A BIT CHILLY.
Peirce

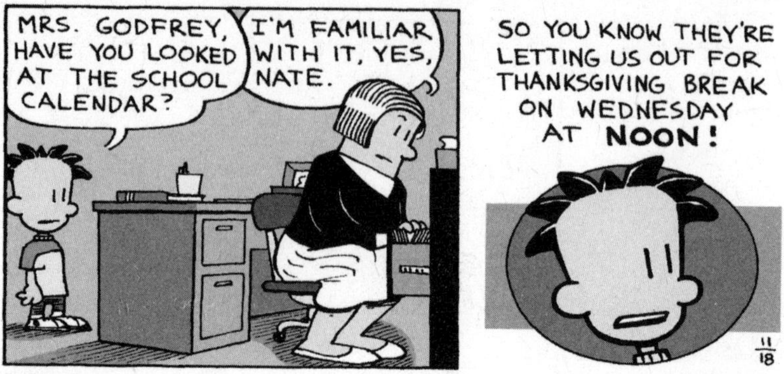
MRS. GODFREY, HAVE YOU LOOKED AT THE SCHOOL CALENDAR?
I'M FAMILIAR WITH IT, YES, NATE.
SO YOU KNOW THEY'RE LETTING US OUT FOR THANKSGIVING BREAK ON WEDNESDAY AT **NOON**!
11/18

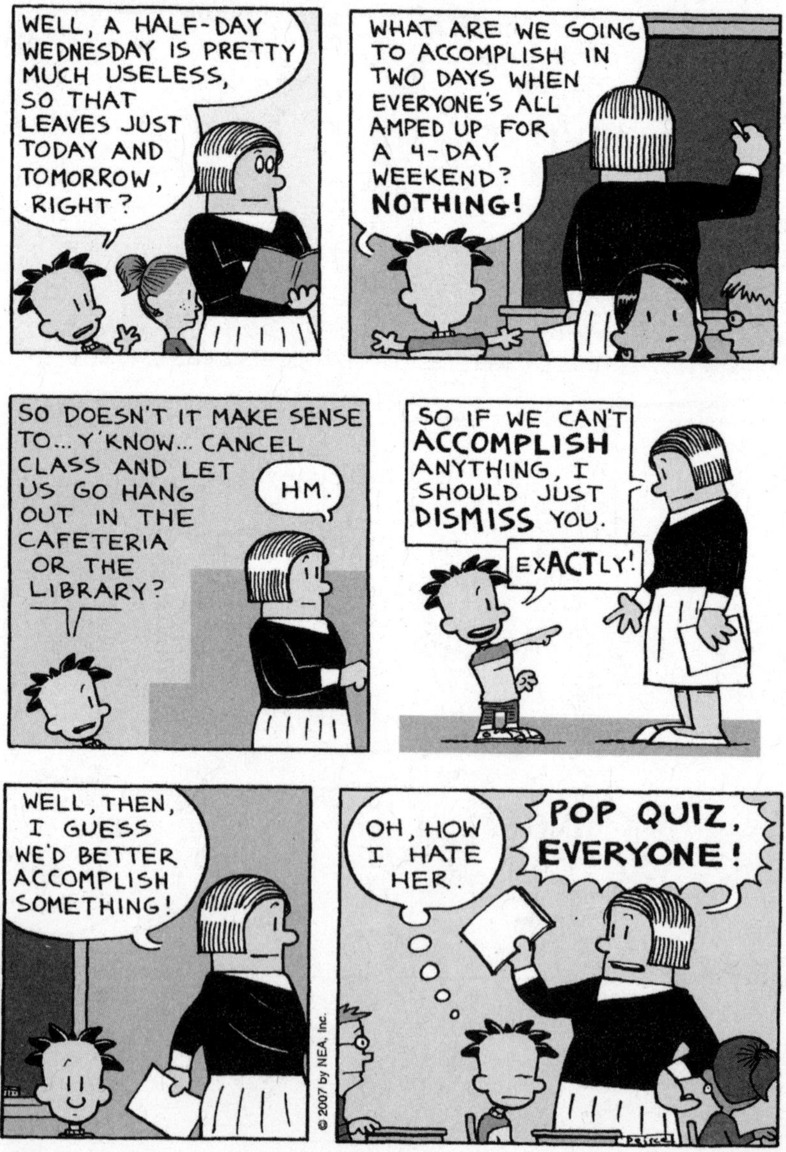
WELL, A HALF-DAY WEDNESDAY IS PRETTY MUCH USELESS, SO THAT LEAVES JUST TODAY AND TOMORROW, RIGHT?
WHAT ARE WE GOING TO ACCOMPLISH IN TWO DAYS WHEN EVERYONE'S ALL AMPED UP FOR A 4-DAY WEEKEND? **NOTHING!**
SO DOESN'T IT MAKE SENSE TO... Y'KNOW... CANCEL CLASS AND LET US GO HANG OUT IN THE CAFETERIA OR THE LIBRARY?
HM.
SO IF WE CAN'T **ACCOMPLISH** ANYTHING, I SHOULD JUST **DISMISS** YOU.
EX**ACT**LY!
WELL, THEN, I GUESS WE'D BETTER ACCOMPLISH SOMETHING!
© 2007 by NEA, Inc.
OH, HOW I HATE HER.
POP QUIZ, EVERYONE!

WHO WANTS TO PLAY SOCIAL STUDIES JEOPARDY?

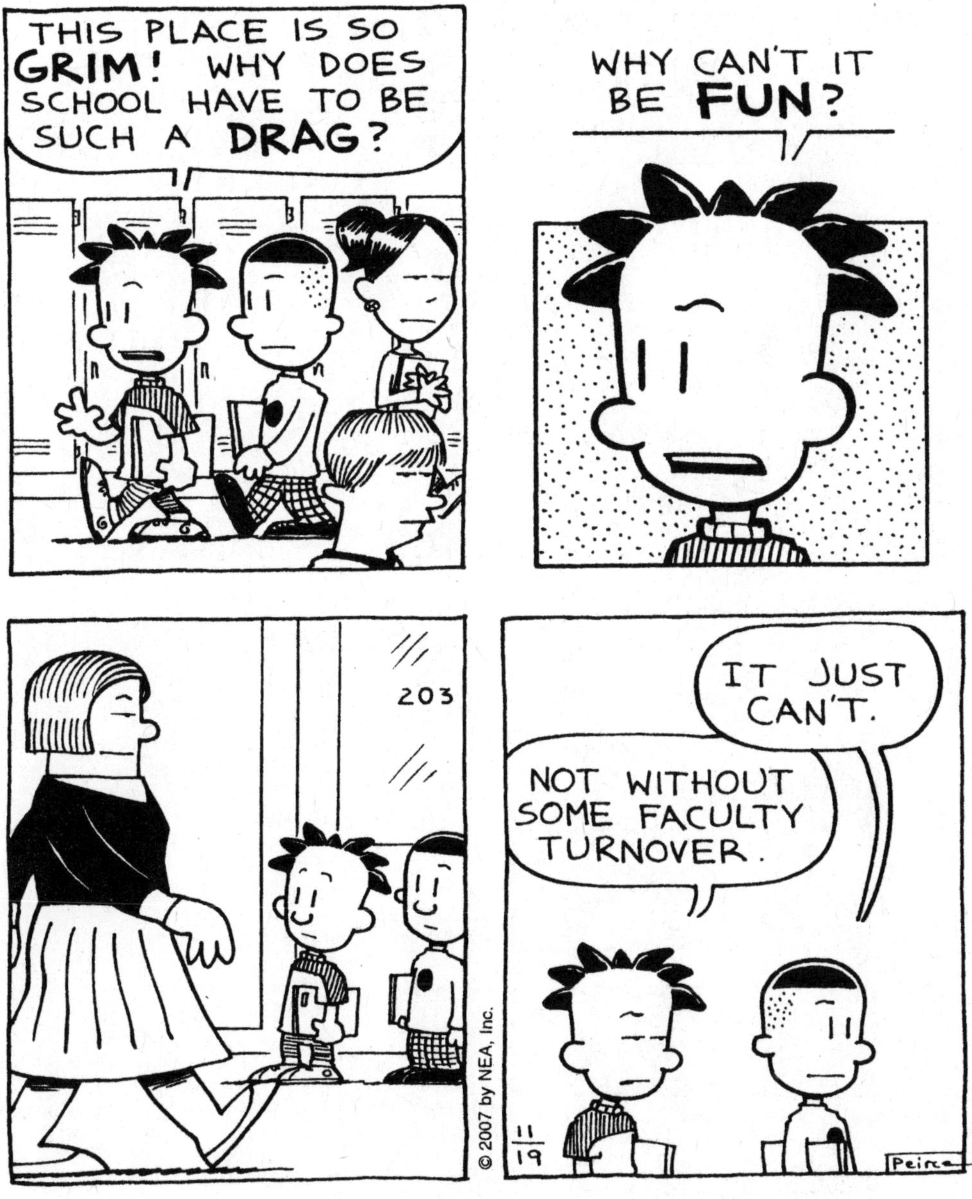
THIS PLACE IS SO GRIM! WHY DOES SCHOOL HAVE TO BE SUCH A DRAG?
WHY CAN'T IT BE FUN?
203
IT JUST CAN'T.
NOT WITHOUT SOME FACULTY TURNOVER.
11/19
Peirce
© 2007 by NEA, Inc.

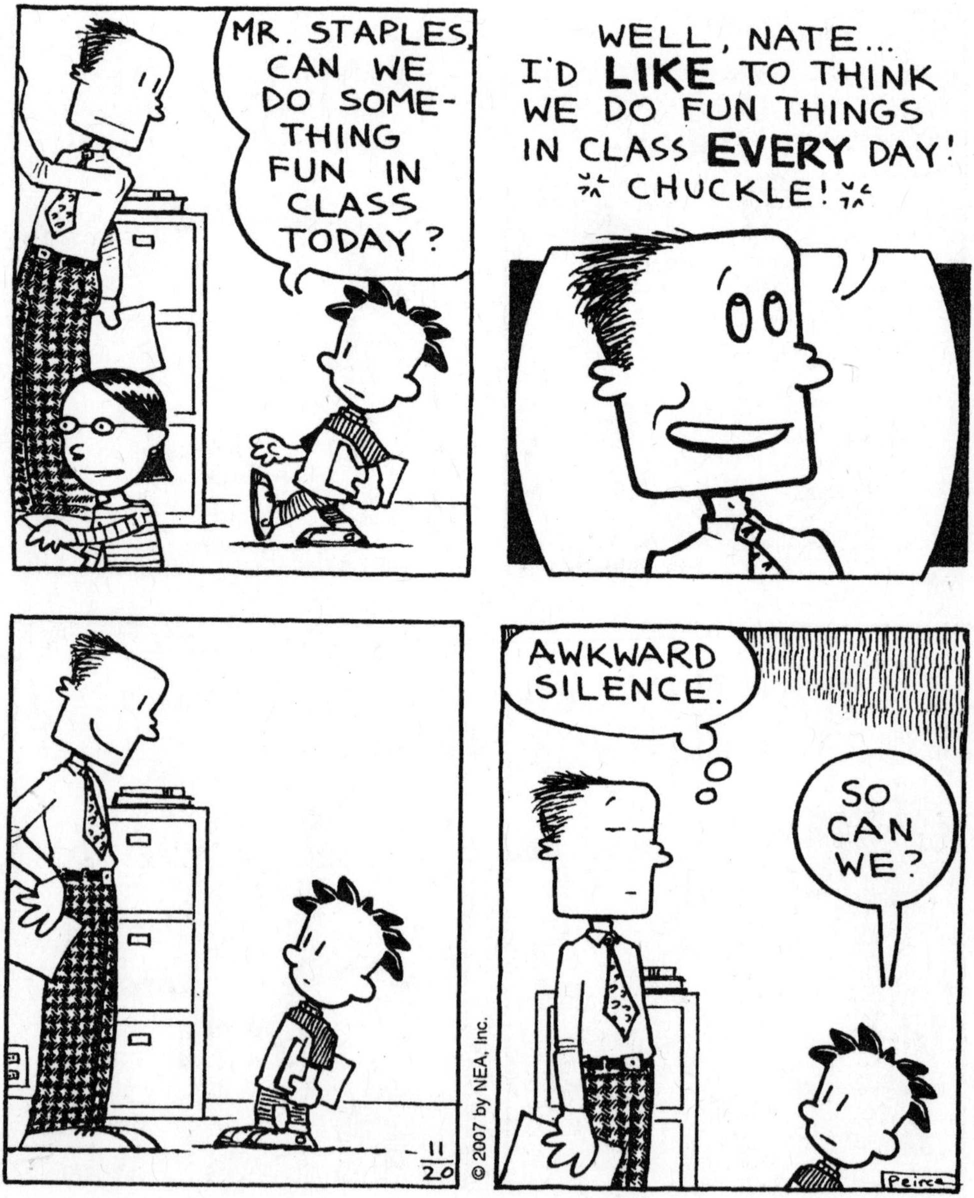
MR. STAPLES, CAN WE DO SOMETHING FUN IN CLASS TODAY?
WELL, NATE... I'D **LIKE** TO THINK WE DO FUN THINGS IN CLASS **EVERY** DAY! CHUCKLE!
AWKWARD SILENCE.
SO CAN WE?
11-20
© 2007 by NEA, Inc.
Peirce

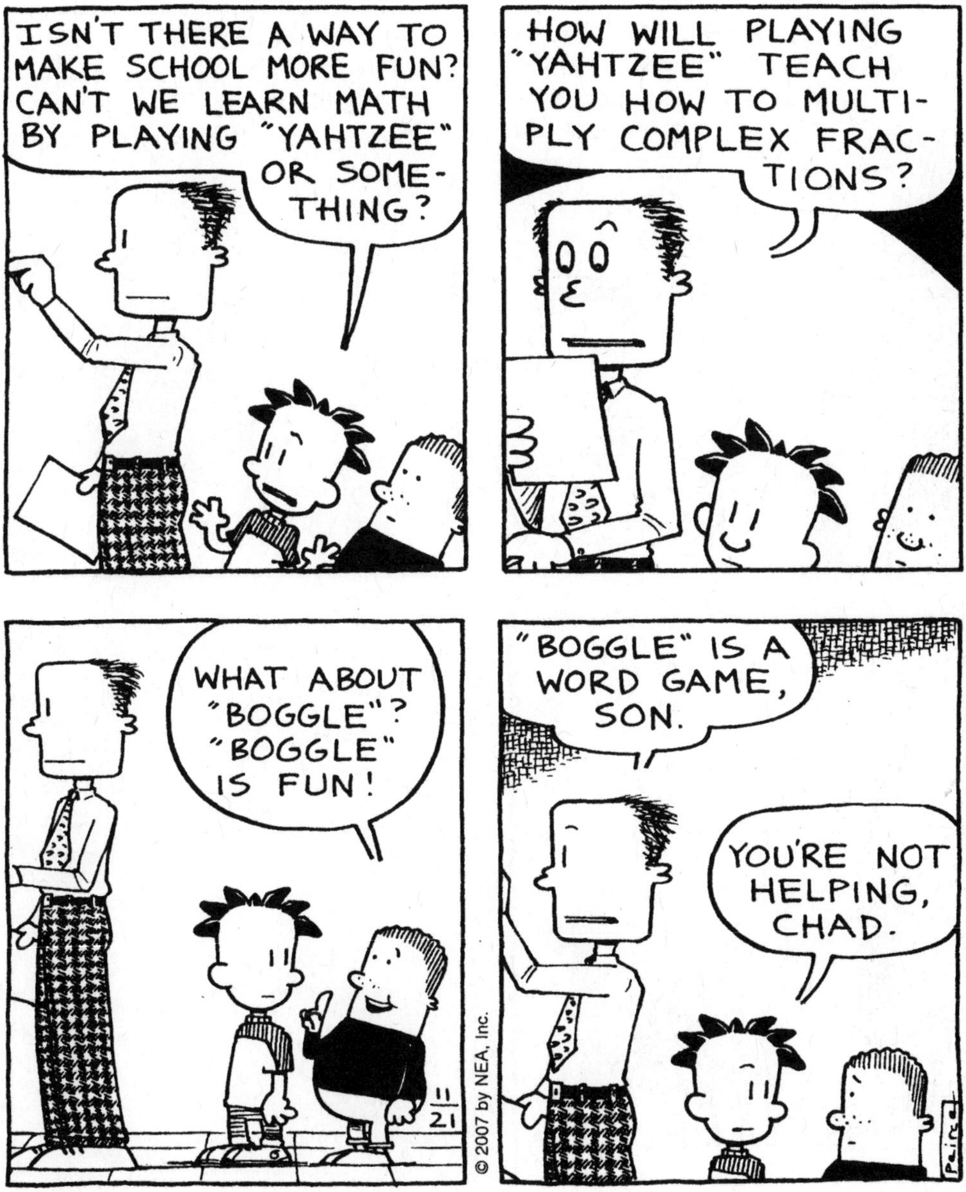
ISN'T THERE A WAY TO MAKE SCHOOL MORE FUN? CAN'T WE LEARN MATH BY PLAYING "YAHTZEE" OR SOMETHING?
HOW WILL PLAYING "YAHTZEE" TEACH YOU HOW TO MULTIPLY COMPLEX FRACTIONS?
WHAT ABOUT "BOGGLE"? "BOGGLE" IS FUN!
11 21
© 2007 by NEA, Inc.
"BOGGLE" IS A WORD GAME, SON.
YOU'RE NOT HELPING, CHAD.
Peirce

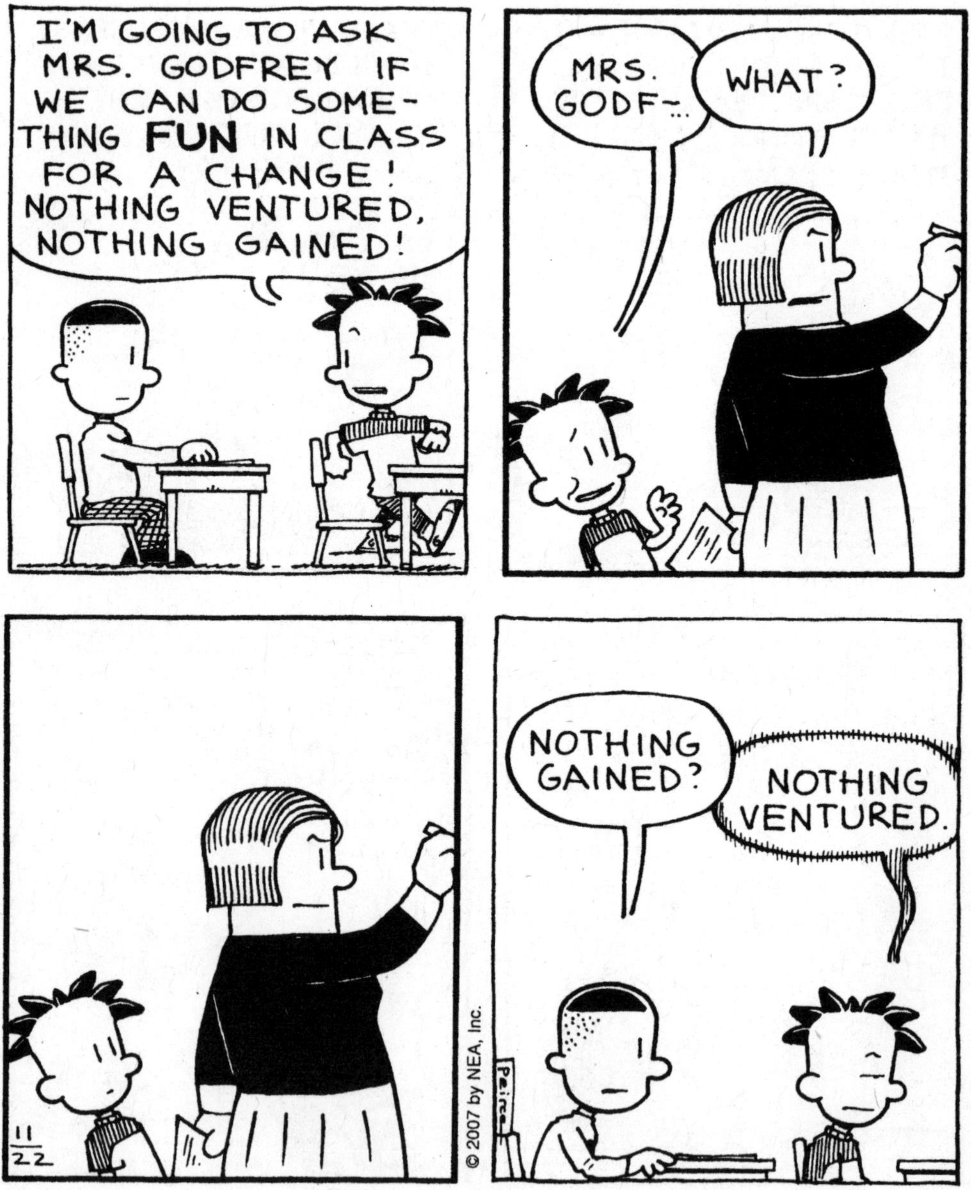
I'M GOING TO ASK MRS. GODFREY IF WE CAN DO SOMETHING **FUN** IN CLASS FOR A CHANGE! NOTHING VENTURED, NOTHING GAINED!
MRS. GODF-...
WHAT?
11/22
© 2007 by NEA, Inc.
Peirce
NOTHING GAINED?
NOTHING VENTURED.

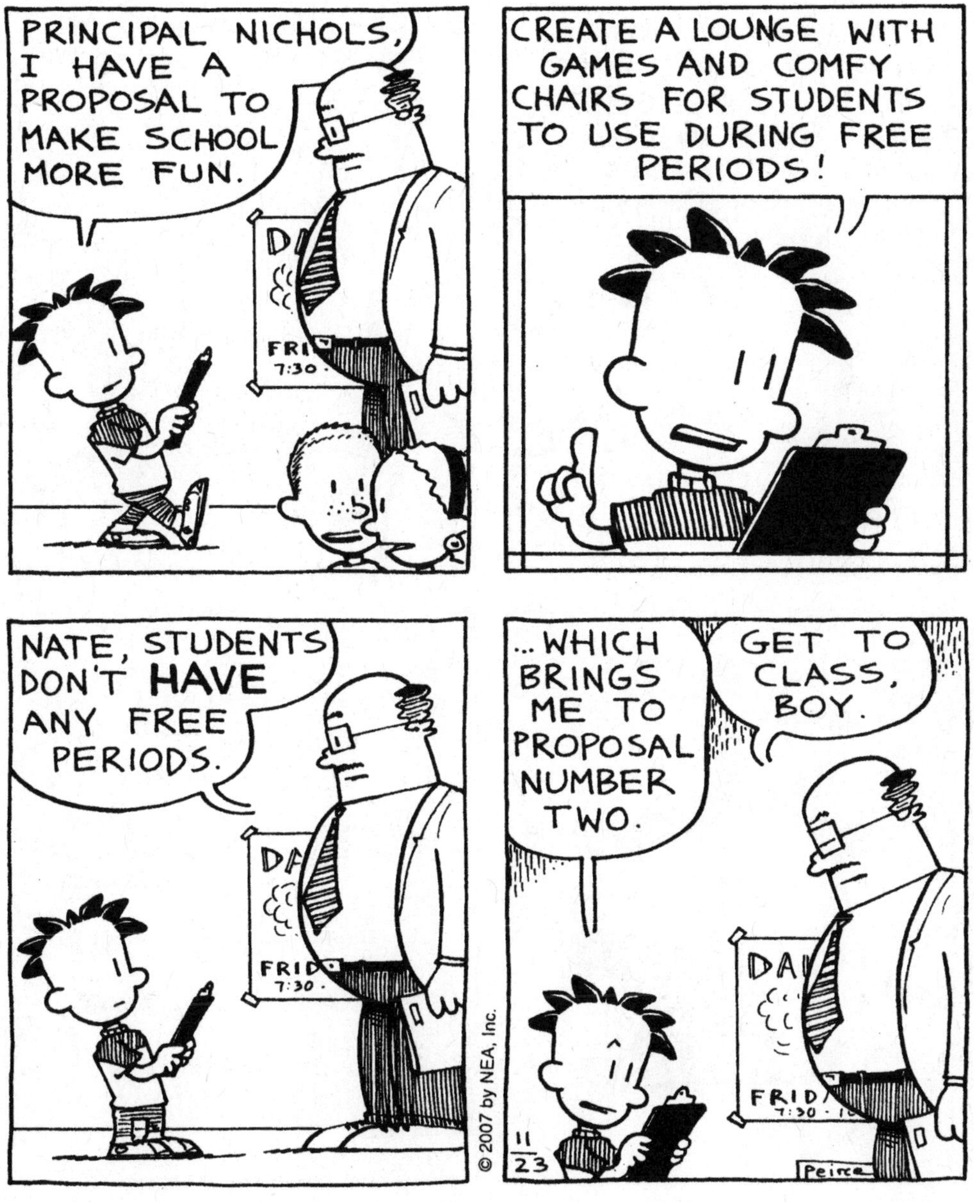
PRINCIPAL NICHOLS, I HAVE A PROPOSAL TO MAKE SCHOOL MORE FUN.
CREATE A LOUNGE WITH GAMES AND COMFY CHAIRS FOR STUDENTS TO USE DURING FREE PERIODS!
NATE, STUDENTS DON'T **HAVE** ANY FREE PERIODS.
...WHICH BRINGS ME TO PROPOSAL NUMBER TWO.
GET TO CLASS, BOY.
© 2007 by NEA, Inc.
11
23
Peirce

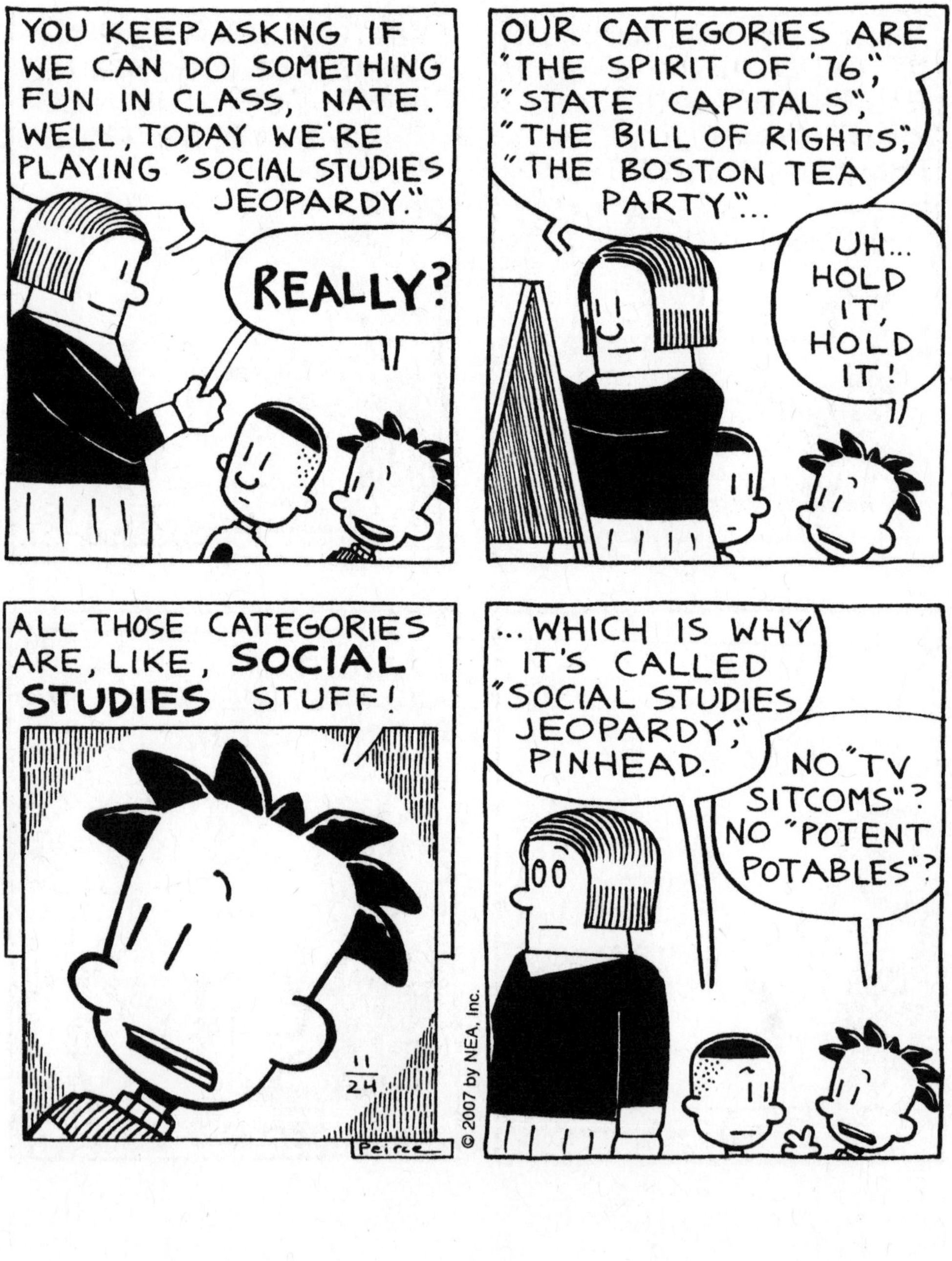
YOU KEEP ASKING IF WE CAN DO SOMETHING FUN IN CLASS, NATE. WELL, TODAY WE'RE PLAYING "SOCIAL STUDIES JEOPARDY."
REALLY?
OUR CATEGORIES ARE "THE SPIRIT OF '76," "STATE CAPITALS," "THE BILL OF RIGHTS," "THE BOSTON TEA PARTY"...
UH... HOLD IT, HOLD IT!
ALL THOSE CATEGORIES ARE, LIKE, SOCIAL STUDIES STUFF!
11/24
Peirce
© 2007 by NEA, Inc.
...WHICH IS WHY IT'S CALLED "SOCIAL STUDIES JEOPARDY," PINHEAD.
NO "TV SITCOMS"? NO "POTENT POTABLES"?

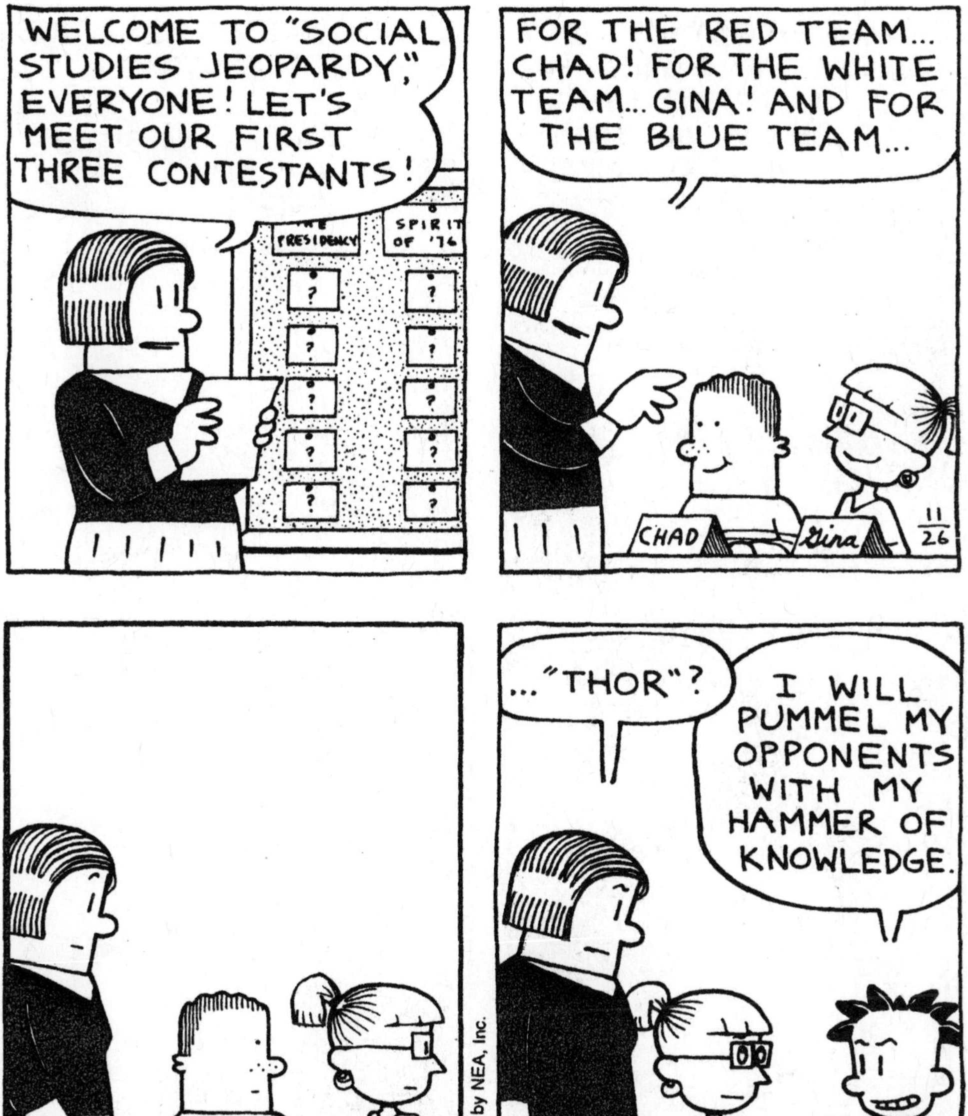
WELCOME TO "SOCIAL STUDIES JEOPARDY," EVERYONE! LET'S MEET OUR FIRST THREE CONTESTANTS!
PRESIDENCY
SPIRIT OF '76
FOR THE RED TEAM... CHAD! FOR THE WHITE TEAM... GINA! AND FOR THE BLUE TEAM...
CHAD
Gina
11/26
CHAD
Gina
© 2007 by NEA, Inc.
..."THOR"?
I WILL PUMMEL MY OPPONENTS WITH MY HAMMER OF KNOWLEDGE.
Gina
THOR
peirce

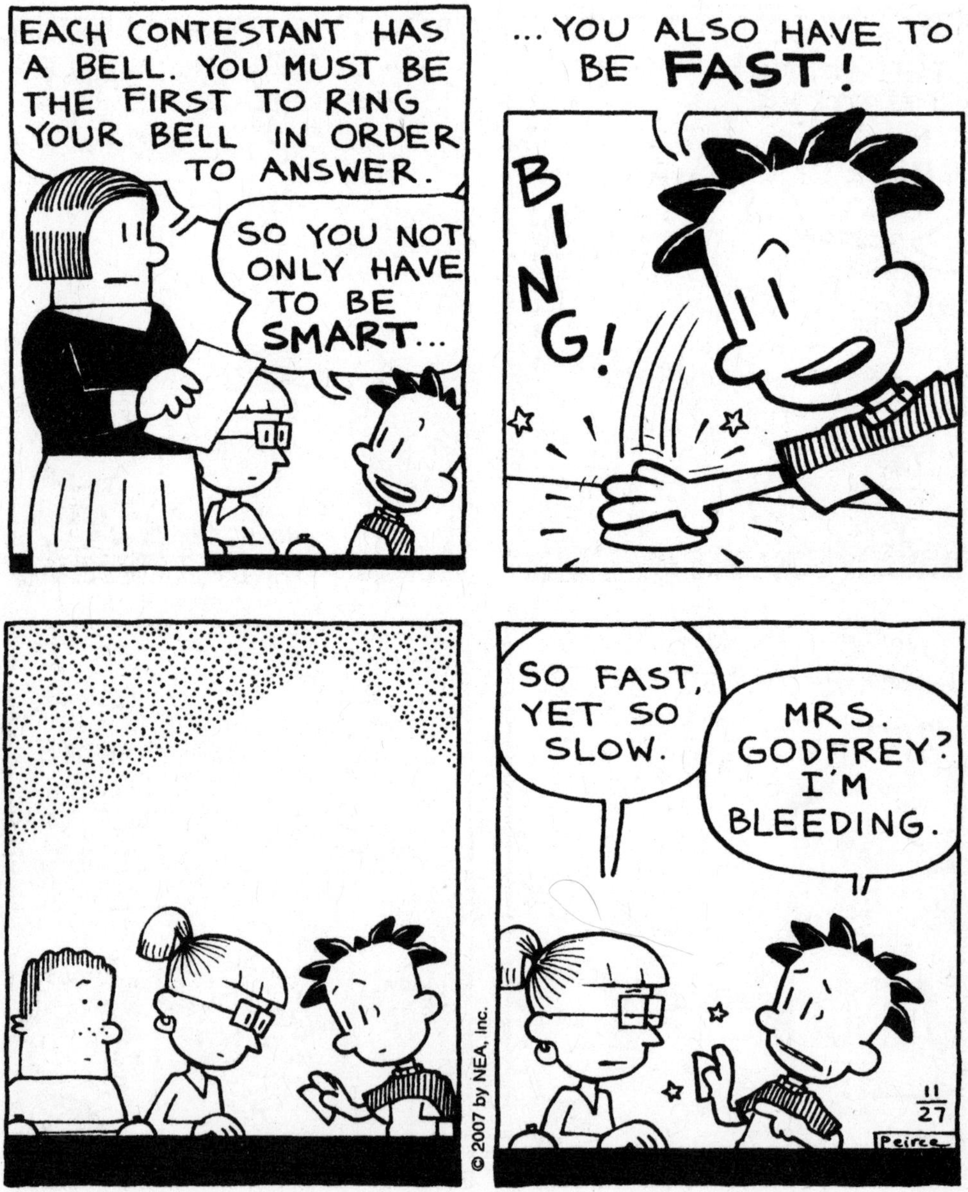
EACH CONTESTANT HAS A BELL. YOU MUST BE THE FIRST TO RING YOUR BELL IN ORDER TO ANSWER.
SO YOU NOT ONLY HAVE TO BE SMART...
...YOU ALSO HAVE TO BE FAST!
BING!
SO FAST, YET SO SLOW.
MRS. GODFREY? I'M BLEEDING.
© 2007 by NEA, Inc.
11/27
Peirce

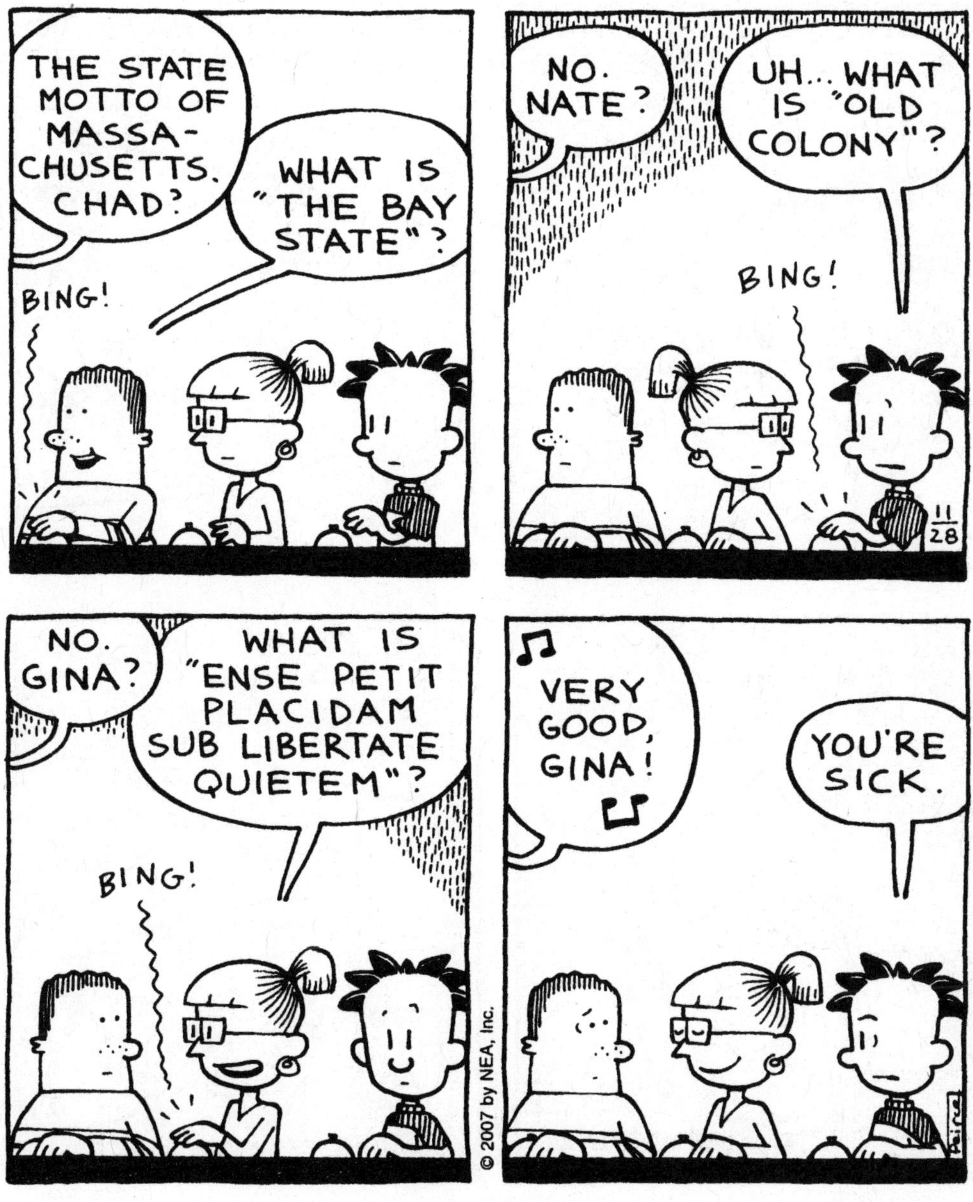
THE STATE MOTTO OF MASSA-CHUSETTS, CHAD?
WHAT IS "THE BAY STATE"?
BING!
NO. NATE?
UH... WHAT IS "OLD COLONY"?
BING!
11 28
NO. GINA?
WHAT IS "ENSE PETIT PLACIDAM SUB LIBERTATE QUIETEM"?
BING!
VERY GOOD, GINA!
YOU'RE SICK.
Peirce

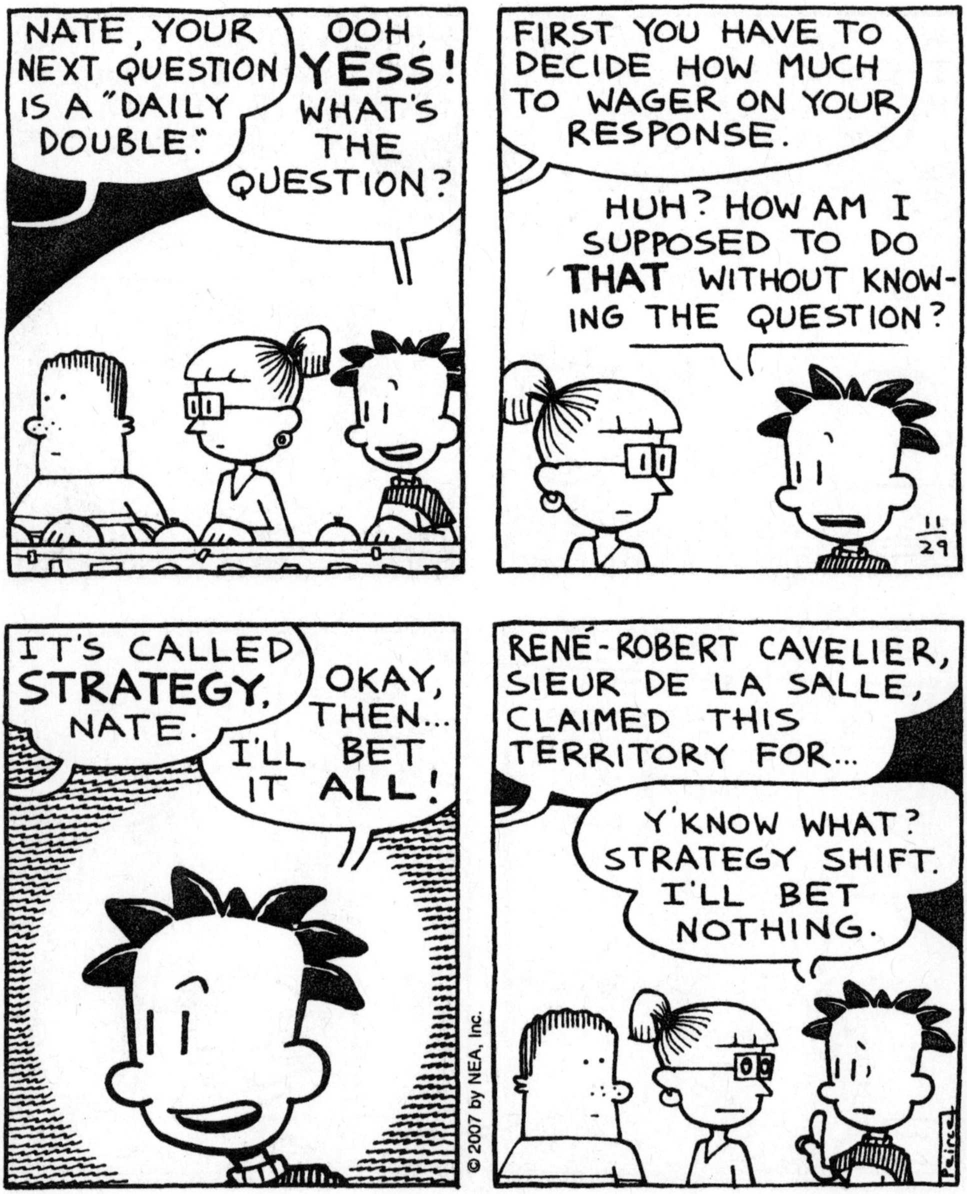
NATE, YOUR NEXT QUESTION IS A "DAILY DOUBLE."
OOH, YESS! WHAT'S THE QUESTION?
FIRST YOU HAVE TO DECIDE HOW MUCH TO WAGER ON YOUR RESPONSE.
HUH? HOW AM I SUPPOSED TO DO THAT WITHOUT KNOWING THE QUESTION?
11/29
IT'S CALLED STRATEGY, NATE.
OKAY, THEN... I'LL BET IT ALL!
© 2007 by NEA, Inc.
RENÉ-ROBERT CAVELIER, SIEUR DE LA SALLE, CLAIMED THIS TERRITORY FOR...
Y'KNOW WHAT? STRATEGY SHIFT. I'LL BET NOTHING.
Peirce

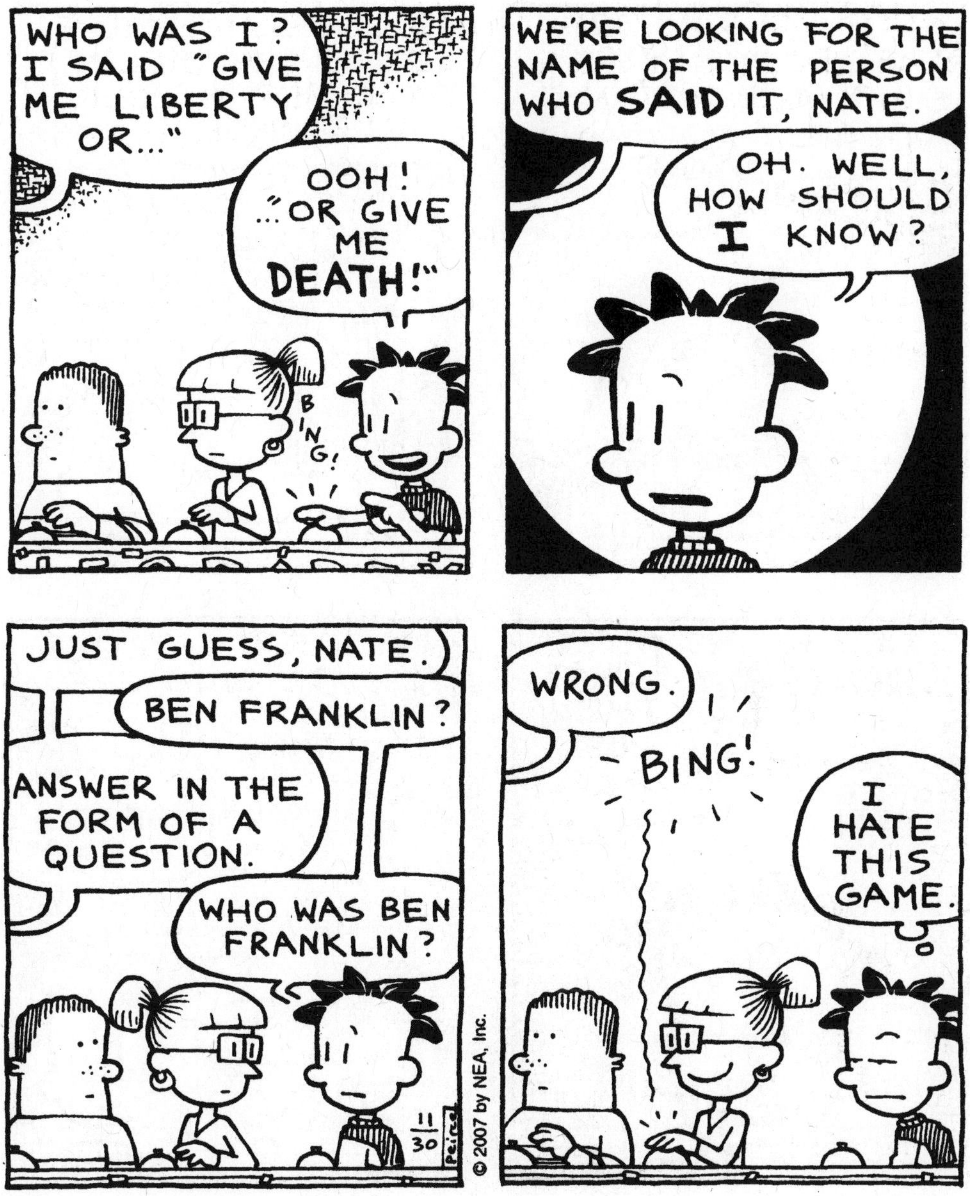
WHO WAS I? I SAID "GIVE ME LIBERTY OR..."
OOH! ..."OR GIVE ME DEATH!"
BING!
WE'RE LOOKING FOR THE NAME OF THE PERSON WHO SAID IT, NATE.
OH. WELL, HOW SHOULD I KNOW?
JUST GUESS, NATE.
BEN FRANKLIN?
ANSWER IN THE FORM OF A QUESTION.
WHO WAS BEN FRANKLIN?
Peirce
11/30
© 2007 by NEA, Inc.
WRONG.
BING!
I HATE THIS GAME.

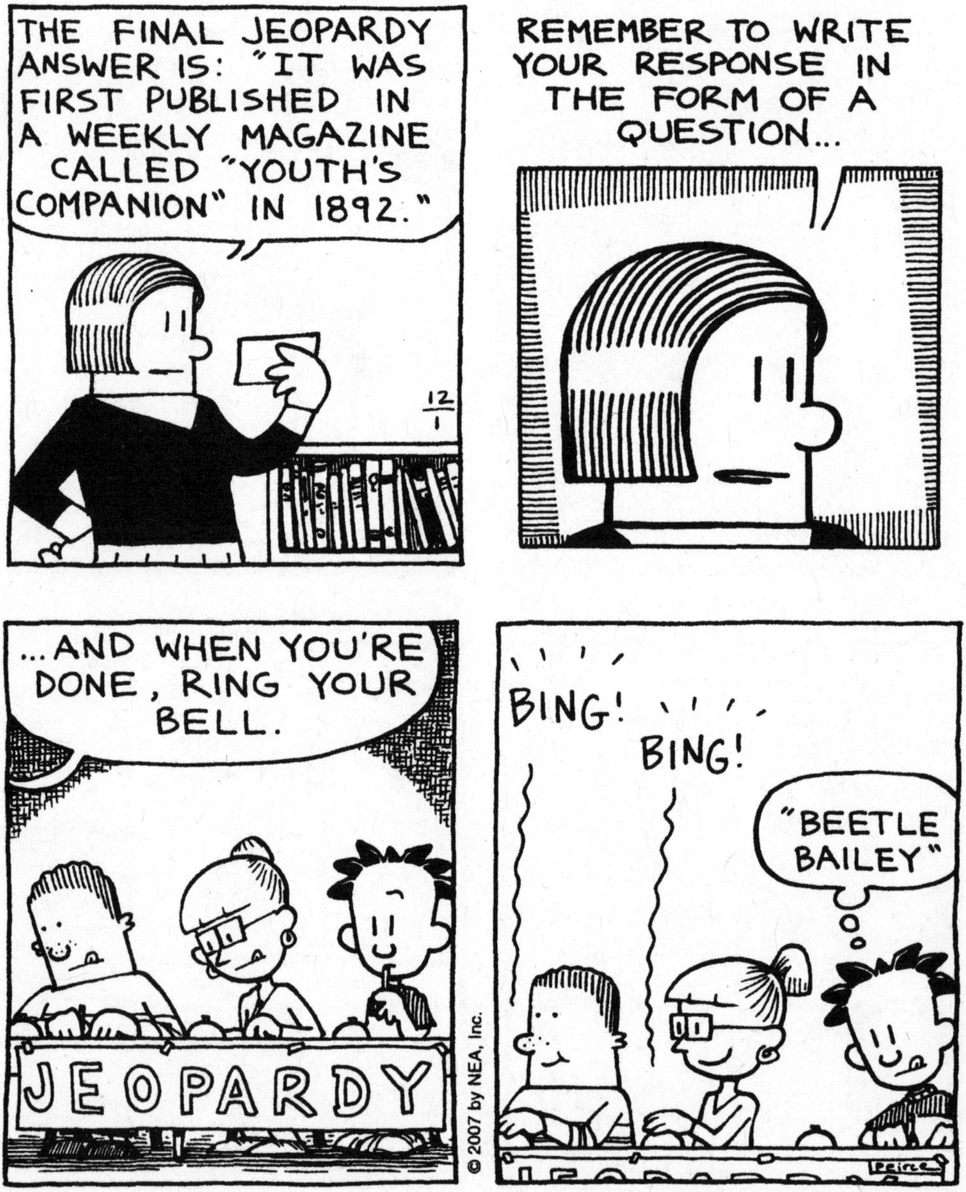
THE FINAL JEOPARDY ANSWER IS: "IT WAS FIRST PUBLISHED IN A WEEKLY MAGAZINE CALLED "YOUTH'S COMPANION" IN 1892."
12/1
REMEMBER TO WRITE YOUR RESPONSE IN THE FORM OF A QUESTION...
...AND WHEN YOU'RE DONE, RING YOUR BELL.
JEOPARDY
© 2007 by NEA, Inc.
BING!
BING!
"BEETLE BAILEY"
Peirce

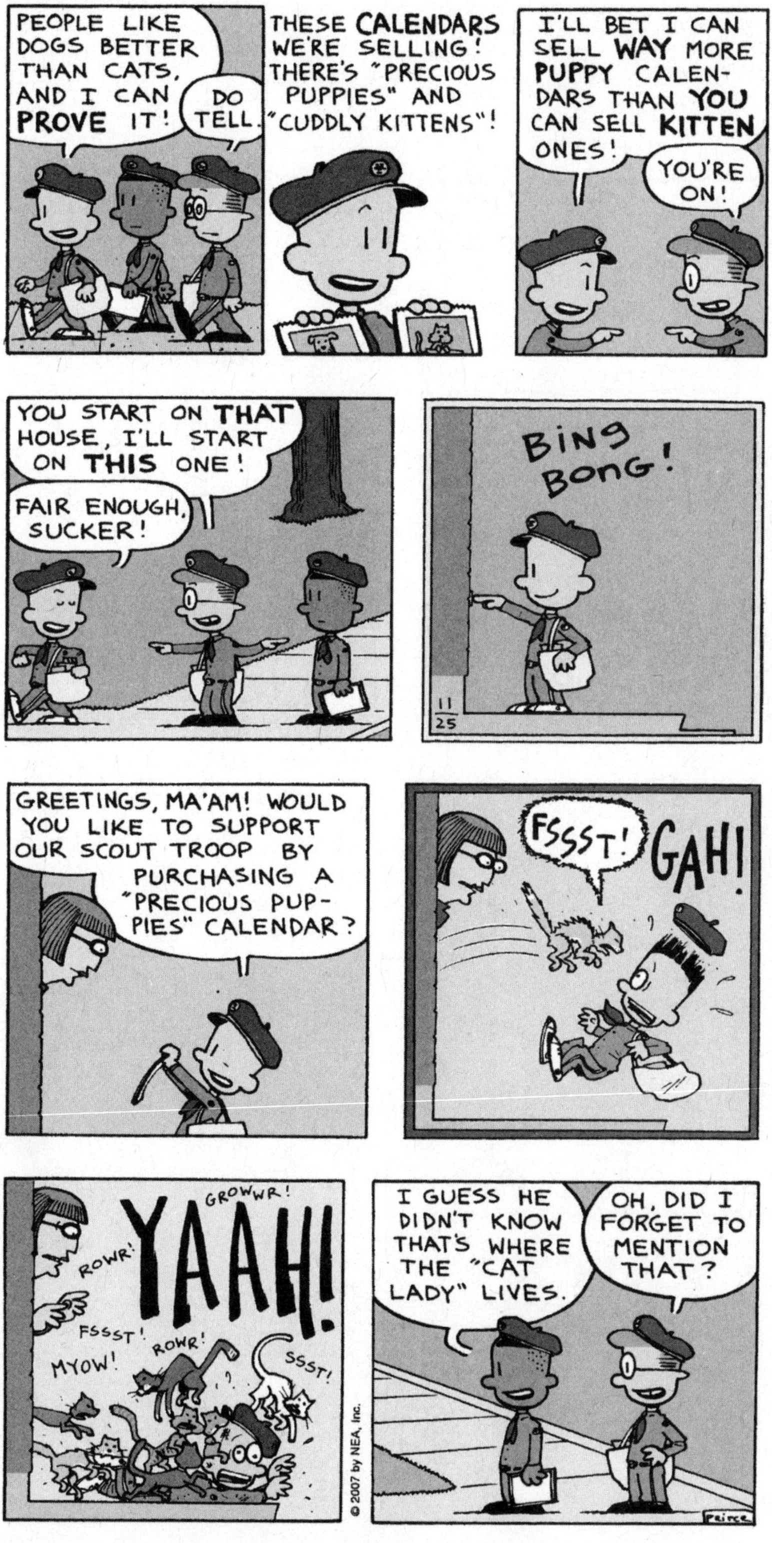
PEOPLE LIKE DOGS BETTER THAN CATS, AND I CAN PROVE IT!
DO TELL.
THESE CALENDARS WE'RE SELLING! THERE'S "PRECIOUS PUPPIES" AND "CUDDLY KITTENS"!
I'LL BET I CAN SELL WAY MORE PUPPY CALENDARS THAN YOU CAN SELL KITTEN ONES!
YOU'RE ON!
YOU START ON THAT HOUSE, I'LL START ON THIS ONE!
FAIR ENOUGH, SUCKER!
BING BONG!
11
25
GREETINGS, MA'AM! WOULD YOU LIKE TO SUPPORT OUR SCOUT TROOP BY PURCHASING A "PRECIOUS PUPPIES" CALENDAR?
FSSST!
GAH!
GROWWR!
ROWR!
YAAH!
FSSST!
ROWR!
MYOW!
SSST!
© 2007 by NEA, Inc.
I GUESS HE DIDN'T KNOW THAT'S WHERE THE "CAT LADY" LIVES.
OH, DID I FORGET TO MENTION THAT?
PEIRCE

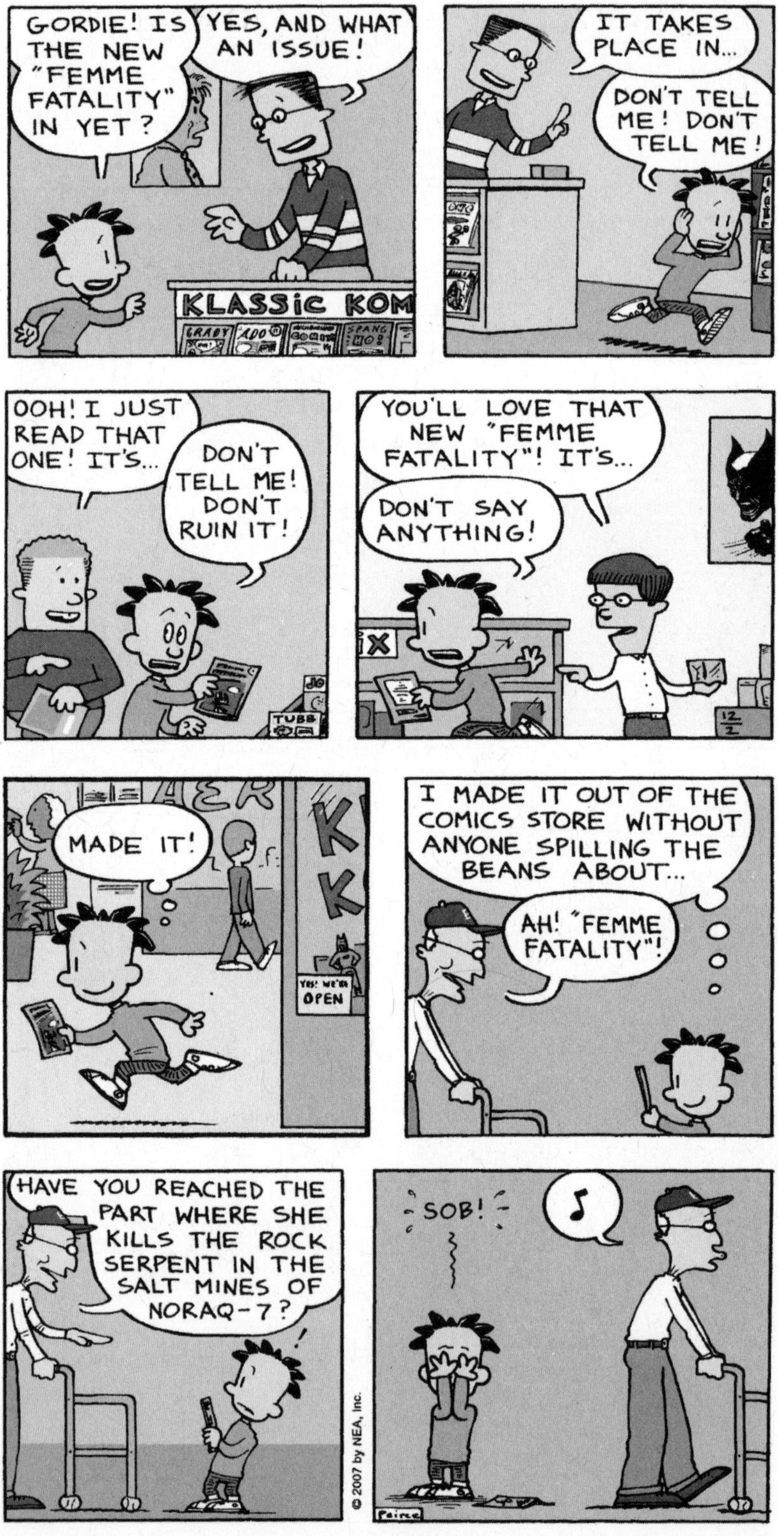
GORDIE! IS THE NEW "FEMME FATALITY" IN YET?
YES, AND WHAT AN ISSUE!
KLASSIC KOM
IT TAKES PLACE IN...
DON'T TELL ME! DON'T TELL ME!
OOH! I JUST READ THAT ONE! IT'S...
DON'T TELL ME! DON'T RUIN IT!
YOU'LL LOVE THAT NEW "FEMME FATALITY"! IT'S...
DON'T SAY ANYTHING!
MADE IT!
YES! WE'RE OPEN
I MADE IT OUT OF THE COMICS STORE WITHOUT ANYONE SPILLING THE BEANS ABOUT...
AH! "FEMME FATALITY"!
HAVE YOU REACHED THE PART WHERE SHE KILLS THE ROCK SERPENT IN THE SALT MINES OF NORAQ-7?
!
SOB!
© 2007 by NEA, Inc.
Peirce

HERE COMES JENNY!

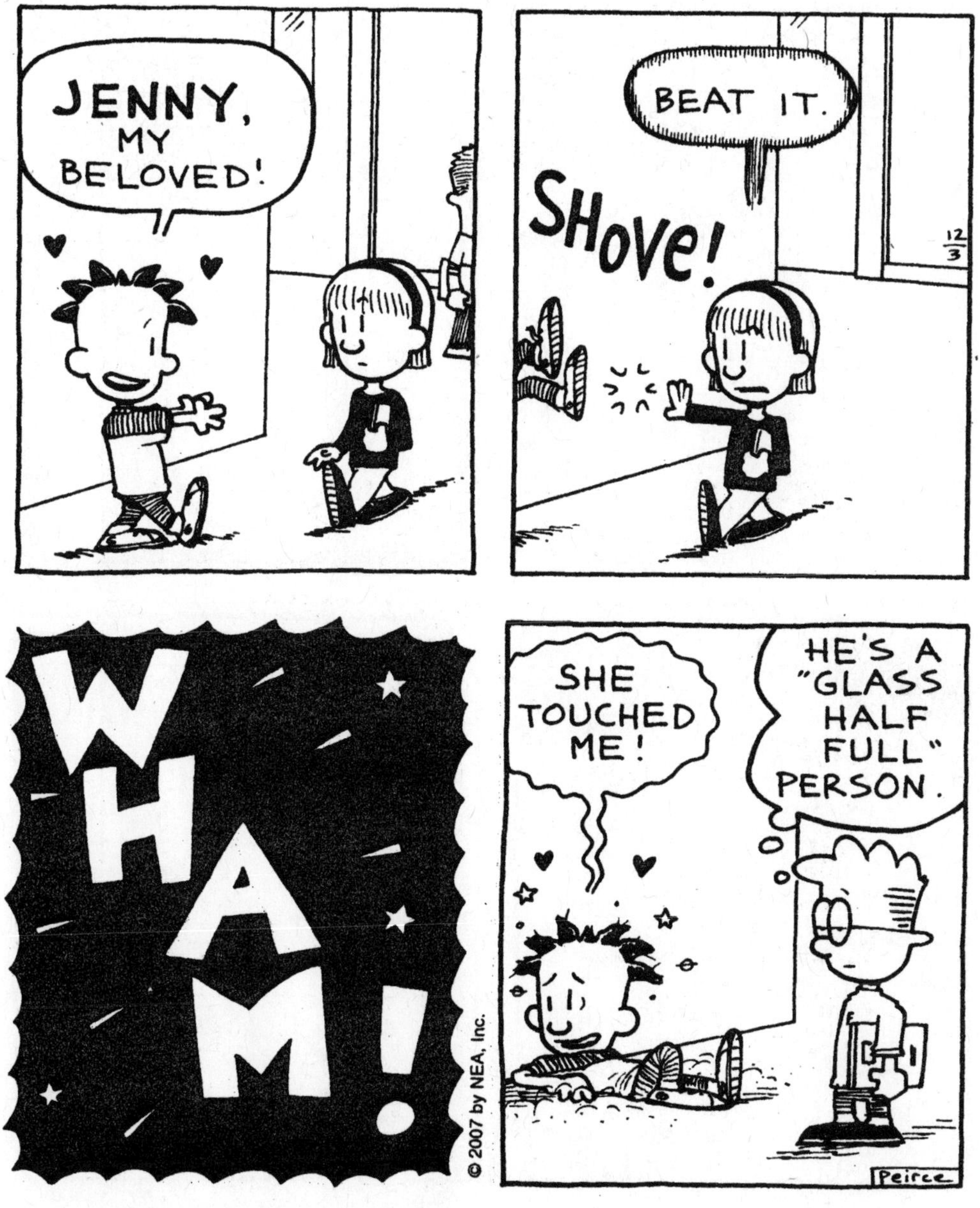
JENNY, MY BELOVED!
BEAT IT.
SHOVE!
12/3
WHAM!
© 2007 by NEA, Inc.
SHE TOUCHED ME!
HE'S A "GLASS HALF FULL" PERSON.
Peirce

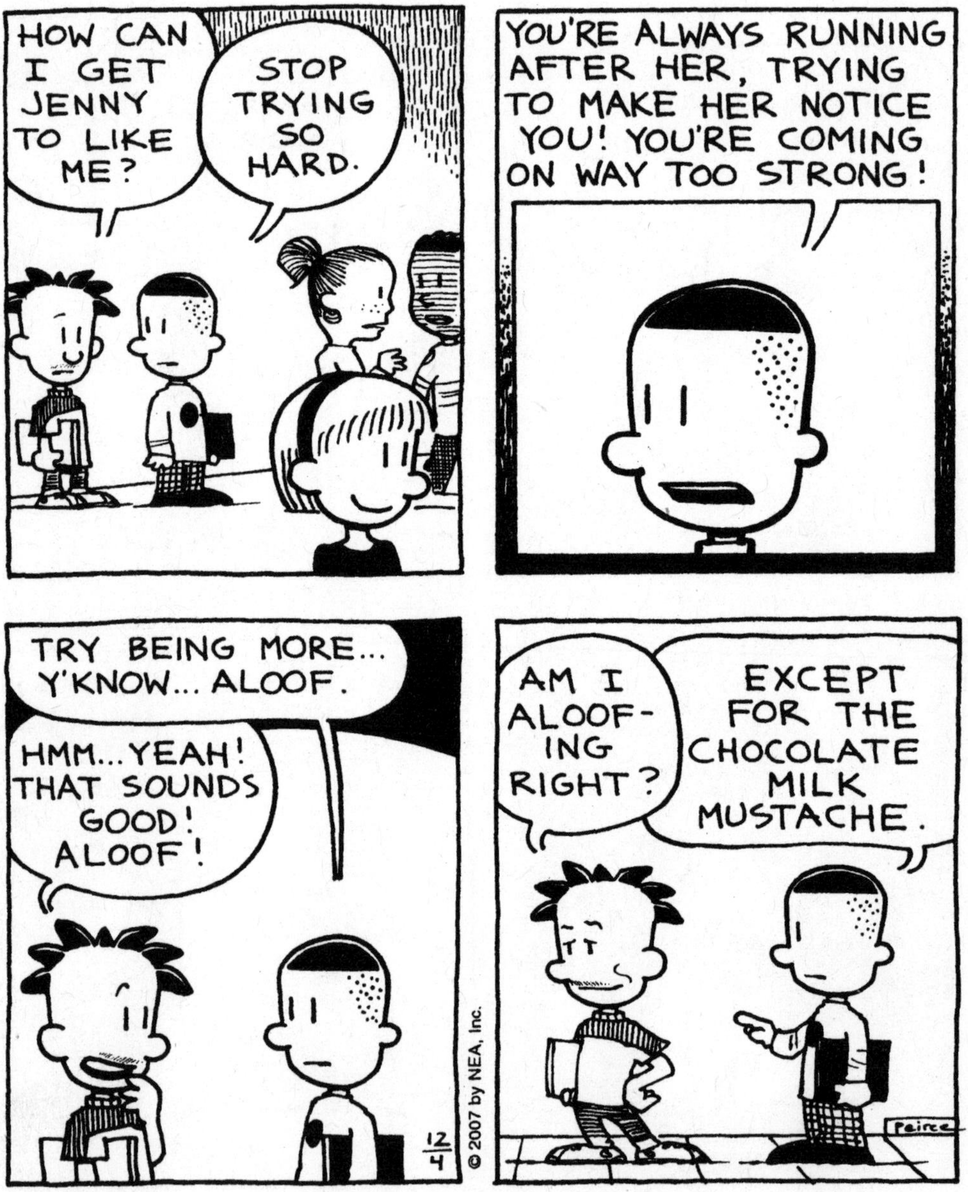
HOW CAN I GET JENNY TO LIKE ME?
STOP TRYING SO HARD.
YOU'RE ALWAYS RUNNING AFTER HER, TRYING TO MAKE HER NOTICE YOU! YOU'RE COMING ON WAY TOO STRONG!
TRY BEING MORE... Y'KNOW... ALOOF.
HMM... YEAH! THAT SOUNDS GOOD! ALOOF!
12/4
© 2007 by NEA, Inc.
AM I ALOOF-ING RIGHT?
EXCEPT FOR THE CHOCOLATE MILK MUSTACHE.
Peirce

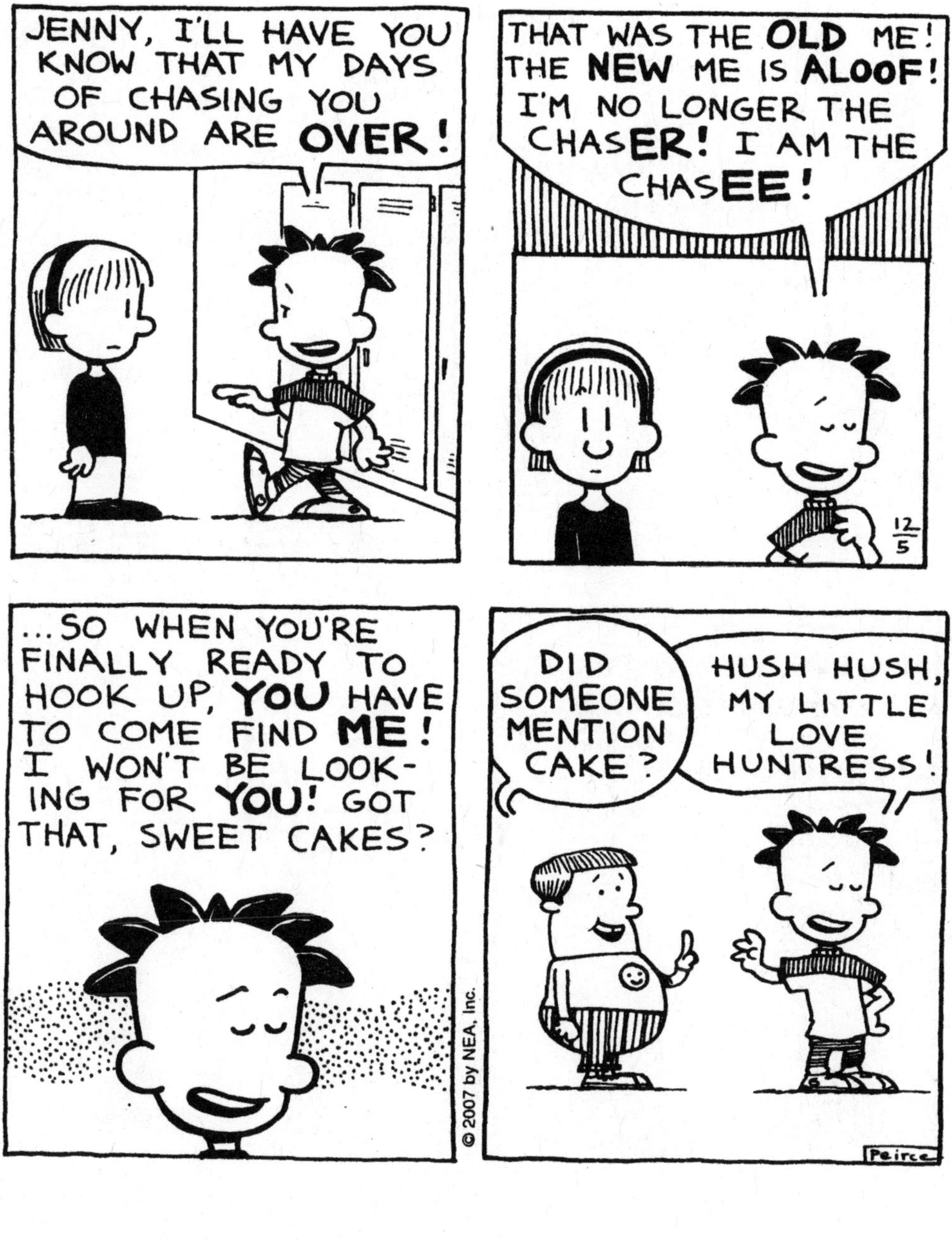
JENNY, I'LL HAVE YOU KNOW THAT MY DAYS OF CHASING YOU AROUND ARE OVER!
THAT WAS THE OLD ME! THE NEW ME IS ALOOF! I'M NO LONGER THE CHASER! I AM THE CHASEE!
12/5
...SO WHEN YOU'RE FINALLY READY TO HOOK UP, YOU HAVE TO COME FIND ME! I WON'T BE LOOKING FOR YOU! GOT THAT, SWEET CAKES?
DID SOMEONE MENTION CAKE?
HUSH HUSH, MY LITTLE LOVE HUNTRESS!
© 2007 by NEA, Inc.
Peirce

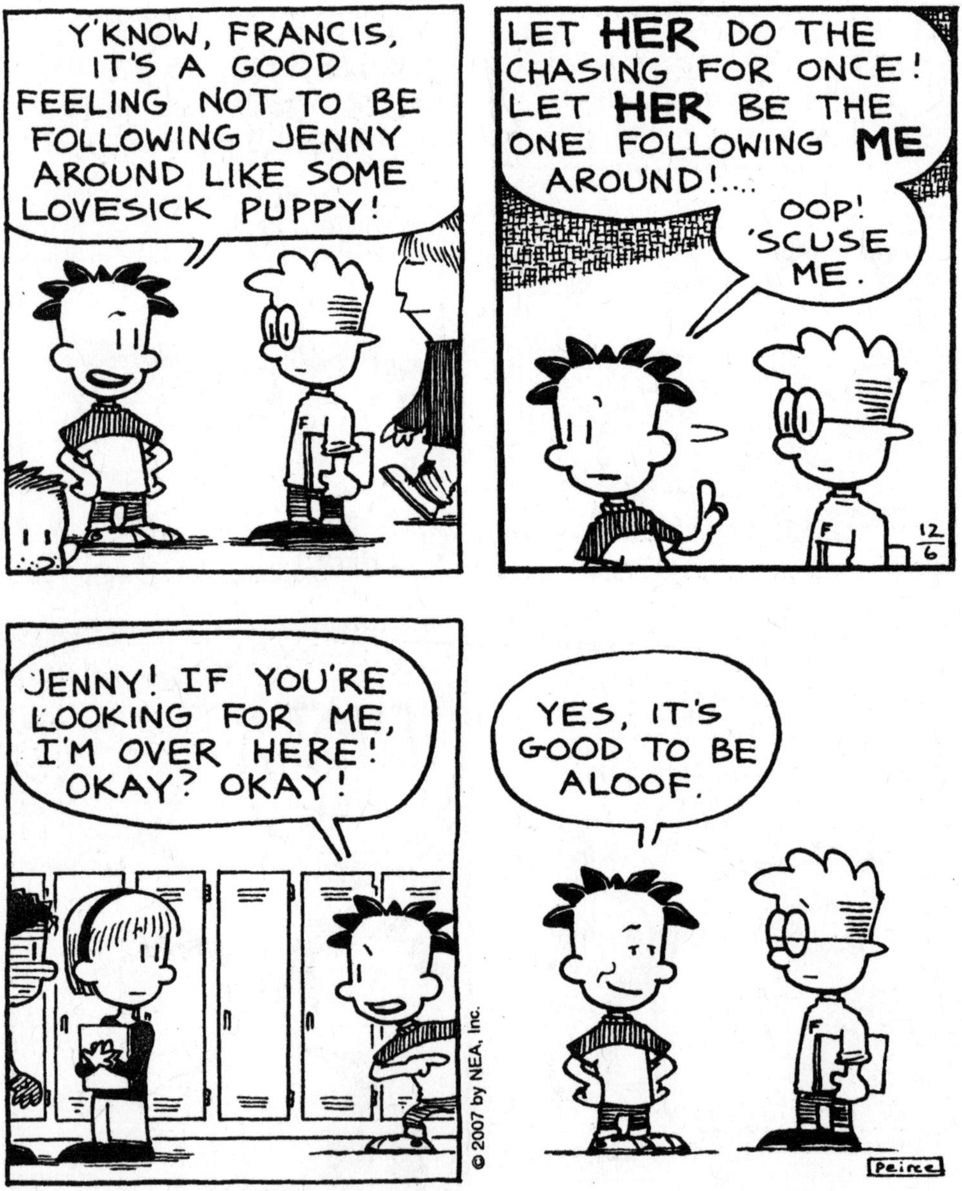
Y'KNOW, FRANCIS, IT'S A GOOD FEELING NOT TO BE FOLLOWING JENNY AROUND LIKE SOME LOVESICK PUPPY!
LET **HER** DO THE CHASING FOR ONCE! LET **HER** BE THE ONE FOLLOWING **ME** AROUND!....
OOP! 'SCUSE ME.
12/6
JENNY! IF YOU'RE LOOKING FOR ME, I'M OVER HERE! OKAY? OKAY!
YES, IT'S GOOD TO BE ALOOF.
Peirce

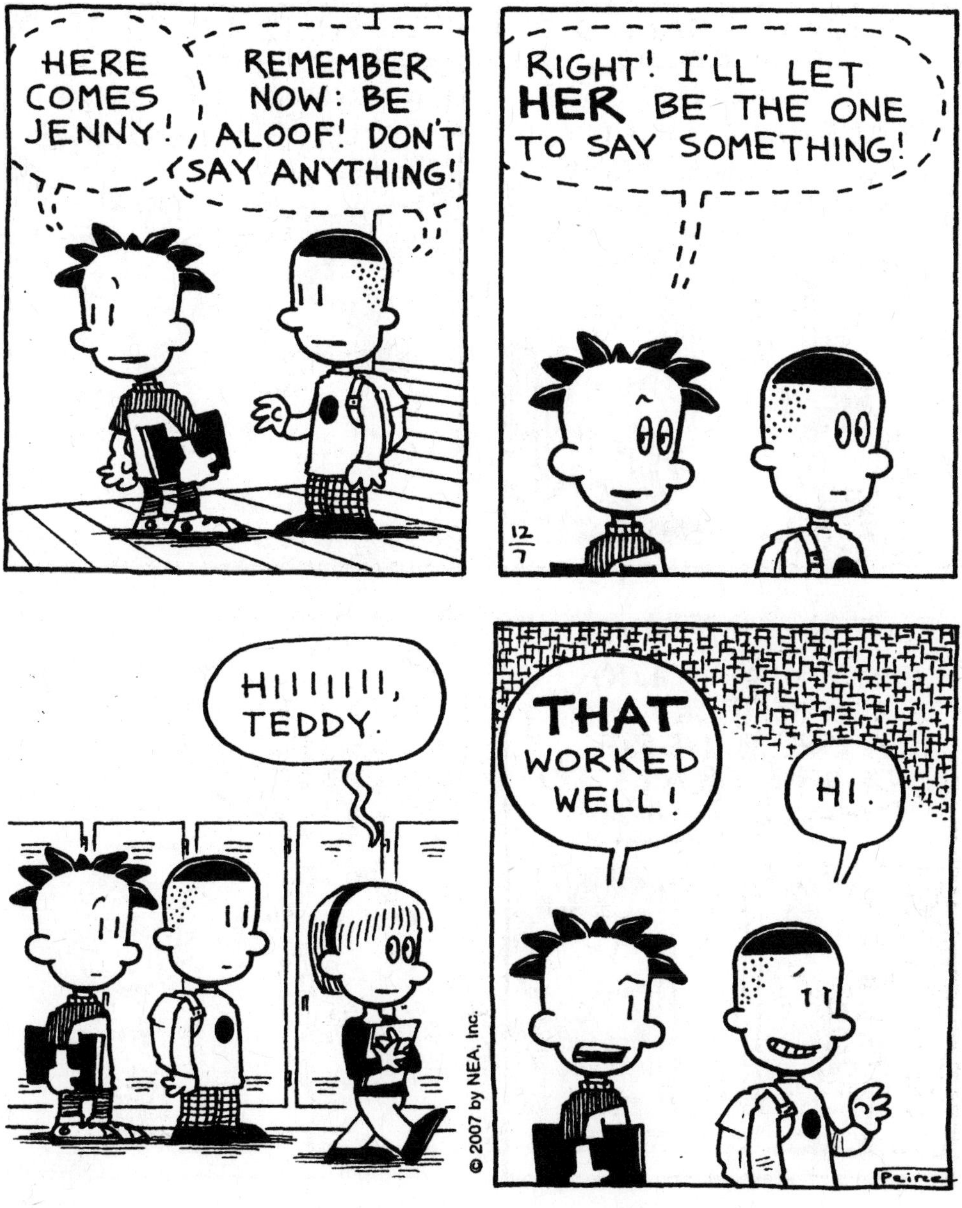
HERE COMES JENNY!
REMEMBER NOW: BE ALOOF! DON'T SAY ANYTHING!
RIGHT! I'LL LET **HER** BE THE ONE TO SAY SOMETHING!
HIIIIIII, TEDDY.
HI.
THAT WORKED WELL!
© 2007 by NEA, Inc.

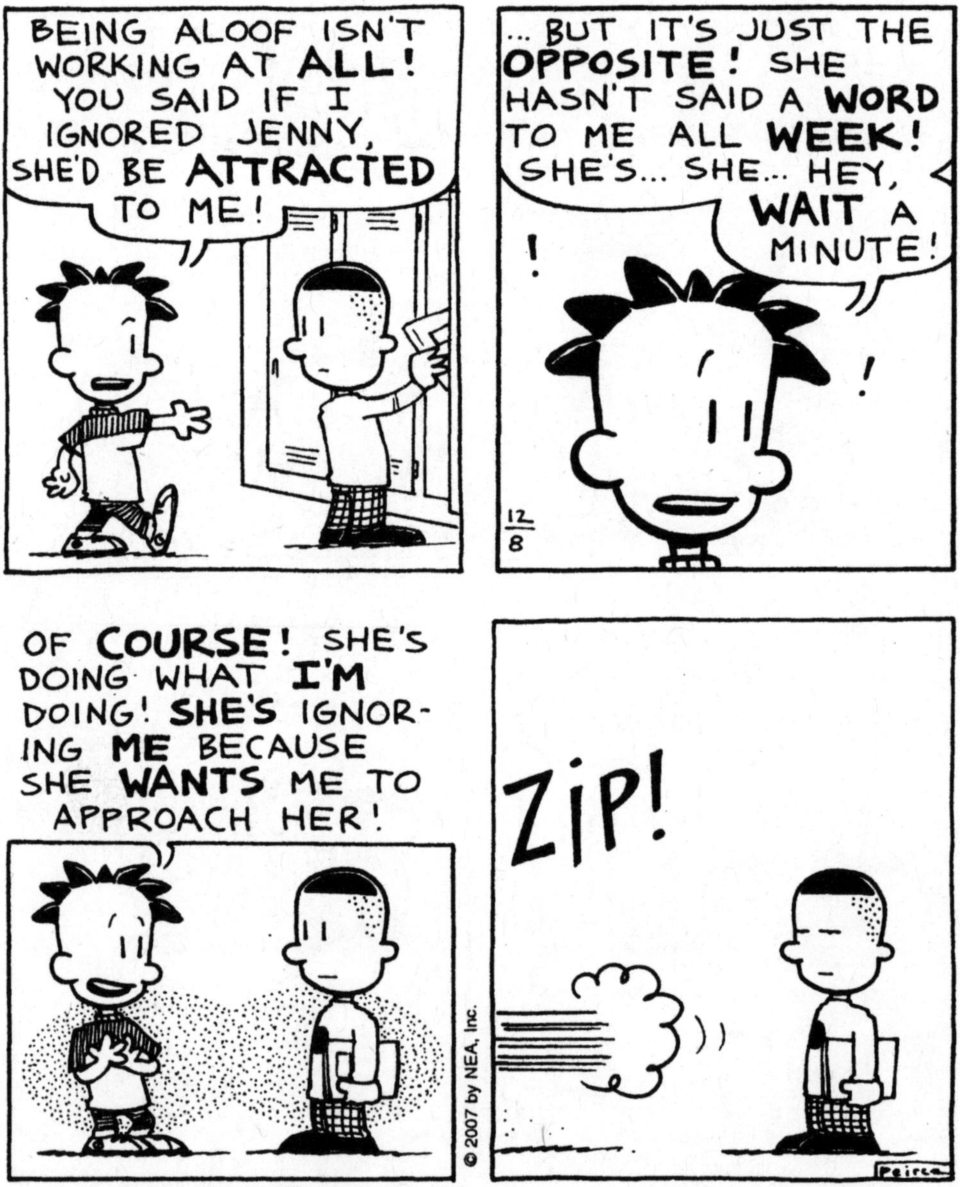
BEING ALOOF ISN'T WORKING AT ALL! YOU SAID IF I IGNORED JENNY, SHE'D BE ATTRACTED TO ME!
... BUT IT'S JUST THE OPPOSITE! SHE HASN'T SAID A WORD TO ME ALL WEEK! SHE'S... SHE... HEY, WAIT A MINUTE!
!
!
12
8
OF COURSE! SHE'S DOING WHAT I'M DOING! SHE'S IGNORING ME BECAUSE SHE WANTS ME TO APPROACH HER!
© 2007 by NEA, Inc.
ZIP!
Peirce

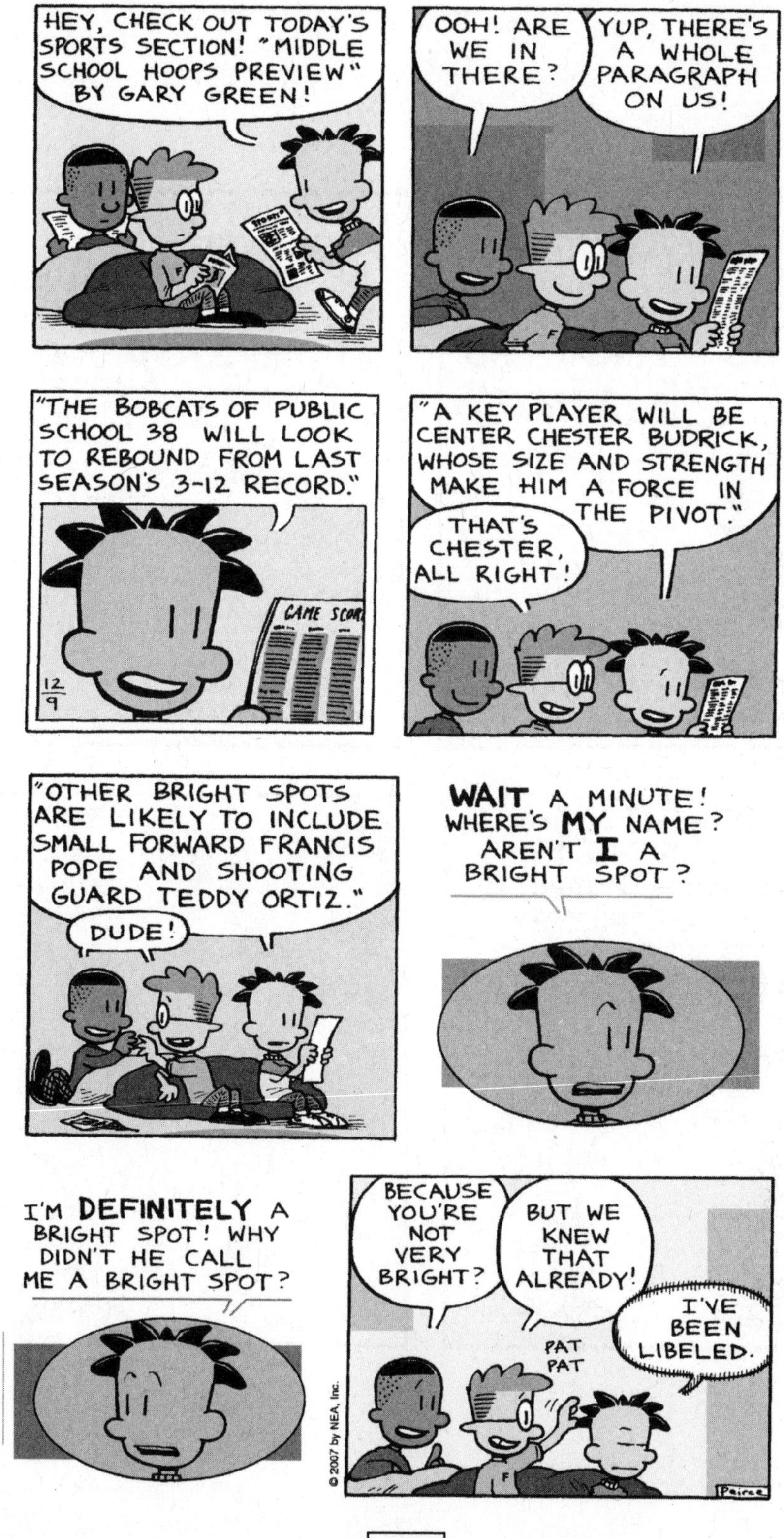

HEY, CHECK OUT TODAY'S SPORTS SECTION! "MIDDLE SCHOOL HOOPS PREVIEW" BY GARY GREEN!
OOH! ARE WE IN THERE?
YUP, THERE'S A WHOLE PARAGRAPH ON US!
"THE BOBCATS OF PUBLIC SCHOOL 38 WILL LOOK TO REBOUND FROM LAST SEASON'S 3-12 RECORD."
GAME SCOR
12/9
"A KEY PLAYER WILL BE CENTER CHESTER BUDRICK, WHOSE SIZE AND STRENGTH MAKE HIM A FORCE IN THE PIVOT."
THAT'S CHESTER, ALL RIGHT!
"OTHER BRIGHT SPOTS ARE LIKELY TO INCLUDE SMALL FORWARD FRANCIS POPE AND SHOOTING GUARD TEDDY ORTIZ."
DUDE!
WAIT A MINUTE! WHERE'S MY NAME? AREN'T I A BRIGHT SPOT?
I'M DEFINITELY A BRIGHT SPOT! WHY DIDN'T HE CALL ME A BRIGHT SPOT?
BECAUSE YOU'RE NOT VERY BRIGHT?
BUT WE KNEW THAT ALREADY!
I'VE BEEN LIBELED.
PAT PAT
© 2007 by NEA, Inc.
Peirce

CHAMPS, OR NOT?

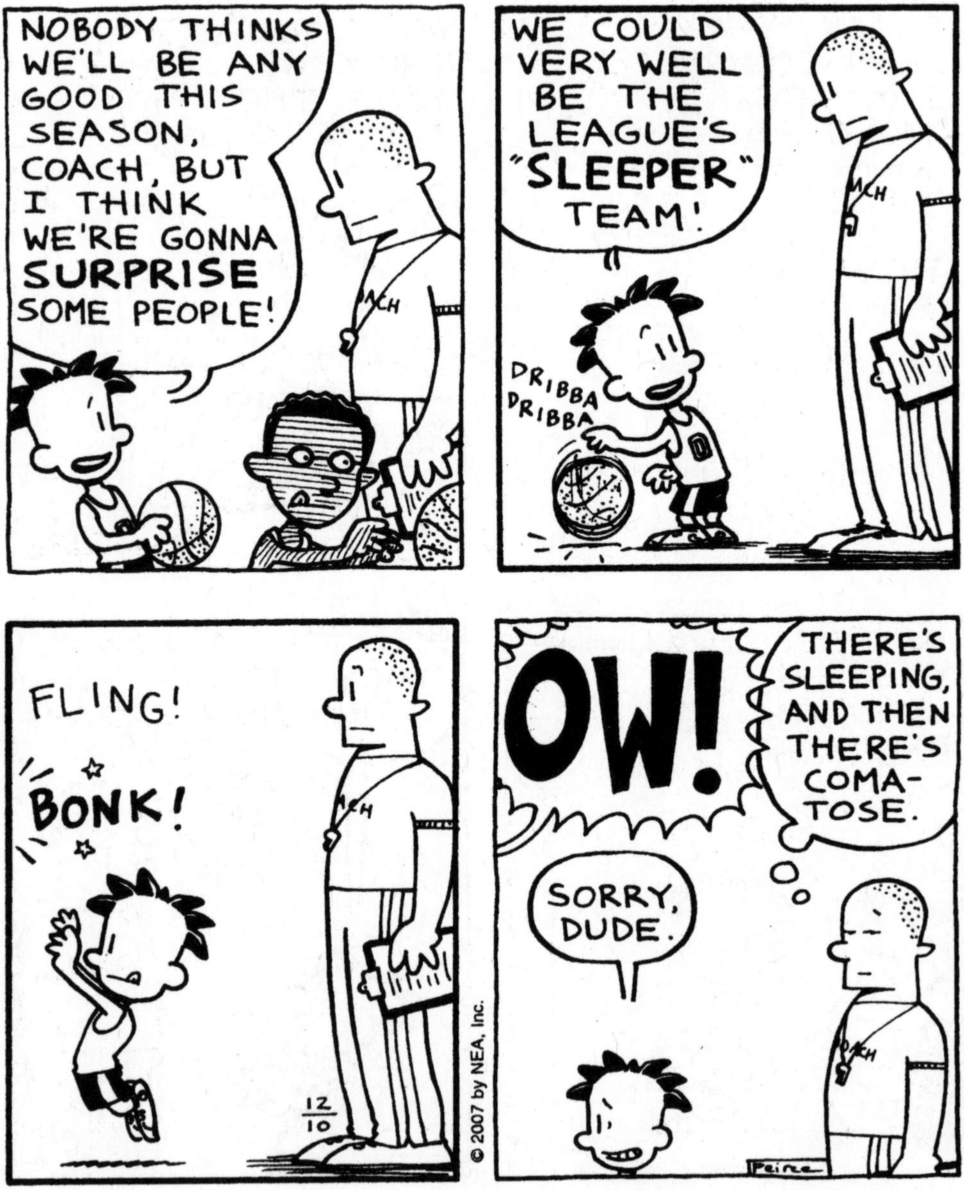
NOBODY THINKS WE'LL BE ANY GOOD THIS SEASON, COACH, BUT I THINK WE'RE GONNA SURPRISE SOME PEOPLE!
WE COULD VERY WELL BE THE LEAGUE'S "SLEEPER" TEAM!
DRIBBA DRIBBA
FLING!
BONK!
OW!
THERE'S SLEEPING, AND THEN THERE'S COMA-TOSE.
SORRY, DUDE.
© 2007 by NEA, Inc.

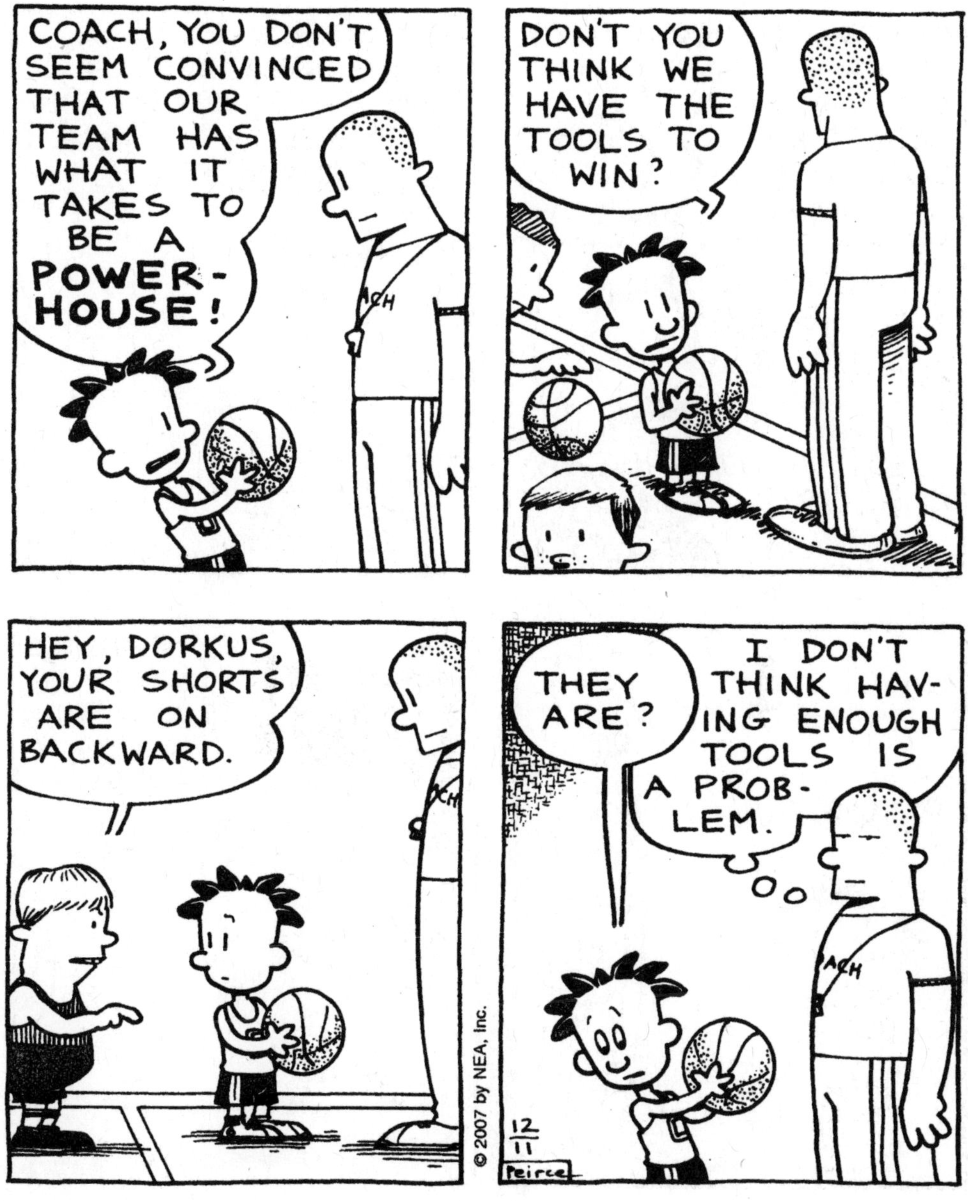
COACH, YOU DON'T SEEM CONVINCED THAT OUR TEAM HAS WHAT IT TAKES TO BE A **POWER-HOUSE!**
DON'T YOU THINK WE HAVE THE TOOLS TO WIN?
HEY, DORKUS, YOUR SHORTS ARE ON BACKWARD.
THEY ARE?
I DON'T THINK HAVING ENOUGH TOOLS IS A PROBLEM.
© 2007 by NEA, Inc.
12/11
Peirce

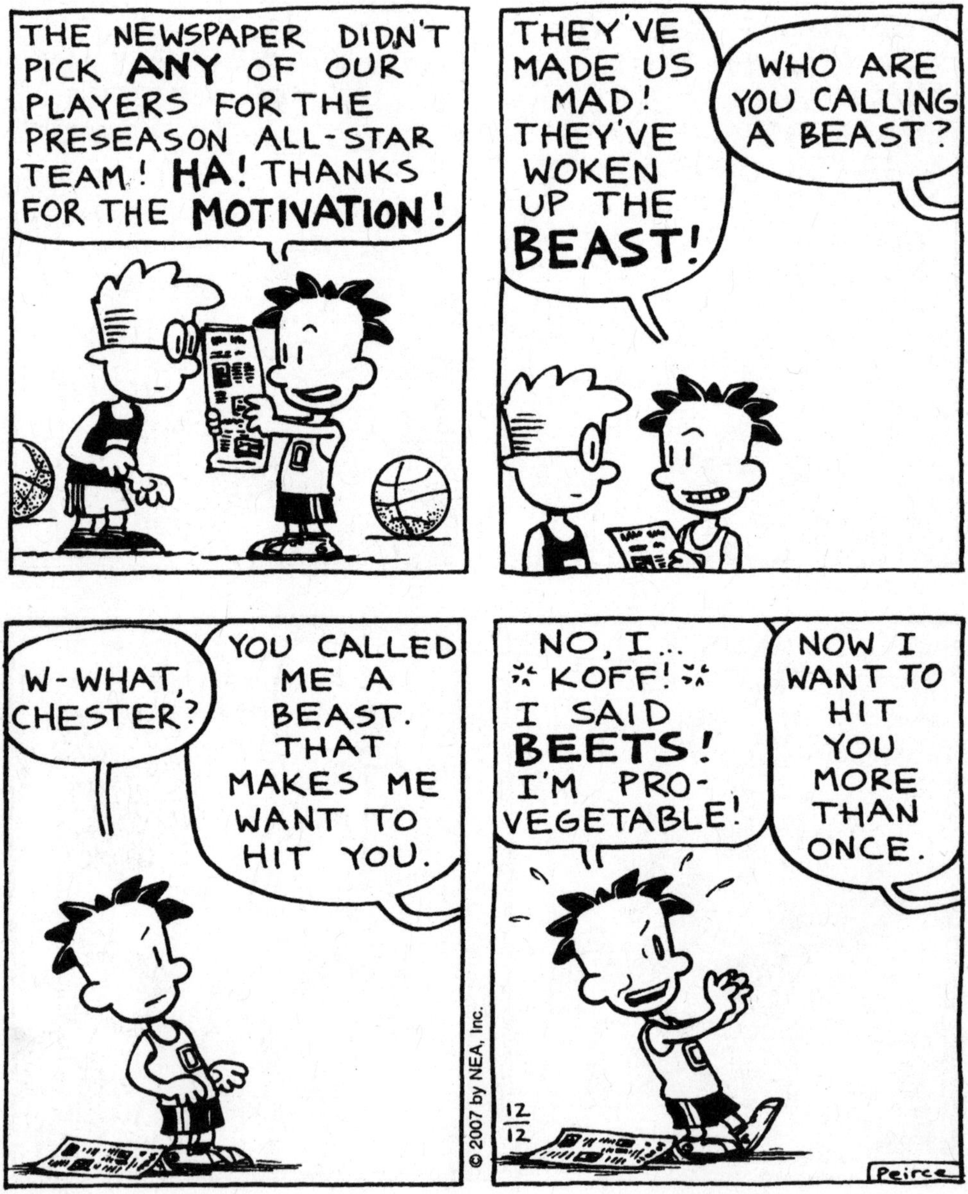
THE NEWSPAPER DIDN'T PICK ANY OF OUR PLAYERS FOR THE PRESEASON ALL-STAR TEAM! HA! THANKS FOR THE MOTIVATION!
THEY'VE MADE US MAD! THEY'VE WOKEN UP THE BEAST!
WHO ARE YOU CALLING A BEAST?
W-WHAT, CHESTER?
YOU CALLED ME A BEAST. THAT MAKES ME WANT TO HIT YOU.
NO, I... KOFF! I SAID BEETS! I'M PRO-VEGETABLE!
NOW I WANT TO HIT YOU MORE THAN ONCE.
© 2007 by NEA, Inc.
12/12
Peirce

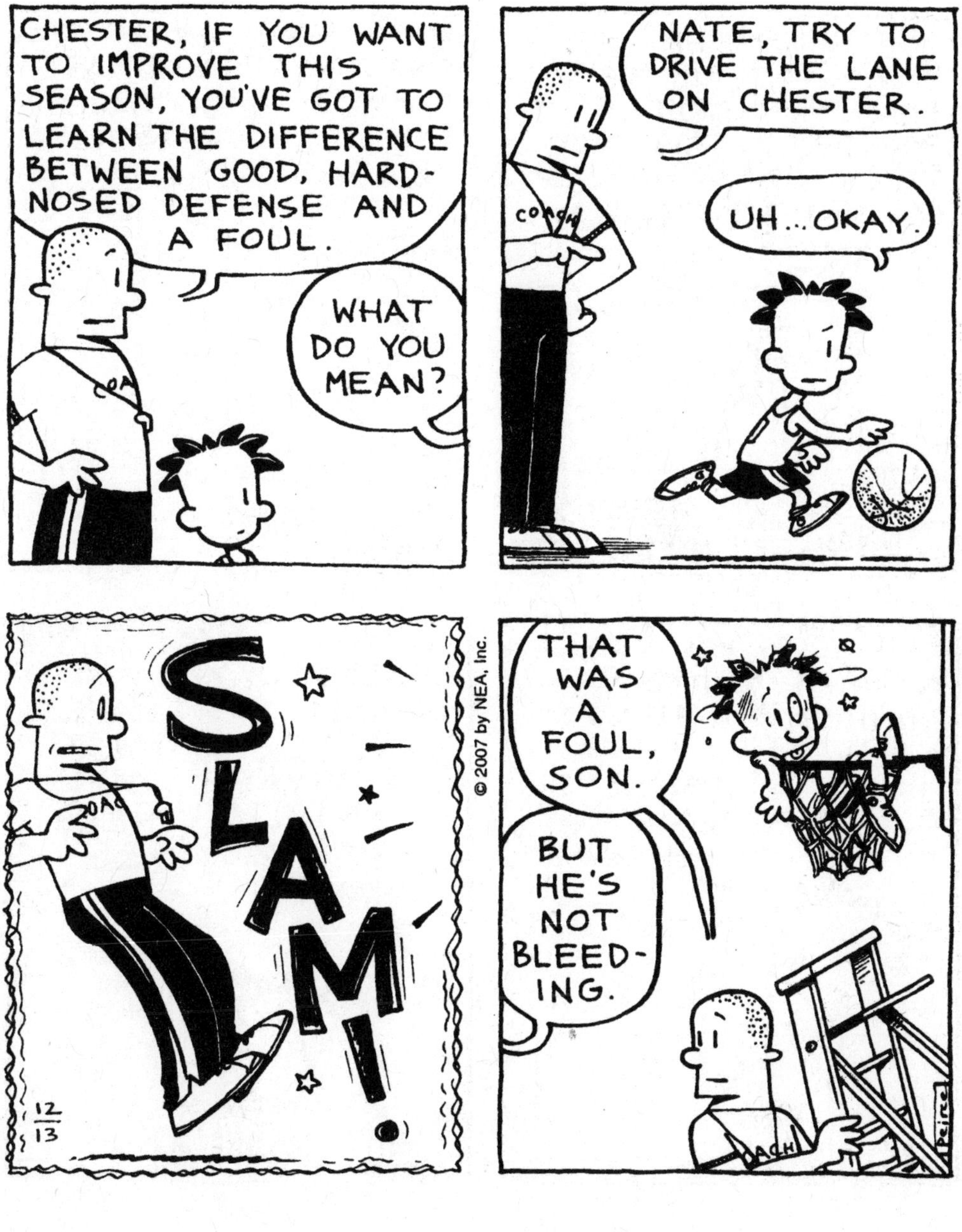
CHESTER, IF YOU WANT TO IMPROVE THIS SEASON, YOU'VE GOT TO LEARN THE DIFFERENCE BETWEEN GOOD, HARD-NOSED DEFENSE AND A FOUL.
WHAT DO YOU MEAN?
NATE, TRY TO DRIVE THE LANE ON CHESTER.
UH...OKAY.
SLAM!
THAT WAS A FOUL, SON.
BUT HE'S NOT BLEEDING.

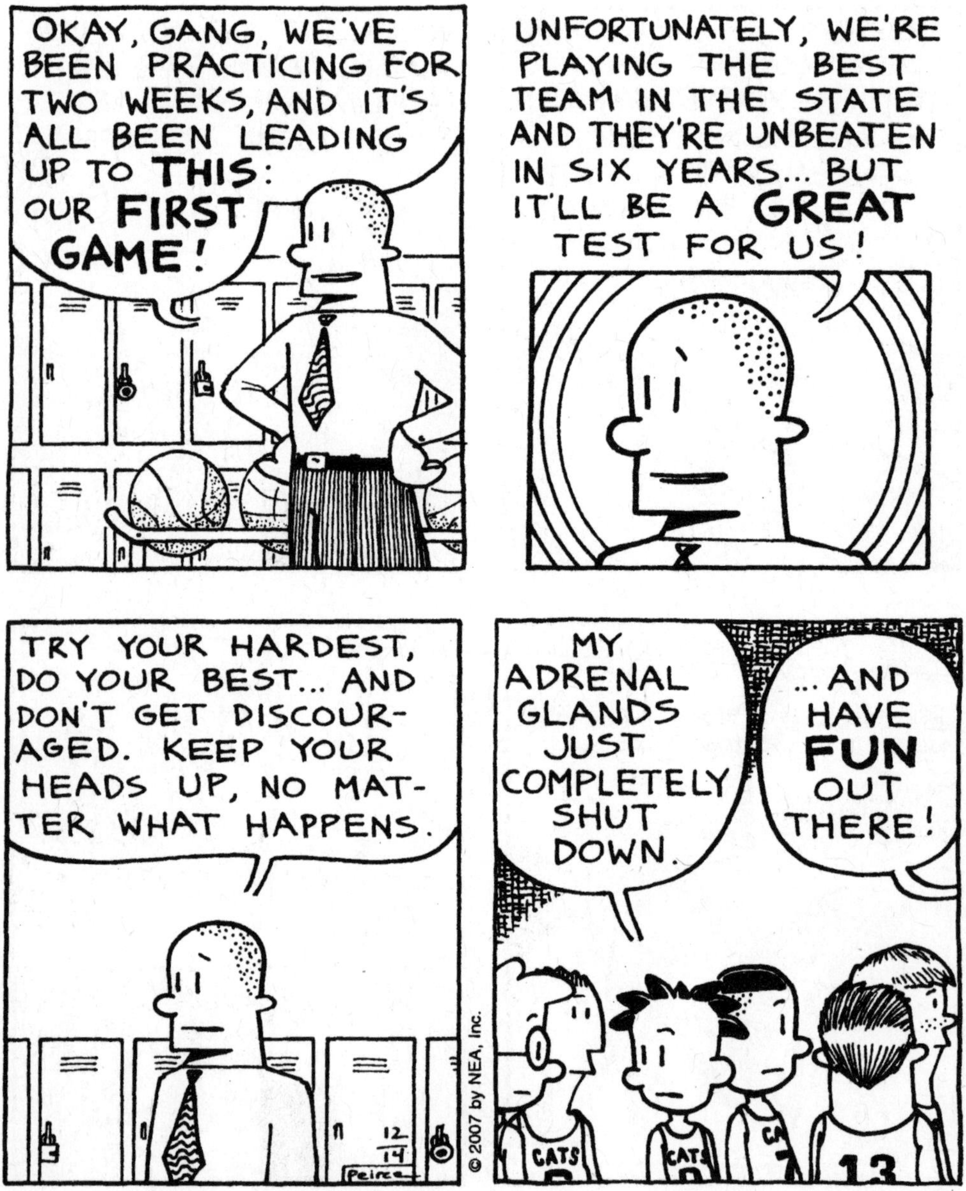
OKAY, GANG, WE'VE BEEN PRACTICING FOR TWO WEEKS, AND IT'S ALL BEEN LEADING UP TO THIS: OUR FIRST GAME!
UNFORTUNATELY, WE'RE PLAYING THE BEST TEAM IN THE STATE AND THEY'RE UNBEATEN IN SIX YEARS... BUT IT'LL BE A GREAT TEST FOR US!
TRY YOUR HARDEST, DO YOUR BEST... AND DON'T GET DISCOURAGED. KEEP YOUR HEADS UP, NO MATTER WHAT HAPPENS.
...AND HAVE FUN OUT THERE!
MY ADRENAL GLANDS JUST COMPLETELY SHUT DOWN.
12/14
Peirce
CATS
CATS
13

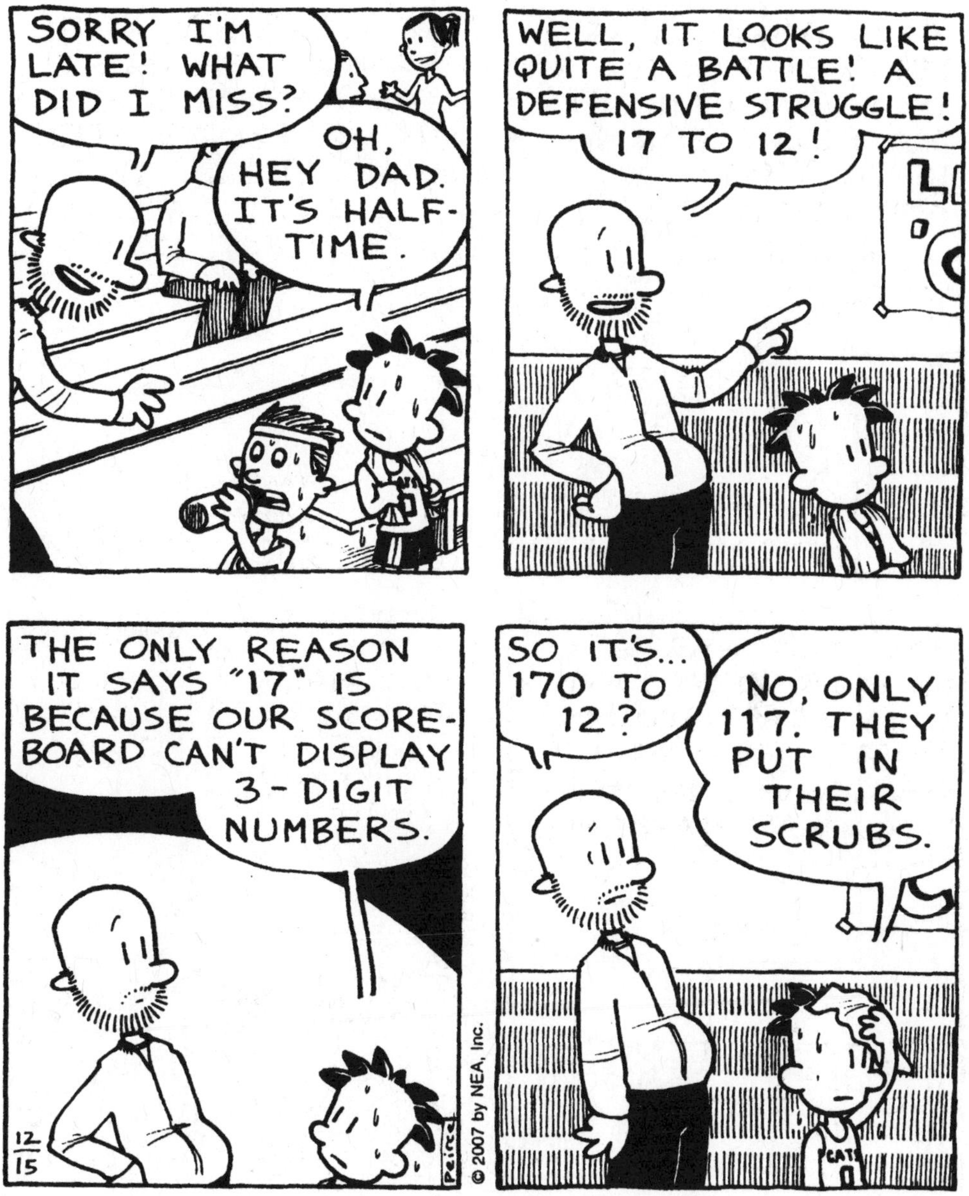
SORRY I'M LATE! WHAT DID I MISS?
OH, HEY DAD. IT'S HALF-TIME.
WELL, IT LOOKS LIKE QUITE A BATTLE! A DEFENSIVE STRUGGLE! 17 TO 12!
THE ONLY REASON IT SAYS "17" IS BECAUSE OUR SCORE-BOARD CAN'T DISPLAY 3-DIGIT NUMBERS.
SO IT'S... 170 TO 12?
NO, ONLY 117. THEY PUT IN THEIR SCRUBS.
12/15
Peirce
© 2007 by NEA, Inc.

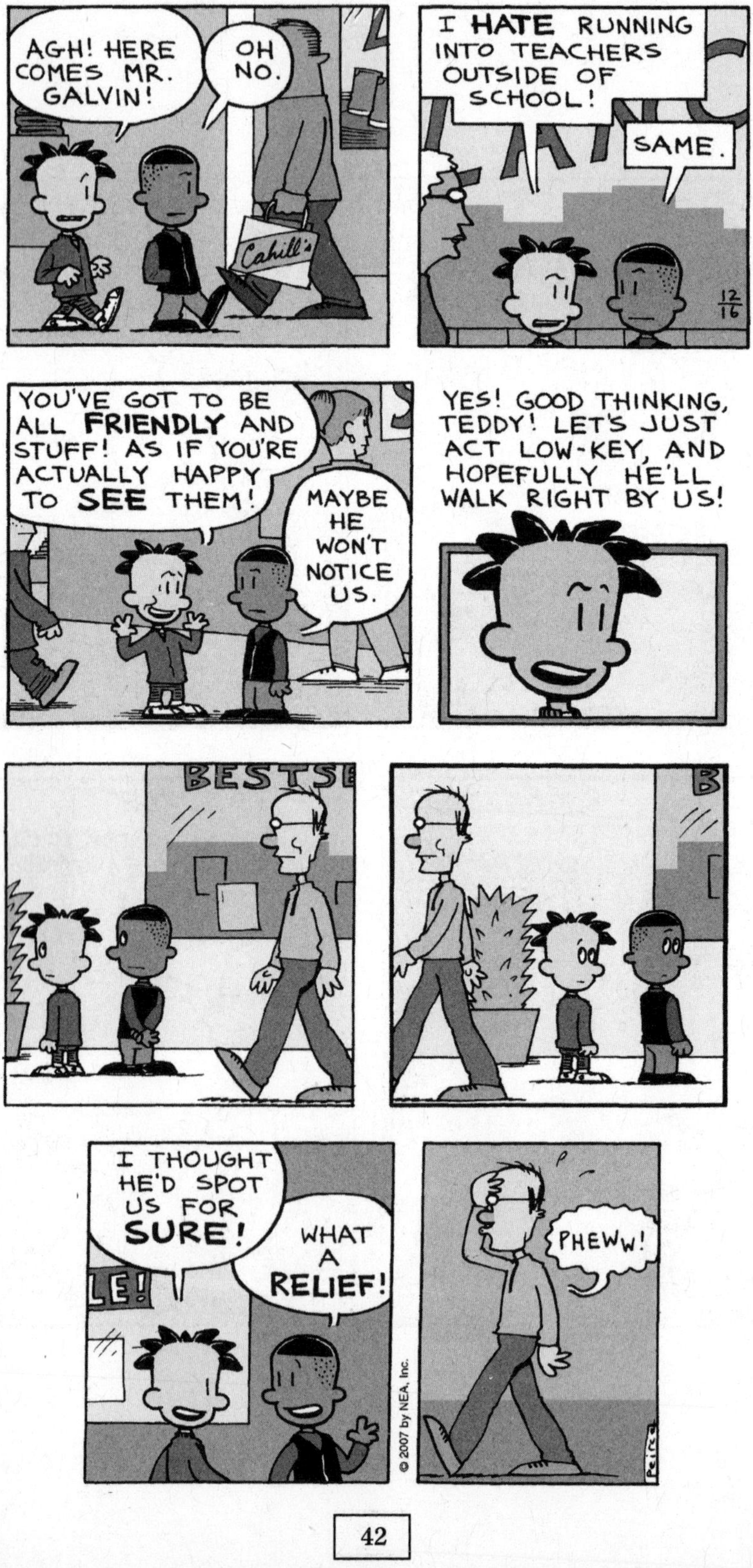
AGH! HERE COMES MR. GALVIN!
OH NO.
Cahill's
I **HATE** RUNNING INTO TEACHERS OUTSIDE OF SCHOOL!
SAME.
12/16
YOU'VE GOT TO BE ALL **FRIENDLY** AND STUFF! AS IF YOU'RE ACTUALLY HAPPY TO **SEE** THEM!
MAYBE HE WON'T NOTICE US.
YES! GOOD THINKING, TEDDY! LET'S JUST ACT LOW-KEY, AND HOPEFULLY HE'LL WALK RIGHT BY US!
BESTSE
I THOUGHT HE'D SPOT US FOR **SURE**!
WHAT A **RELIEF**!
PHEWW!
© 2007 by NEA, Inc.

DOGS VS. CATS

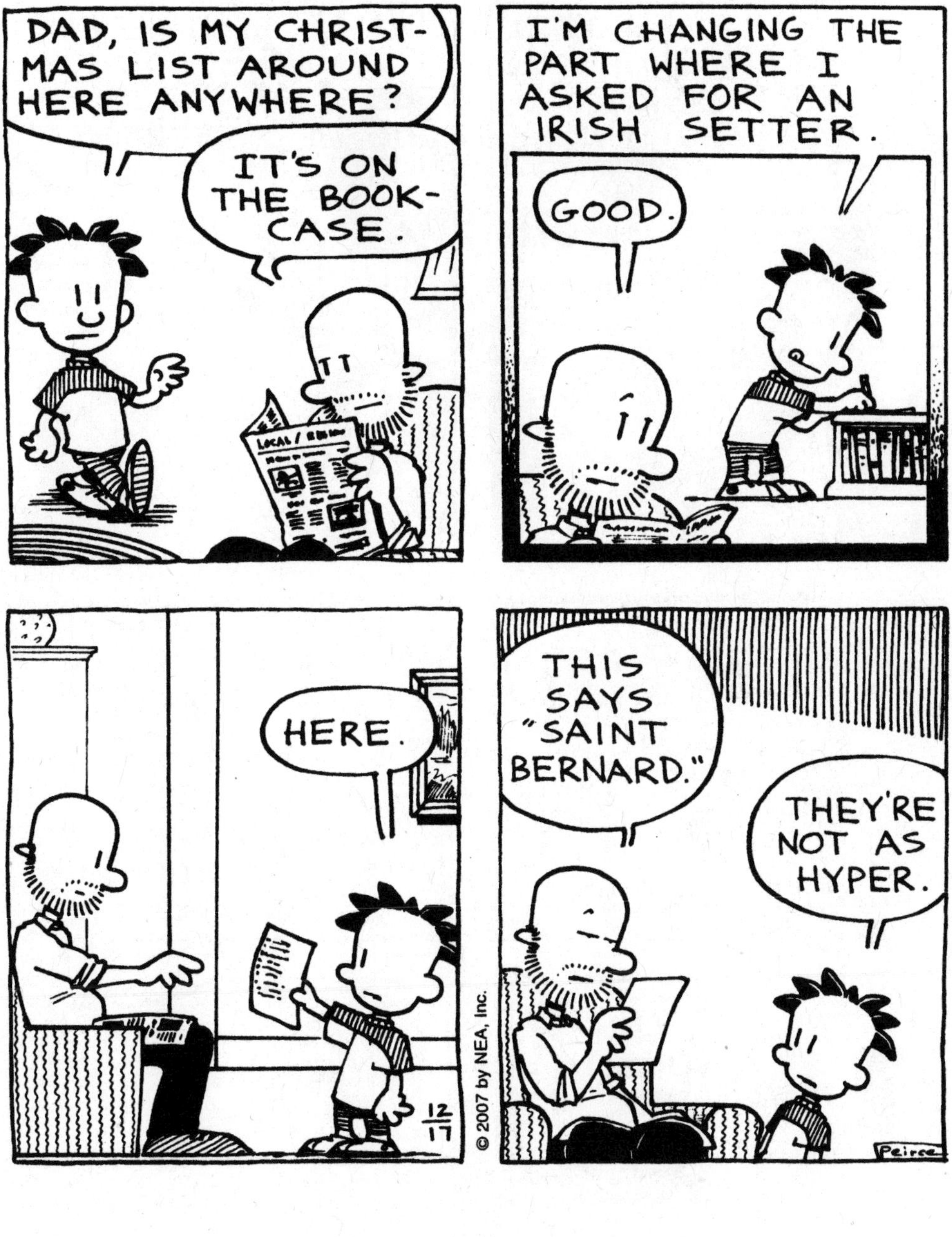
DAD, IS MY CHRISTMAS LIST AROUND HERE ANYWHERE?
IT'S ON THE BOOKCASE.
I'M CHANGING THE PART WHERE I ASKED FOR AN IRISH SETTER.
GOOD.
HERE.
12/17
© 2007 by NEA, Inc.
THIS SAYS "SAINT BERNARD."
THEY'RE NOT AS HYPER.
Peirce

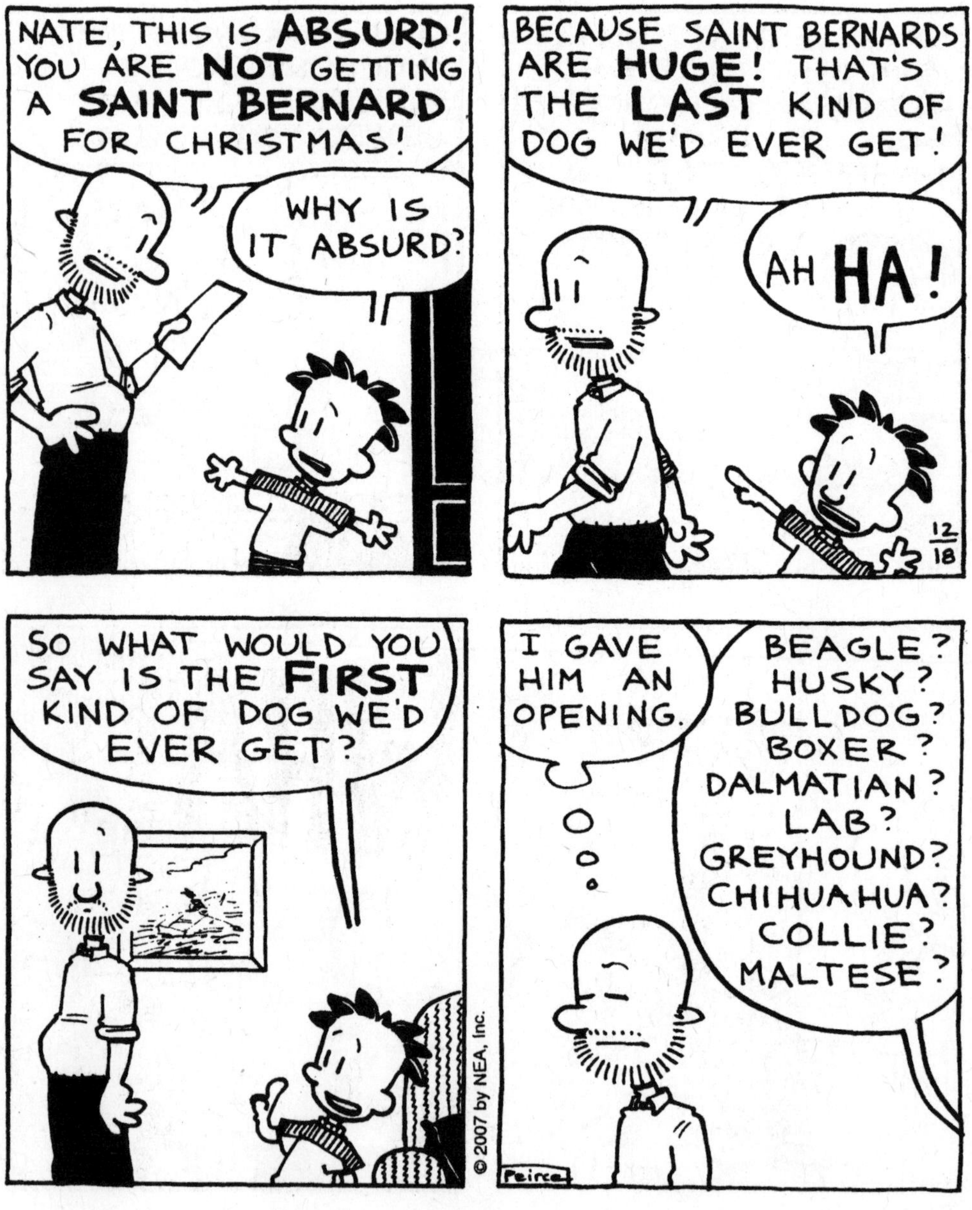
NATE, THIS IS ABSURD! YOU ARE NOT GETTING A SAINT BERNARD FOR CHRISTMAS!
WHY IS IT ABSURD?
BECAUSE SAINT BERNARDS ARE HUGE! THAT'S THE LAST KIND OF DOG WE'D EVER GET!
AH HA!
12/18
SO WHAT WOULD YOU SAY IS THE FIRST KIND OF DOG WE'D EVER GET?
© 2007 by NEA, Inc.
I GAVE HIM AN OPENING.
BEAGLE? HUSKY? BULLDOG? BOXER? DALMATIAN? LAB? GREYHOUND? CHIHUAHUA? COLLIE? MALTESE?
Peirce

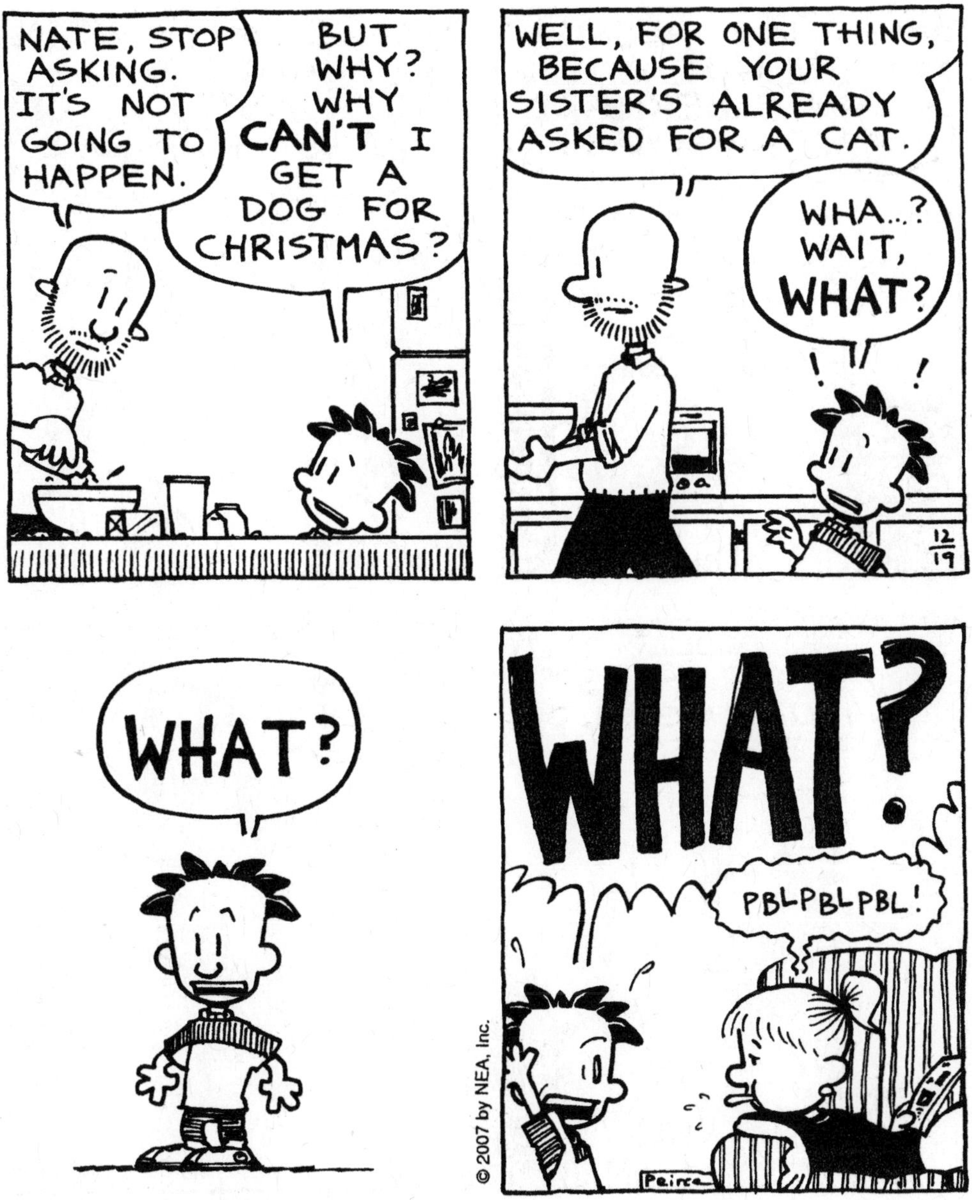
NATE, STOP ASKING. IT'S NOT GOING TO HAPPEN.
BUT WHY? WHY **CAN'T** I GET A DOG FOR CHRISTMAS?
WELL, FOR ONE THING, BECAUSE YOUR SISTER'S ALREADY ASKED FOR A CAT.
WHA...? WAIT, **WHAT?**
WHAT?
WHAT?
PBLPBLPBL!

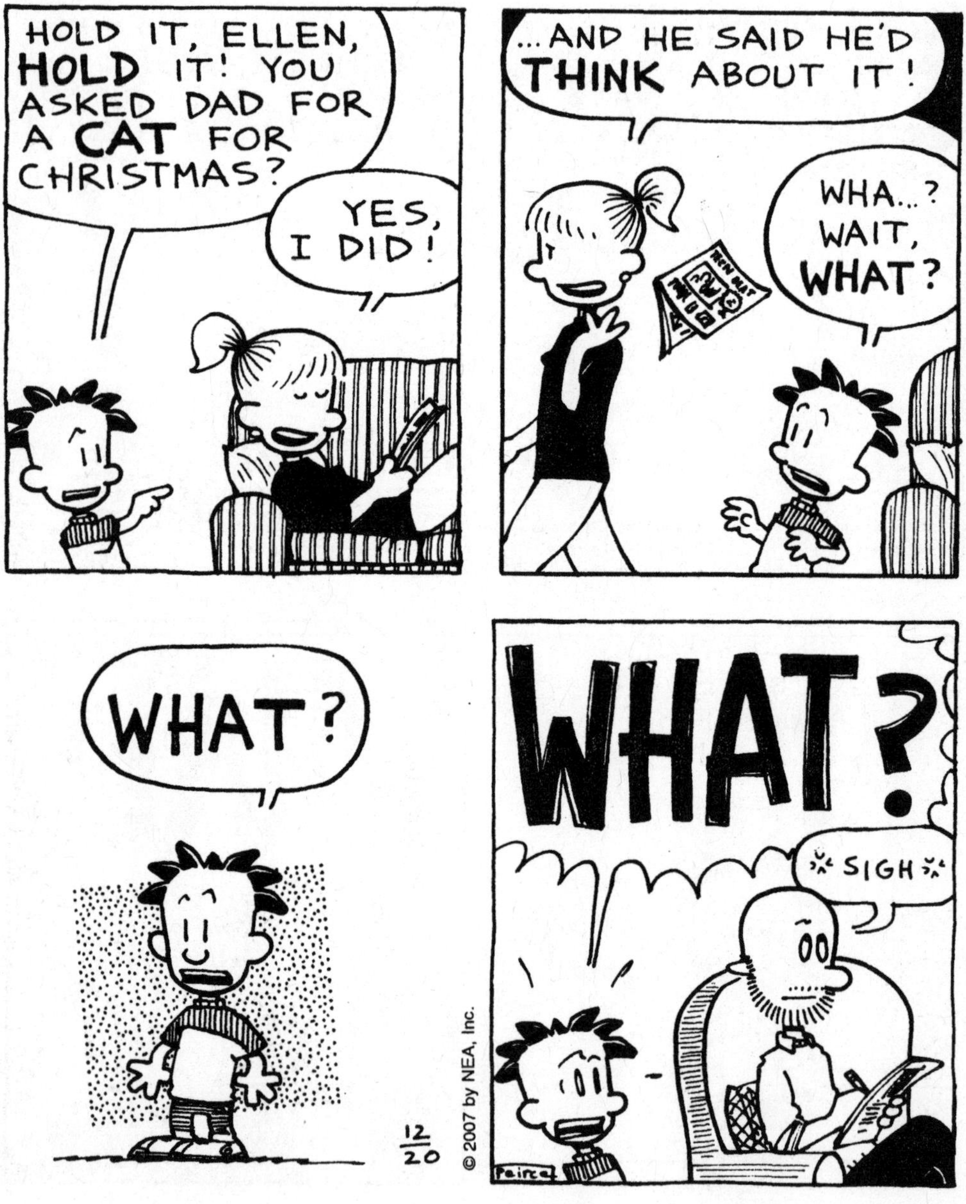
HOLD IT, ELLEN, **HOLD** IT! YOU ASKED DAD FOR A **CAT** FOR CHRISTMAS?
YES, I DID!
...AND HE SAID HE'D **THINK** ABOUT IT!
WHA...? WAIT, **WHAT**?
WHAT?
12/20
© 2007 by NEA, Inc.
WHAT?
SIGH
Peirce

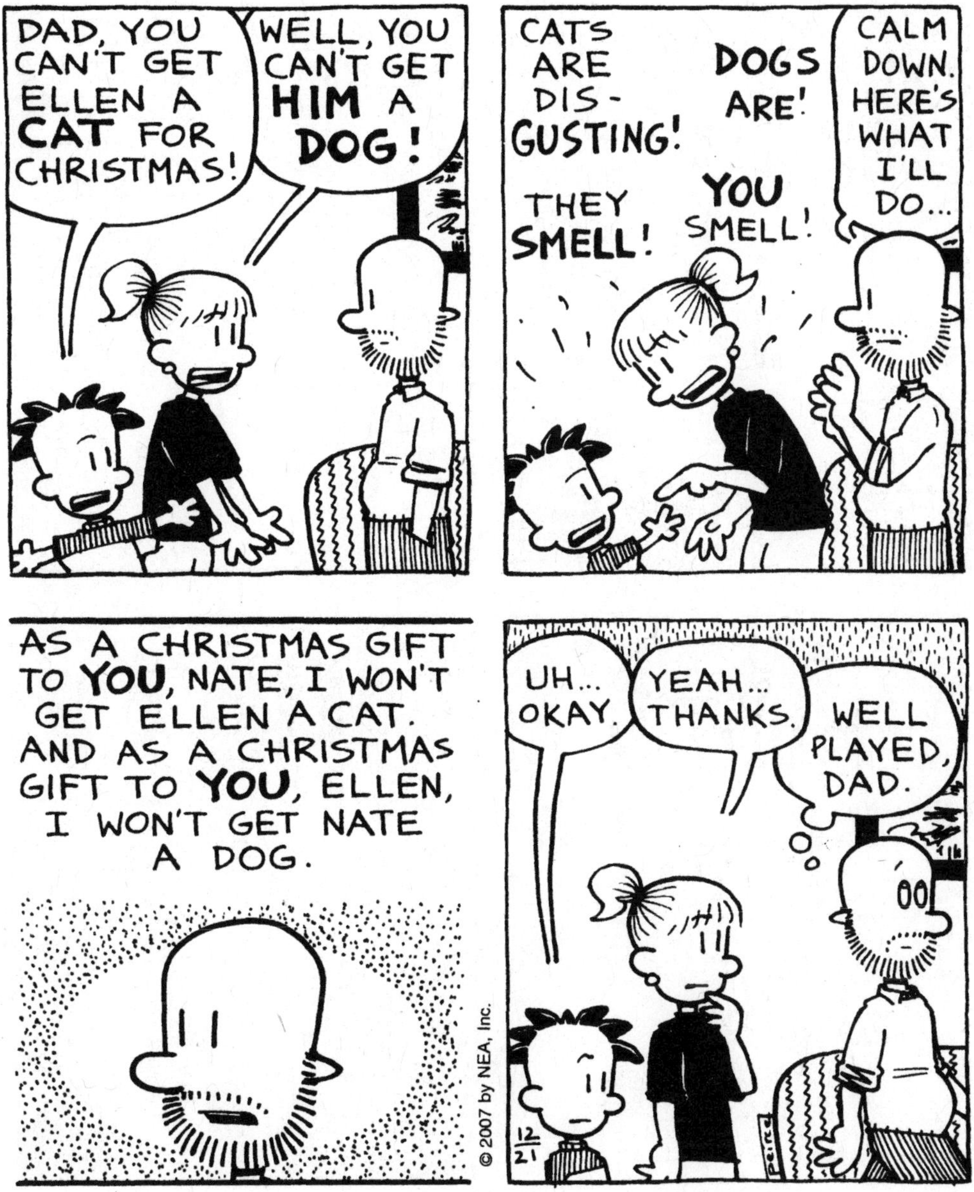
DAD, YOU CAN'T GET ELLEN A CAT FOR CHRISTMAS!
WELL, YOU CAN'T GET HIM A DOG!
CATS ARE DIS-GUSTING!
DOGS ARE!
THEY SMELL!
YOU SMELL!
CALM DOWN. HERE'S WHAT I'LL DO...
AS A CHRISTMAS GIFT TO YOU, NATE, I WON'T GET ELLEN A CAT. AND AS A CHRISTMAS GIFT TO YOU, ELLEN, I WON'T GET NATE A DOG.
© 2007 by NEA, Inc.
UH... OKAY.
YEAH... THANKS.
WELL PLAYED, DAD.
12 21

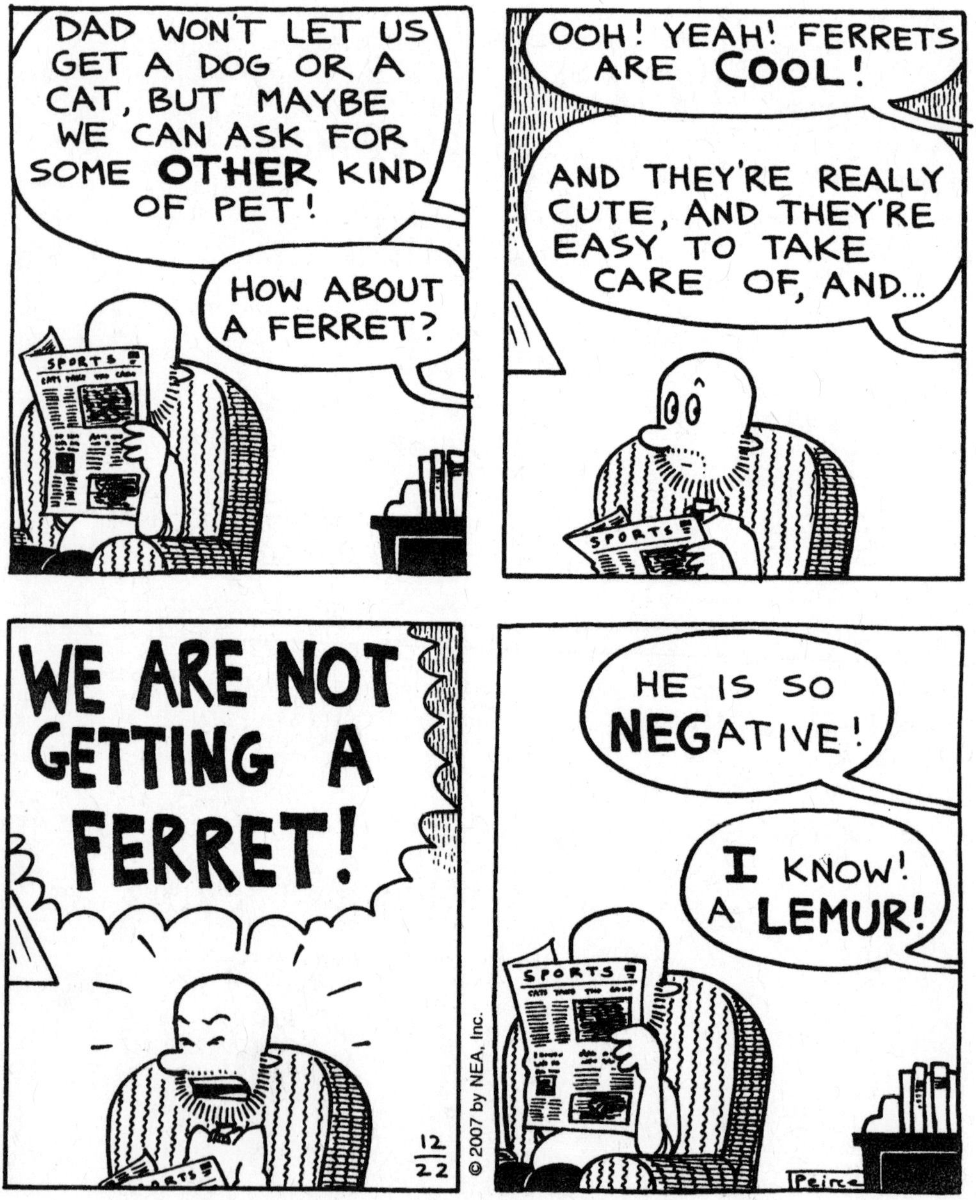
DAD WON'T LET US GET A DOG OR A CAT, BUT MAYBE WE CAN ASK FOR SOME **OTHER** KIND OF PET!
HOW ABOUT A FERRET?
OOH! YEAH! FERRETS ARE **COOL**!
AND THEY'RE REALLY CUTE, AND THEY'RE EASY TO TAKE CARE OF, AND...
WE ARE NOT GETTING A FERRET!
12/22
HE IS SO **NEG**ATIVE!
I KNOW! A **LEMUR**!
Peirce

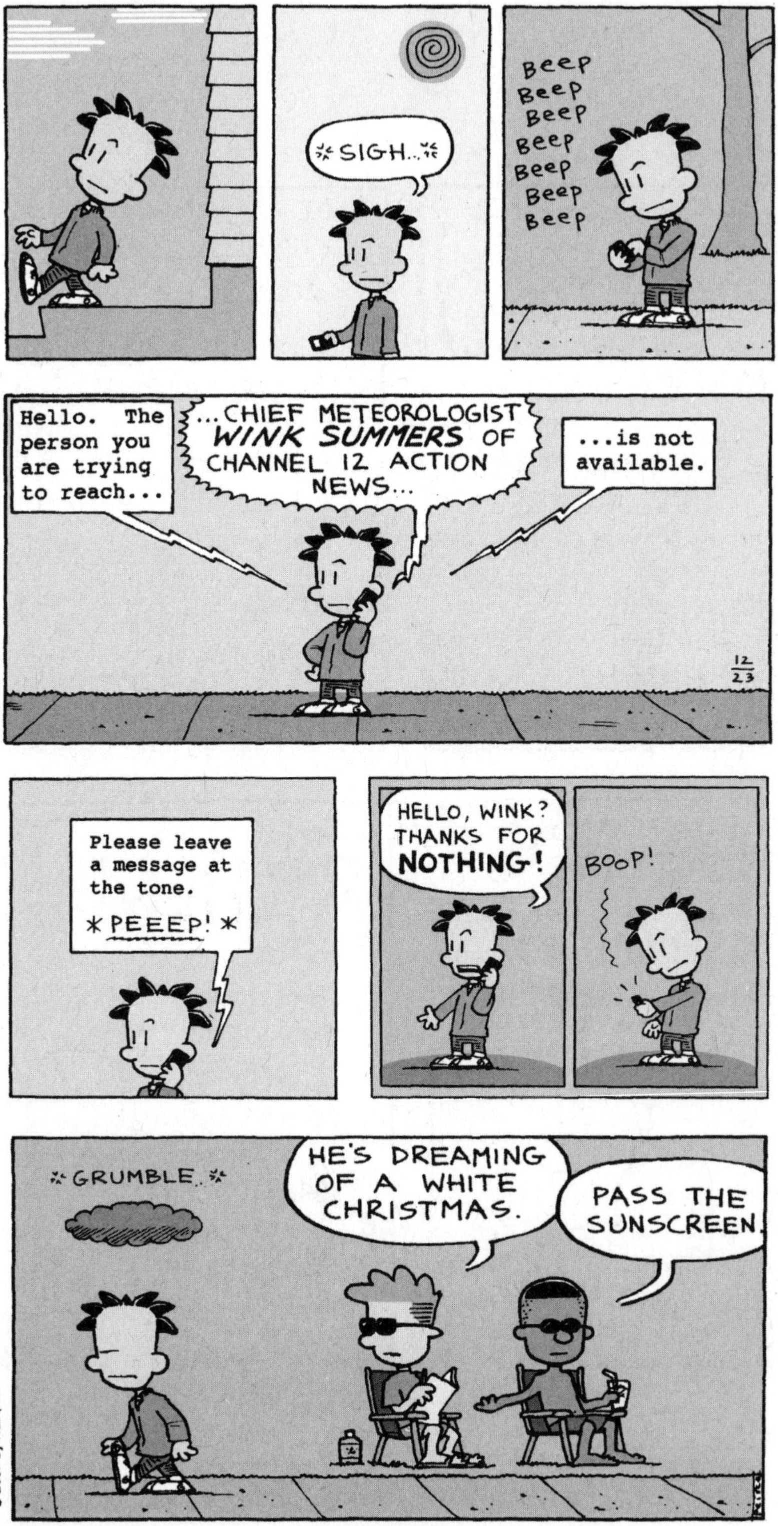
SIGH...
Beep
Beep
Beep
Beep
Beep
Beep
Beep
Hello. The person you are trying to reach...
...CHIEF METEOROLOGIST WINK SUMMERS OF CHANNEL 12 ACTION NEWS...
...is not available.
12/23
Please leave a message at the tone.
PEEEP!
HELLO, WINK? THANKS FOR NOTHING!
BOOP!
GRUMBLE...
HE'S DREAMING OF A WHITE CHRISTMAS.
PASS THE SUNSCREEN.

'TIS THE SEASON

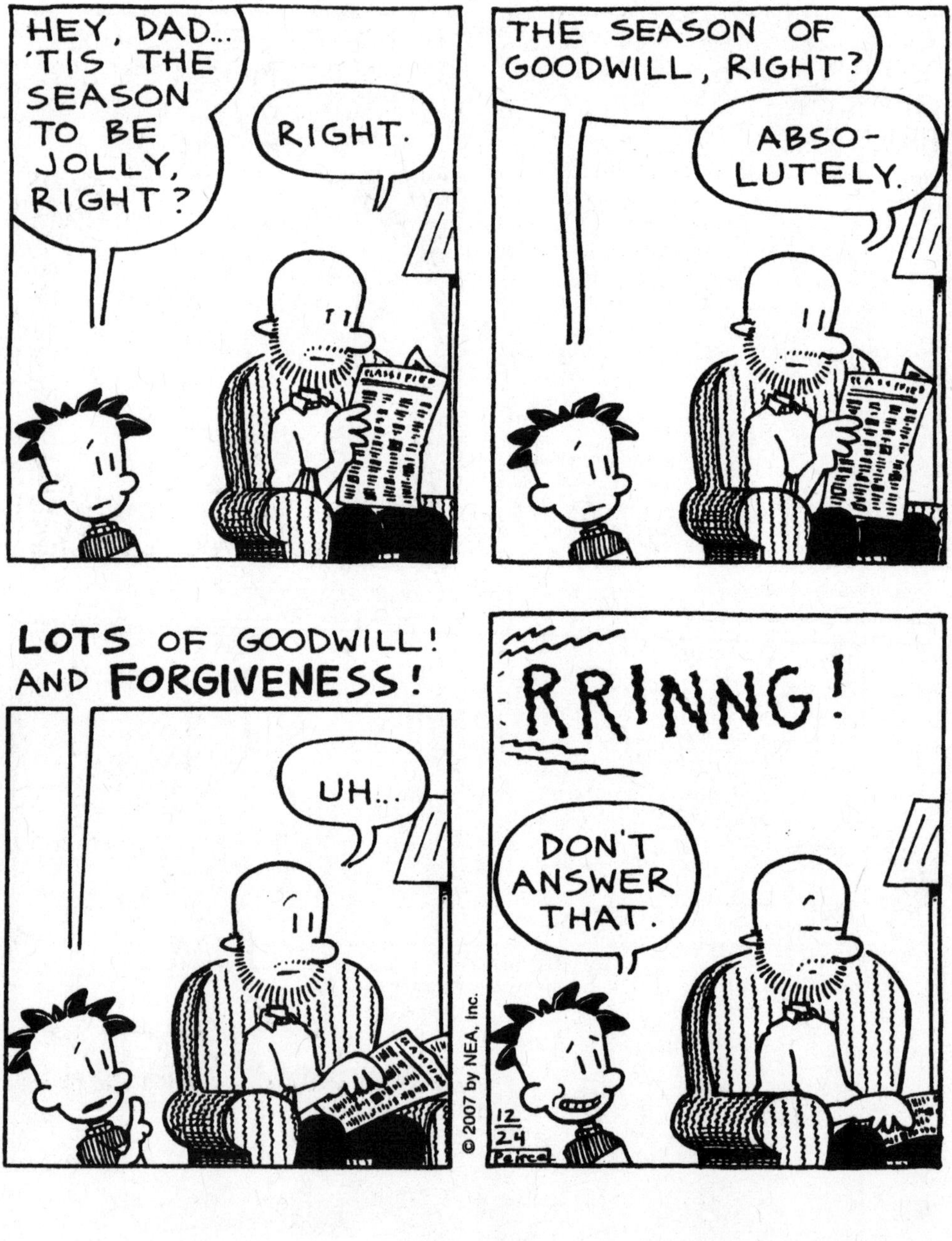
HEY, DAD... 'TIS THE SEASON TO BE JOLLY, RIGHT?
RIGHT.
THE SEASON OF GOODWILL, RIGHT?
ABSO-LUTELY.
LOTS OF GOODWILL! AND FORGIVENESS!
UH...
© 2007 by NEA, Inc.
12 24 Peirce
RRINNG!
DON'T ANSWER THAT.

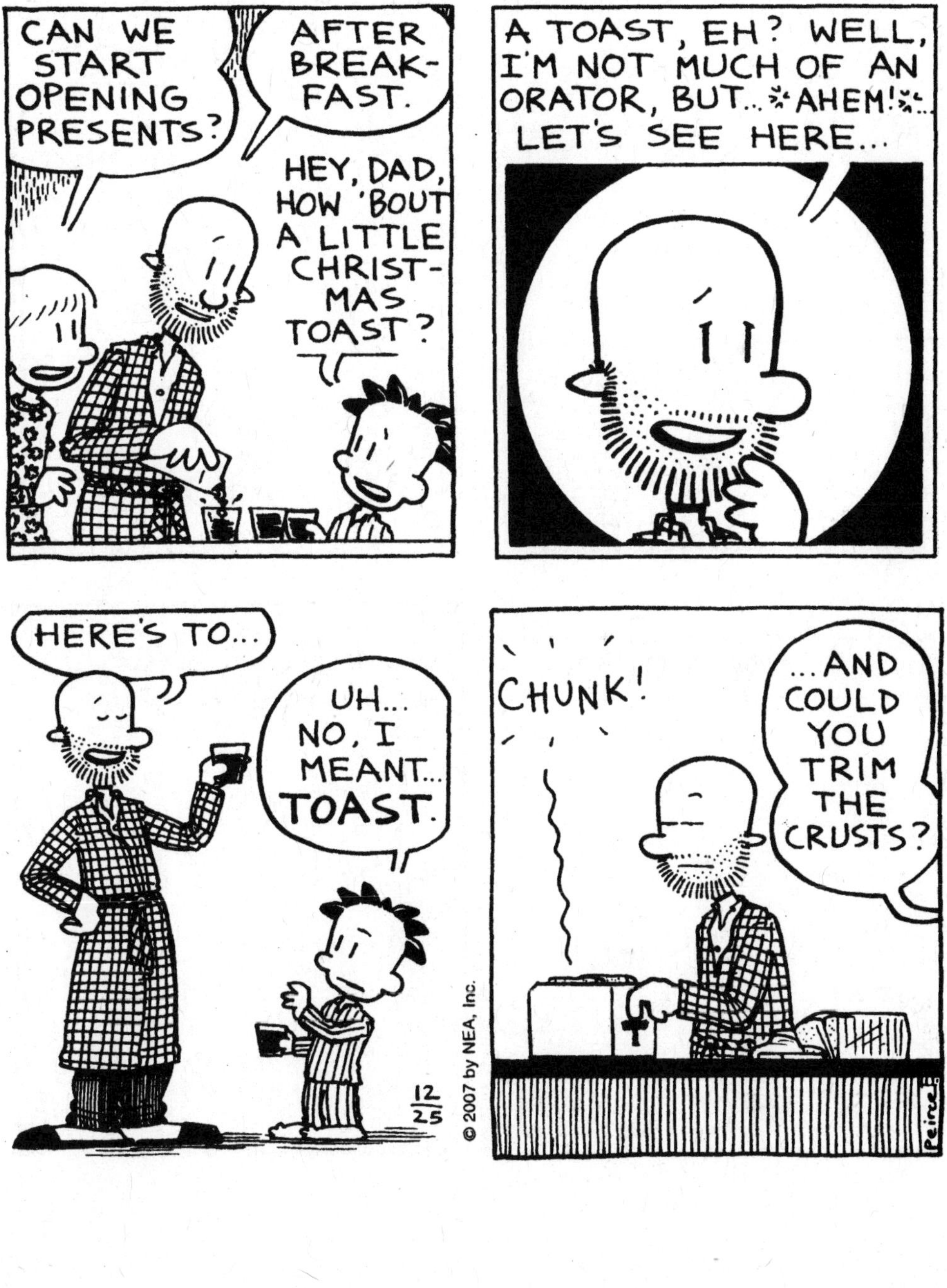
CAN WE START OPENING PRESENTS?
AFTER BREAK-FAST.
HEY, DAD, HOW 'BOUT A LITTLE CHRIST-MAS TOAST?
A TOAST, EH? WELL, I'M NOT MUCH OF AN ORATOR, BUT... AHEM!... LET'S SEE HERE...
HERE'S TO...
UH... NO, I MEANT... TOAST.
12/25
© 2007 by NEA, Inc.
CHUNK!
...AND COULD YOU TRIM THE CRUSTS?
Peirce

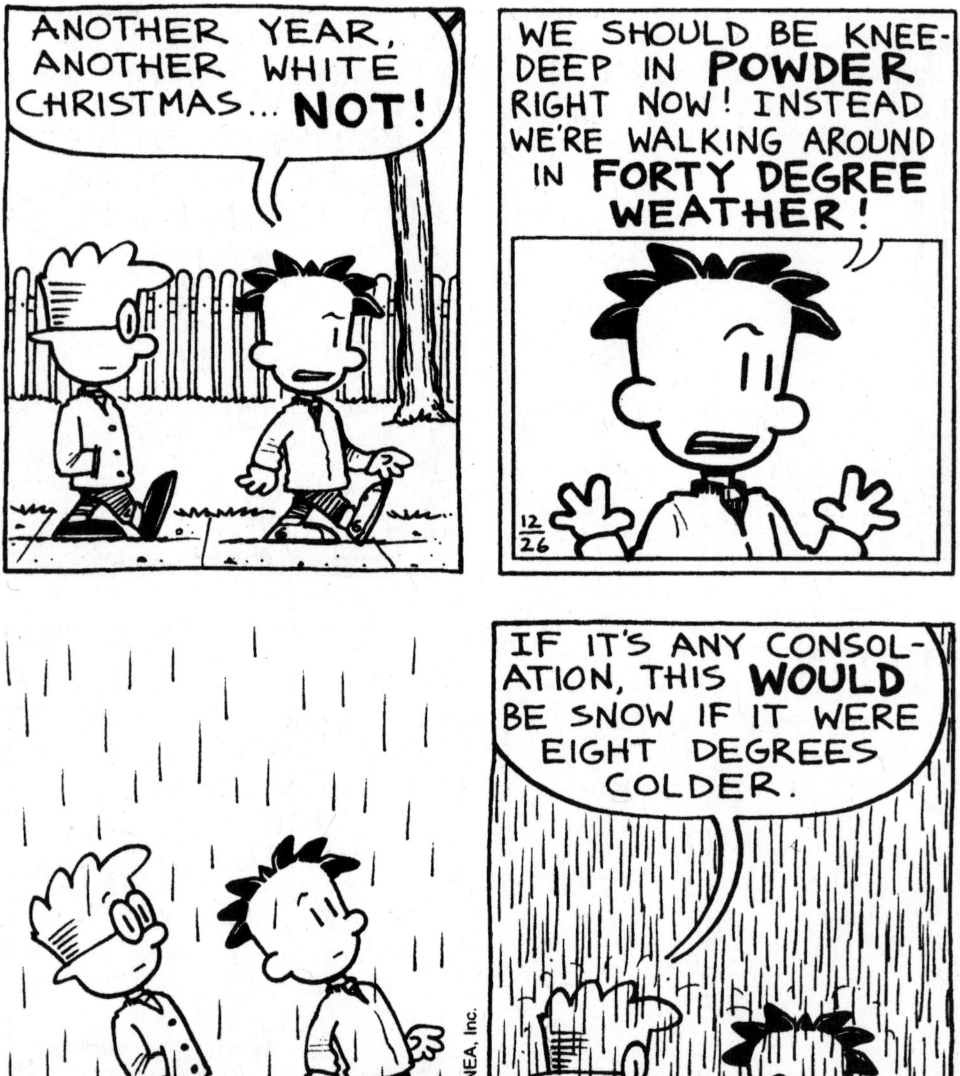
ANOTHER YEAR, ANOTHER WHITE CHRISTMAS... NOT!
WE SHOULD BE KNEE-DEEP IN POWDER RIGHT NOW! INSTEAD WE'RE WALKING AROUND IN FORTY DEGREE WEATHER!
12/26
© 2007 by NEA, Inc.
IF IT'S ANY CONSOLATION, THIS WOULD BE SNOW IF IT WERE EIGHT DEGREES COLDER.

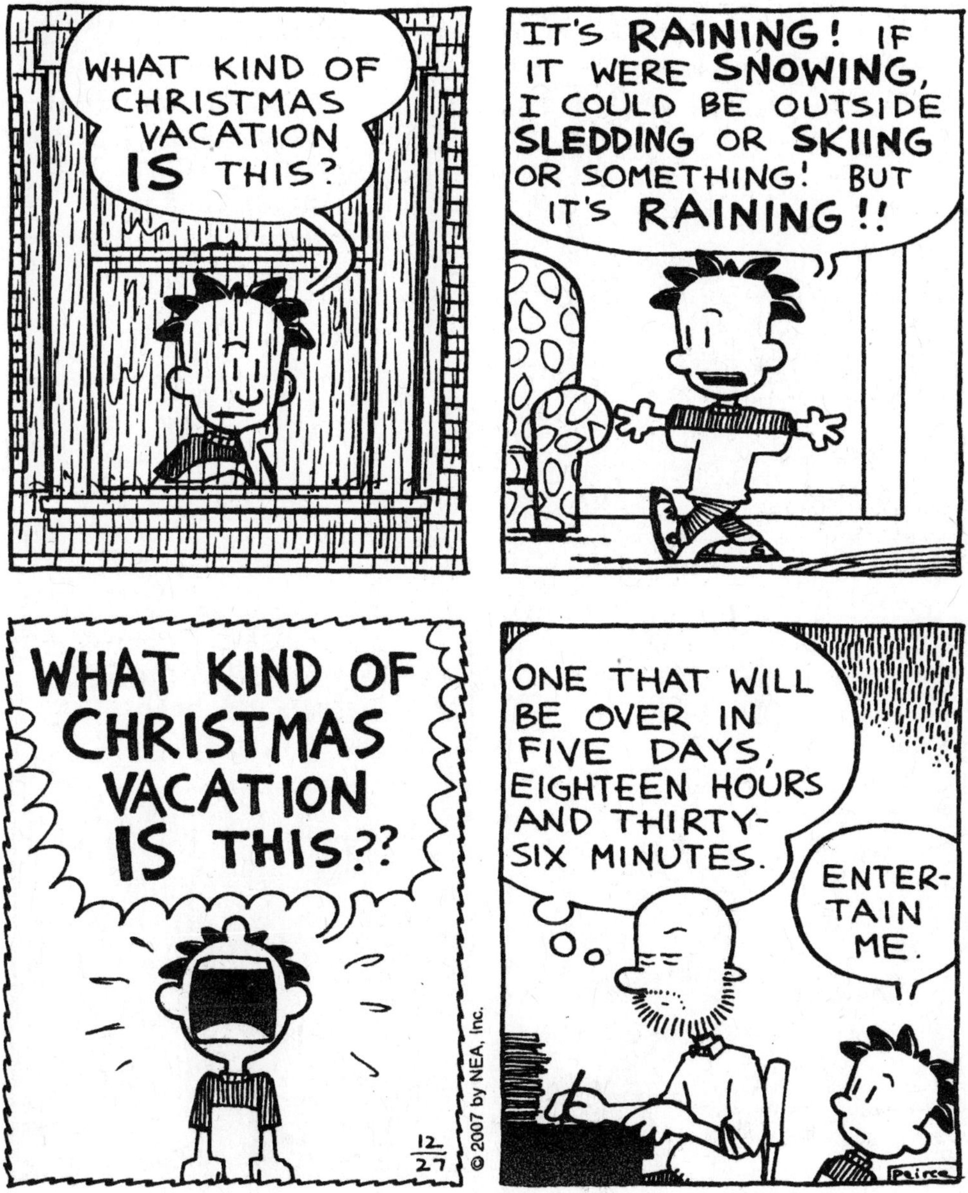
WHAT KIND OF CHRISTMAS VACATION IS THIS?
IT'S RAINING! IF IT WERE SNOWING, I COULD BE OUTSIDE SLEDDING OR SKIING OR SOMETHING! BUT IT'S RAINING!!
WHAT KIND OF CHRISTMAS VACATION IS THIS??
12/27
© 2007 by NEA, Inc.
ONE THAT WILL BE OVER IN FIVE DAYS, EIGHTEEN HOURS AND THIRTY-SIX MINUTES.
ENTERTAIN ME.
Peirce

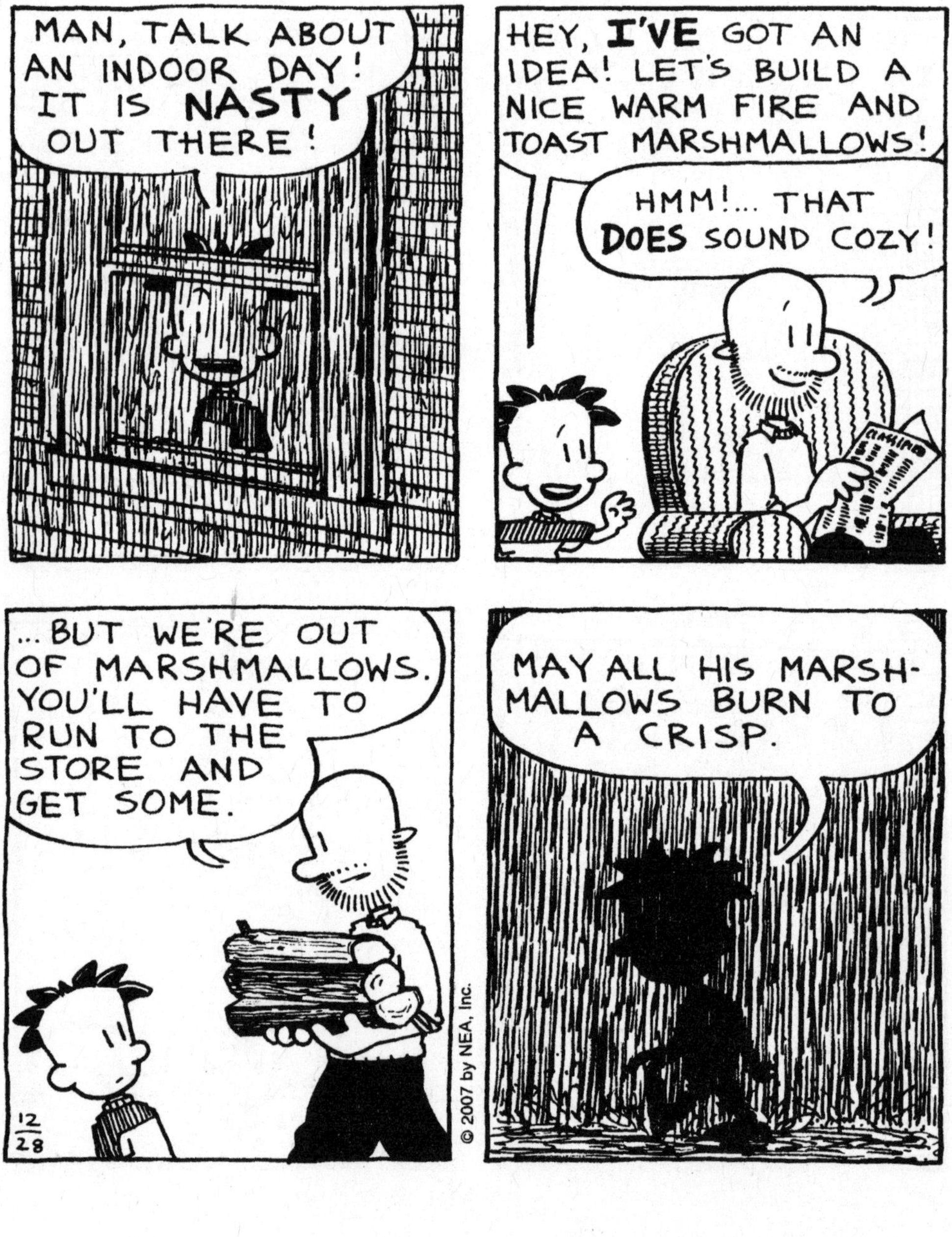
MAN, TALK ABOUT AN INDOOR DAY! IT IS **NASTY** OUT THERE!
HEY, **I'VE** GOT AN IDEA! LET'S BUILD A NICE WARM FIRE AND TOAST MARSHMALLOWS!
HMM!... THAT **DOES** SOUND COZY!
...BUT WE'RE OUT OF MARSHMALLOWS. YOU'LL HAVE TO RUN TO THE STORE AND GET SOME.
12/28
© 2007 by NEA, Inc.
MAY ALL HIS MARSH-MALLOWS BURN TO A CRISP.

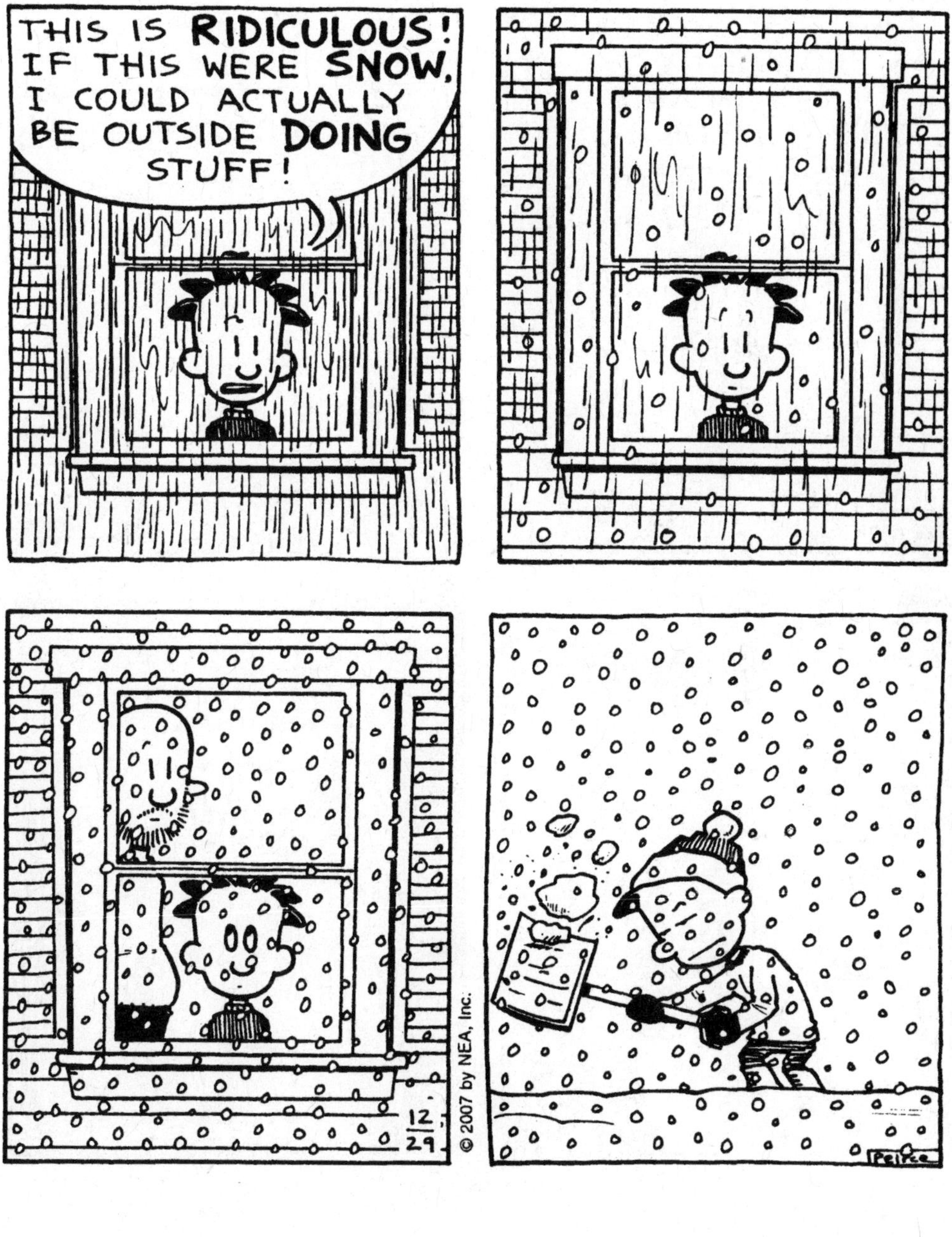
THIS IS RIDICULOUS! IF THIS WERE SNOW, I COULD ACTUALLY BE OUTSIDE DOING STUFF!
12-29
© 2007 by NEA, Inc.
Peirce

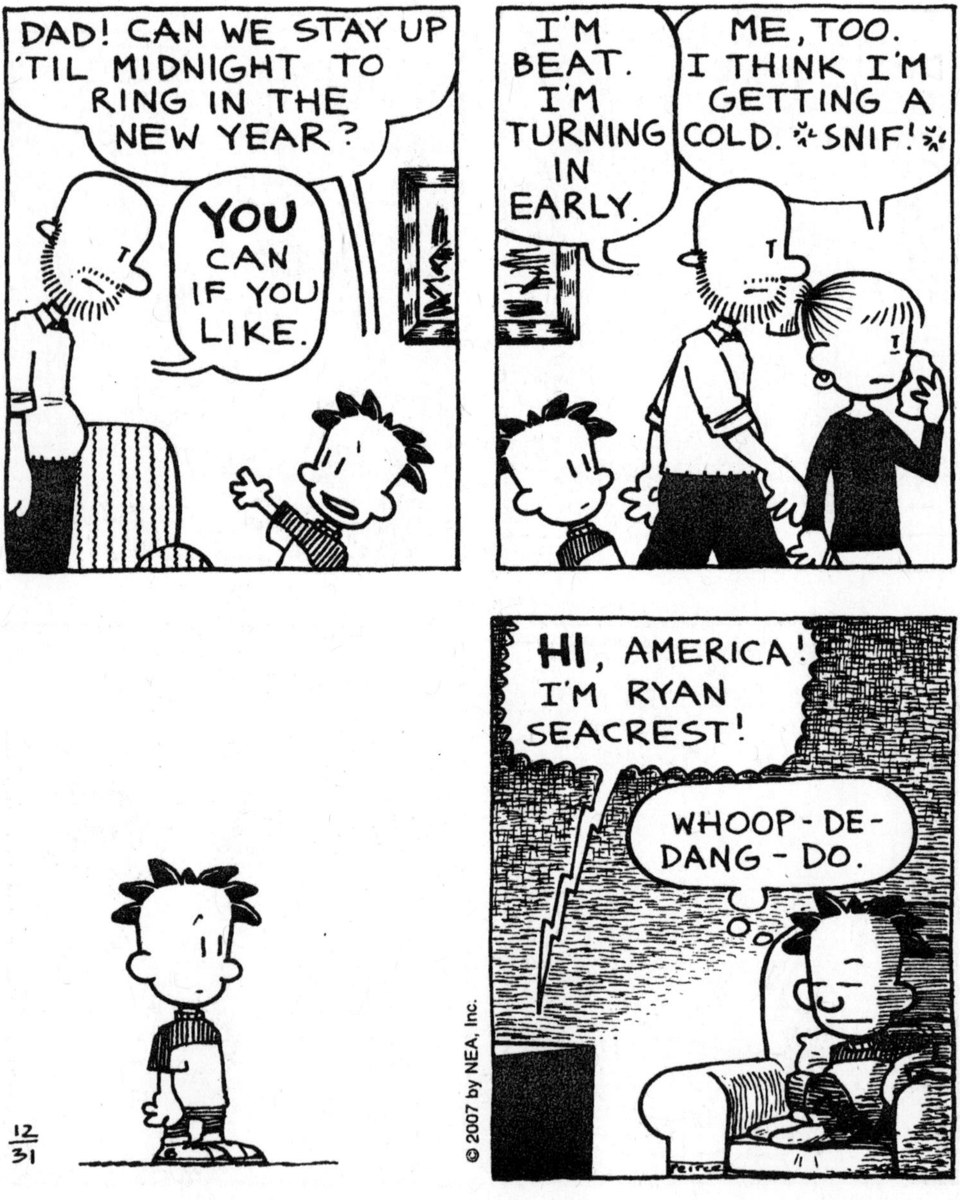
DAD! CAN WE STAY UP 'TIL MIDNIGHT TO RING IN THE NEW YEAR?
YOU CAN IF YOU LIKE.
I'M BEAT. I'M TURNING IN EARLY.
ME, TOO. I THINK I'M GETTING A COLD. SNIF!
12/31
HI, AMERICA! I'M RYAN SEACREST!
WHOOP-DE-DANG-DO.

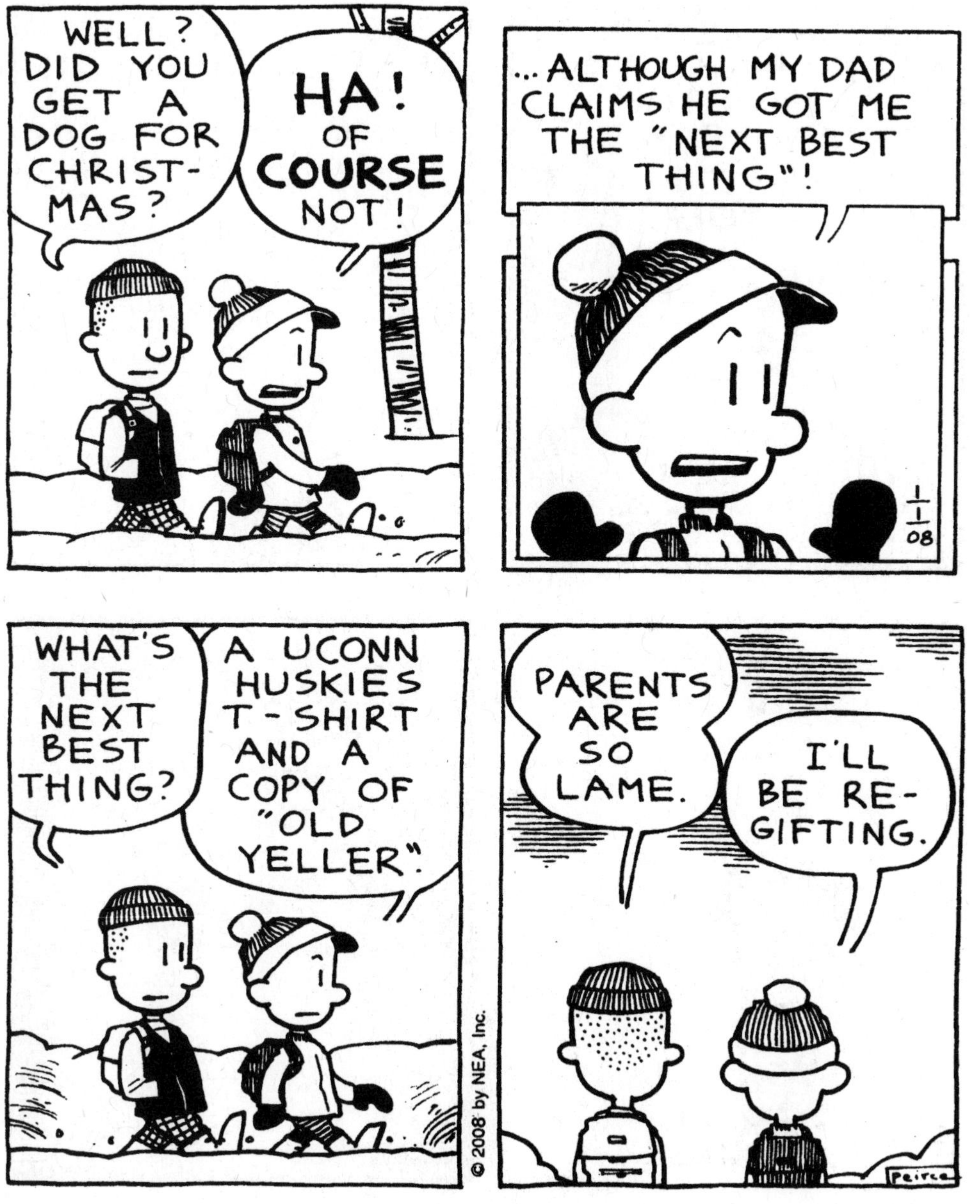
WELL? DID YOU GET A DOG FOR CHRIST-MAS?
HA! OF COURSE NOT!
...ALTHOUGH MY DAD CLAIMS HE GOT ME THE "NEXT BEST THING"!
1/1/08
WHAT'S THE NEXT BEST THING?
A UCONN HUSKIES T-SHIRT AND A COPY OF "OLD YELLER".
PARENTS ARE SO LAME.
I'LL BE RE-GIFTING.
Peirce

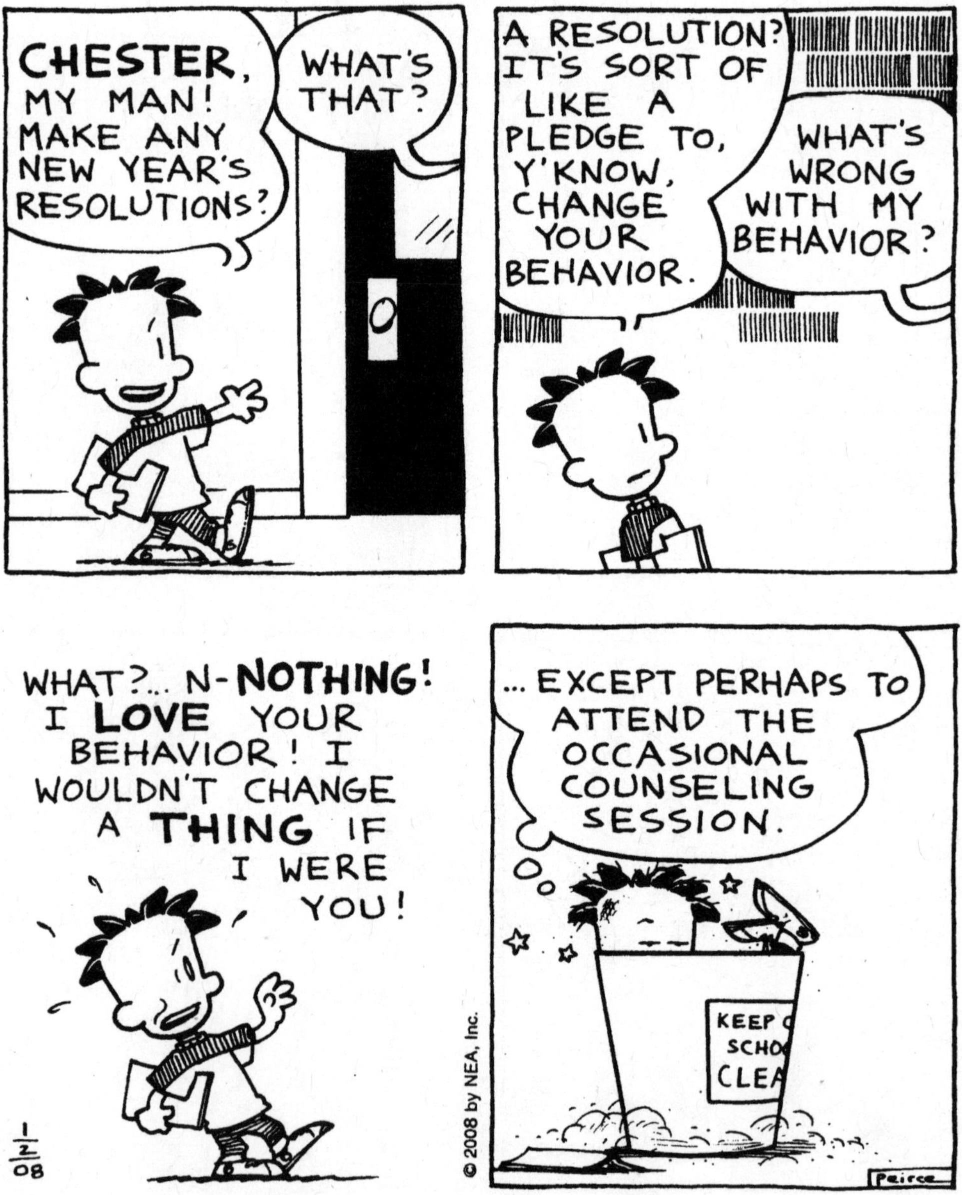

CHESTER, MY MAN! MAKE ANY NEW YEAR'S RESOLUTIONS?
WHAT'S THAT?
A RESOLUTION? IT'S SORT OF LIKE A PLEDGE TO, Y'KNOW, CHANGE YOUR BEHAVIOR.
WHAT'S WRONG WITH MY BEHAVIOR?
WHAT?... N-NOTHING! I LOVE YOUR BEHAVIOR! I WOULDN'T CHANGE A THING IF I WERE YOU!
... EXCEPT PERHAPS TO ATTEND THE OCCASIONAL COUNSELING SESSION.
KEEP O
SCHO
CLEA
1/2/08
© 2008 by NEA, Inc.
Peirce

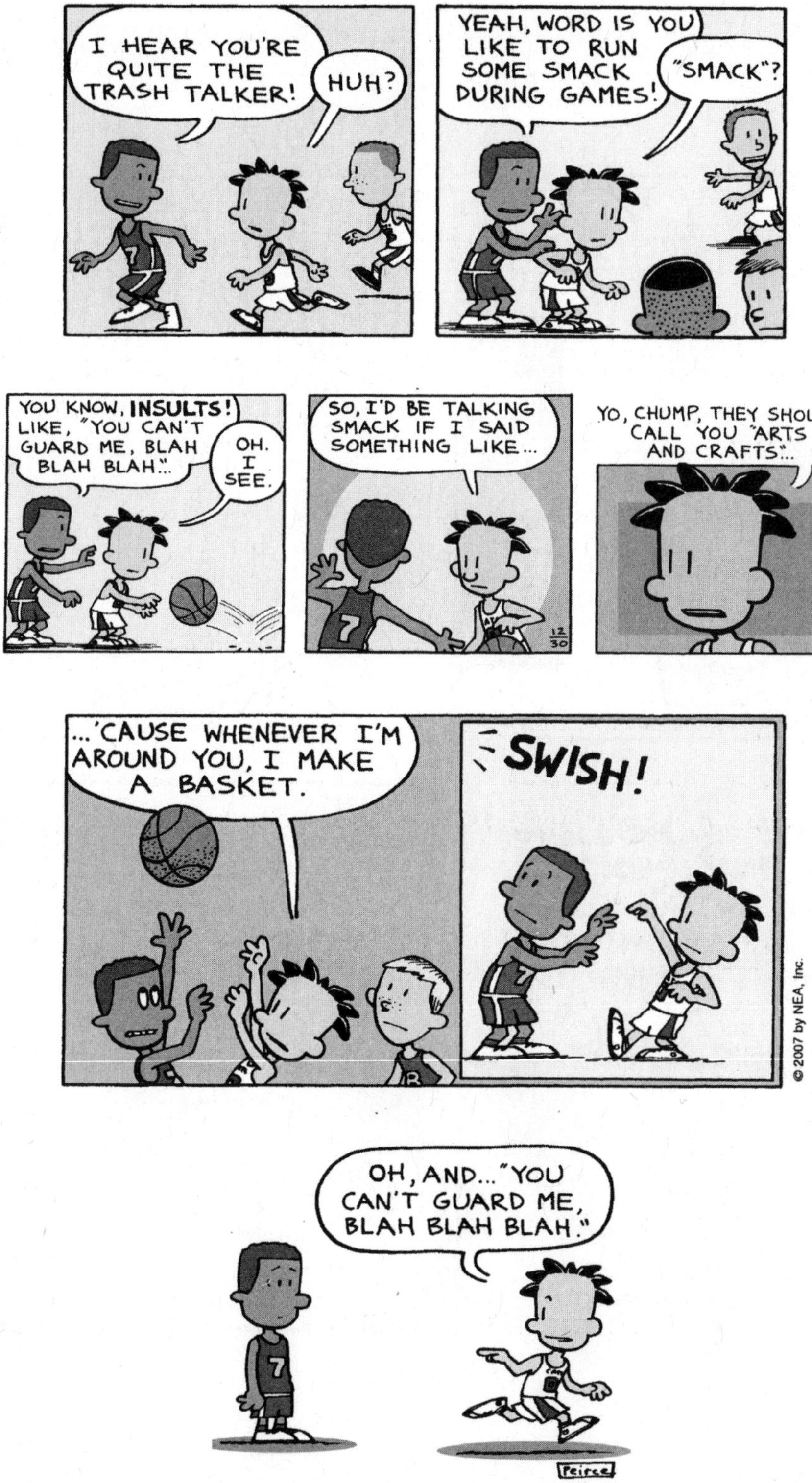
I HEAR YOU'RE QUITE THE TRASH TALKER!
HUH?
YEAH, WORD IS YOU LIKE TO RUN SOME SMACK DURING GAMES!
"SMACK"?
YOU KNOW, INSULTS! LIKE, "YOU CAN'T GUARD ME, BLAH BLAH BLAH"...
OH. I SEE.
SO, I'D BE TALKING SMACK IF I SAID SOMETHING LIKE...
12 30
YO, CHUMP, THEY SHOULD CALL YOU "ARTS AND CRAFTS"...
...'CAUSE WHENEVER I'M AROUND YOU, I MAKE A BASKET.
SWISH!
© 2007 by NEA, Inc.
OH, AND..."YOU CAN'T GUARD ME, BLAH BLAH BLAH."
Peirce

THE BOOK OF FACTS = BOR-ING!

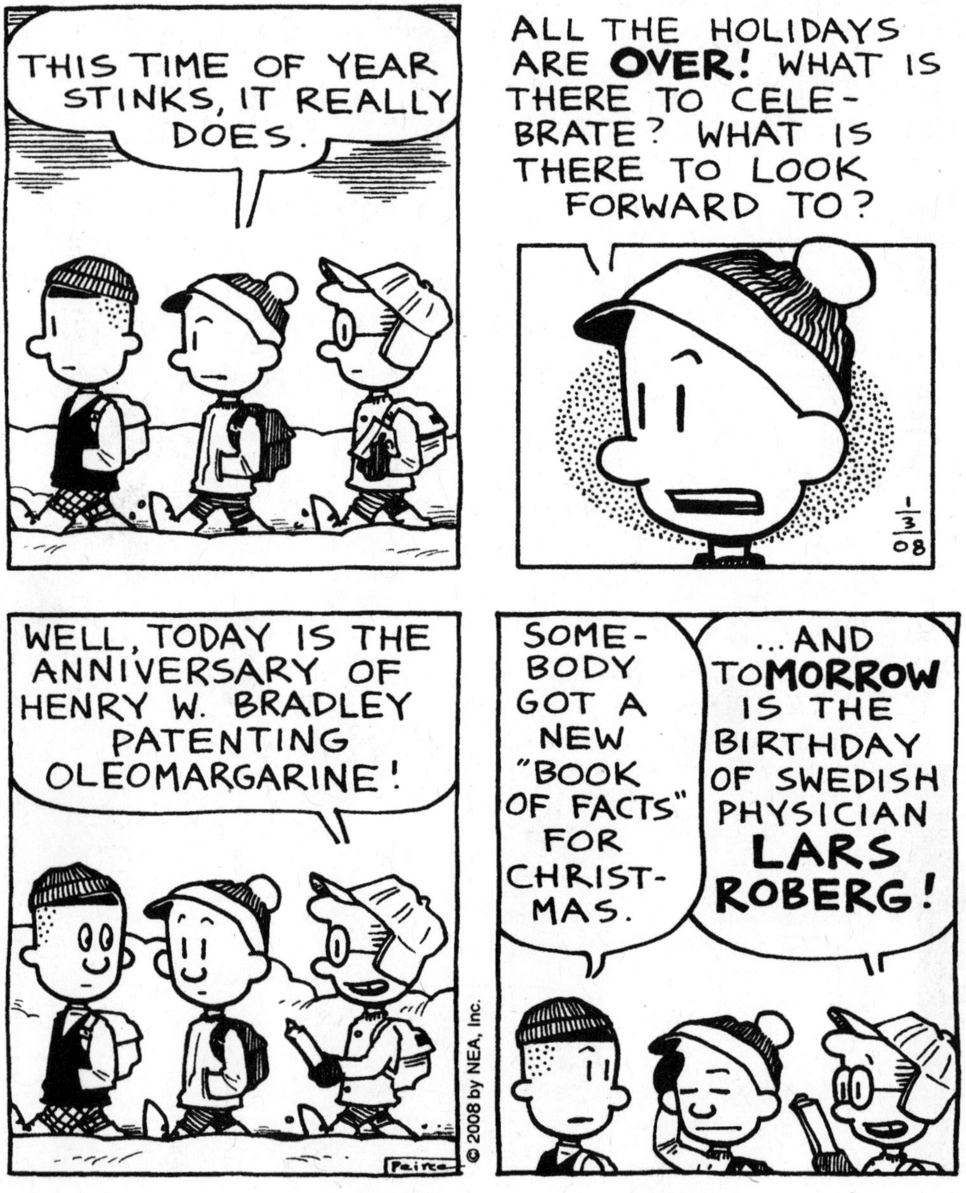
THIS TIME OF YEAR STINKS, IT REALLY DOES.
ALL THE HOLIDAYS ARE **OVER!** WHAT IS THERE TO CELE-BRATE? WHAT IS THERE TO LOOK FORWARD TO?
1/3/08
WELL, TODAY IS THE ANNIVERSARY OF HENRY W. BRADLEY PATENTING OLEOMARGARINE!
SOME-BODY GOT A NEW "BOOK OF FACTS" FOR CHRIST-MAS.
...AND TO**MORROW** IS THE BIRTHDAY OF SWEDISH PHYSICIAN **LARS ROBERG!**
Peirce
© 2008 by NEA, Inc.

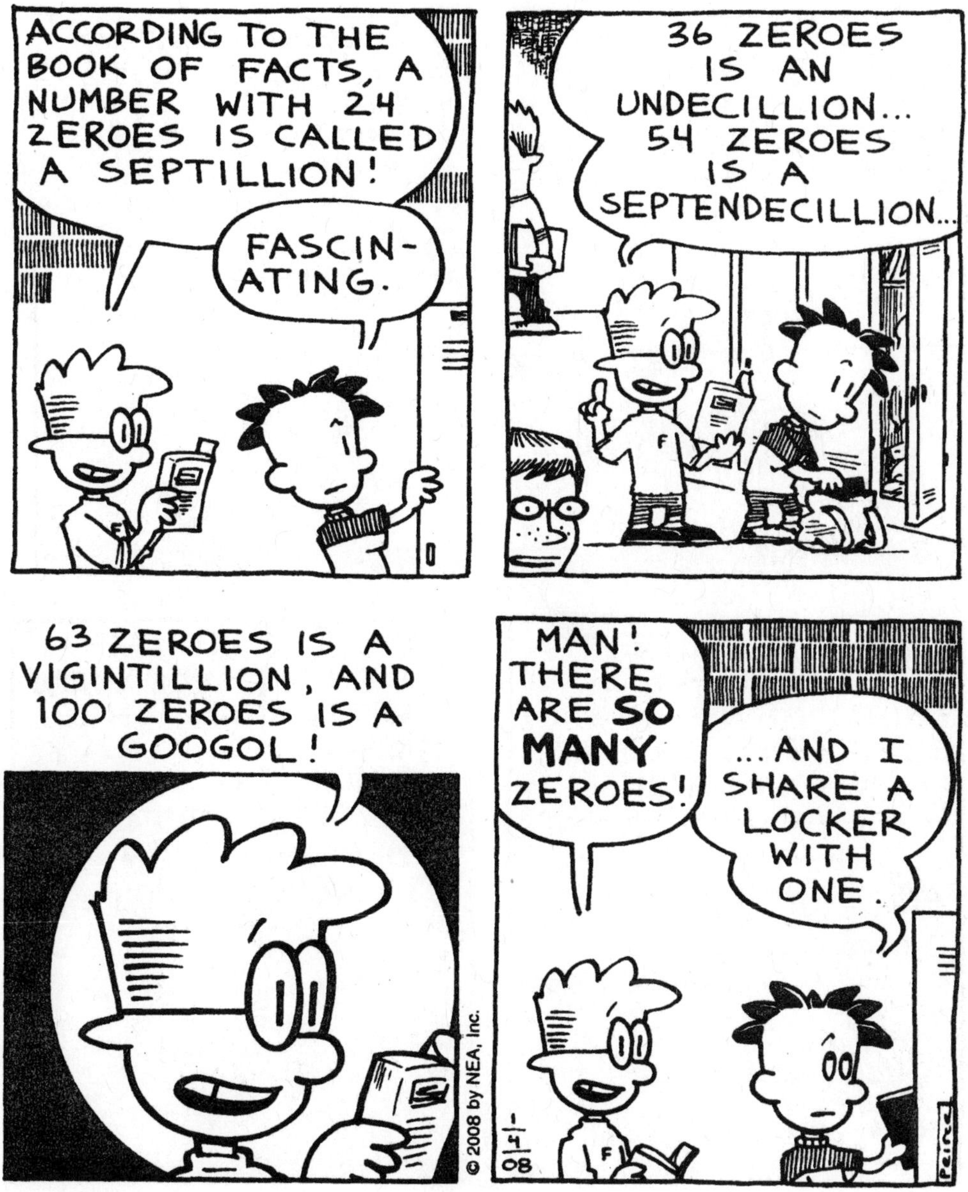
ACCORDING TO THE BOOK OF FACTS, A NUMBER WITH 24 ZEROES IS CALLED A SEPTILLION!
FASCIN-ATING.
36 ZEROES IS AN UNDECILLION... 54 ZEROES IS A SEPTENDECILLION...
63 ZEROES IS A VIGINTILLION, AND 100 ZEROES IS A GOOGOL!
MAN! THERE ARE **SO MANY** ZEROES!
...AND I SHARE A LOCKER WITH ONE.
© 2008 by NEA, Inc.
1-4-08
PEIRCE

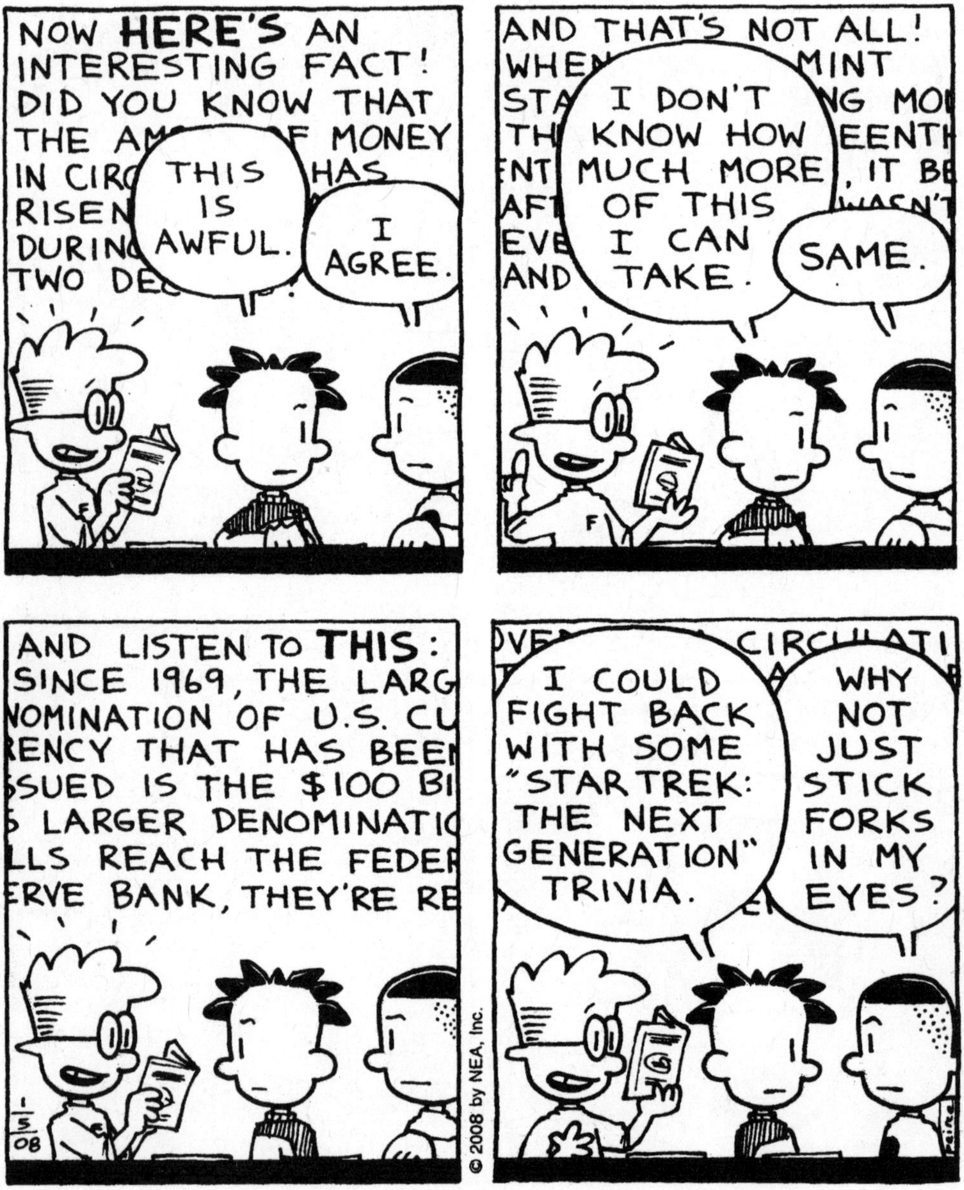
NOW HERE'S AN INTERESTING FACT! DID YOU KNOW THAT THE AM F MONEY IN CIRC HAS RISEN DURING TWO DE
THIS IS AWFUL.
I AGREE.
AND THAT'S NOT ALL! WHEN MINT
I DON'T KNOW HOW MUCH MORE OF THIS I CAN TAKE.
SAME.
AND LISTEN TO THIS: SINCE 1969, THE LARG NOMINATION OF U.S. CU RENCY THAT HAS BEEN SSUED IS THE $100 BI LARGER DENOMINATI LLS REACH THE FEDER ERVE BANK, THEY'RE RE
1/5/08
I COULD FIGHT BACK WITH SOME "STAR TREK: THE NEXT GENERATION" TRIVIA.
WHY NOT JUST STICK FORKS IN MY EYES?

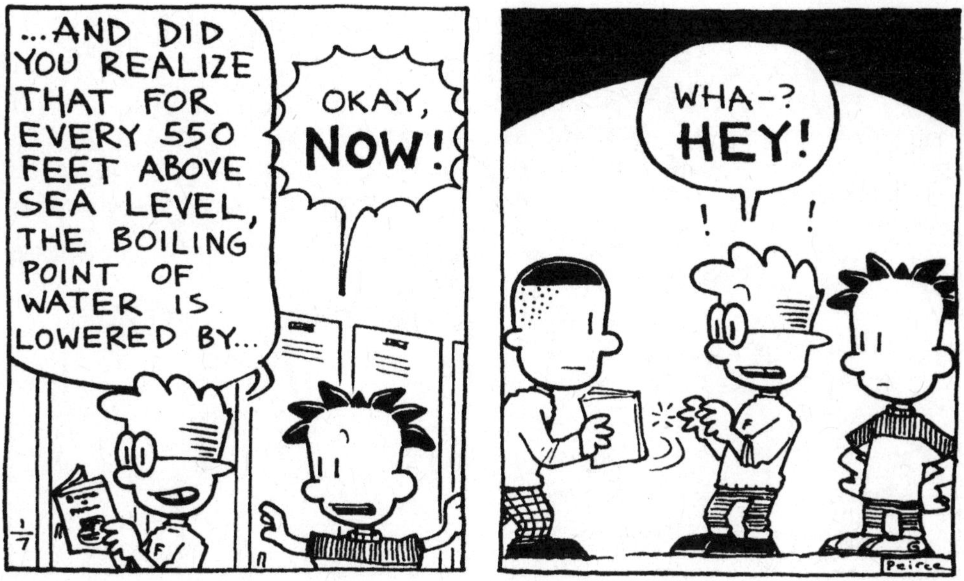

...AND DID YOU REALIZE THAT FOR EVERY 550 FEET ABOVE SEA LEVEL, THE BOILING POINT OF WATER IS LOWERED BY...
OKAY, NOW!
1/7
WHA-? HEY!
Peirce

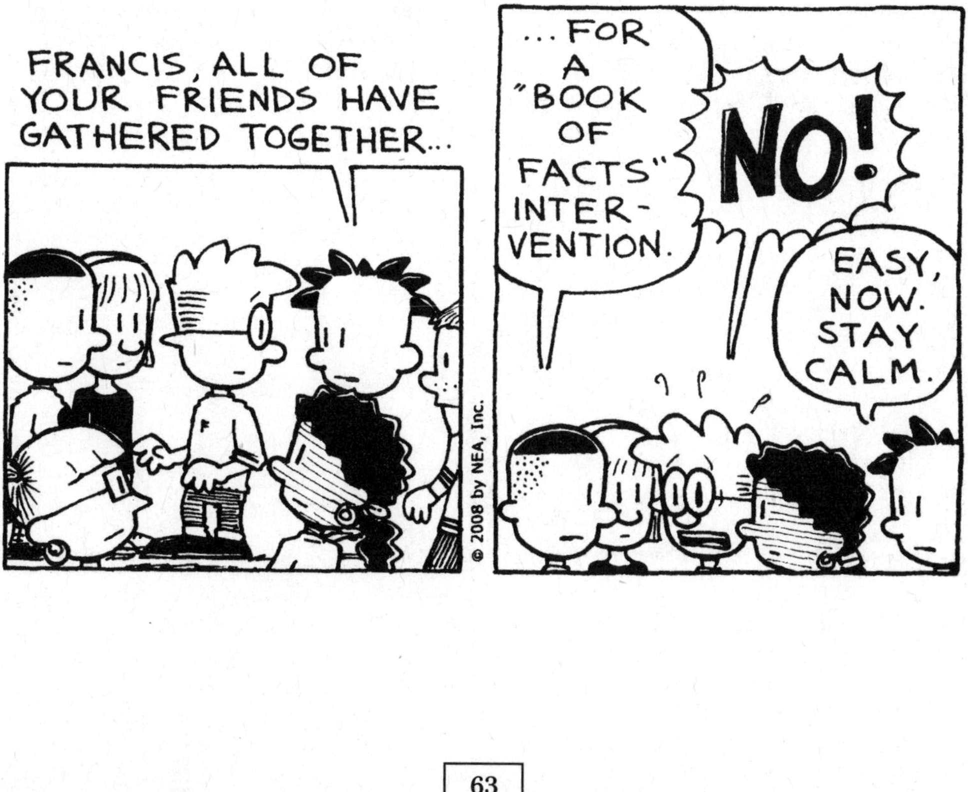

FRANCIS, ALL OF YOUR FRIENDS HAVE GATHERED TOGETHER...
...FOR A "BOOK OF FACTS" INTER-VENTION.
NO!
EASY, NOW. STAY CALM.
© 2008 by NEA, Inc.

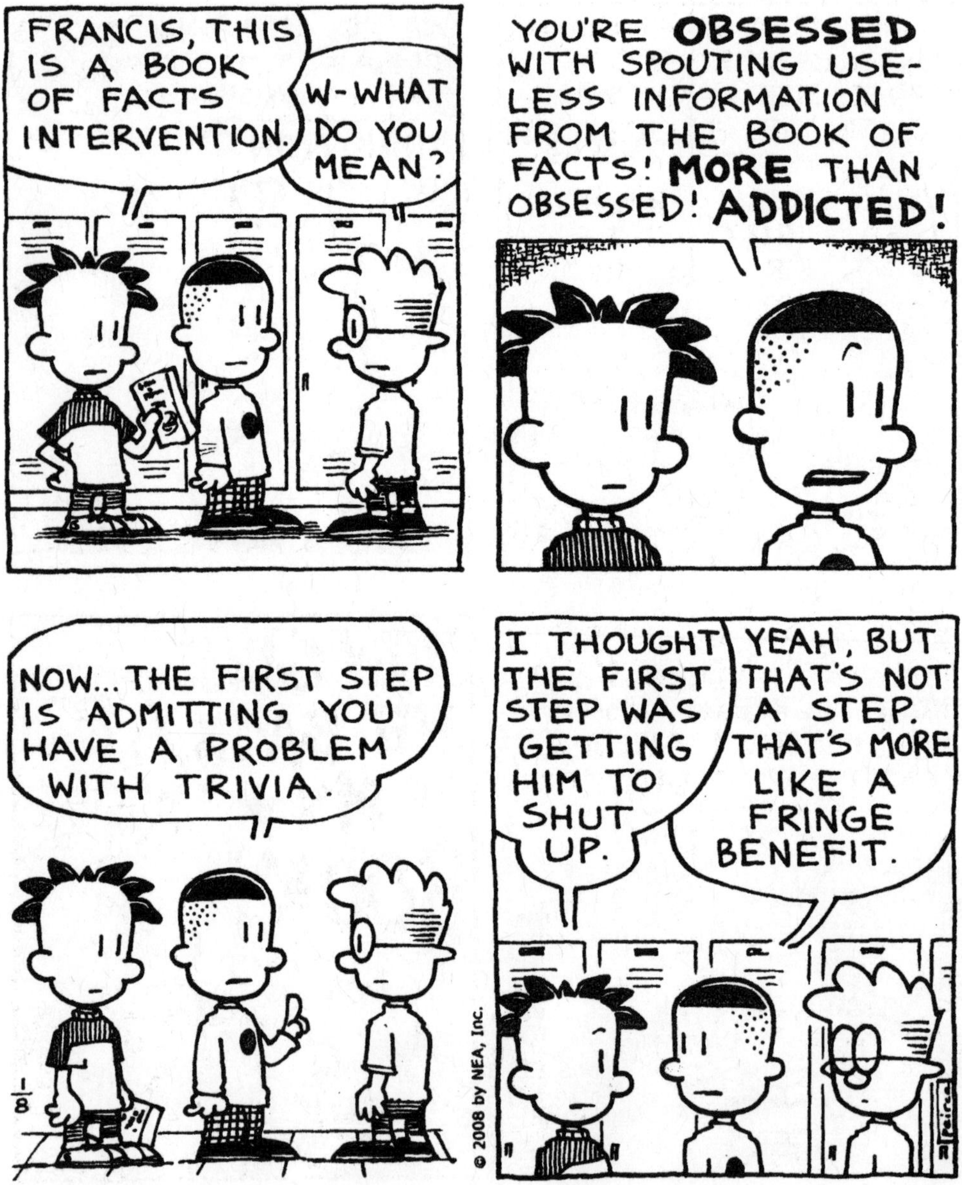
FRANCIS, THIS IS A BOOK OF FACTS INTERVENTION.
W-WHAT DO YOU MEAN?
YOU'RE **OBSESSED** WITH SPOUTING USE-LESS INFORMATION FROM THE BOOK OF FACTS! **MORE** THAN OBSESSED! **ADDICTED!**
NOW... THE FIRST STEP IS ADMITTING YOU HAVE A PROBLEM WITH TRIVIA.
I THOUGHT THE FIRST STEP WAS GETTING HIM TO SHUT UP.
YEAH, BUT THAT'S NOT A STEP. THAT'S MORE LIKE A FRINGE BENEFIT.
1/8
© 2008 by NEA, Inc.
Peirce

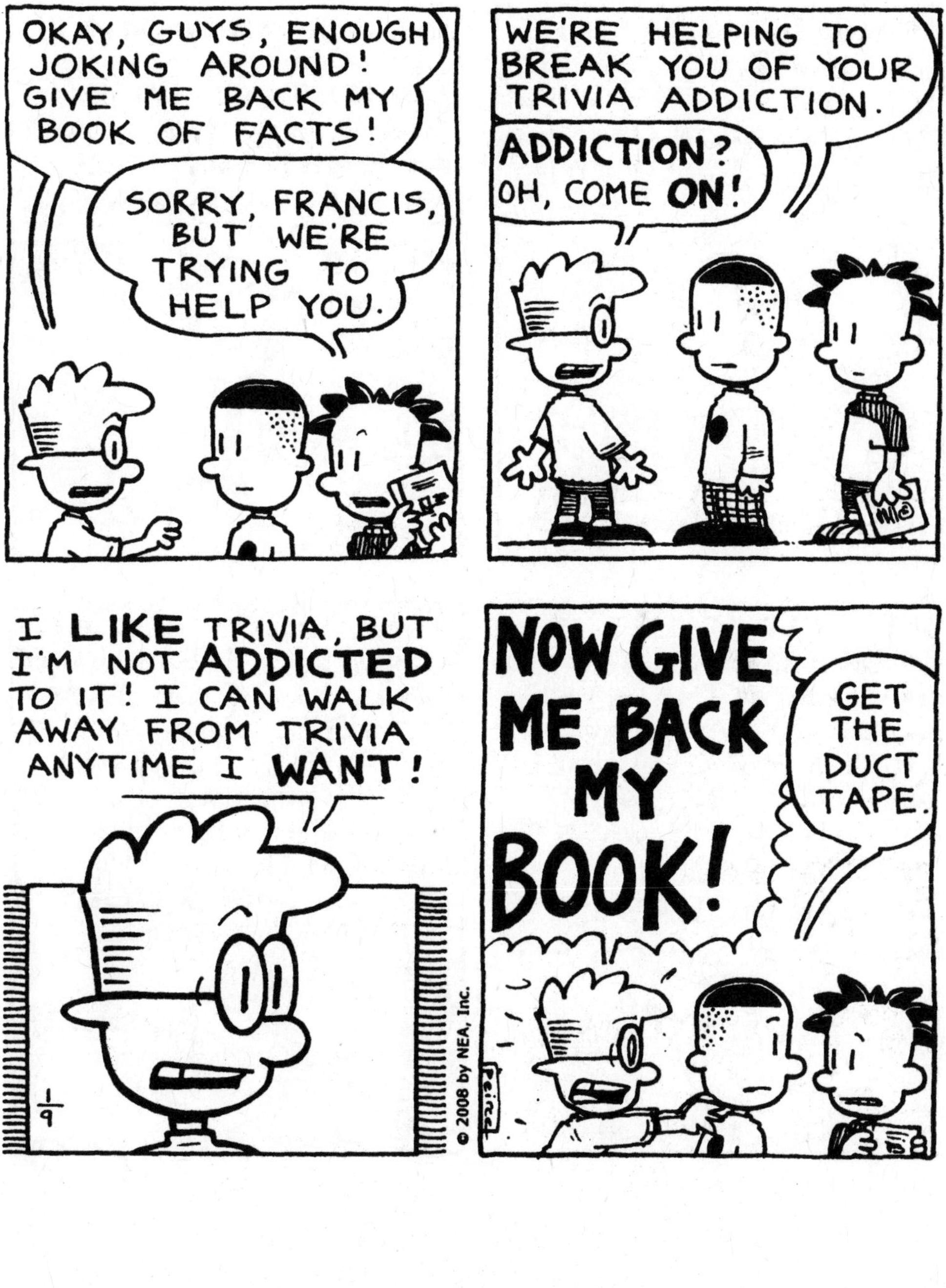
OKAY, GUYS, ENOUGH JOKING AROUND! GIVE ME BACK MY BOOK OF FACTS!
SORRY, FRANCIS, BUT WE'RE TRYING TO HELP YOU.
WE'RE HELPING TO BREAK YOU OF YOUR TRIVIA ADDICTION.
ADDICTION? OH, COME ON!
I LIKE TRIVIA, BUT I'M NOT ADDICTED TO IT! I CAN WALK AWAY FROM TRIVIA ANYTIME I WANT!
NOW GIVE ME BACK MY BOOK!
GET THE DUCT TAPE.
© 2008 by NEA, Inc.

Panel 1: HOW'S FRANCIS DOING WITHOUT HIS BOOK OF FACTS?

NOT GOOD.

Panel 2: DID YOU KNOW THAT THE CAPITAL OF DJIBOUTI IS ROSEAU? WAIT!... NO, THAT CAN'T BE RIGHT... UH... THE CAPITAL OF ROSEAU IS...

Panel 3: UH... HOLD IT, LET ME START OVER!... DID YOU KNOW THAT THE COMPOSER ARTURO "HOT LIPS" O'FARRILL WAS... UM... NO, WAIT, HIS NICKNAME WASN'T "HOT LIPS", IT WAS... DANG, WHAT **WAS** IT?...

1/10

Panel 4: OKAY, LET'S TALK ABOU[T] [RA]ILROADS! THE NUMBER [O]F T[...]S OF TRACK IN[...] 30 WAS O[V] A[...] BRITNEY S[...] W[...] A[...] IN[...] NO, [...] [D]OES[...] SENSE! I'LL HAVE [...] G[...]

HE'S TRYING TO FREE-STYLE.

THIS IS UGLY.

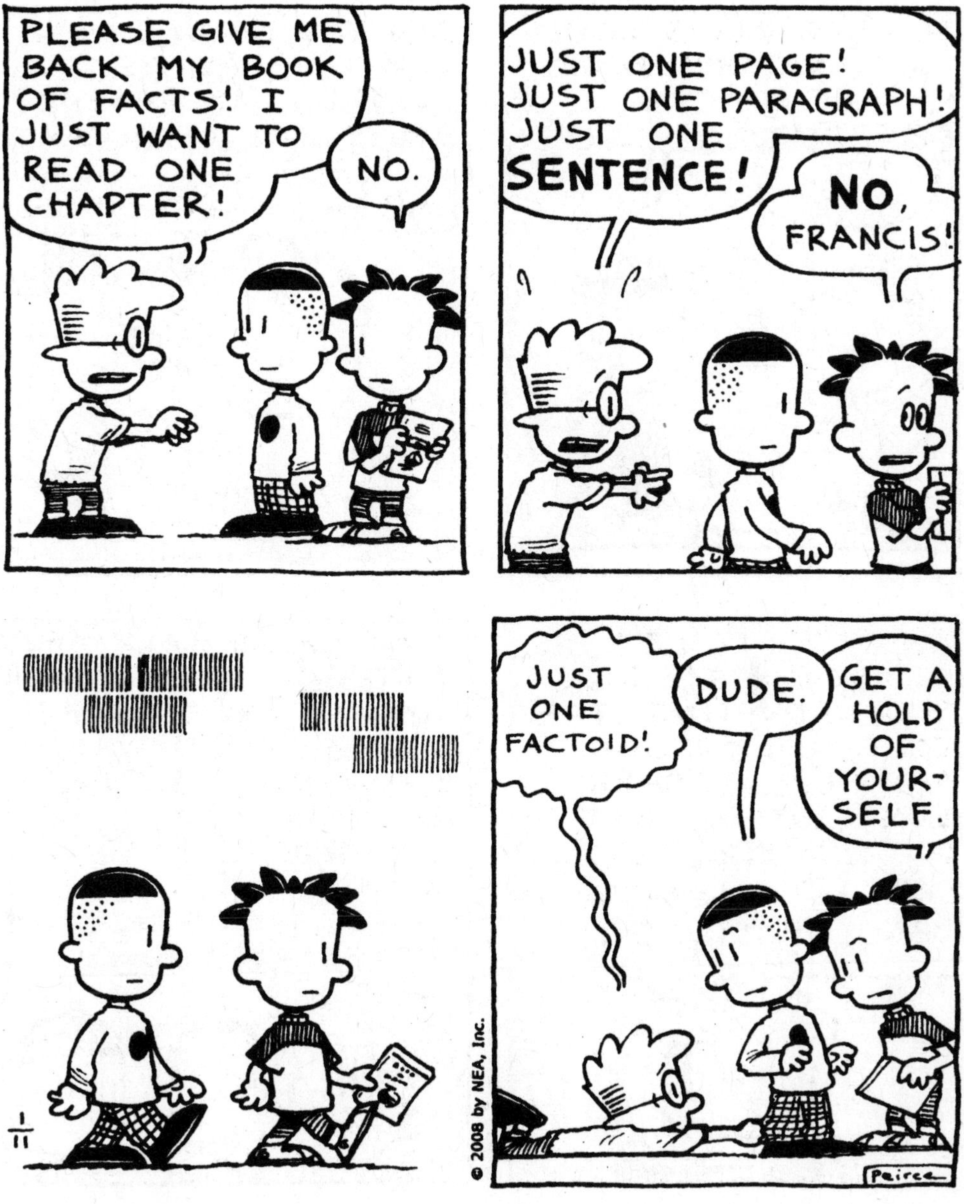
PLEASE GIVE ME BACK MY BOOK OF FACTS! I JUST WANT TO READ ONE CHAPTER!
NO.
JUST ONE PAGE! JUST ONE PARAGRAPH! JUST ONE SENTENCE!
NO, FRANCIS!
1/11
© 2008 by NEA, Inc.
JUST ONE FACTOID!
DUDE.
GET A HOLD OF YOUR-SELF.
Peirce

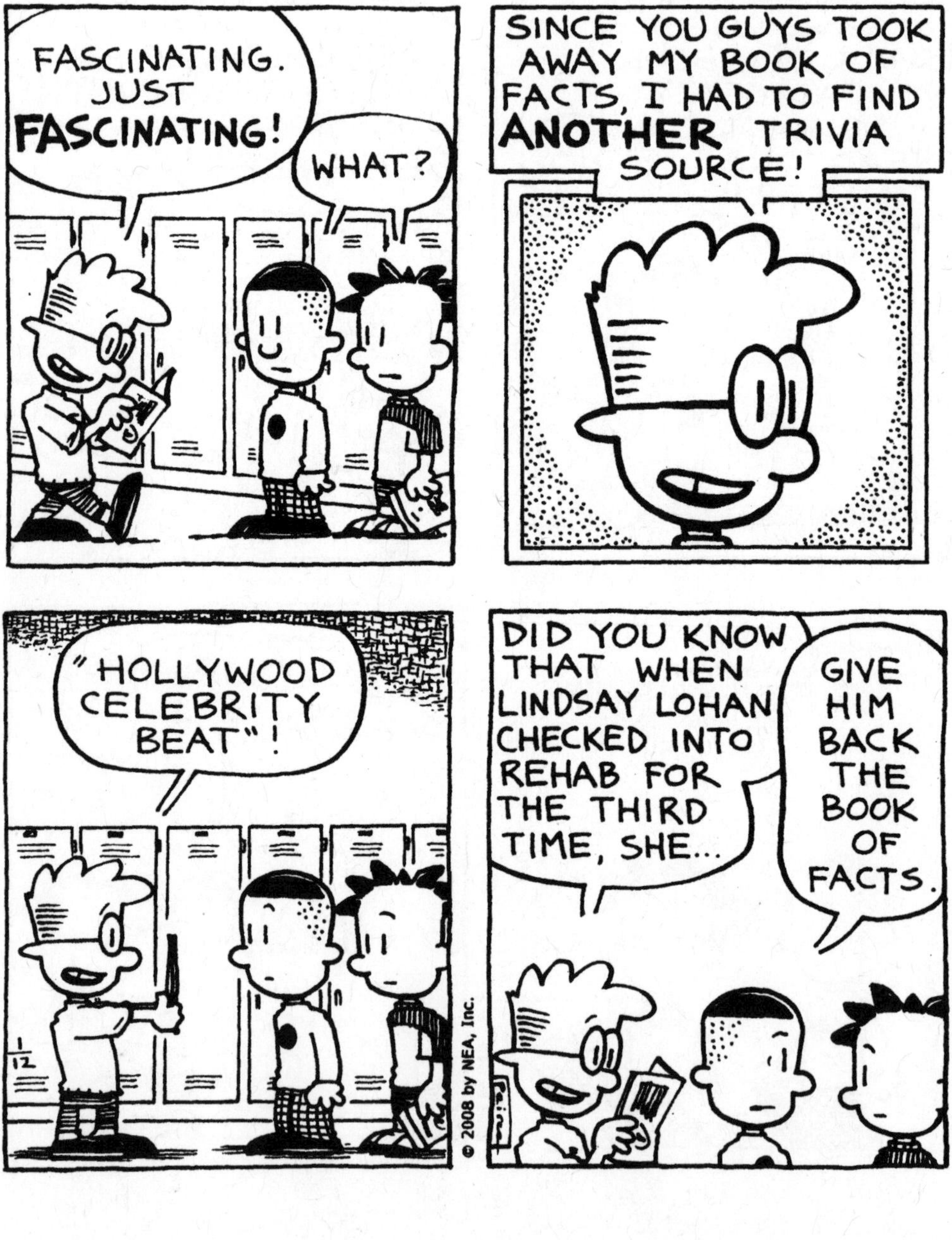
FASCINATING. JUST **FASCINATING**!
WHAT?
SINCE YOU GUYS TOOK AWAY MY BOOK OF FACTS, I HAD TO FIND **ANOTHER** TRIVIA SOURCE!
"HOLLYWOOD CELEBRITY BEAT"!
1/12
© 2008 by NEA, Inc.
DID YOU KNOW THAT WHEN LINDSAY LOHAN CHECKED INTO REHAB FOR THE THIRD TIME, SHE...
GIVE HIM BACK THE BOOK OF FACTS.

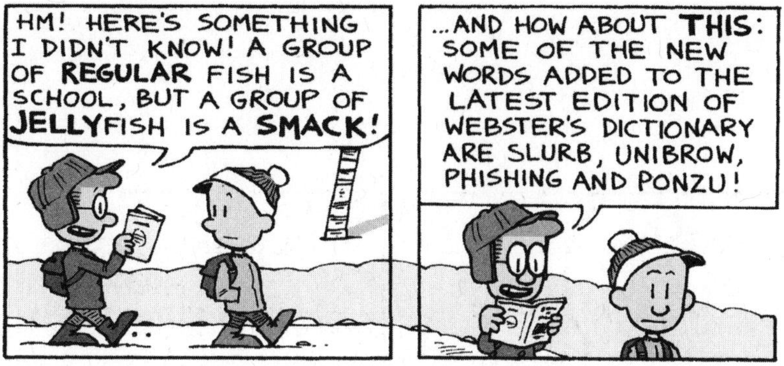
HM! HERE'S SOMETHING I DIDN'T KNOW! A GROUP OF **REGULAR** FISH IS A SCHOOL, BUT A GROUP OF **JELLY**FISH IS A **SMACK**!
...AND HOW ABOUT **THIS**: SOME OF THE NEW WORDS ADDED TO THE LATEST EDITION OF WEBSTER'S DICTIONARY ARE SLURB, UNIBROW, PHISHING AND PONZU!

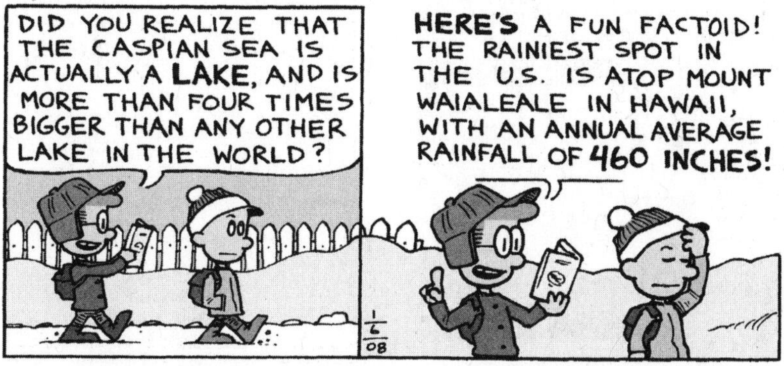
DID YOU REALIZE THAT THE CASPIAN SEA IS ACTUALLY A **LAKE**, AND IS MORE THAN FOUR TIMES BIGGER THAN ANY OTHER LAKE IN THE WORLD?
1/6/08
HERE'S A FUN FACTOID! THE RAINIEST SPOT IN THE U.S. IS ATOP MOUNT WAIALEALE IN HAWAII, WITH AN ANNUAL AVERAGE RAINFALL OF **460 INCHES**!

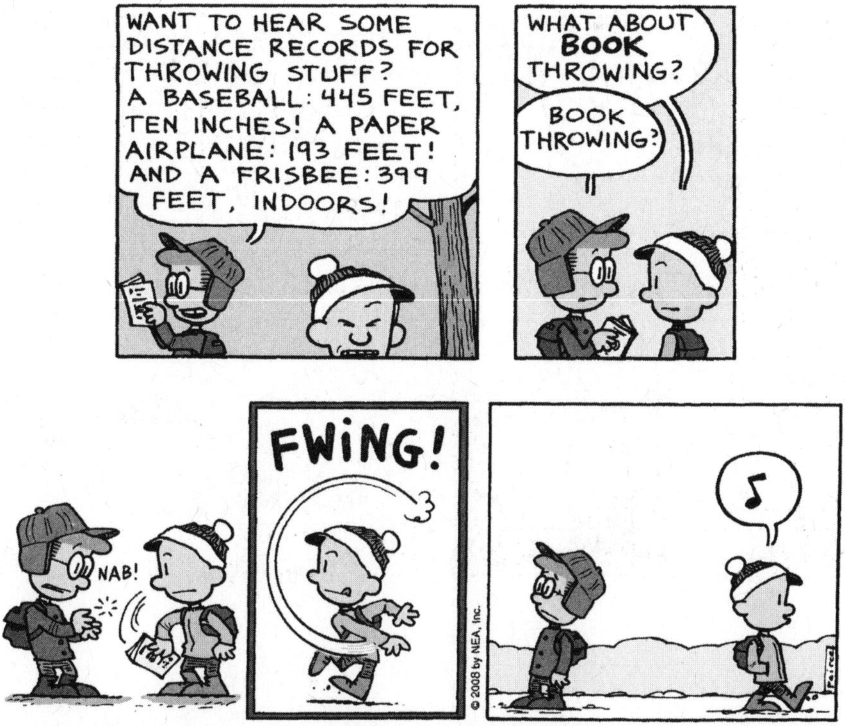
WANT TO HEAR SOME DISTANCE RECORDS FOR THROWING STUFF? A BASEBALL: 445 FEET, TEN INCHES! A PAPER AIRPLANE: 193 FEET! AND A FRISBEE: 399 FEET, INDOORS!
WHAT ABOUT **BOOK** THROWING?
BOOK THROWING?
NAB!
FWING!
♪
© 2008 by NEA, Inc.
Peirce

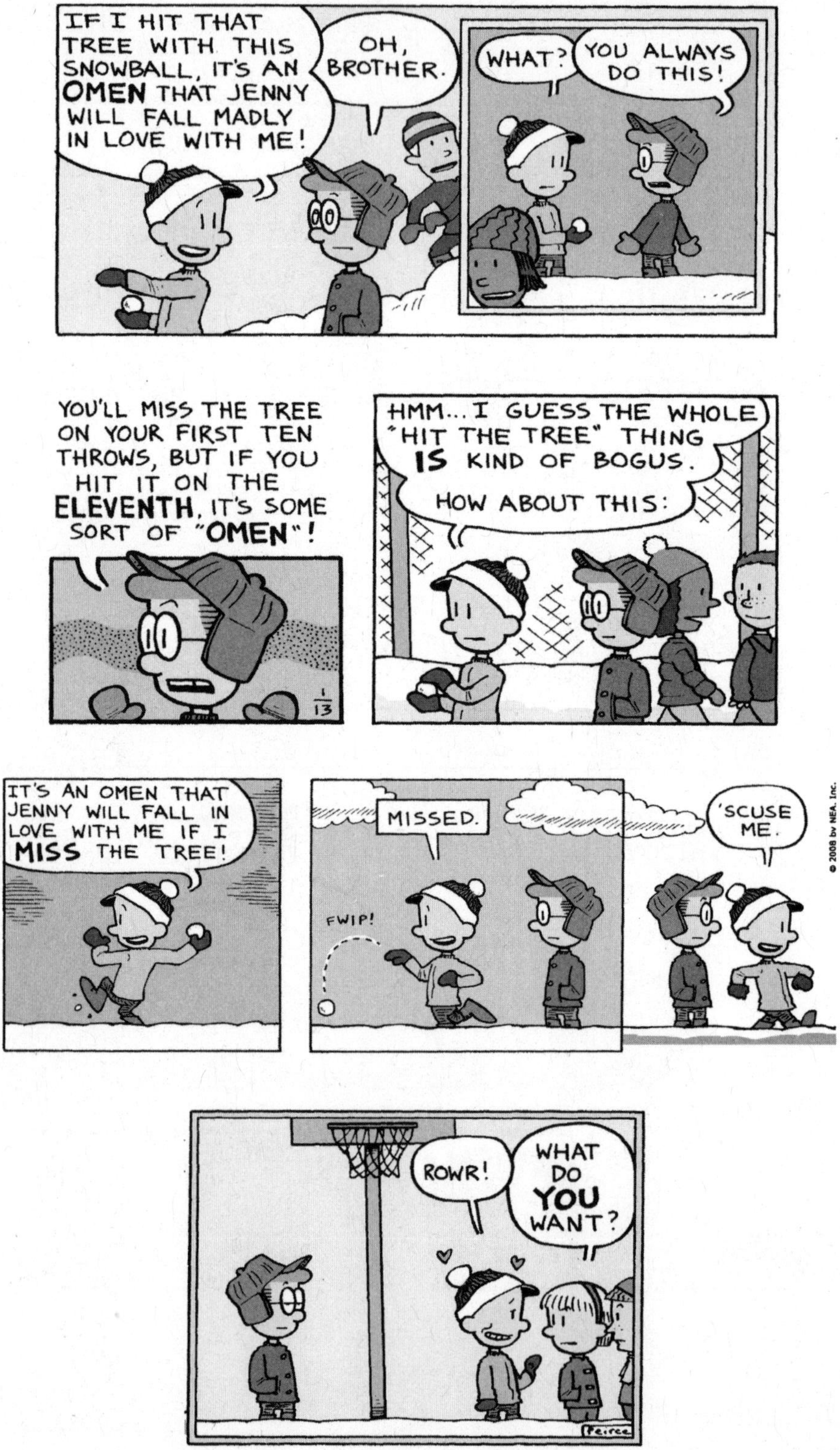
IF I HIT THAT TREE WITH THIS SNOWBALL, IT'S AN OMEN THAT JENNY WILL FALL MADLY IN LOVE WITH ME!
OH, BROTHER.
WHAT?
YOU ALWAYS DO THIS!
YOU'LL MISS THE TREE ON YOUR FIRST TEN THROWS, BUT IF YOU HIT IT ON THE ELEVENTH, IT'S SOME SORT OF "OMEN"!
1/13
HMM... I GUESS THE WHOLE "HIT THE TREE" THING IS KIND OF BOGUS.
HOW ABOUT THIS:
IT'S AN OMEN THAT JENNY WILL FALL IN LOVE WITH ME IF I MISS THE TREE!
FWIP!
MISSED.
'SCUSE ME.
© 2008 by NEA, Inc.
ROWR!
WHAT DO YOU WANT?
Peirce

RELAX...OR ELSE!

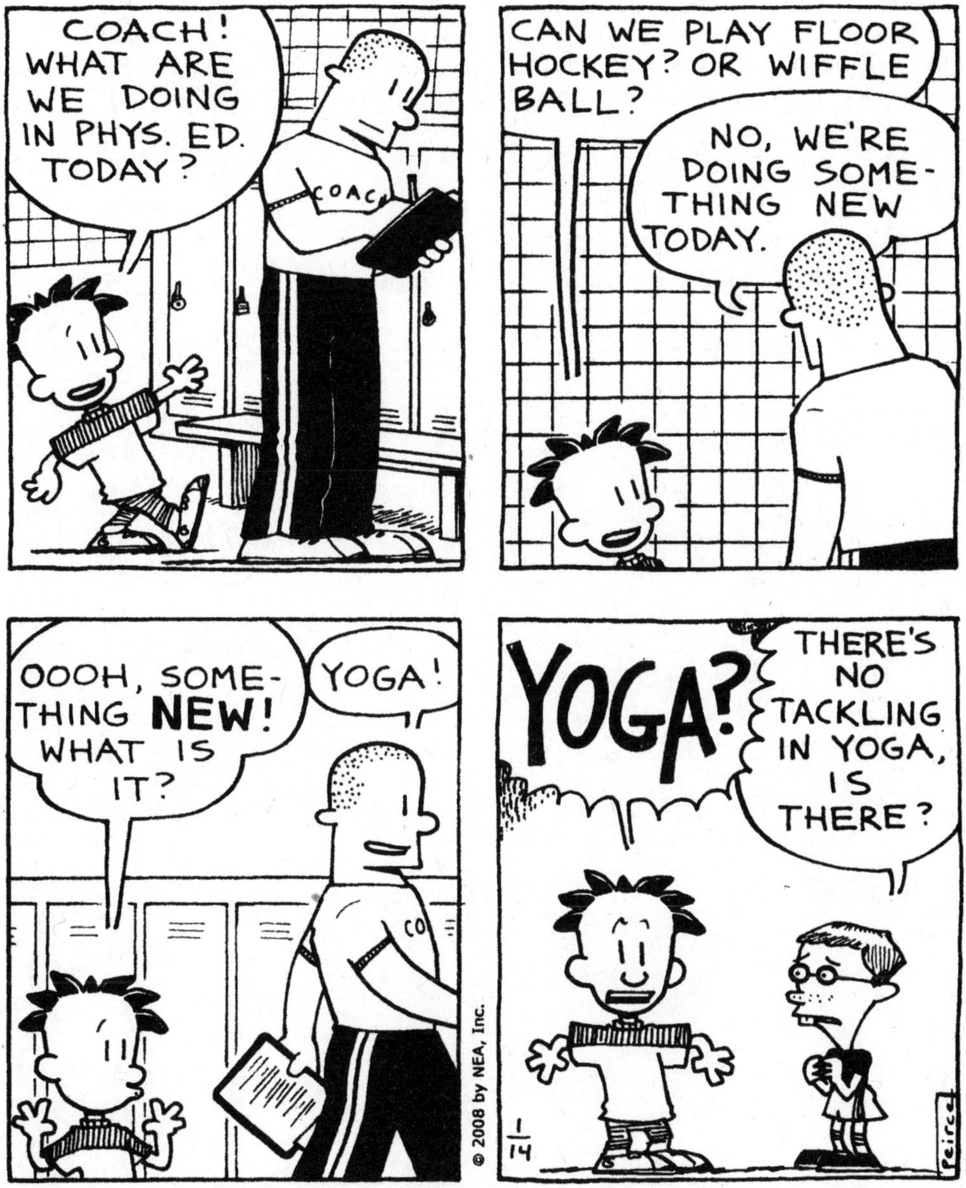
COACH! WHAT ARE WE DOING IN PHYS. ED. TODAY?
COACH
CAN WE PLAY FLOOR HOCKEY? OR WIFFLE BALL?
NO, WE'RE DOING SOME-THING NEW TODAY.
OOOH, SOME-THING **NEW**! WHAT IS IT?
YOGA!
CO
© 2008 by NEA, Inc.
YOGA?
THERE'S NO TACKLING IN YOGA, IS THERE?
1/14
Peirce

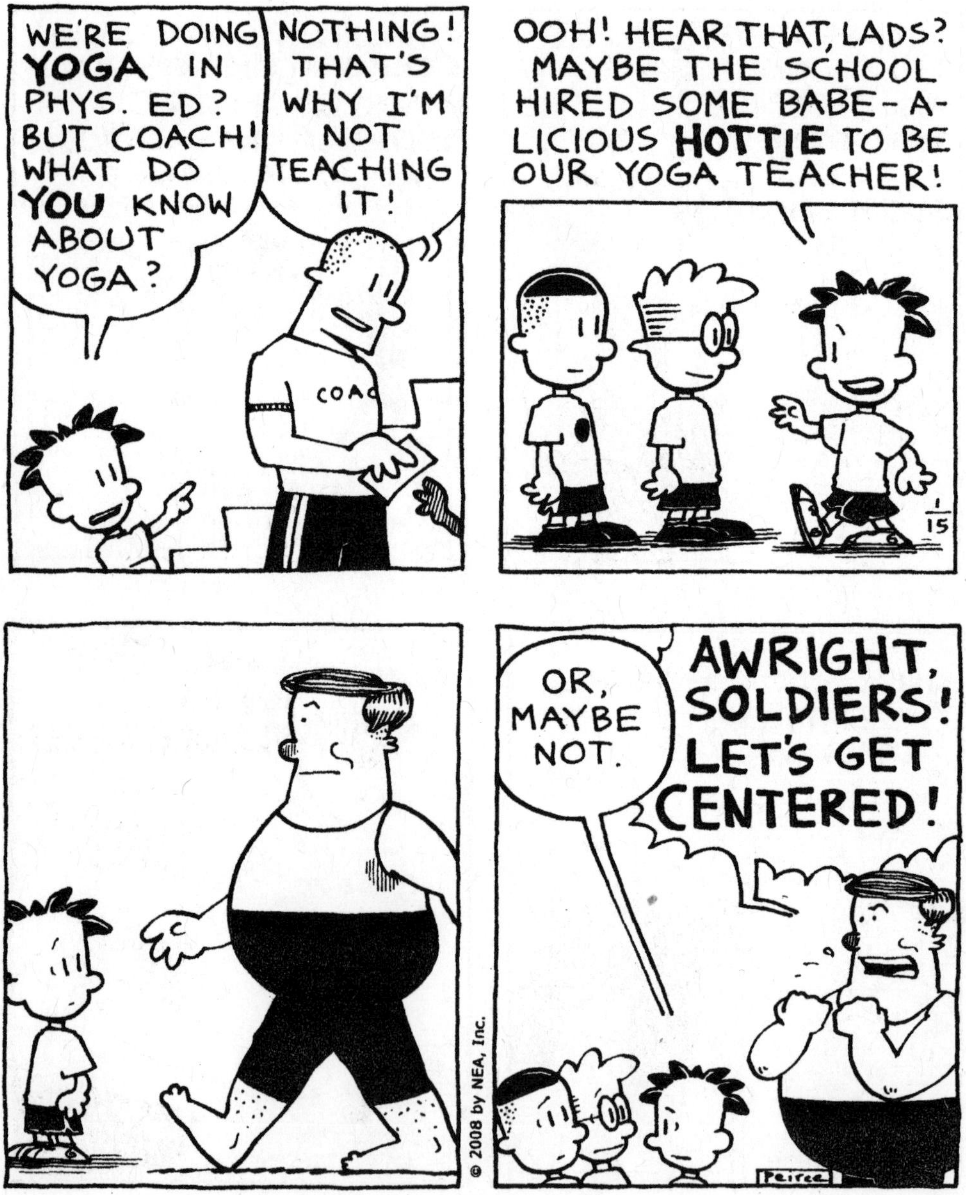

WE'RE DOING YOGA IN PHYS. ED? BUT COACH! WHAT DO YOU KNOW ABOUT YOGA?
NOTHING! THAT'S WHY I'M NOT TEACHING IT!
COAC
OOH! HEAR THAT, LADS? MAYBE THE SCHOOL HIRED SOME BABE-A-LICIOUS HOTTIE TO BE OUR YOGA TEACHER!
1/15
© 2008 by NEA, Inc.
AWRIGHT, SOLDIERS! LET'S GET CENTERED!
OR, MAYBE NOT.
Peirce

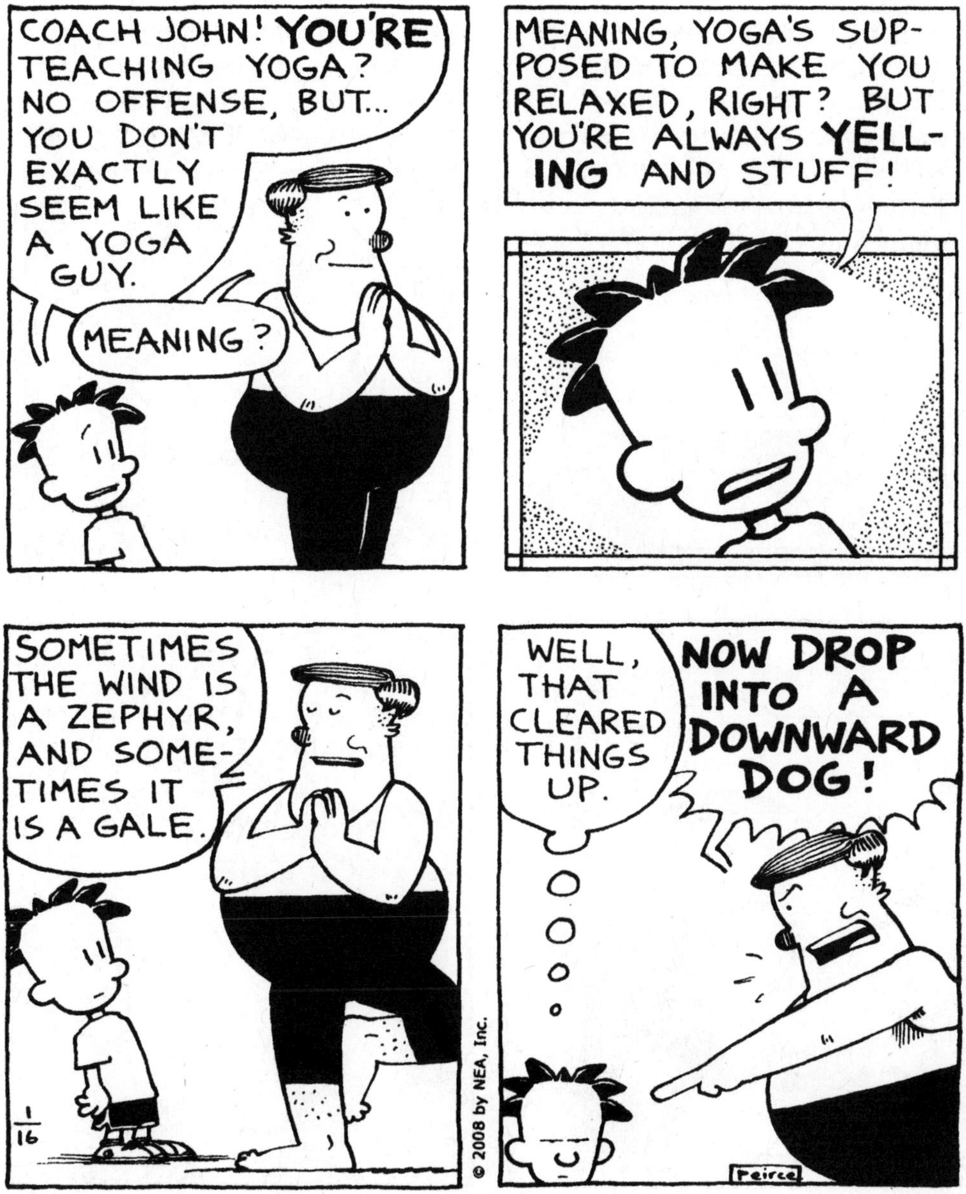

COACH JOHN! YOU'RE TEACHING YOGA? NO OFFENSE, BUT... YOU DON'T EXACTLY SEEM LIKE A YOGA GUY.
MEANING?
MEANING, YOGA'S SUP- POSED TO MAKE YOU RELAXED, RIGHT? BUT YOU'RE ALWAYS YELL- ING AND STUFF!
SOMETIMES THE WIND IS A ZEPHYR, AND SOME- TIMES IT IS A GALE.
1/16
© 2008 by NEA, Inc.
WELL, THAT CLEARED THINGS UP.
NOW DROP INTO A DOWNWARD DOG!
Peirce

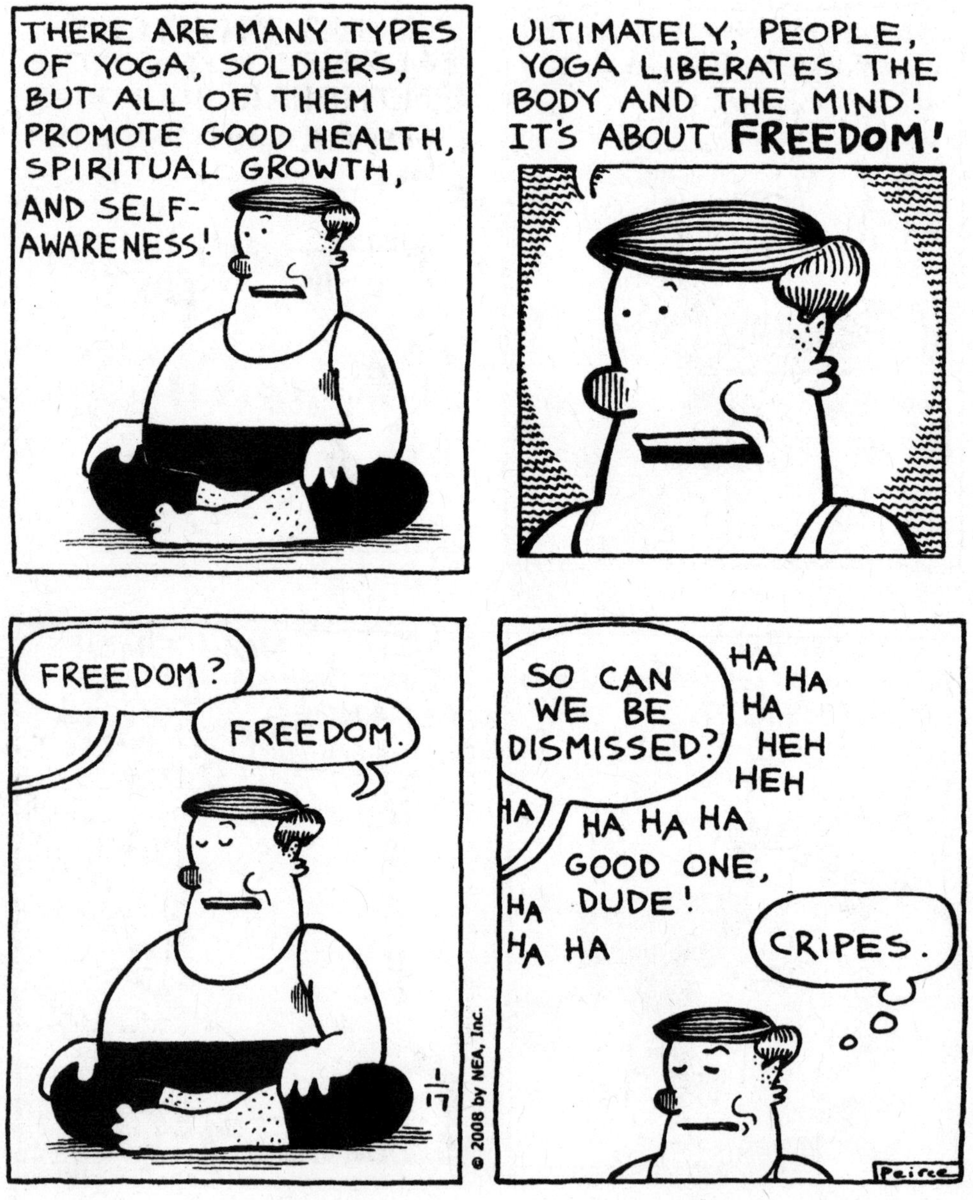
THERE ARE MANY TYPES OF YOGA, SOLDIERS, BUT ALL OF THEM PROMOTE GOOD HEALTH, SPIRITUAL GROWTH, AND SELF-AWARENESS!
ULTIMATELY, PEOPLE, YOGA LIBERATES THE BODY AND THE MIND! IT'S ABOUT FREEDOM!
FREEDOM?
FREEDOM.
1/17
© 2008 by NEA, Inc.
SO CAN WE BE DISMISSED?
HA HA HA HEH HEH
HA
HA HA HA
GOOD ONE, DUDE!
HA HA HA
CRIPES.
Peirce

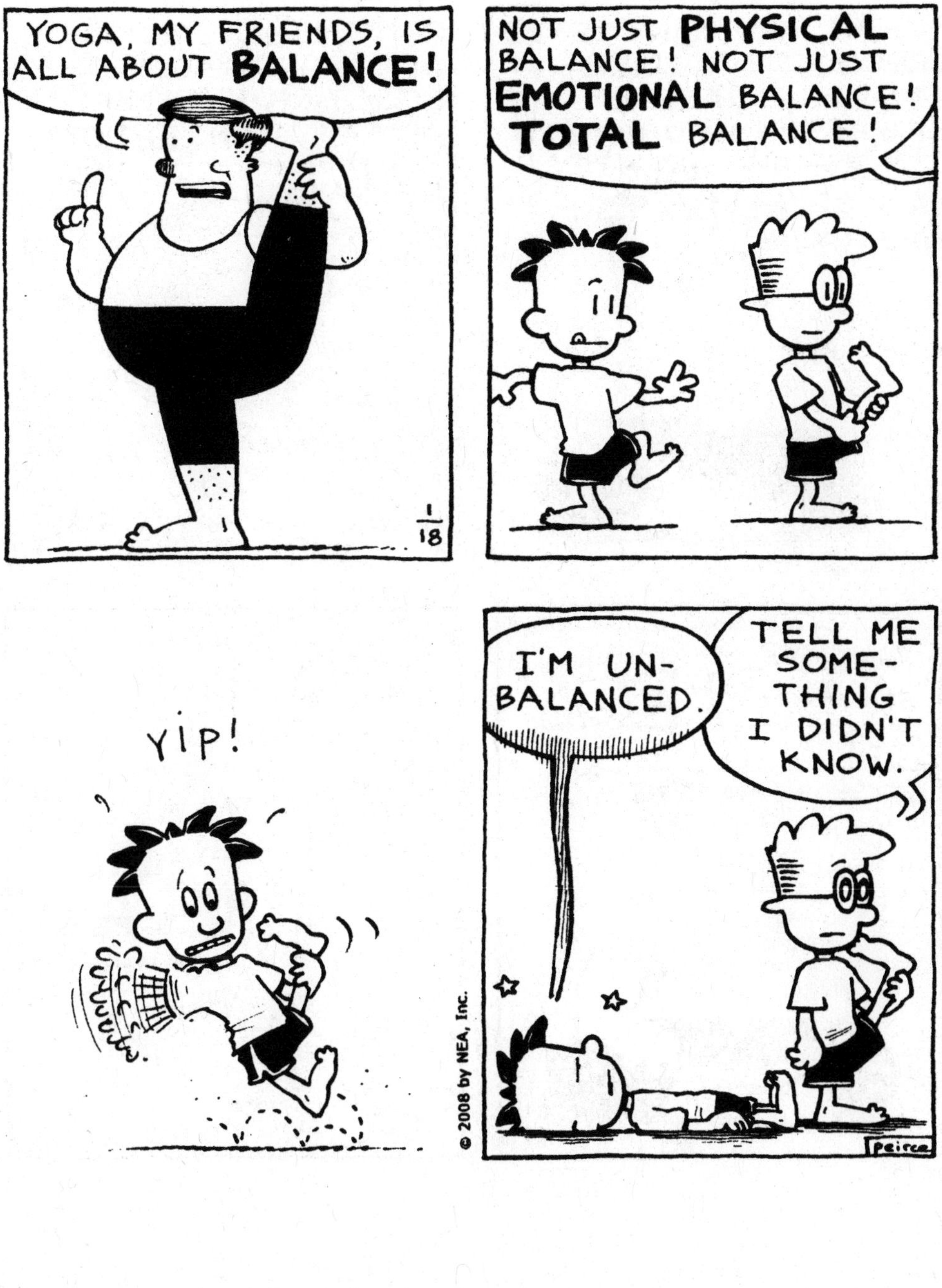
YOGA, MY FRIENDS, IS ALL ABOUT **BALANCE**!
1/18
NOT JUST **PHYSICAL** BALANCE! NOT JUST **EMOTIONAL** BALANCE! **TOTAL** BALANCE!
YIP!
I'M UN-BALANCED.
TELL ME SOME-THING I DIDN'T KNOW.
© 2008 by NEA, Inc.
peirce

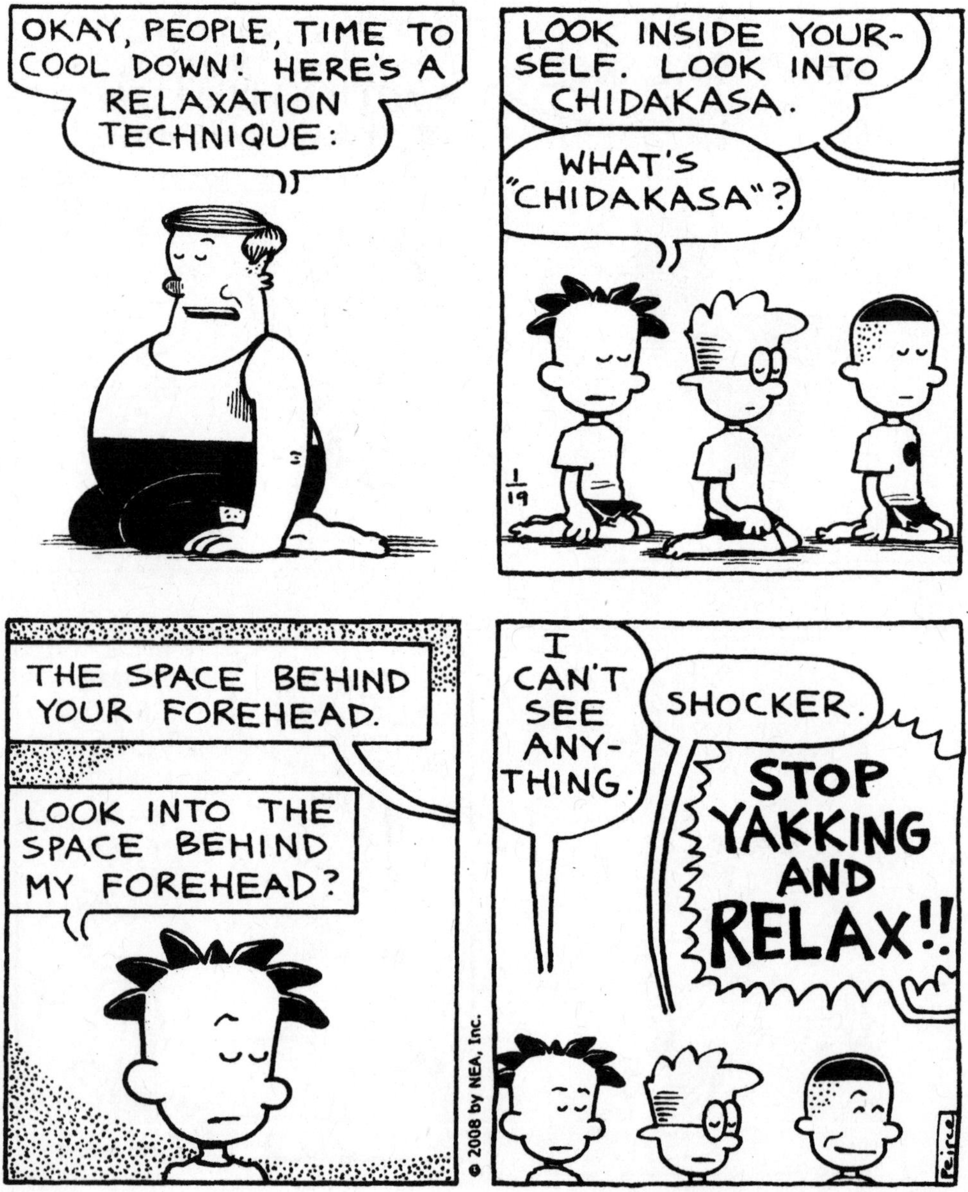
OKAY, PEOPLE, TIME TO COOL DOWN! HERE'S A RELAXATION TECHNIQUE:
LOOK INSIDE YOURSELF. LOOK INTO CHIDAKASA.
WHAT'S "CHIDAKASA"?
1/19
THE SPACE BEHIND YOUR FOREHEAD.
LOOK INTO THE SPACE BEHIND MY FOREHEAD?
© 2008 by NEA, Inc.
I CAN'T SEE ANYTHING.
SHOCKER.
STOP YAKKING AND RELAX!!
Peirce

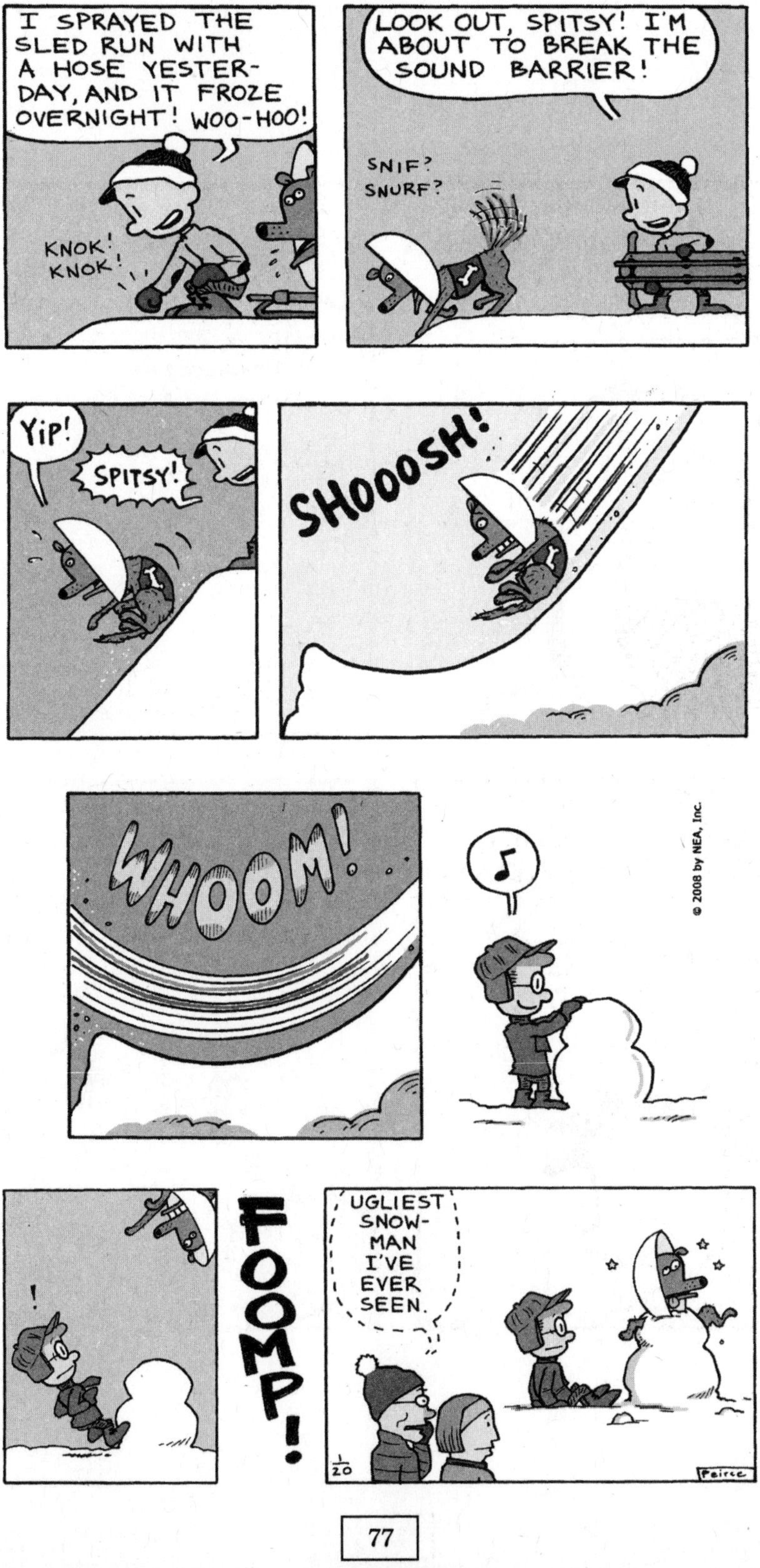

I SPRAYED THE SLED RUN WITH A HOSE YESTER-DAY, AND IT FROZE OVERNIGHT! WOO-HOO!
KNOK! KNOK!
LOOK OUT, SPITSY! I'M ABOUT TO BREAK THE SOUND BARRIER!
SNIF? SNURF?
YIP!
SPITSY!
SHOOOSH!
WHOOM!
♪
!
FOOMP!
UGLIEST SNOW-MAN I'VE EVER SEEN.
1/20
Peirce

ART À LA NATE

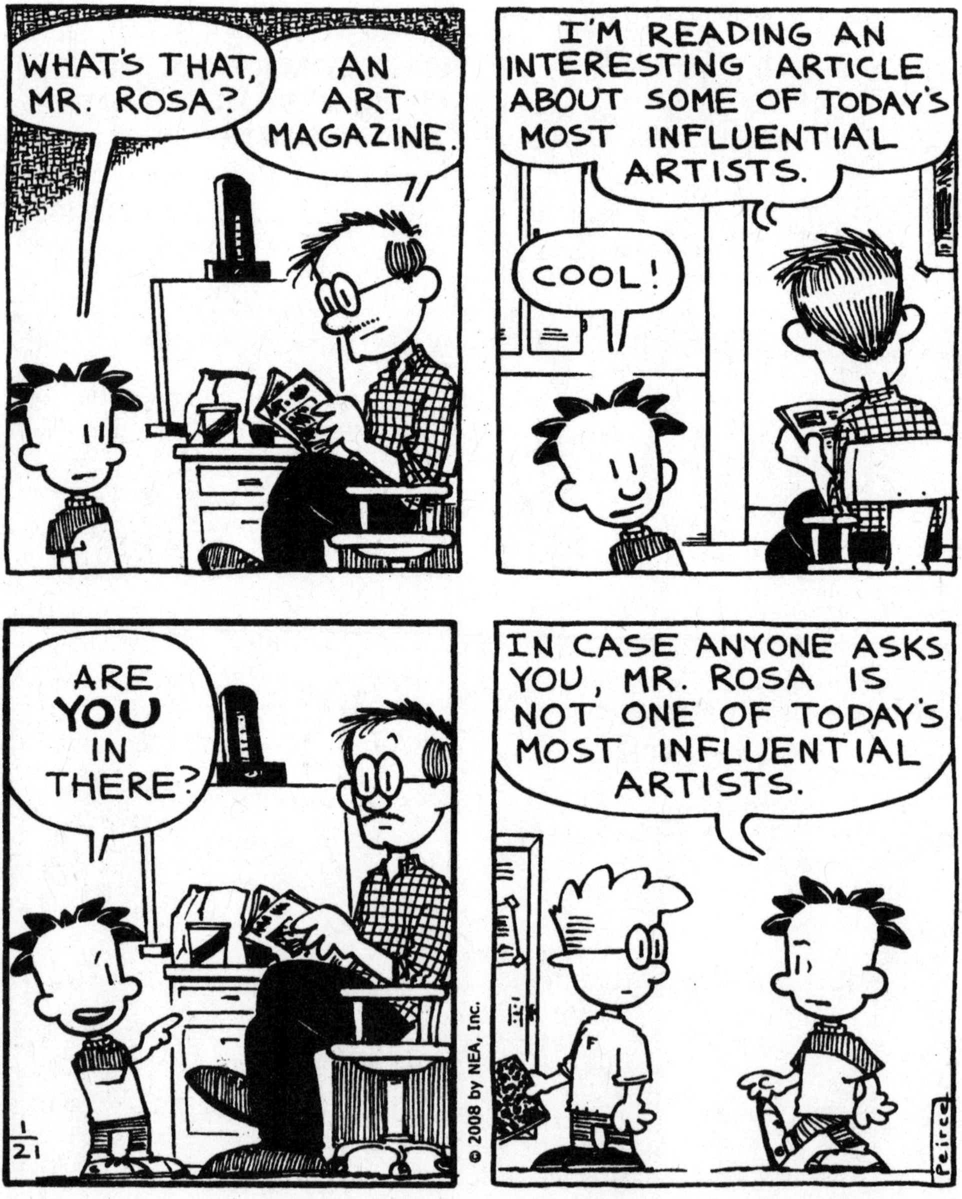
WHAT'S THAT, MR. ROSA?
AN ART MAGAZINE.
I'M READING AN INTERESTING ARTICLE ABOUT SOME OF TODAY'S MOST INFLUENTIAL ARTISTS.
COOL!
ARE YOU IN THERE?
IN CASE ANYONE ASKS YOU, MR. ROSA IS NOT ONE OF TODAY'S MOST INFLUENTIAL ARTISTS.
1/21
© 2008 by NEA, Inc.
Peirce

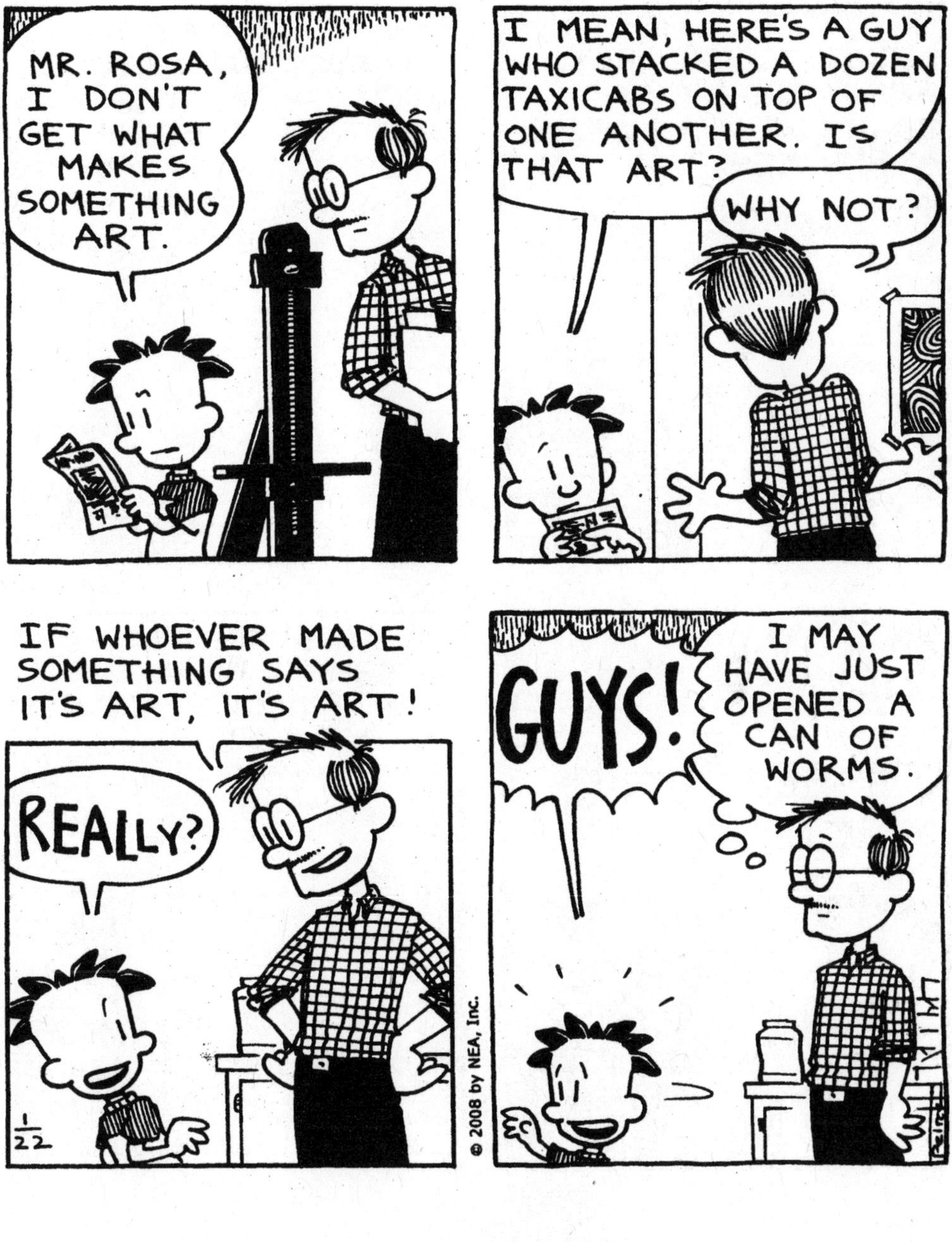
MR. ROSA, I DON'T GET WHAT MAKES SOMETHING ART.
I MEAN, HERE'S A GUY WHO STACKED A DOZEN TAXICABS ON TOP OF ONE ANOTHER. IS THAT ART?
WHY NOT?
IF WHOEVER MADE SOMETHING SAYS IT'S ART, IT'S ART!
REALLY?
1/22
GUYS!
I MAY HAVE JUST OPENED A CAN OF WORMS.
© 2008 by NEA, Inc.

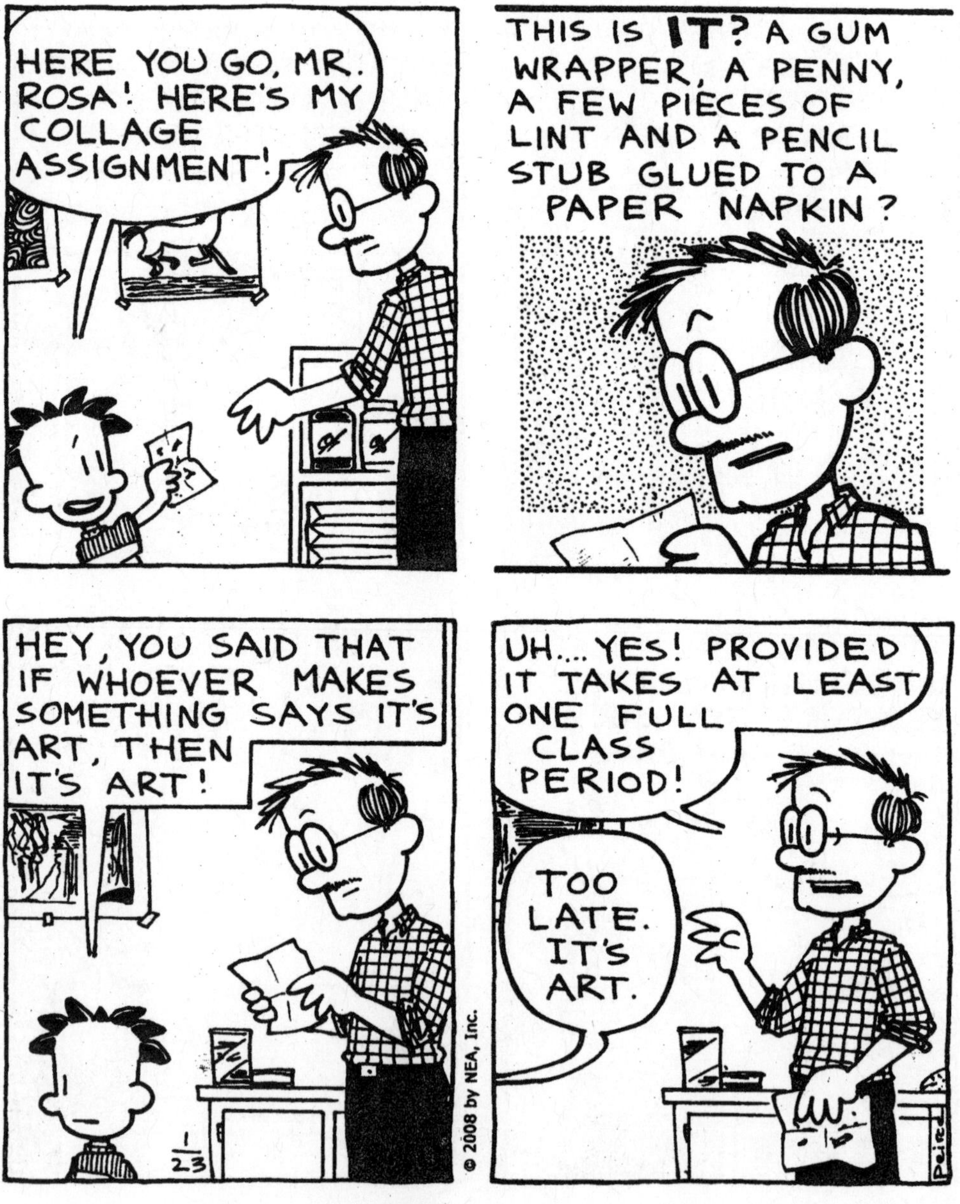
HERE YOU GO, MR. ROSA! HERE'S MY COLLAGE ASSIGNMENT!
THIS IS IT? A GUM WRAPPER, A PENNY, A FEW PIECES OF LINT AND A PENCIL STUB GLUED TO A PAPER NAPKIN?
HEY, YOU SAID THAT IF WHOEVER MAKES SOMETHING SAYS IT'S ART, THEN IT'S ART!
1/23
© 2008 by NEA, Inc.
UH.... YES! PROVIDED IT TAKES AT LEAST ONE FULL CLASS PERIOD!
TOO LATE. IT'S ART.
Peirce

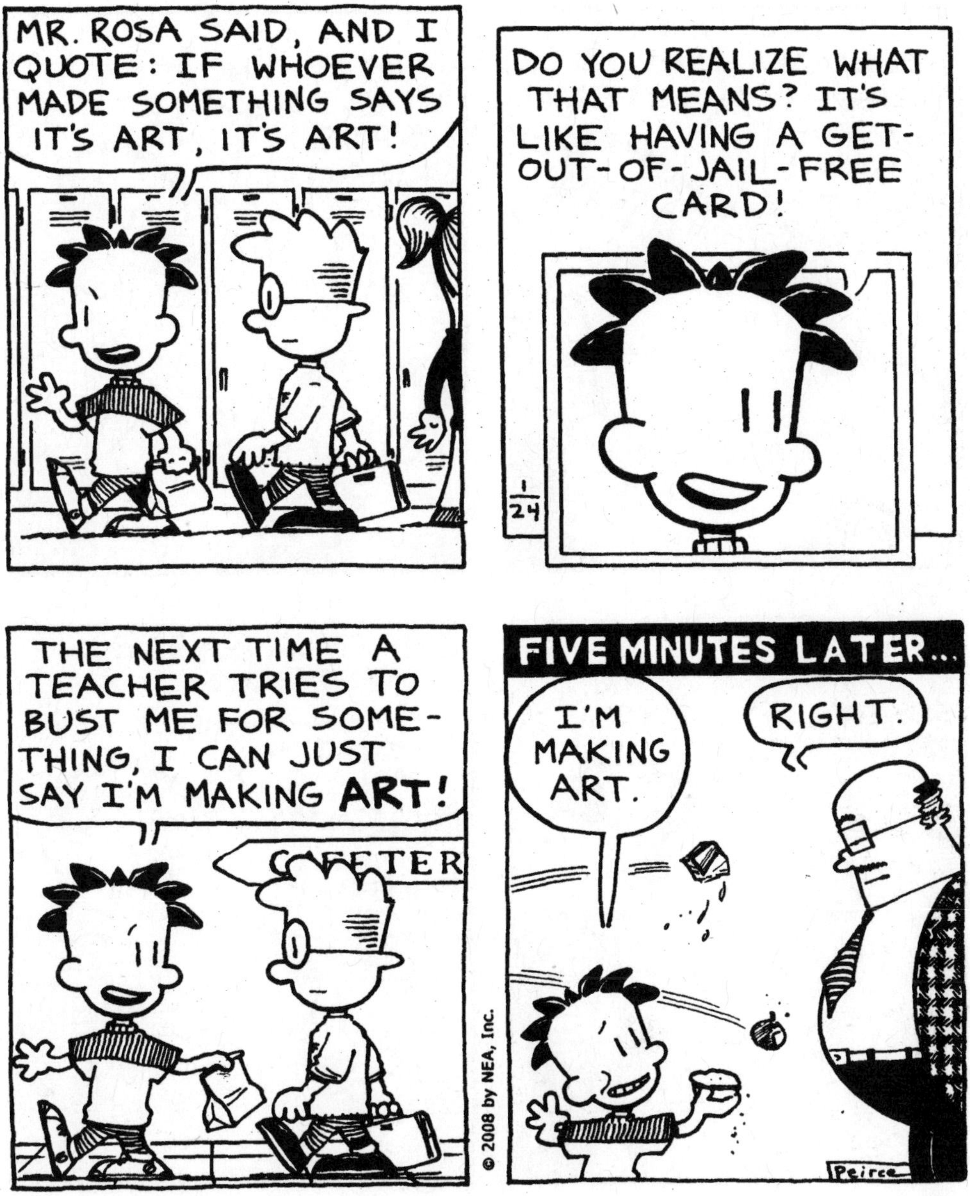
MR. ROSA SAID, AND I QUOTE: IF WHOEVER MADE SOMETHING SAYS IT'S ART, IT'S ART!
DO YOU REALIZE WHAT THAT MEANS? IT'S LIKE HAVING A GET-OUT-OF-JAIL-FREE CARD!
1/24
THE NEXT TIME A TEACHER TRIES TO BUST ME FOR SOMETHING, I CAN JUST SAY I'M MAKING **ART**!
© 2008 by NEA, Inc.
FIVE MINUTES LATER...
I'M MAKING ART.
RIGHT.
Peirce

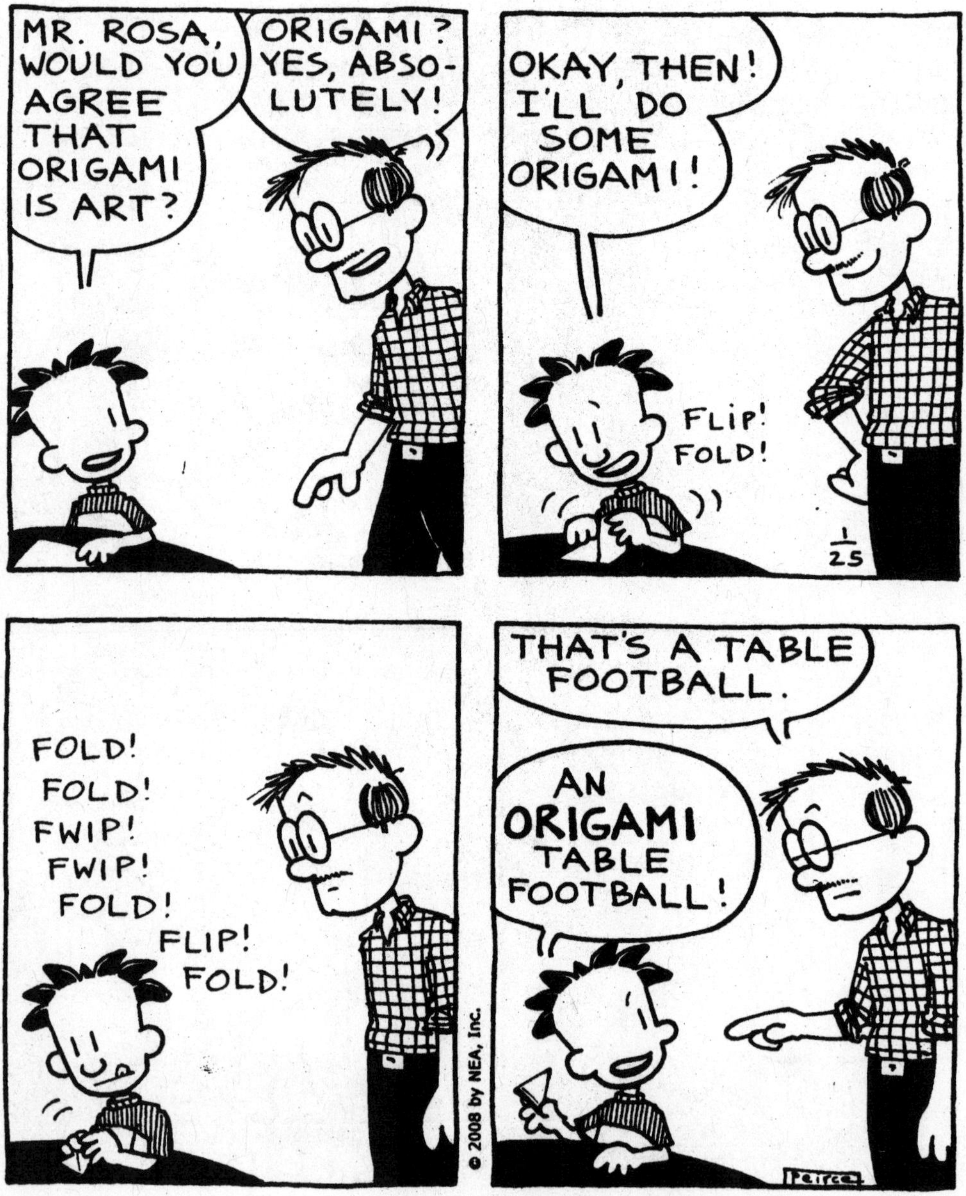
MR. ROSA, WOULD YOU AGREE THAT ORIGAMI IS ART?
ORIGAMI? YES, ABSOLUTELY!
OKAY, THEN! I'LL DO SOME ORIGAMI!
FLIP! FOLD!
1/25
FOLD! FOLD! FWIP! FWIP! FOLD! FLIP! FOLD!
© 2008 by NEA, Inc.
THAT'S A TABLE FOOTBALL.
AN **ORIGAMI** TABLE FOOTBALL!
PEIRCE

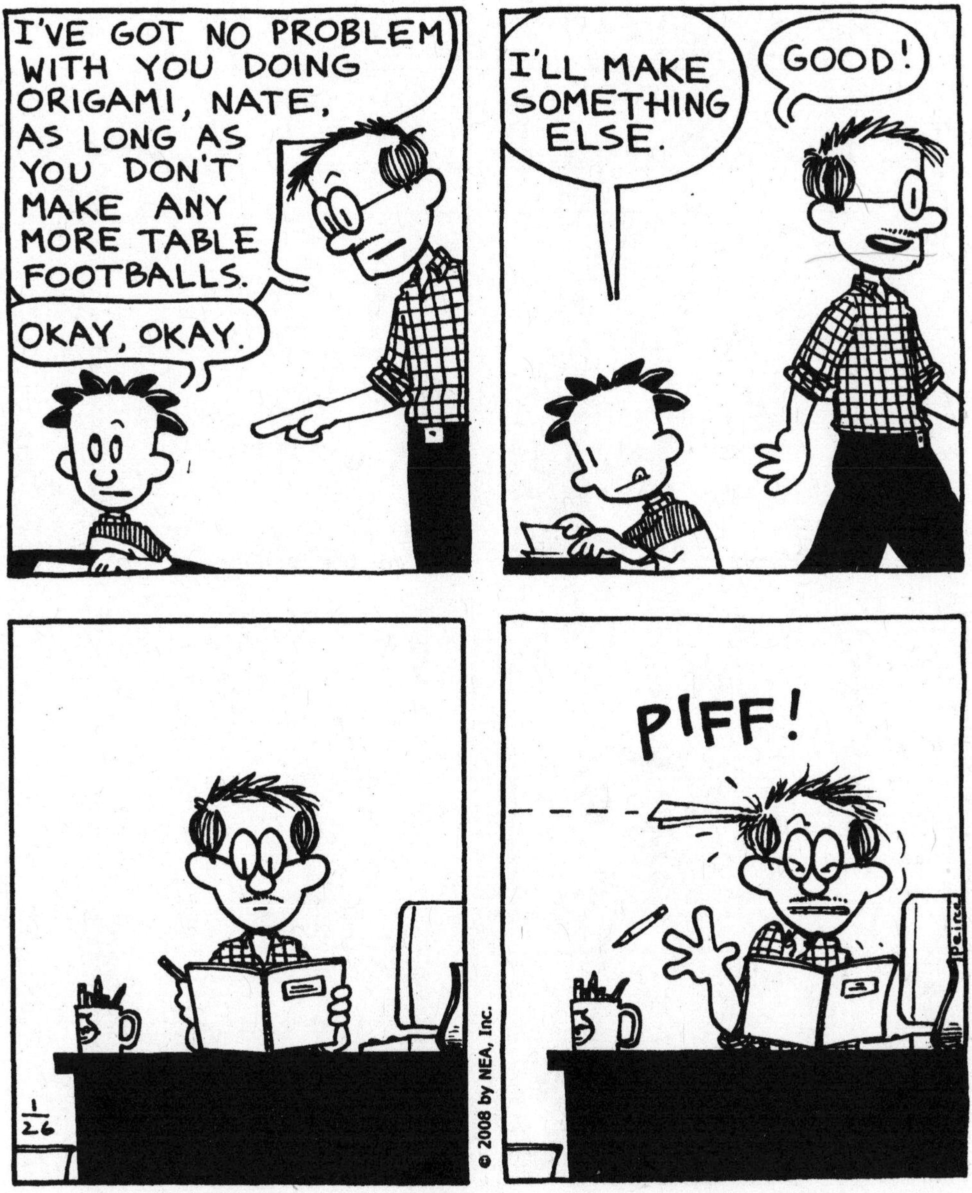
I'VE GOT NO PROBLEM WITH YOU DOING ORIGAMI, NATE, AS LONG AS YOU DON'T MAKE ANY MORE TABLE FOOTBALLS.
OKAY, OKAY.
I'LL MAKE SOMETHING ELSE.
GOOD!
1/26
© 2008 by NEA, Inc.
PIFF!
Peirce

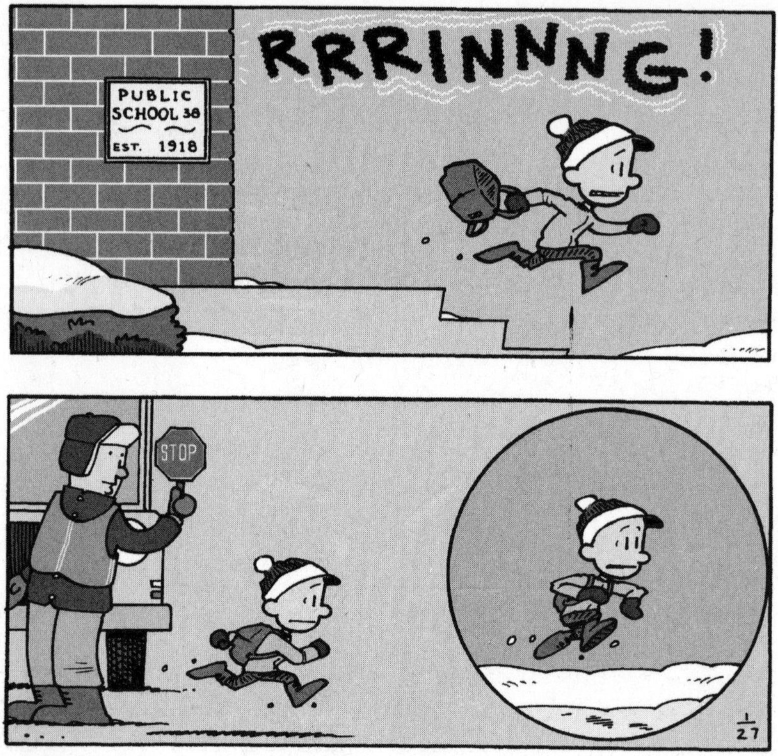
RRRINNNG!
PUBLIC SCHOOL 38 EST. 1918
STOP
1/27

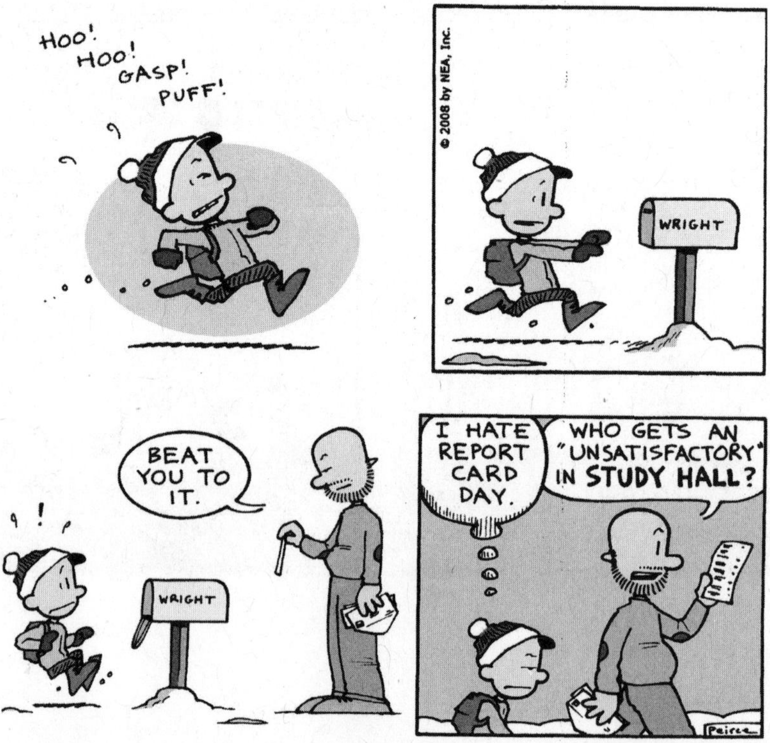
© 2008 by NEA, Inc.
HOO! HOO! GASP! PUFF!
WRIGHT
!
BEAT YOU TO IT.
WRIGHT
I HATE REPORT CARD DAY.
WHO GETS AN "UNSATISFACTORY" IN STUDY HALL?
Peirce

WHO'S THE PERFECT COUPLE?

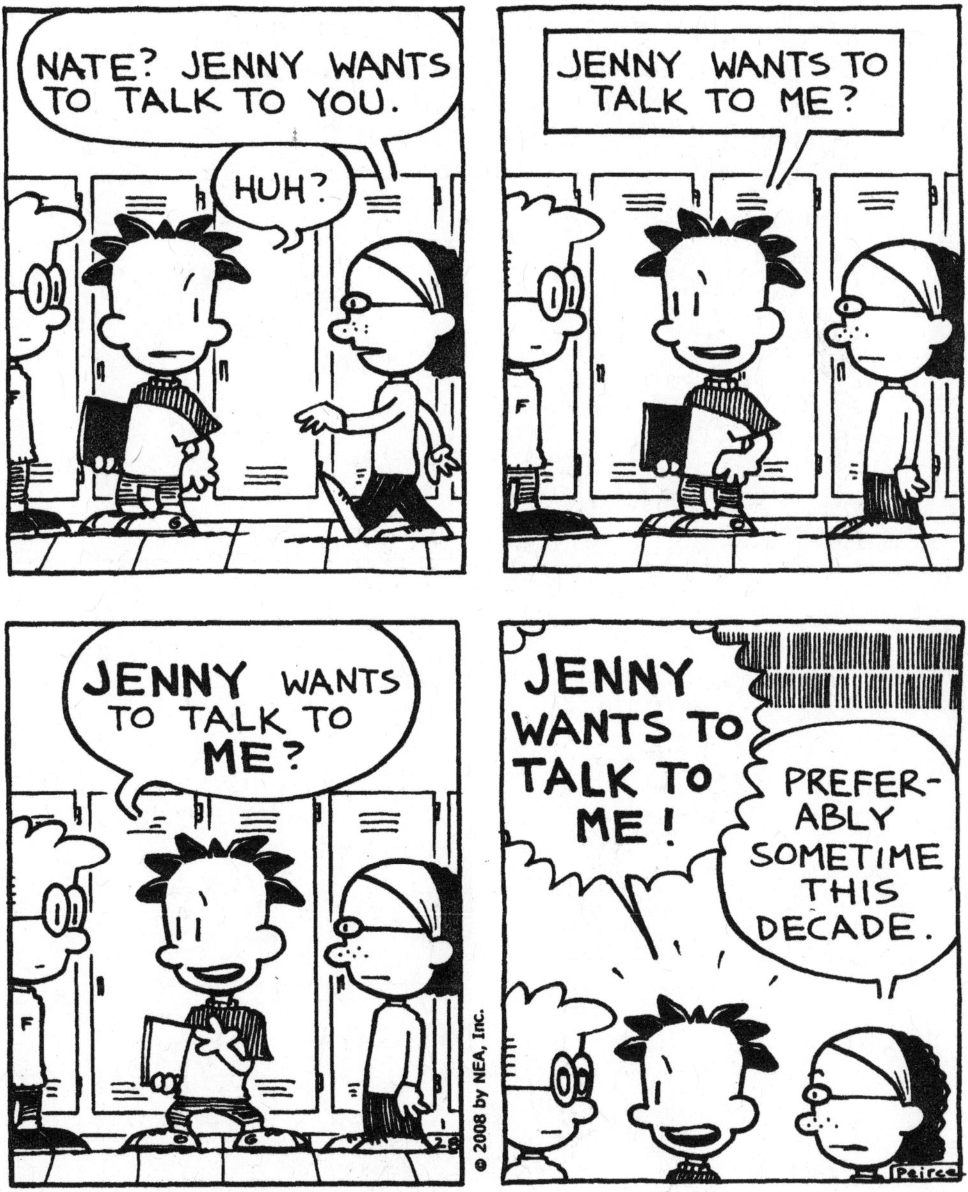

NATE? JENNY WANTS TO TALK TO YOU.
HUH?
JENNY WANTS TO TALK TO ME?
JENNY WANTS TO TALK TO ME?
JENNY WANTS TO TALK TO ME!
PREFER-ABLY SOMETIME THIS DECADE.
© 2008 by NEA, Inc.
Peirce

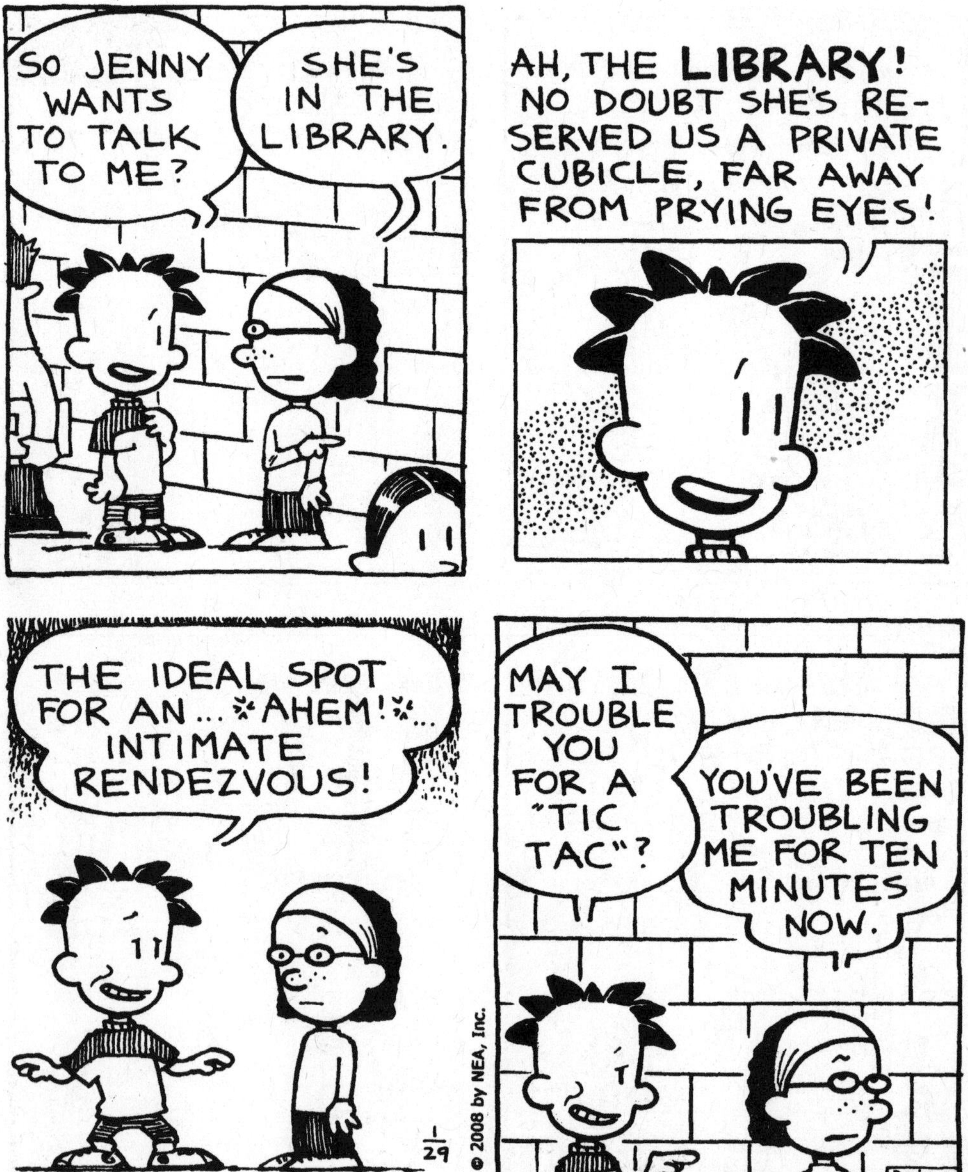
SO JENNY WANTS TO TALK TO ME?
SHE'S IN THE LIBRARY.
AH, THE LIBRARY! NO DOUBT SHE'S RE-SERVED US A PRIVATE CUBICLE, FAR AWAY FROM PRYING EYES!
THE IDEAL SPOT FOR AN... *AHEM!*... INTIMATE RENDEZVOUS!
1/29
© 2008 by NEA, Inc.
MAY I TROUBLE YOU FOR A "TIC TAC"?
YOU'VE BEEN TROUBLING ME FOR TEN MINUTES NOW.
Peirce

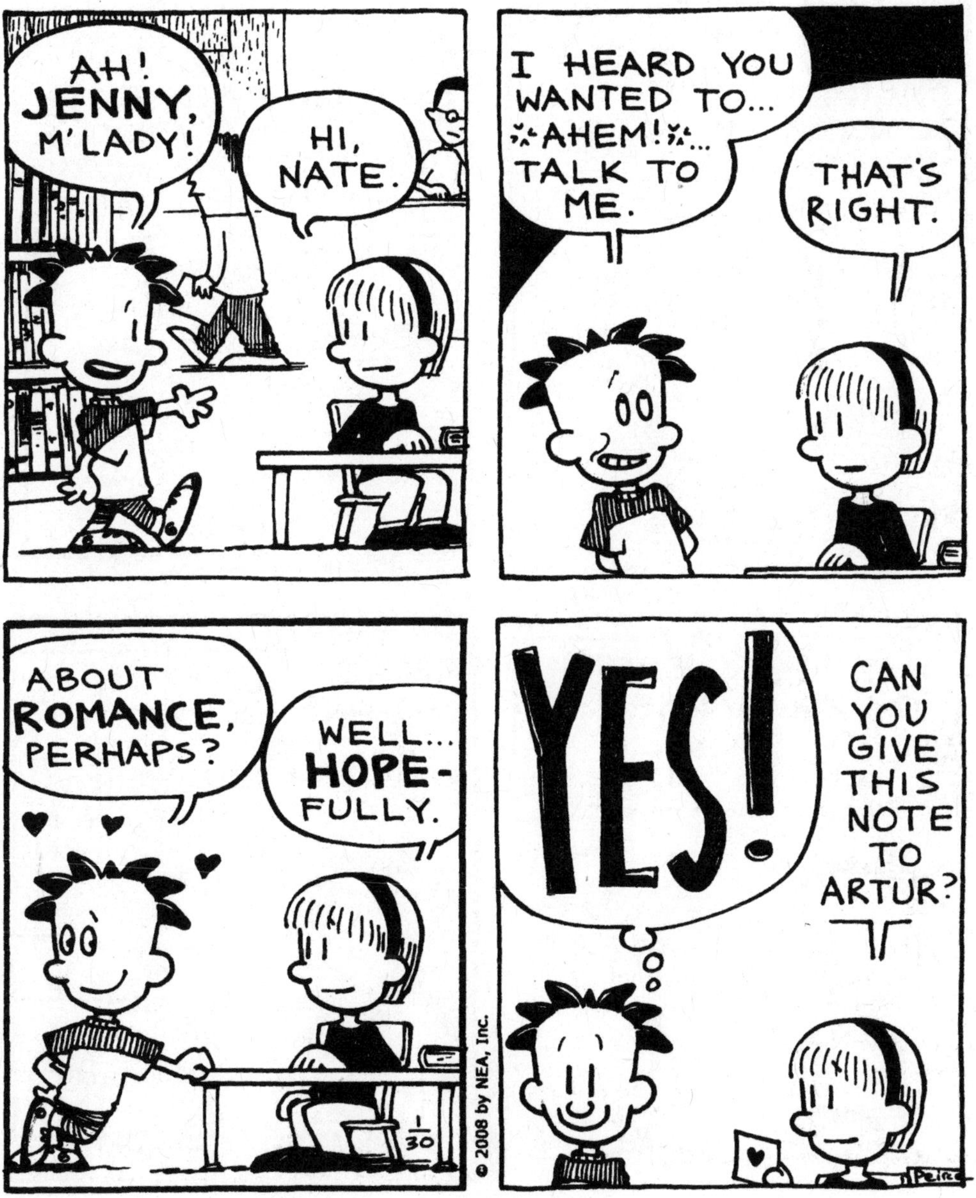
AH! JENNY, M'LADY!
HI, NATE.
I HEARD YOU WANTED TO... AHEM!... TALK TO ME.
THAT'S RIGHT.
ABOUT ROMANCE, PERHAPS?
WELL... HOPE-FULLY.
YES!
CAN YOU GIVE THIS NOTE TO ARTUR?
1/30
© 2008 by NEA, Inc.

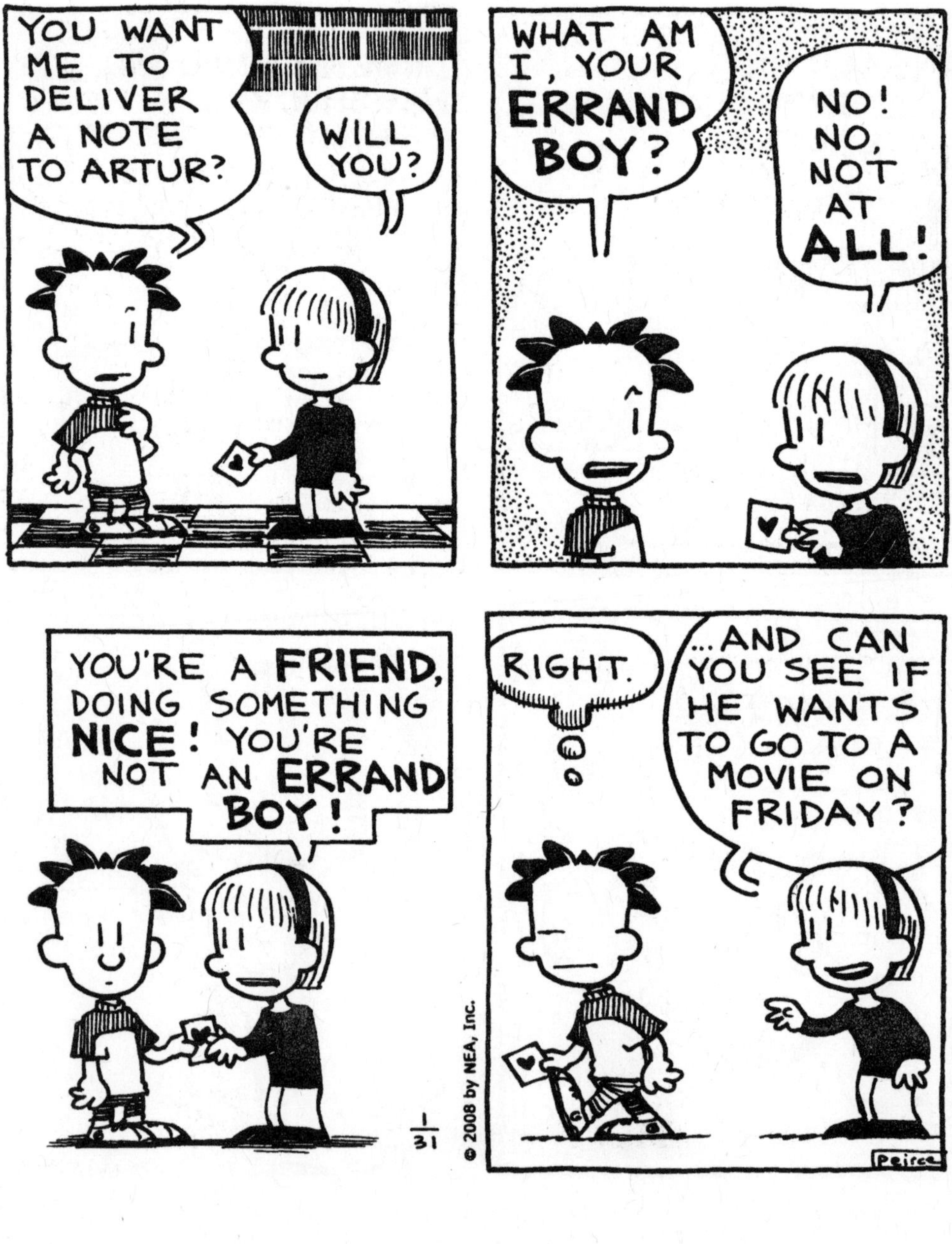
YOU WANT ME TO DELIVER A NOTE TO ARTUR?
WILL YOU?
WHAT AM I, YOUR ERRAND BOY?
NO! NO, NOT AT ALL!
YOU'RE A FRIEND, DOING SOMETHING NICE! YOU'RE NOT AN ERRAND BOY!
RIGHT.
...AND CAN YOU SEE IF HE WANTS TO GO TO A MOVIE ON FRIDAY?
1/31
© 2008 by NEA, Inc.
Peirce

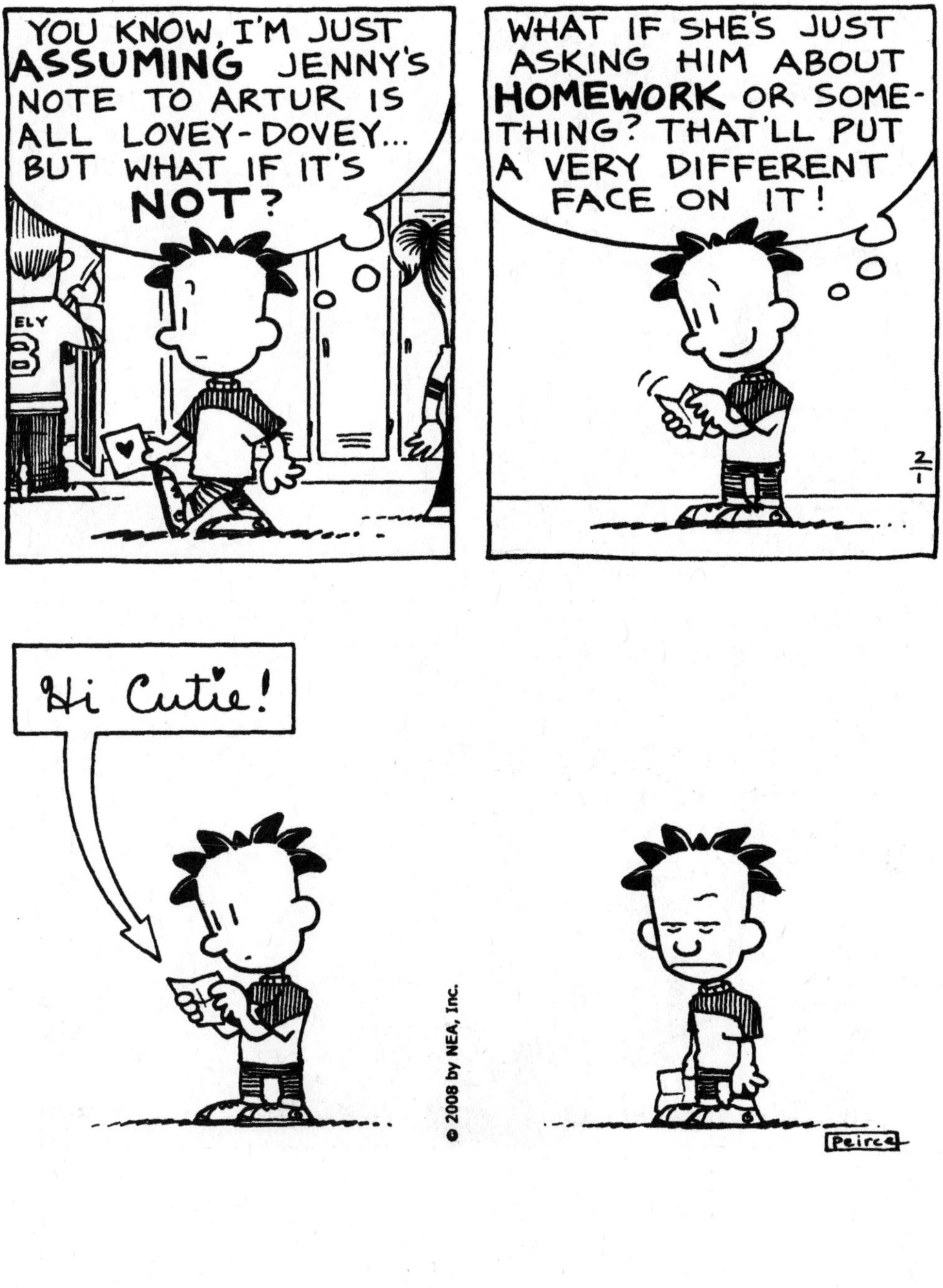
YOU KNOW, I'M JUST ASSUMING JENNY'S NOTE TO ARTUR IS ALL LOVEY-DOVEY... BUT WHAT IF IT'S NOT?
ELY
WHAT IF SHE'S JUST ASKING HIM ABOUT HOMEWORK OR SOMETHING? THAT'LL PUT A VERY DIFFERENT FACE ON IT!
2/1
Hi Cutie!
© 2008 by NEA, Inc.
Peirce

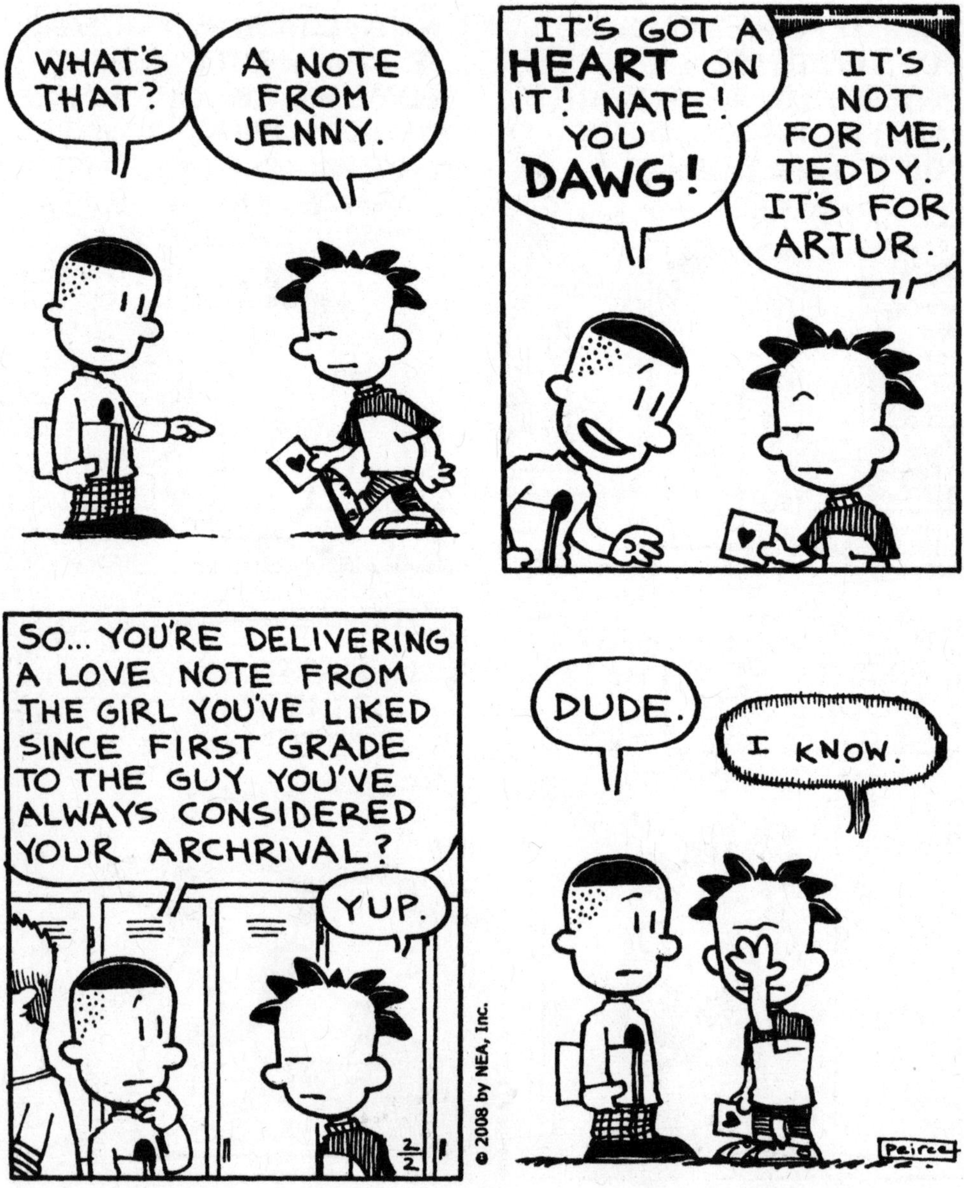
WHAT'S THAT?
A NOTE FROM JENNY.
IT'S GOT A HEART ON IT! NATE! YOU DAWG!
IT'S NOT FOR ME, TEDDY. IT'S FOR ARTUR.
SO... YOU'RE DELIVERING A LOVE NOTE FROM THE GIRL YOU'VE LIKED SINCE FIRST GRADE TO THE GUY YOU'VE ALWAYS CONSIDERED YOUR ARCHRIVAL?
YUP.
© 2008 by NEA, Inc.
DUDE.
I KNOW.
Peirce

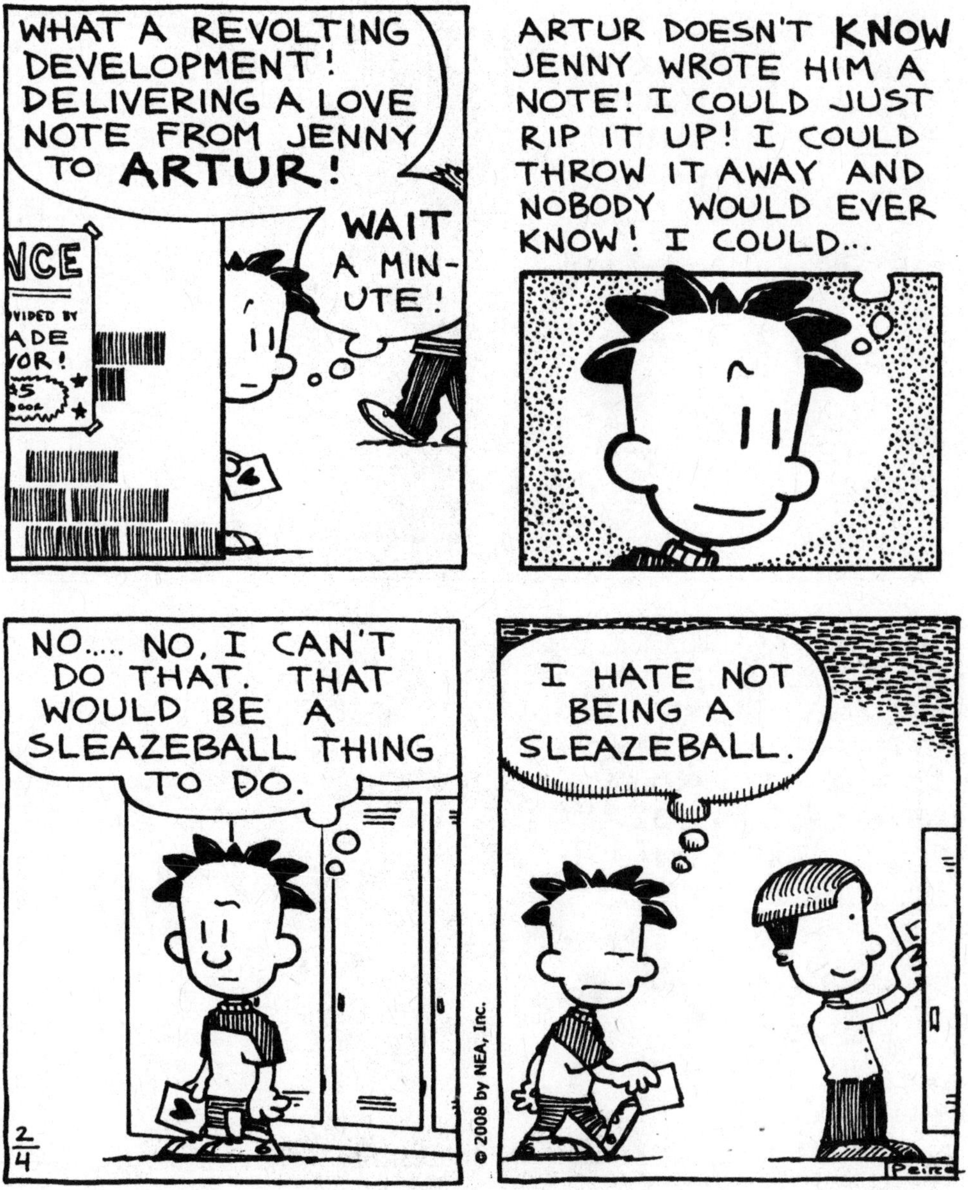
WHAT A REVOLTING DEVELOPMENT! DELIVERING A LOVE NOTE FROM JENNY TO ARTUR!
WAIT A MIN-UTE!
ARTUR DOESN'T KNOW JENNY WROTE HIM A NOTE! I COULD JUST RIP IT UP! I COULD THROW IT AWAY AND NOBODY WOULD EVER KNOW! I COULD...
NO..... NO, I CAN'T DO THAT. THAT WOULD BE A SLEAZEBALL THING TO DO.
I HATE NOT BEING A SLEAZEBALL.
2/4
© 2008 by NEA, Inc.

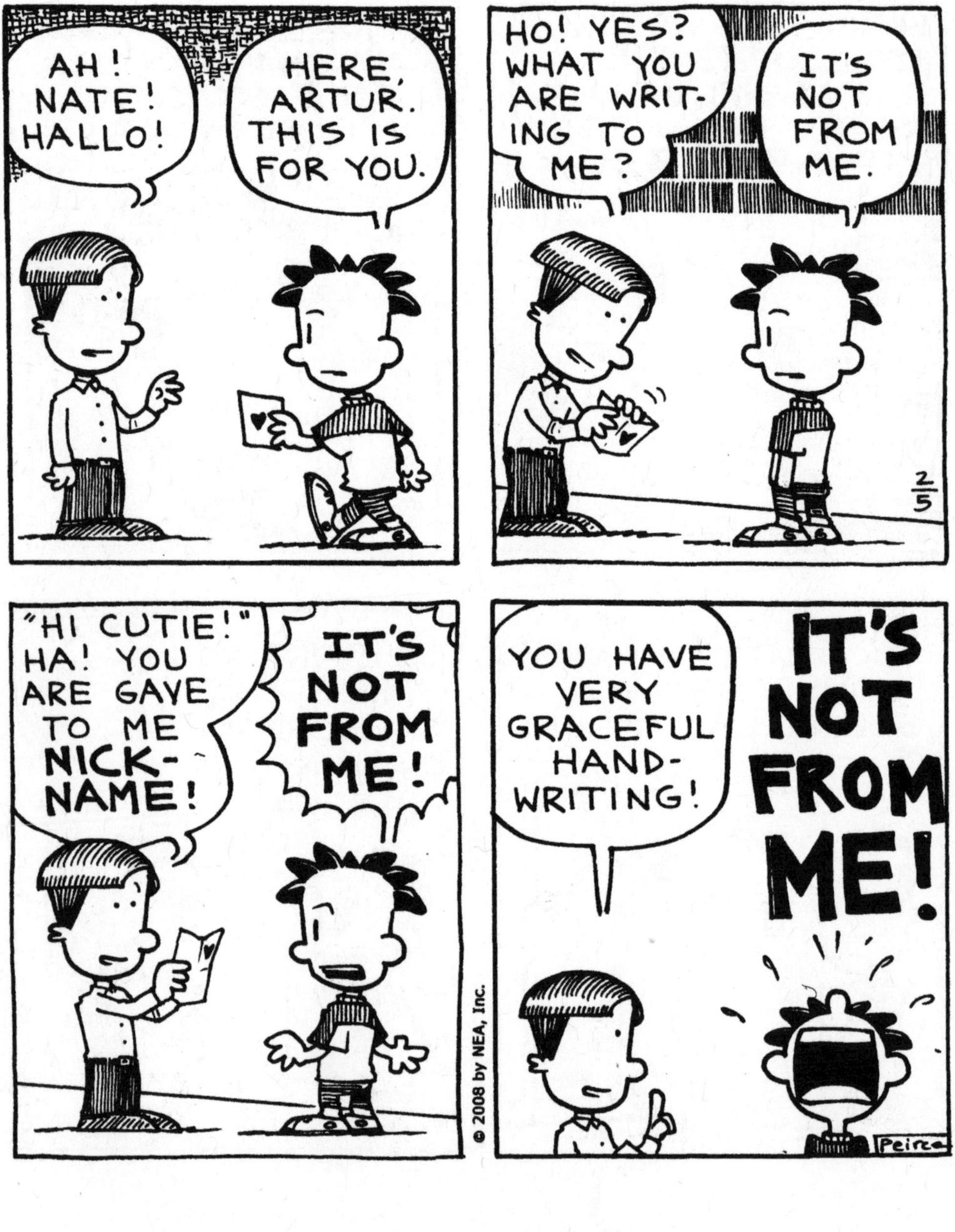
AH! NATE! HALLO!
HERE, ARTUR. THIS IS FOR YOU.
HO! YES? WHAT YOU ARE WRITING TO ME?
IT'S NOT FROM ME.
2/5
"HI CUTIE!" HA! YOU ARE GAVE TO ME NICKNAME!
IT'S NOT FROM ME!
© 2008 by NEA, Inc.
YOU HAVE VERY GRACEFUL HANDWRITING!
IT'S NOT FROM ME!
Peirce

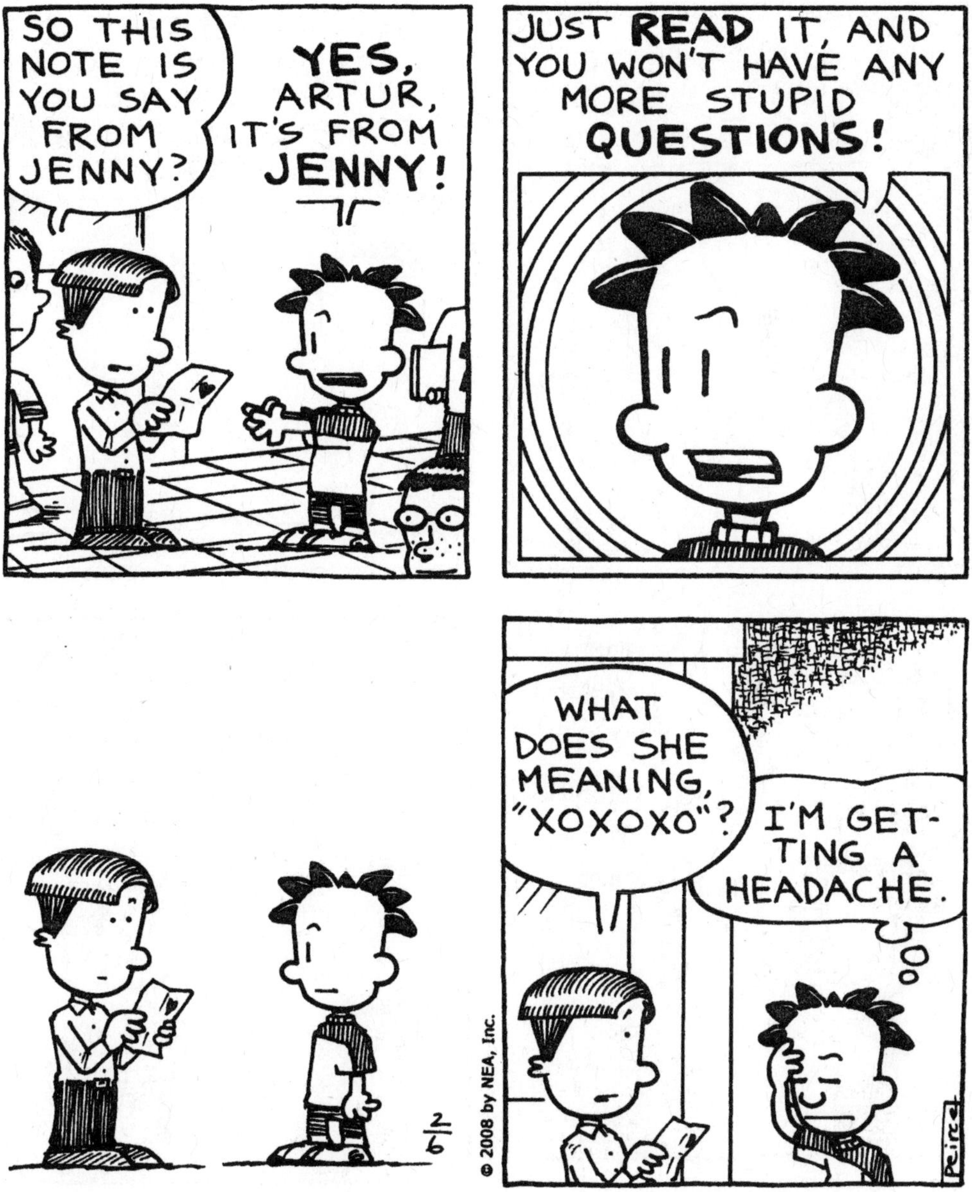
SO THIS NOTE IS YOU SAY FROM JENNY?
YES, ARTUR, IT'S FROM JENNY!
JUST READ IT, AND YOU WON'T HAVE ANY MORE STUPID QUESTIONS!
WHAT DOES SHE MEANING, "XOXOXO"?
I'M GETTING A HEADACHE.
2/6
© 2008 by NEA, Inc.
Peirce

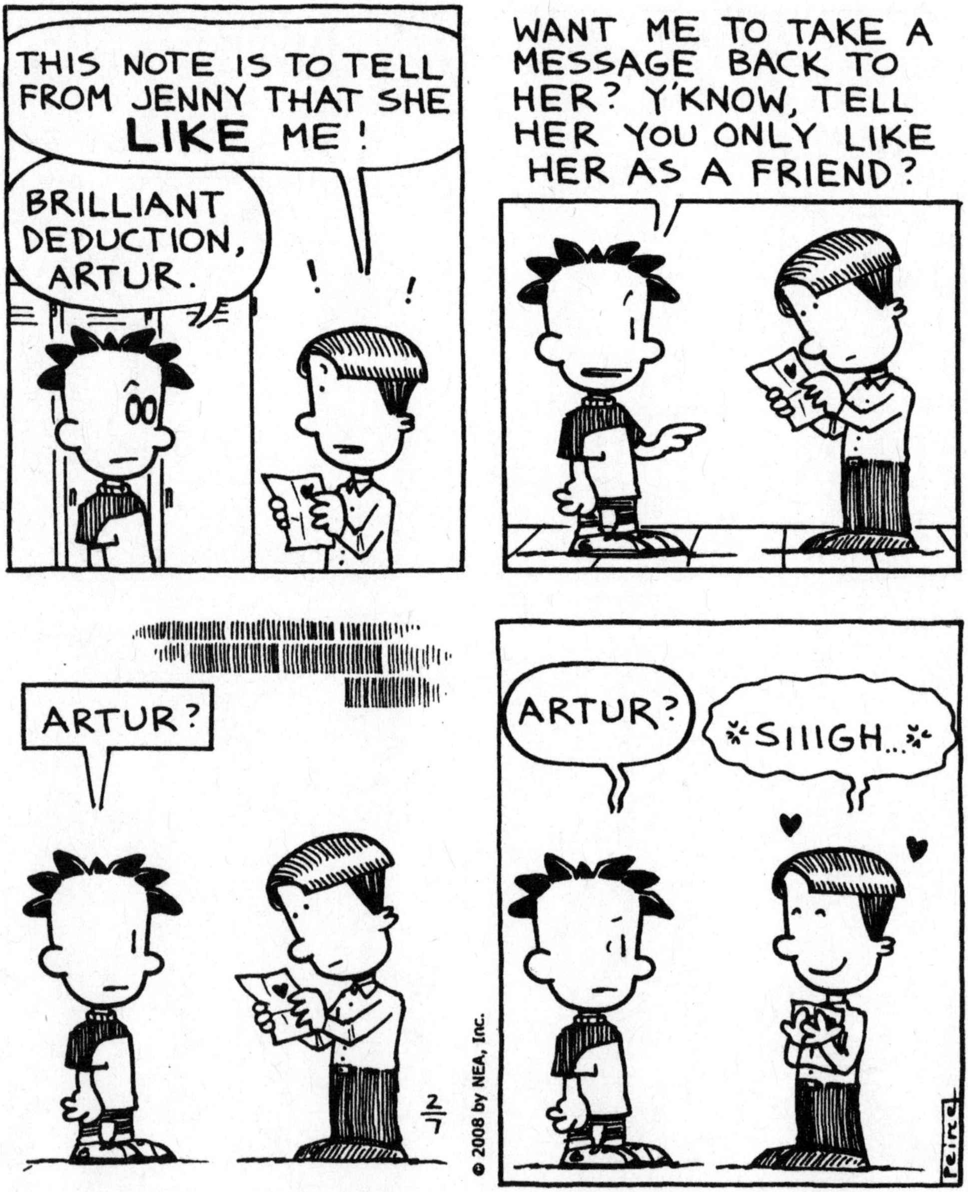
THIS NOTE IS TO TELL FROM JENNY THAT SHE LIKE ME!
BRILLIANT DEDUCTION, ARTUR.
! !
WANT ME TO TAKE A MESSAGE BACK TO HER? Y'KNOW, TELL HER YOU ONLY LIKE HER AS A FRIEND?
ARTUR?
ARTUR?
SIIIGH...
2/7
© 2008 by NEA, Inc.
Peirce

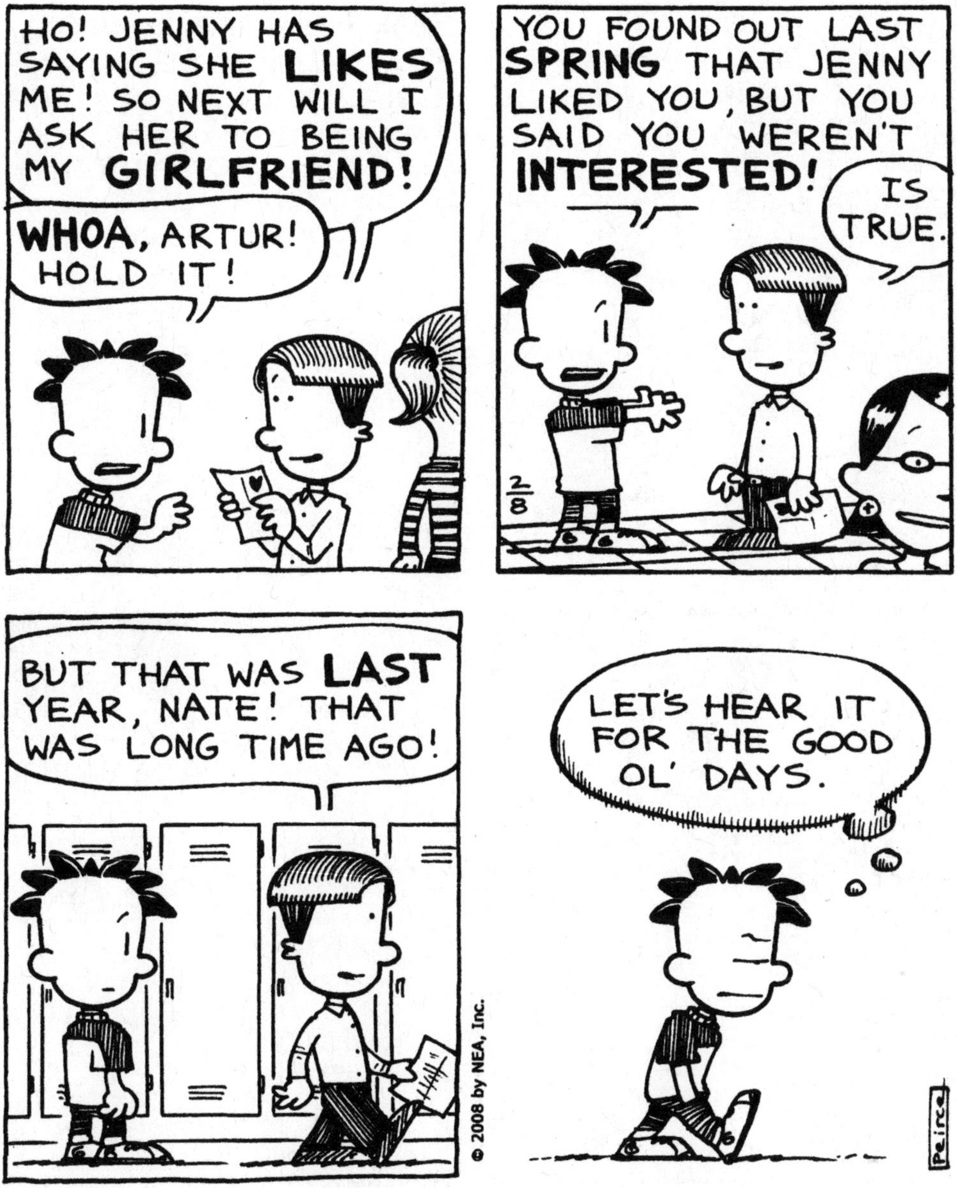
HO! JENNY HAS SAYING SHE LIKES ME! SO NEXT WILL I ASK HER TO BEING MY GIRLFRIEND!
WHOA, ARTUR! HOLD IT!
YOU FOUND OUT LAST SPRING THAT JENNY LIKED YOU, BUT YOU SAID YOU WEREN'T INTERESTED!
IS TRUE.
2/8
BUT THAT WAS LAST YEAR, NATE! THAT WAS LONG TIME AGO!
© 2008 by NEA, Inc.
LET'S HEAR IT FOR THE GOOD OL' DAYS.
Peirce

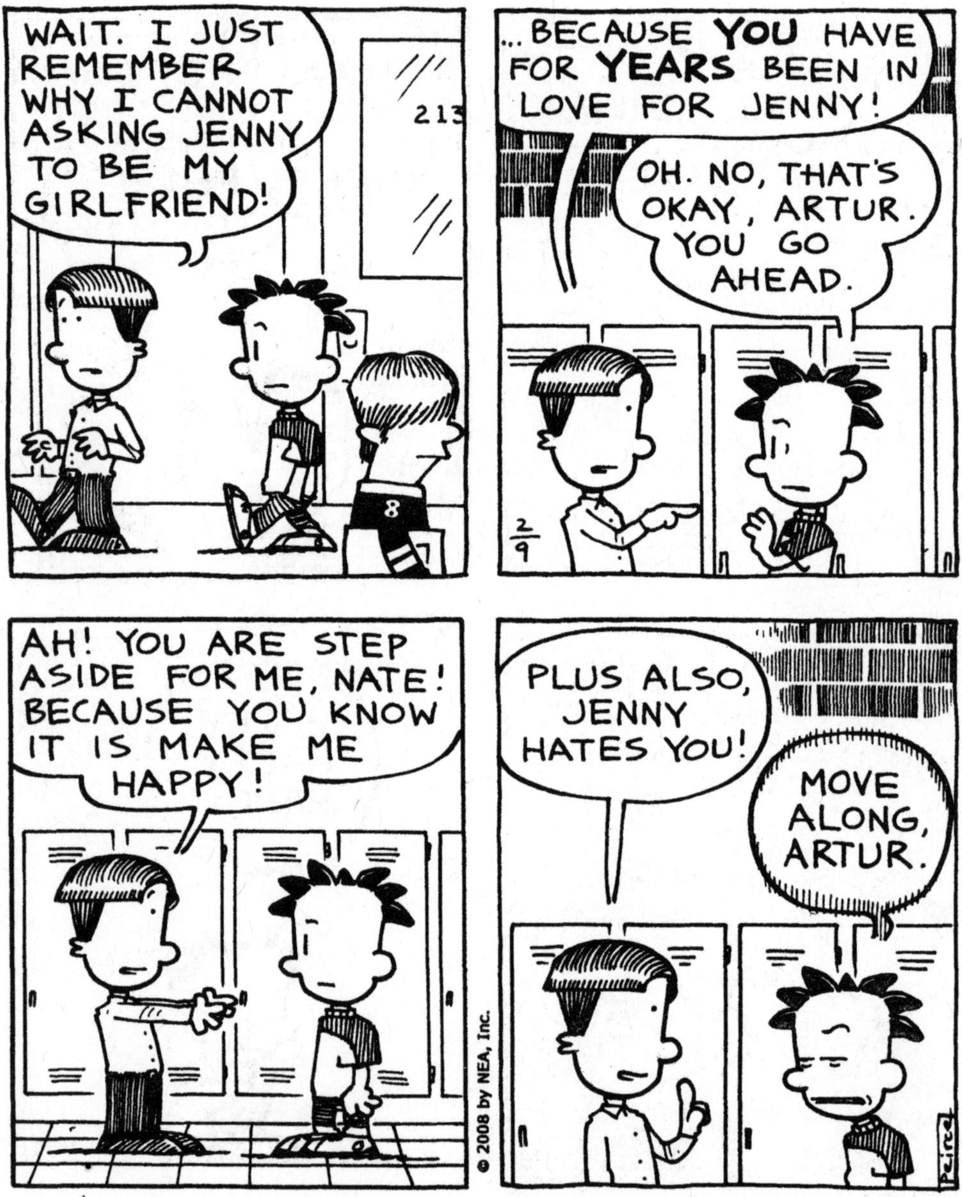
WAIT. I JUST REMEMBER WHY I CANNOT ASKING JENNY TO BE MY GIRLFRIEND!
213
...BECAUSE **YOU** HAVE FOR **YEARS** BEEN IN LOVE FOR JENNY!
OH. NO, THAT'S OKAY, ARTUR. YOU GO AHEAD.
2/9
AH! YOU ARE STEP ASIDE FOR ME, NATE! BECAUSE YOU KNOW IT IS MAKE ME HAPPY!
© 2008 by NEA, Inc.
PLUS ALSO, JENNY HATES YOU!
MOVE ALONG, ARTUR.
PEIRCE

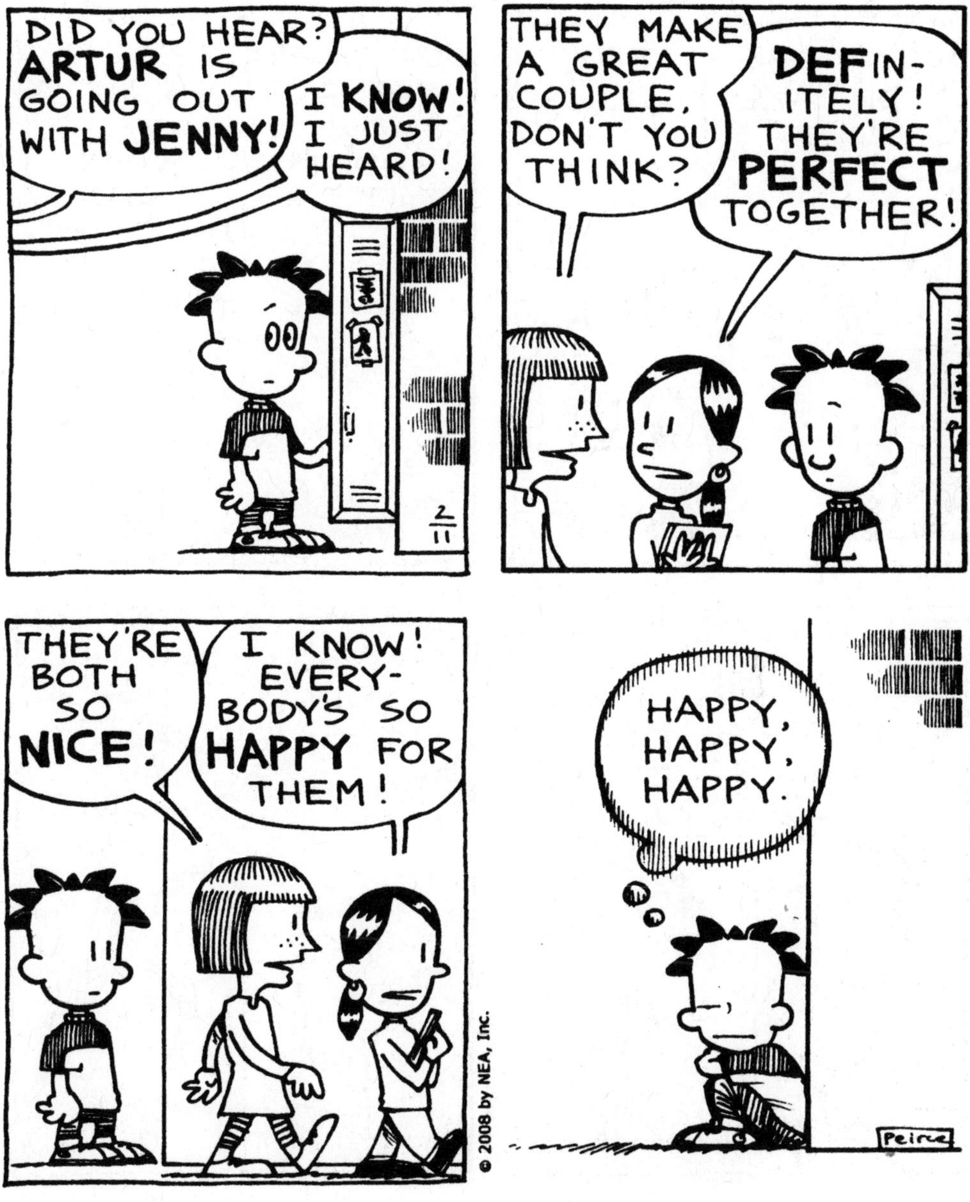
DID YOU HEAR? ARTUR IS GOING OUT WITH JENNY!
I KNOW! I JUST HEARD!
2/11
THEY MAKE A GREAT COUPLE, DON'T YOU THINK?
DEFINITELY! THEY'RE PERFECT TOGETHER!
THEY'RE BOTH SO NICE!
I KNOW! EVERYBODY'S SO HAPPY FOR THEM!
© 2008 by NEA, Inc.
HAPPY, HAPPY, HAPPY.
Peirce

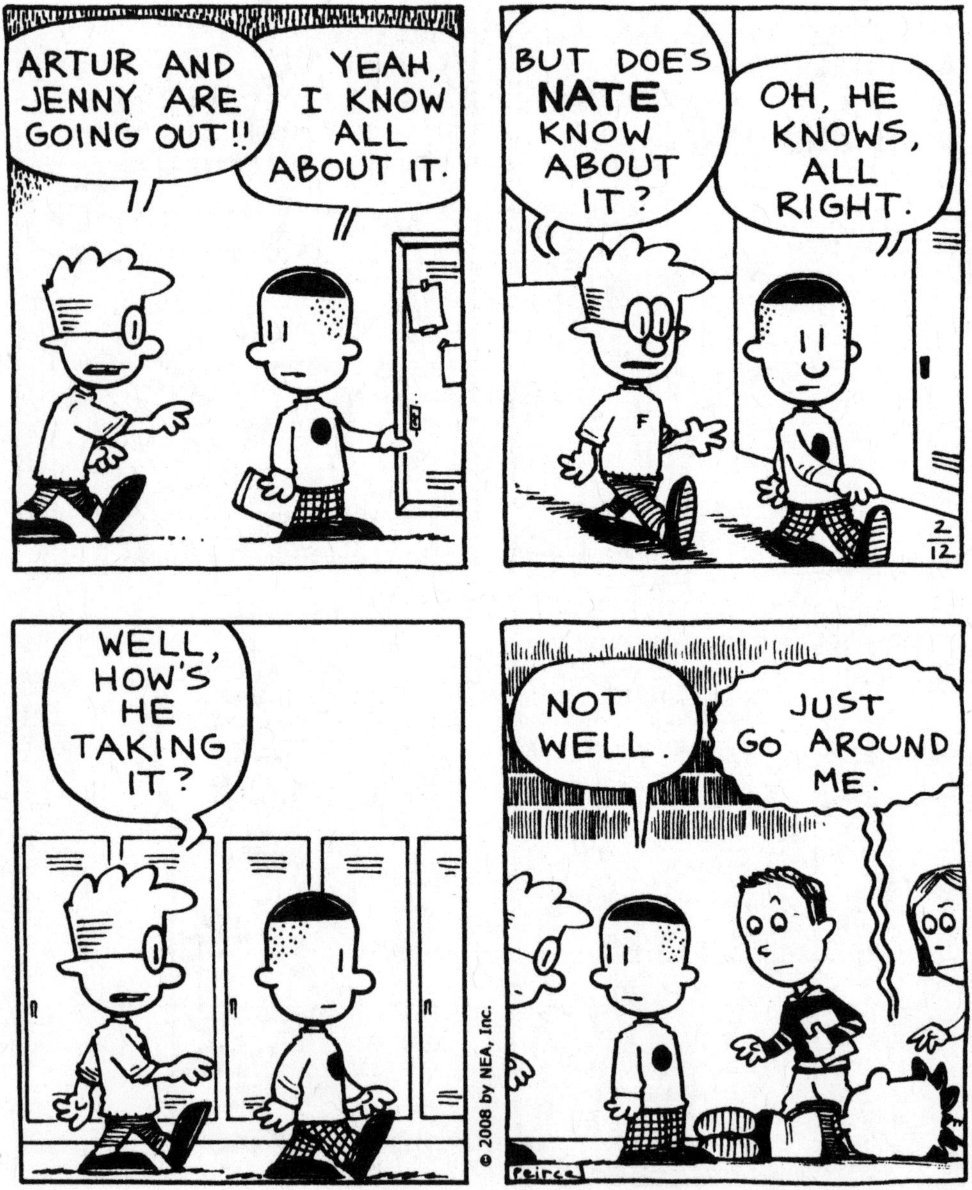
ARTUR AND JENNY ARE GOING OUT!!
YEAH, I KNOW ALL ABOUT IT.
BUT DOES NATE KNOW ABOUT IT?
OH, HE KNOWS, ALL RIGHT.
2/12
WELL, HOW'S HE TAKING IT?
NOT WELL.
JUST GO AROUND ME.
© 2008 by NEA, Inc.
Peirce

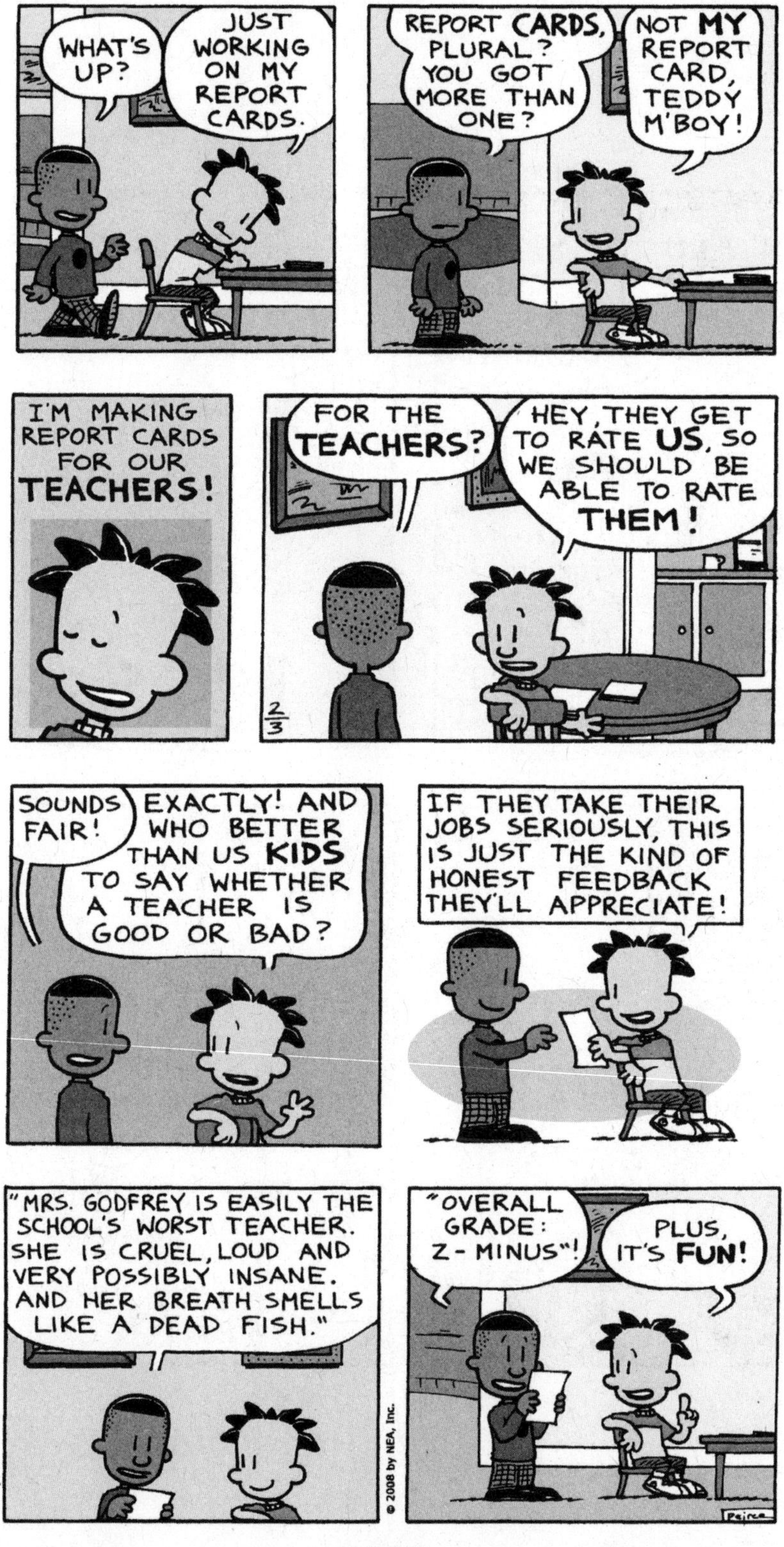
WHAT'S UP?
JUST WORKING ON MY REPORT CARDS.
REPORT CARDS, PLURAL? YOU GOT MORE THAN ONE?
NOT MY REPORT CARD, TEDDY M'BOY!
I'M MAKING REPORT CARDS FOR OUR TEACHERS!
FOR THE TEACHERS?
HEY, THEY GET TO RATE US, SO WE SHOULD BE ABLE TO RATE THEM!
2/3
SOUNDS FAIR!
EXACTLY! AND WHO BETTER THAN US KIDS TO SAY WHETHER A TEACHER IS GOOD OR BAD?
IF THEY TAKE THEIR JOBS SERIOUSLY, THIS IS JUST THE KIND OF HONEST FEEDBACK THEY'LL APPRECIATE!
"MRS. GODFREY IS EASILY THE SCHOOL'S WORST TEACHER. SHE IS CRUEL, LOUD AND VERY POSSIBLY INSANE. AND HER BREATH SMELLS LIKE A DEAD FISH."
© 2008 by NEA, Inc.
"OVERALL GRADE: Z-MINUS"!
PLUS, IT'S FUN!
Peirce

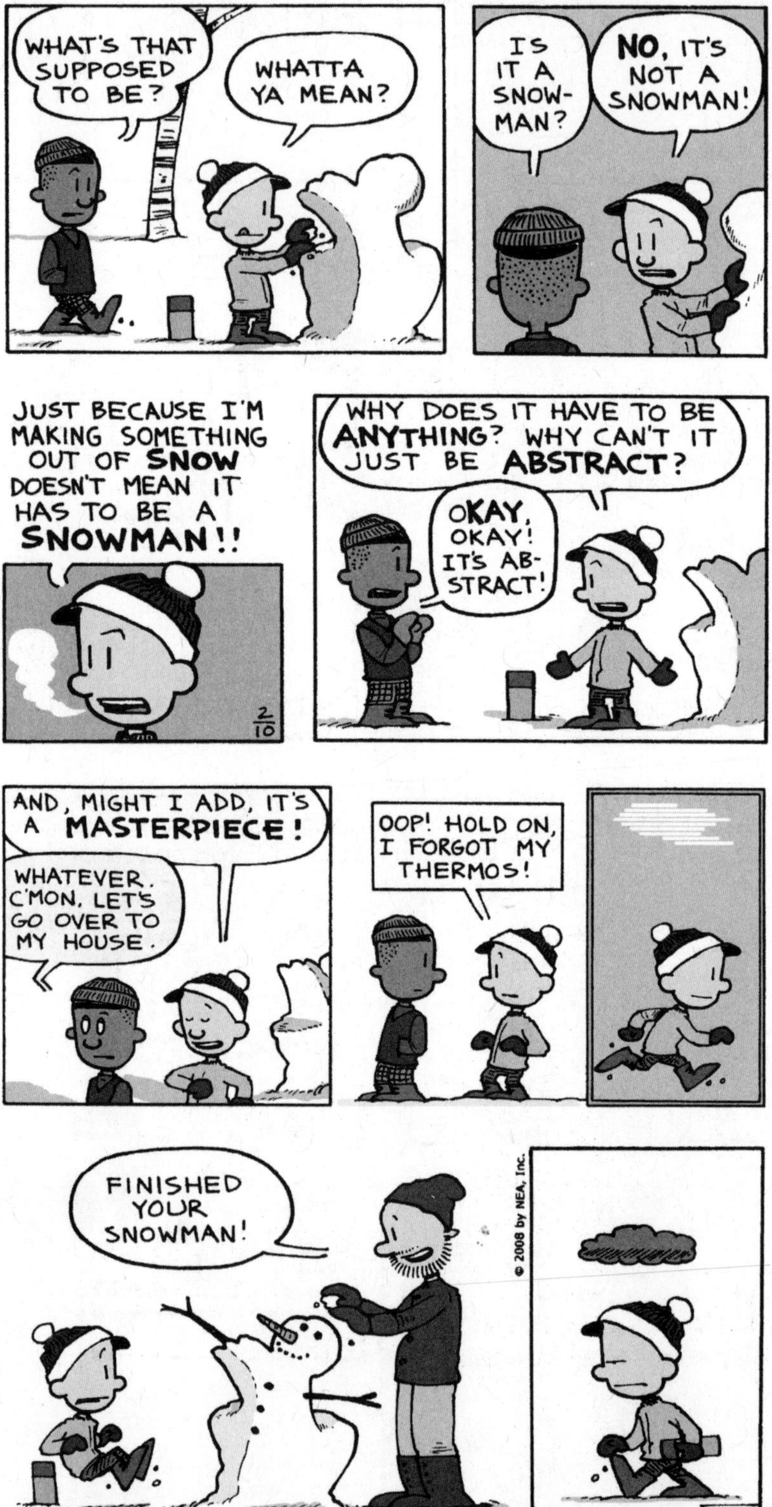
WHAT'S THAT SUPPOSED TO BE?
WHATTA YA MEAN?
IS IT A SNOW-MAN?
NO, IT'S NOT A SNOWMAN!
JUST BECAUSE I'M MAKING SOMETHING OUT OF SNOW DOESN'T MEAN IT HAS TO BE A SNOWMAN!!
2/10
WHY DOES IT HAVE TO BE ANYTHING? WHY CAN'T IT JUST BE ABSTRACT?
OKAY, OKAY! IT'S AB-STRACT!
AND, MIGHT I ADD, IT'S A MASTERPIECE!
WHATEVER. C'MON, LET'S GO OVER TO MY HOUSE.
OOP! HOLD ON, I FORGOT MY THERMOS!
FINISHED YOUR SNOWMAN!
© 2008 by NEA, Inc.
Peirce

LUNCH BLUES

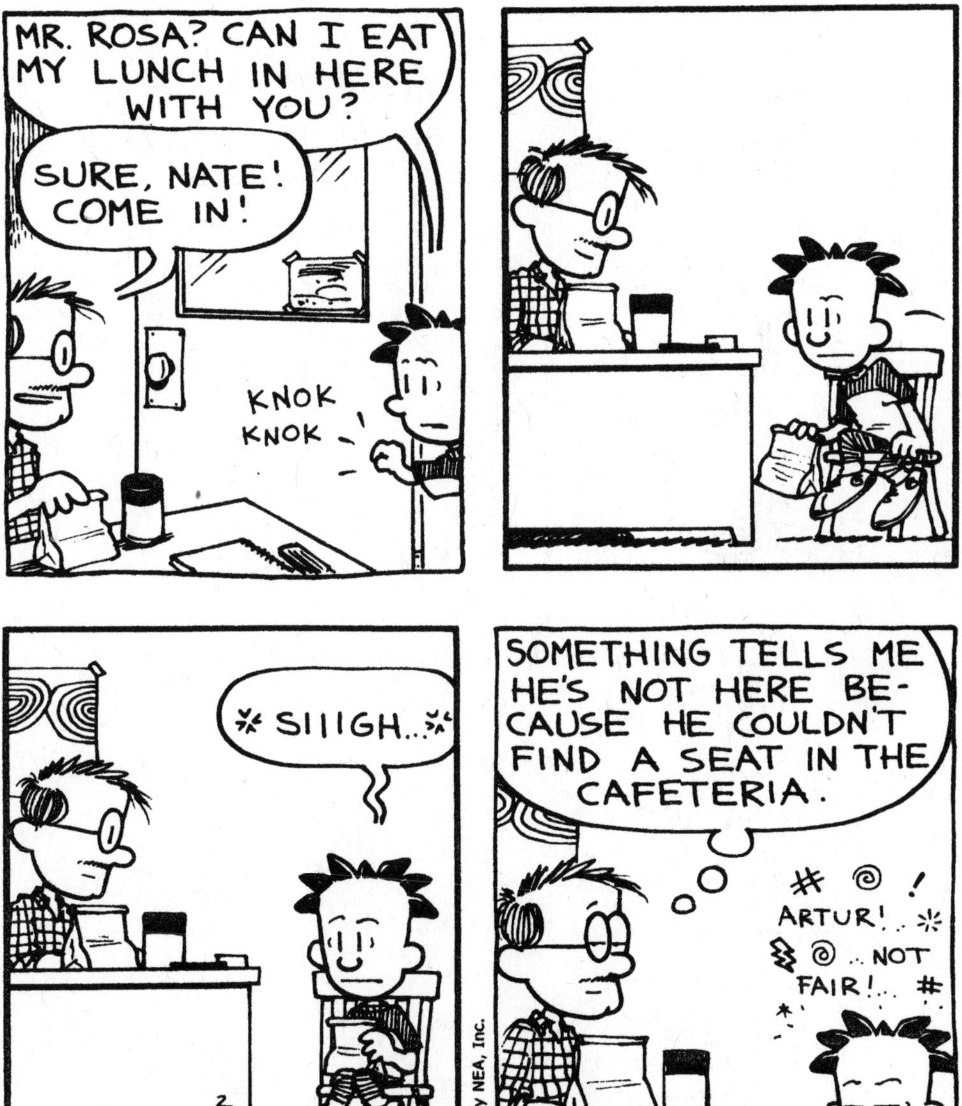
MR. ROSA? CAN I EAT MY LUNCH IN HERE WITH YOU?
SURE, NATE! COME IN!
KNOK KNOK
SIIIGH...
SOMETHING TELLS ME HE'S NOT HERE BE-CAUSE HE COULDN'T FIND A SEAT IN THE CAFETERIA.
ARTUR! ... NOT FAIR!...
2/13
© 2008 by NEA, Inc.
Peirce

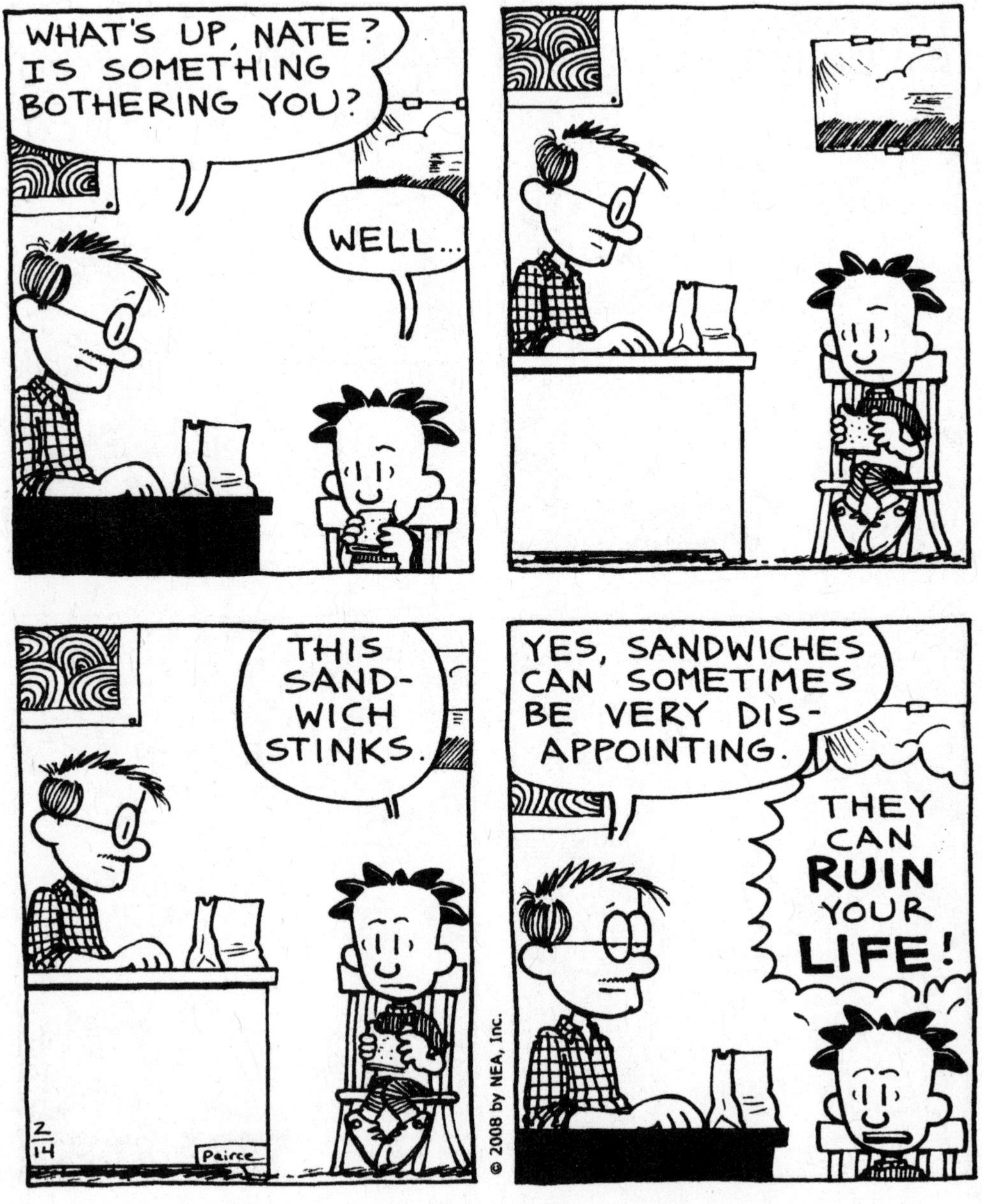
WHAT'S UP, NATE? IS SOMETHING BOTHERING YOU?
WELL...
THIS SAND-WICH STINKS.
2/14
Peirce
© 2008 by NEA, Inc.
YES, SANDWICHES CAN SOMETIMES BE VERY DIS-APPOINTING.
THEY CAN RUIN YOUR LIFE!

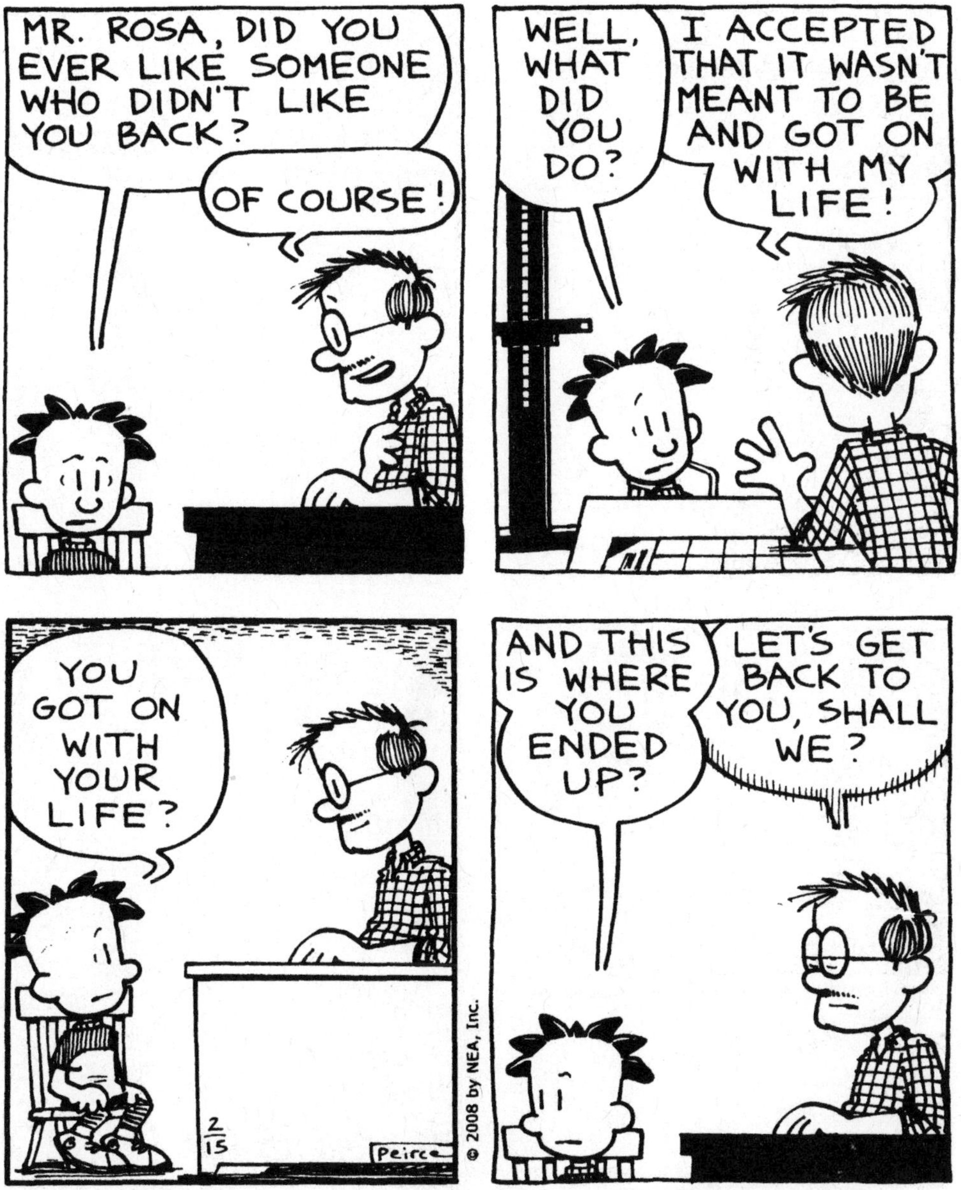
MR. ROSA, DID YOU EVER LIKE SOMEONE WHO DIDN'T LIKE YOU BACK?
OF COURSE!
WELL, WHAT DID YOU DO?
I ACCEPTED THAT IT WASN'T MEANT TO BE AND GOT ON WITH MY LIFE!
YOU GOT ON WITH YOUR LIFE?
AND THIS IS WHERE YOU ENDED UP?
LET'S GET BACK TO YOU, SHALL WE?
2/15
Peirce
© 2008 by NEA, Inc.

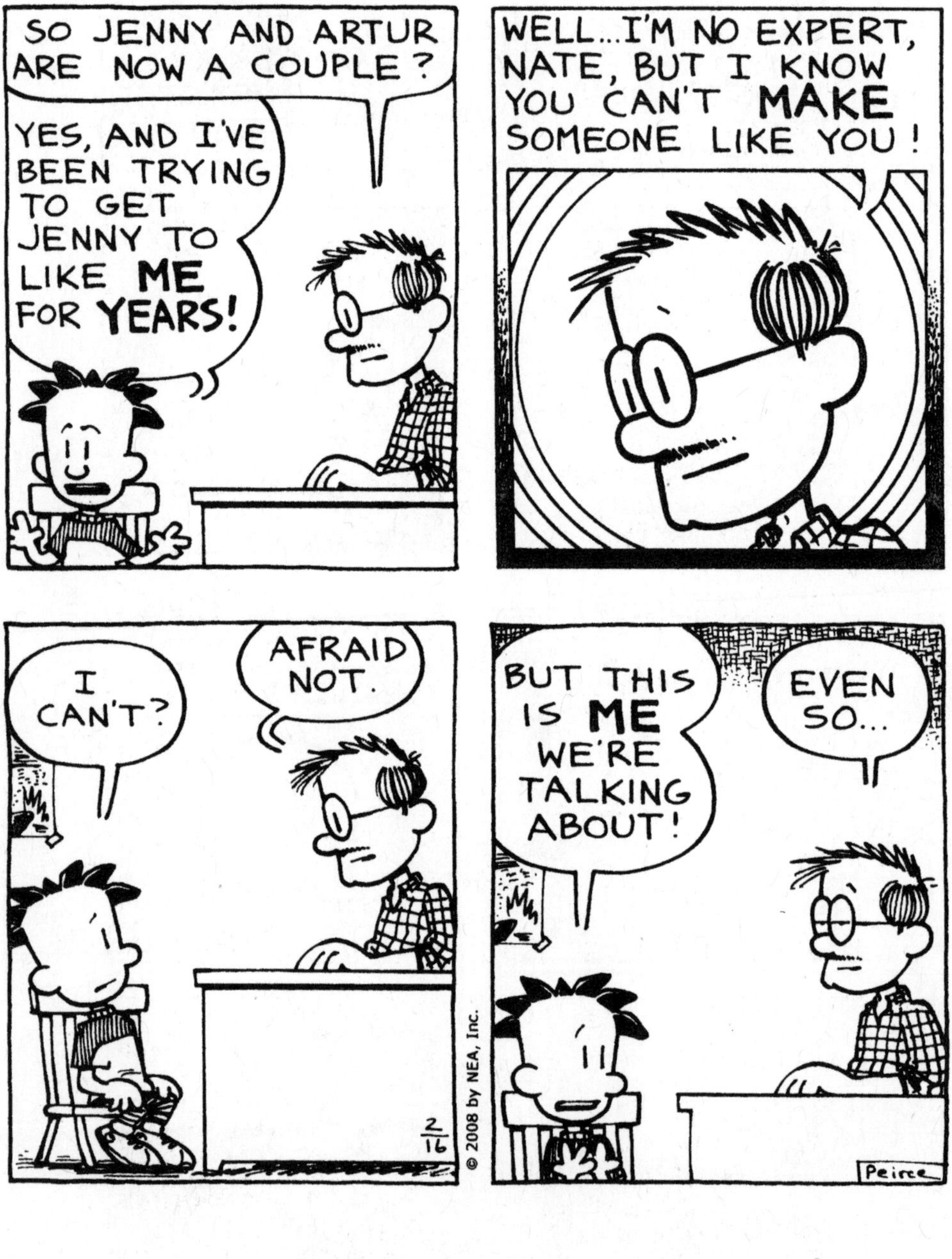
SO JENNY AND ARTUR ARE NOW A COUPLE?
YES, AND I'VE BEEN TRYING TO GET JENNY TO LIKE ME FOR YEARS!
WELL... I'M NO EXPERT, NATE, BUT I KNOW YOU CAN'T MAKE SOMEONE LIKE YOU!
I CAN'T?
AFRAID NOT.
BUT THIS IS ME WE'RE TALKING ABOUT!
EVEN SO...
2/16
© 2008 by NEA, Inc.
Peirce

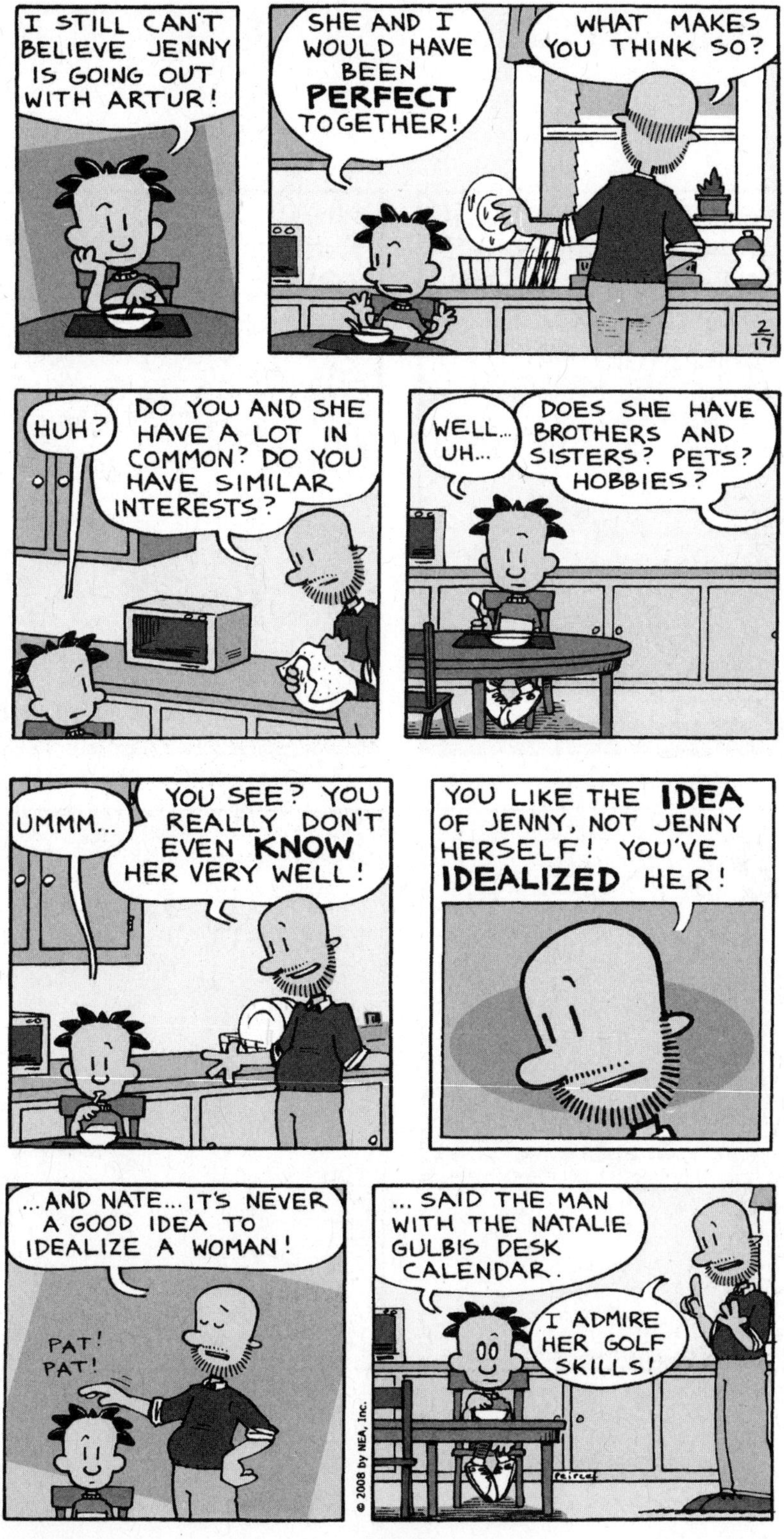
I STILL CAN'T BELIEVE JENNY IS GOING OUT WITH ARTUR!
SHE AND I WOULD HAVE BEEN **PERFECT** TOGETHER!
WHAT MAKES YOU THINK SO?
2/17
HUH?
DO YOU AND SHE HAVE A LOT IN COMMON? DO YOU HAVE SIMILAR INTERESTS?
WELL... UH...
DOES SHE HAVE BROTHERS AND SISTERS? PETS? HOBBIES?
UMMM...
YOU SEE? YOU REALLY DON'T EVEN **KNOW** HER VERY WELL!
YOU LIKE THE **IDEA** OF JENNY, NOT JENNY HERSELF! YOU'VE **IDEALIZED** HER!
...AND NATE...IT'S NEVER A GOOD IDEA TO IDEALIZE A WOMAN!
PAT! PAT!
...SAID THE MAN WITH THE NATALIE GULBIS DESK CALENDAR.
I ADMIRE HER GOLF SKILLS!
© 2008 by NEA, Inc.
PEIRCE

NATE WRIGHT, FOOD CRITIC

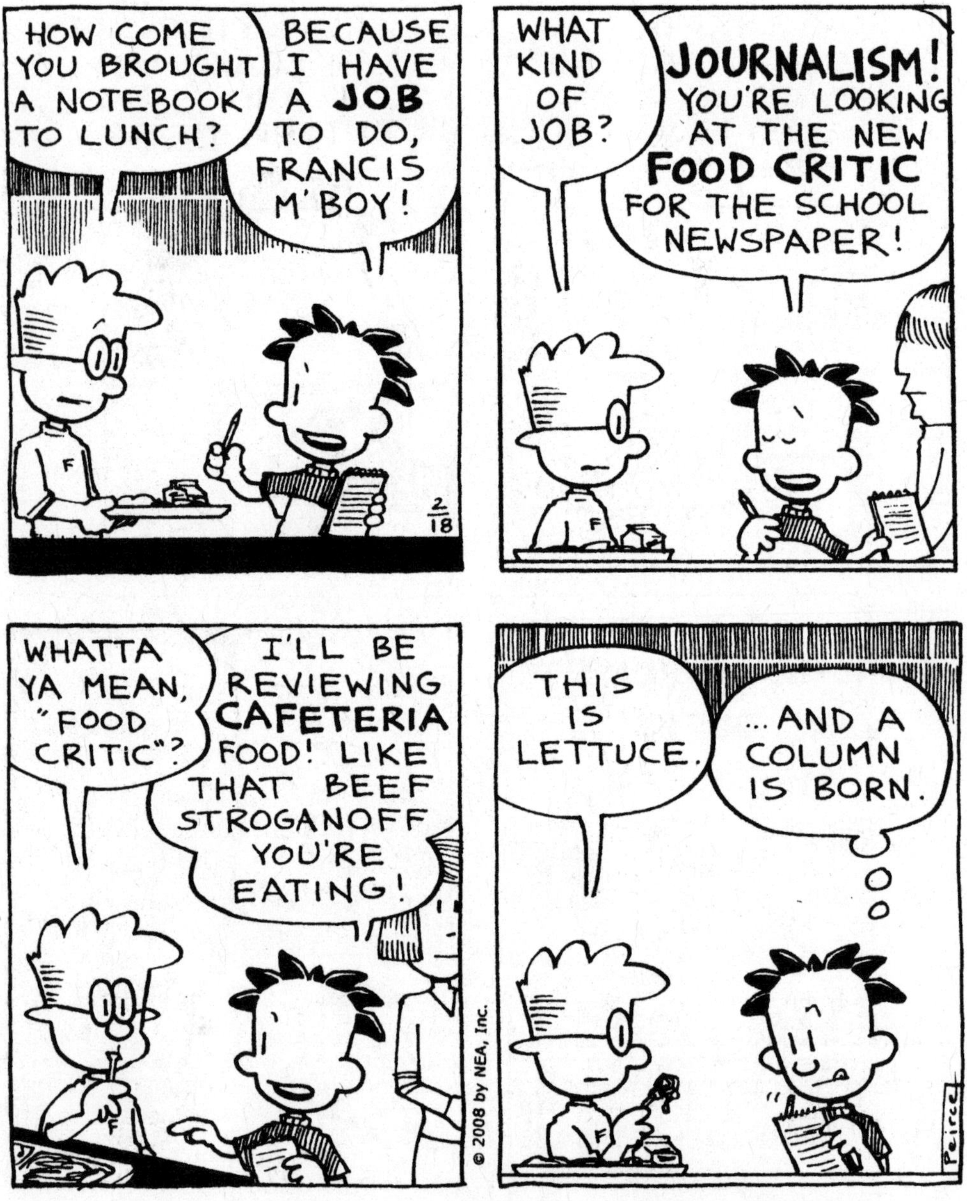
HOW COME YOU BROUGHT A NOTEBOOK TO LUNCH?
BECAUSE I HAVE A **JOB** TO DO, FRANCIS M'BOY!
2/18
WHAT KIND OF JOB?
JOURNALISM! YOU'RE LOOKING AT THE NEW **FOOD CRITIC** FOR THE SCHOOL NEWSPAPER!
WHATTA YA MEAN, "FOOD CRITIC"?
I'LL BE REVIEWING **CAFETERIA** FOOD! LIKE THAT BEEF STROGANOFF YOU'RE EATING!
© 2008 by NEA, Inc.
THIS IS LETTUCE.
...AND A COLUMN IS BORN.
Peirce

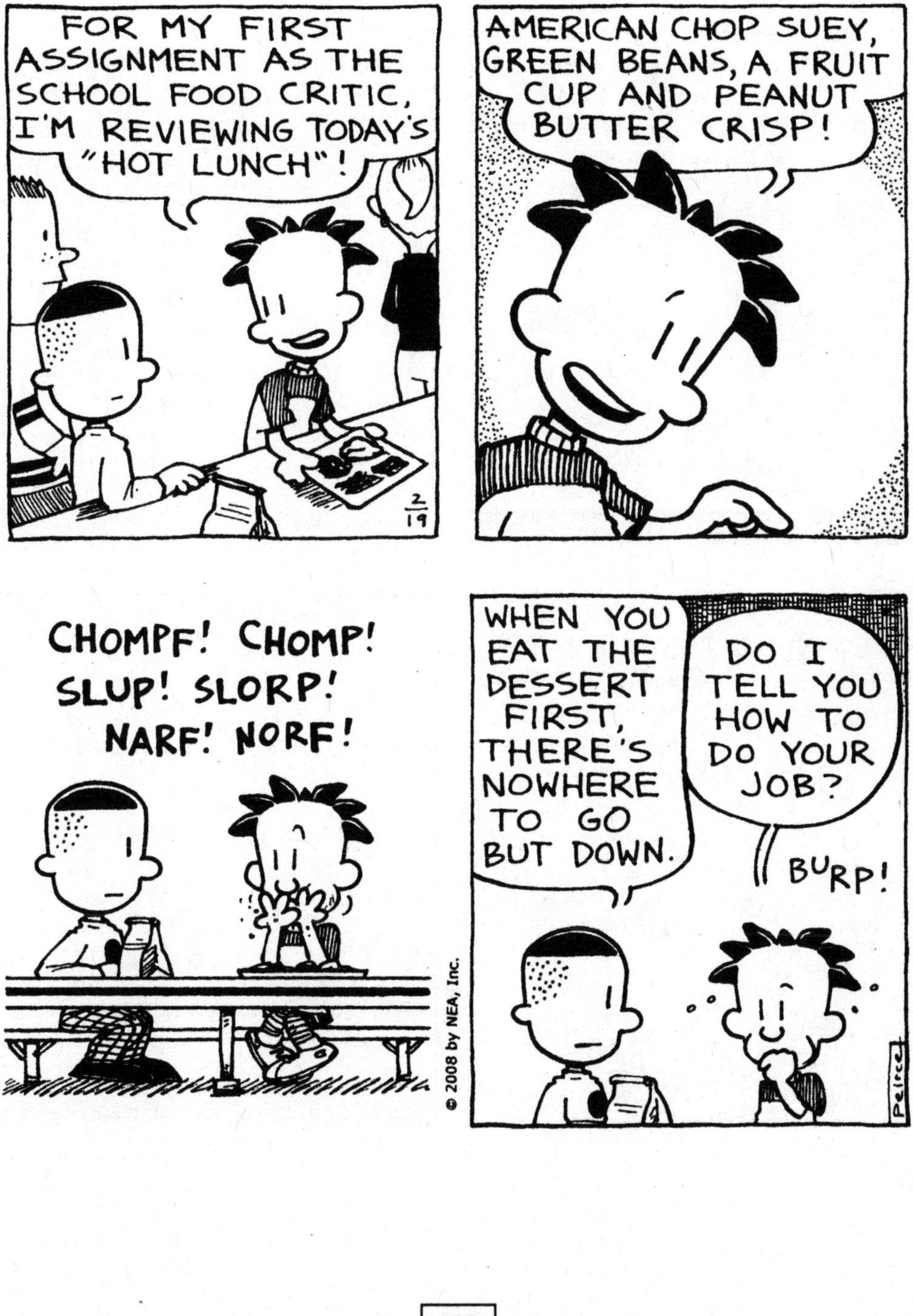
FOR MY FIRST ASSIGNMENT AS THE SCHOOL FOOD CRITIC, I'M REVIEWING TODAY'S "HOT LUNCH"!
2/19
AMERICAN CHOP SUEY, GREEN BEANS, A FRUIT CUP AND PEANUT BUTTER CRISP!
CHOMPF! CHOMP! SLUP! SLORP! NARF! NORF!
© 2008 by NEA, Inc.
WHEN YOU EAT THE DESSERT FIRST, THERE'S NOWHERE TO GO BUT DOWN.
DO I TELL YOU HOW TO DO YOUR JOB?
BURP!
Peirce

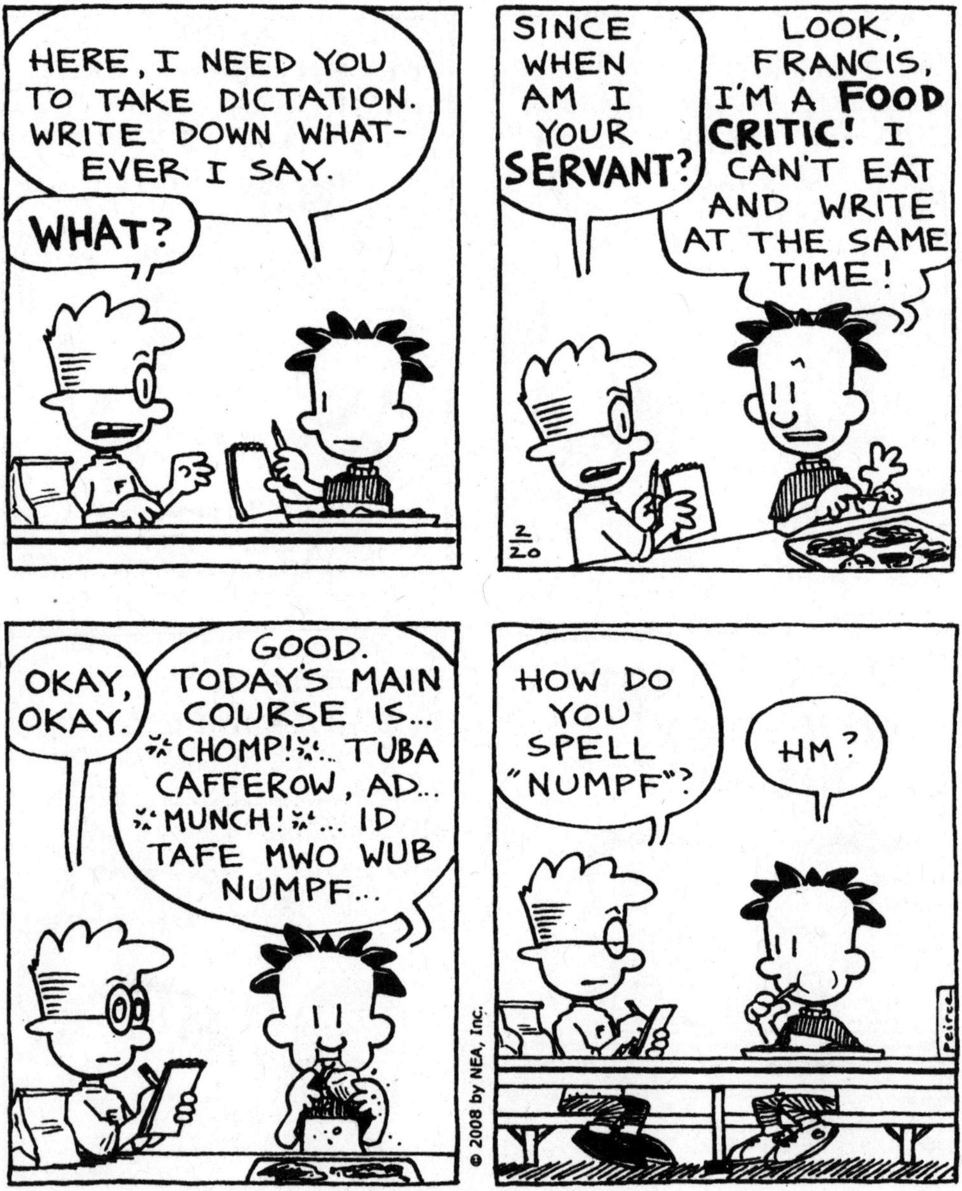
HERE, I NEED YOU TO TAKE DICTATION. WRITE DOWN WHAT-EVER I SAY.
WHAT?
SINCE WHEN AM I YOUR SERVANT?
LOOK, FRANCIS, I'M A FOOD CRITIC! I CAN'T EAT AND WRITE AT THE SAME TIME!
2
20
OKAY, OKAY.
GOOD. TODAY'S MAIN COURSE IS... CHOMP!... TUBA CAFFEROW, AD... MUNCH!... ID TAFE MWO WUB NUMPF...
© 2008 by NEA, Inc.
HOW DO YOU SPELL "NUMPF"?
HM?
Peirce

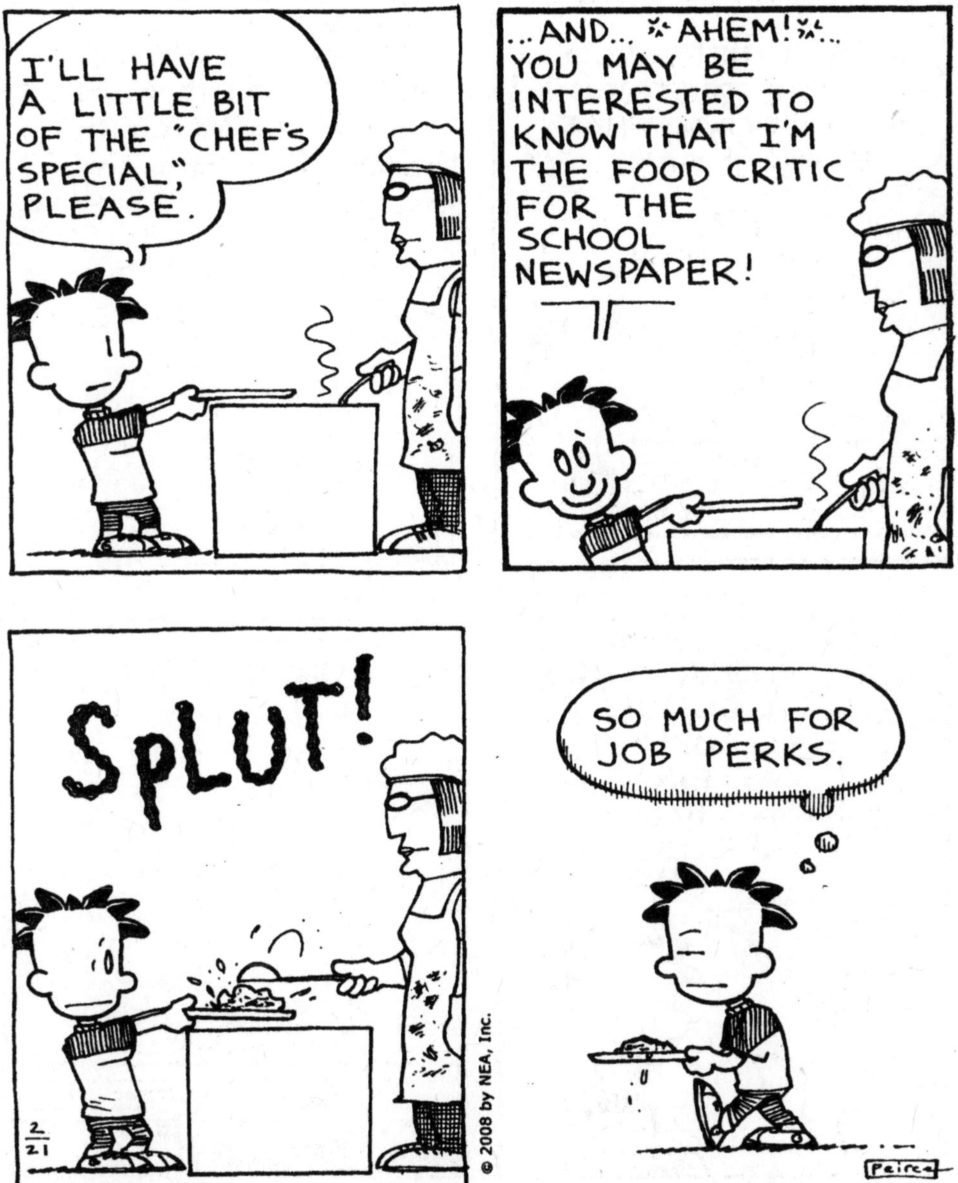
I'LL HAVE A LITTLE BIT OF THE "CHEF'S SPECIAL," PLEASE.
...AND... *AHEM!*... YOU MAY BE INTERESTED TO KNOW THAT I'M THE FOOD CRITIC FOR THE SCHOOL NEWSPAPER!
SPLUT!
2/21
© 2008 by NEA, Inc.
SO MUCH FOR JOB PERKS.
Peirce

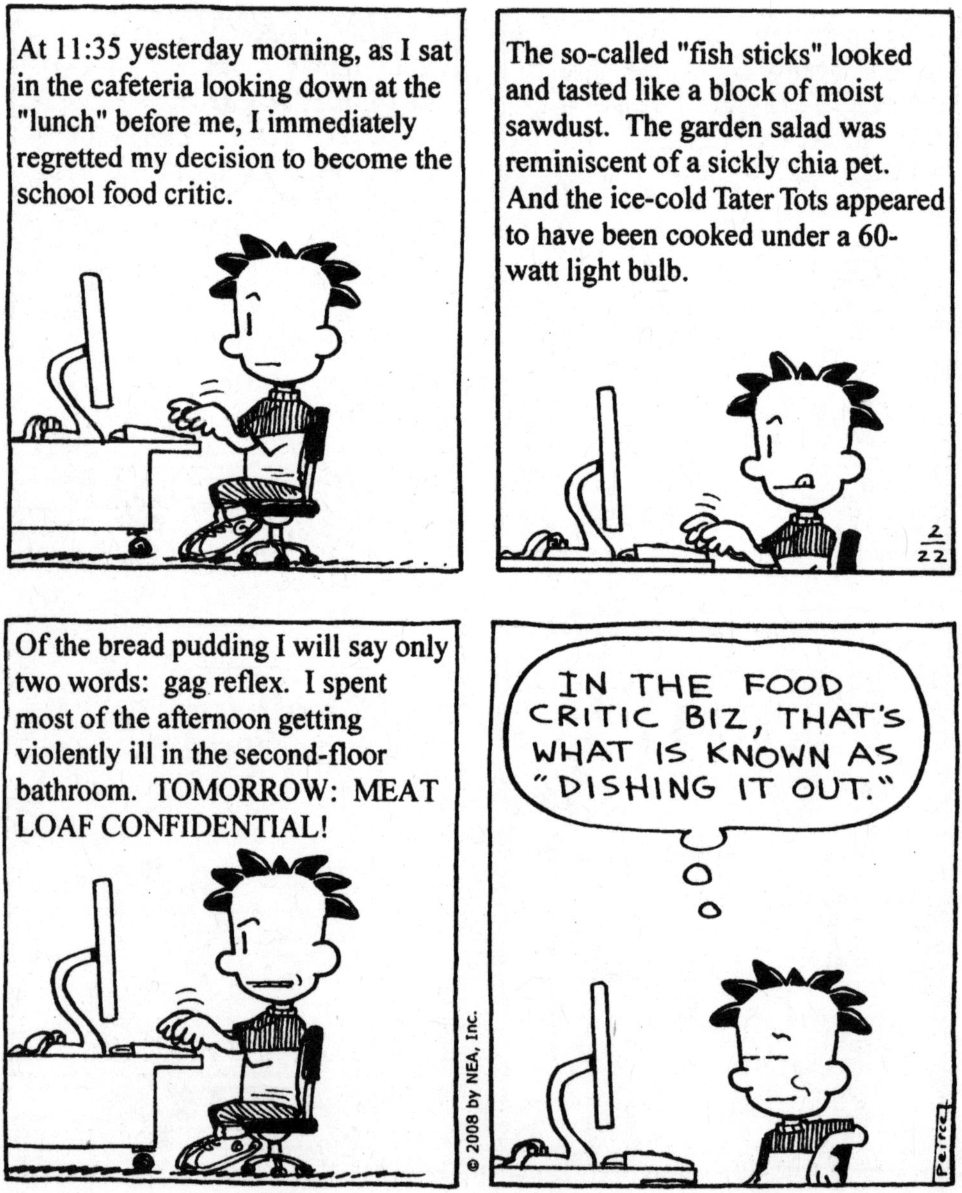
At 11:35 yesterday morning, as I sat in the cafeteria looking down at the "lunch" before me, I immediately regretted my decision to become the school food critic.
The so-called "fish sticks" looked and tasted like a block of moist sawdust. The garden salad was reminiscent of a sickly chia pet. And the ice-cold Tater Tots appeared to have been cooked under a 60-watt light bulb.
2/22
Of the bread pudding I will say only two words: gag reflex. I spent most of the afternoon getting violently ill in the second-floor bathroom. TOMORROW: MEAT LOAF CONFIDENTIAL!
© 2008 by NEA, Inc.
IN THE FOOD CRITIC BIZ, THAT'S WHAT IS KNOWN AS "DISHING IT OUT."
Peirce

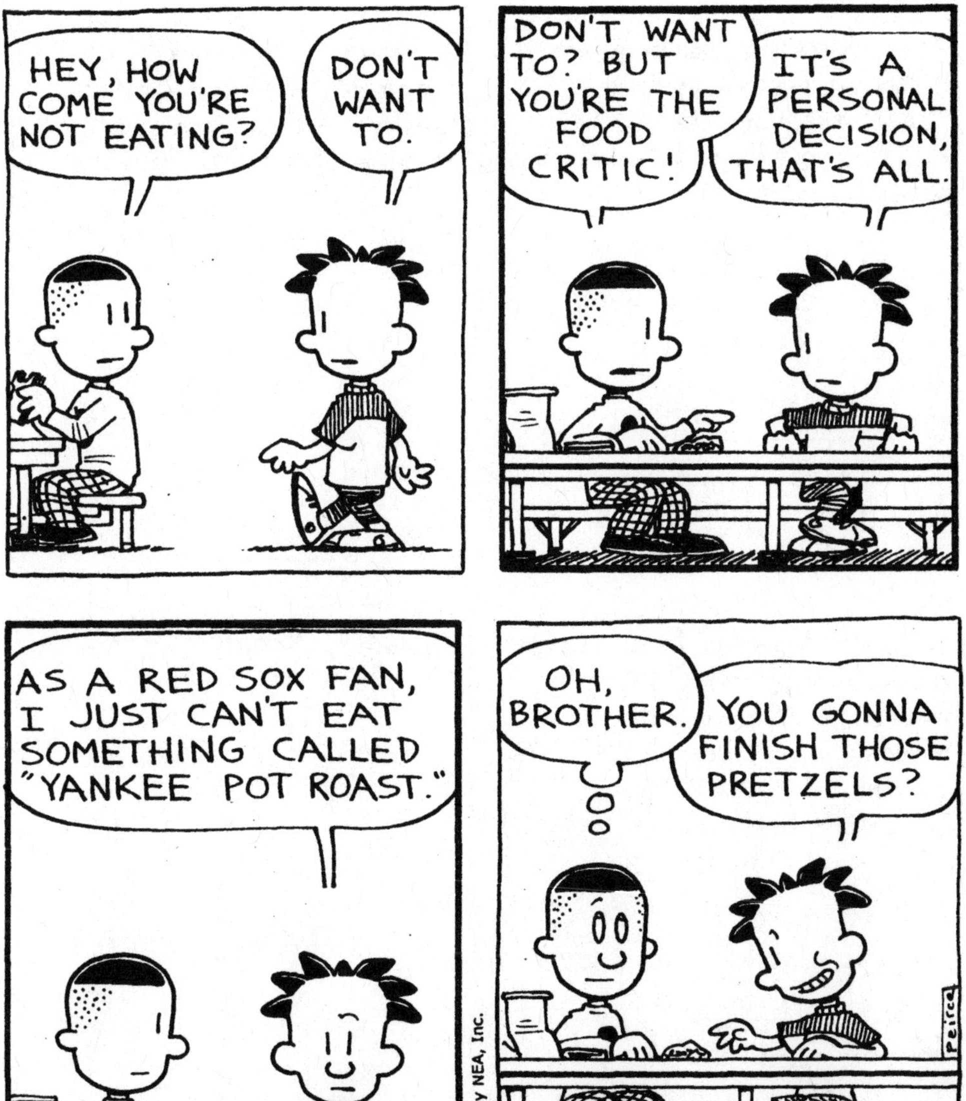
HEY, HOW COME YOU'RE NOT EATING?
DON'T WANT TO.
DON'T WANT TO? BUT YOU'RE THE FOOD CRITIC!
IT'S A PERSONAL DECISION, THAT'S ALL.
AS A RED SOX FAN, I JUST CAN'T EAT SOMETHING CALLED "YANKEE POT ROAST."
2/23
© 2008 by NEA, Inc.
OH, BROTHER.
YOU GONNA FINISH THOSE PRETZELS?
Peirce

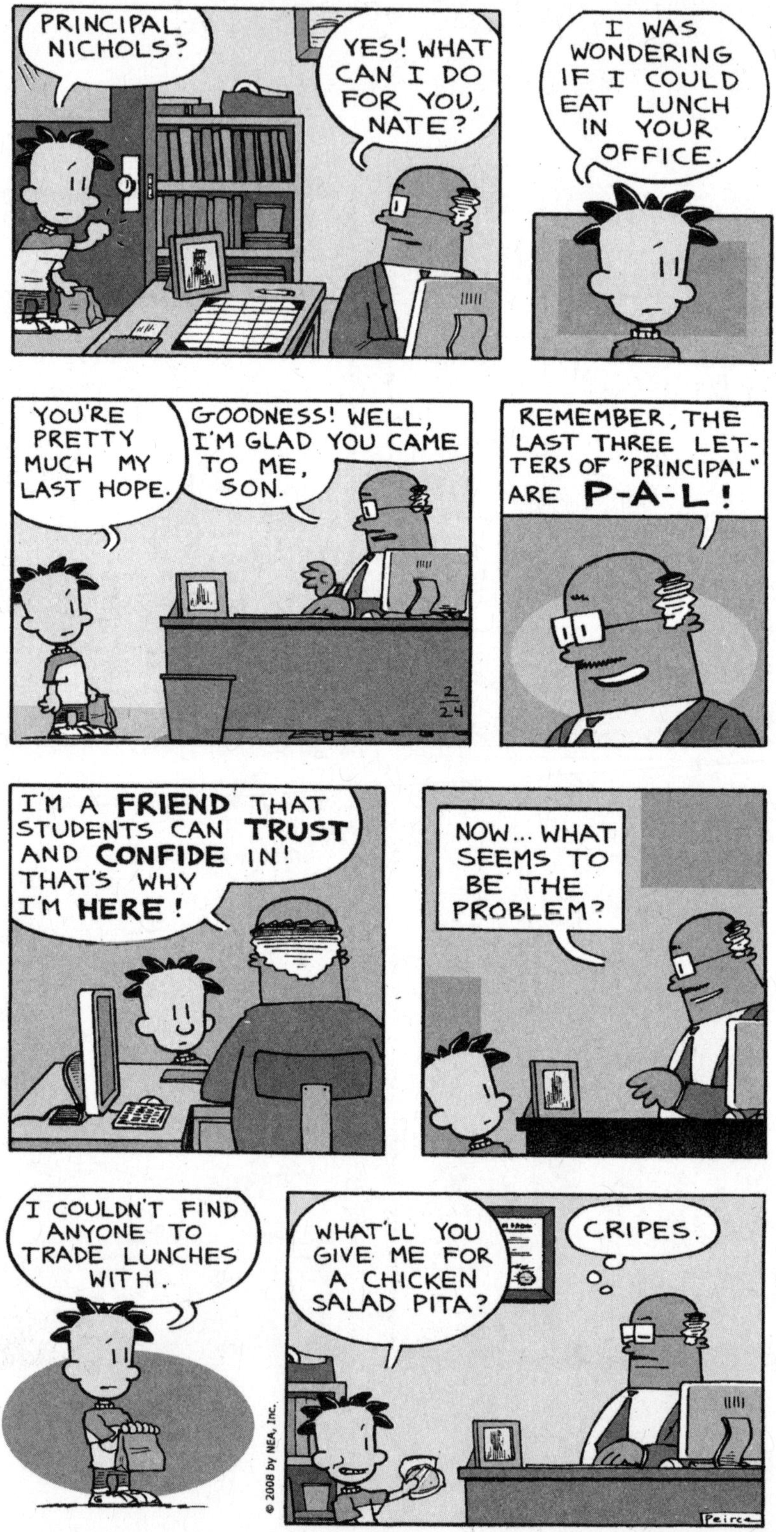
PRINCIPAL NICHOLS?
YES! WHAT CAN I DO FOR YOU, NATE?
I WAS WONDERING IF I COULD EAT LUNCH IN YOUR OFFICE.
YOU'RE PRETTY MUCH MY LAST HOPE.
GOODNESS! WELL, I'M GLAD YOU CAME TO ME, SON.
2/24
REMEMBER, THE LAST THREE LETTERS OF "PRINCIPAL" ARE P-A-L!
I'M A FRIEND THAT STUDENTS CAN TRUST AND CONFIDE IN! THAT'S WHY I'M HERE!
NOW... WHAT SEEMS TO BE THE PROBLEM?
I COULDN'T FIND ANYONE TO TRADE LUNCHES WITH.
WHAT'LL YOU GIVE ME FOR A CHICKEN SALAD PITA?
CRIPES.
© 2008 by NEA, Inc.
Peirce

WHAT'S WITH BODY LANGUAGE?

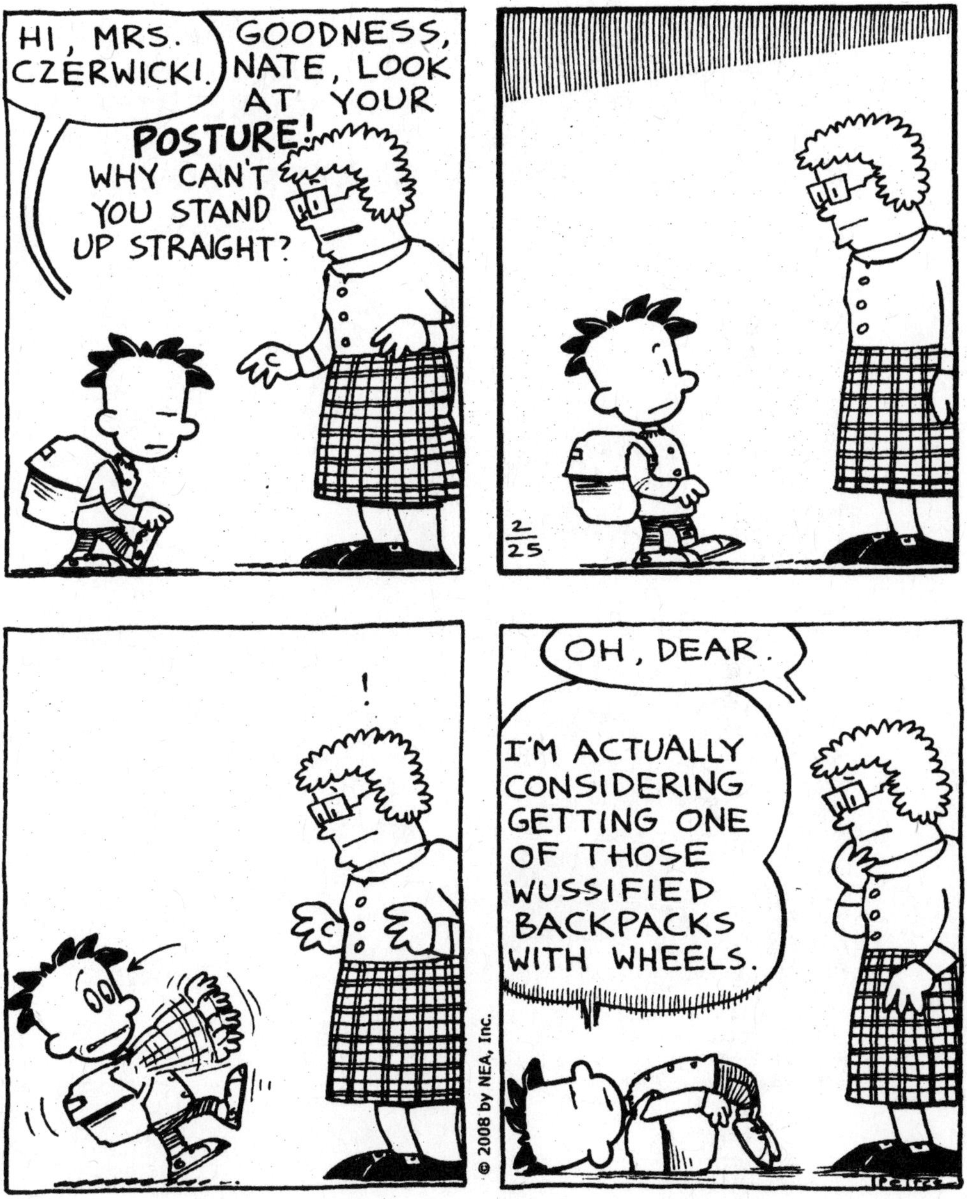
HI, MRS. CZERWICKI.
GOODNESS, NATE, LOOK AT YOUR **POSTURE**! WHY CAN'T YOU STAND UP STRAIGHT?
2/25
!
OH, DEAR.
I'M ACTUALLY CONSIDERING GETTING ONE OF THOSE WUSSIFIED BACKPACKS WITH WHEELS.
© 2008 by NEA, Inc.

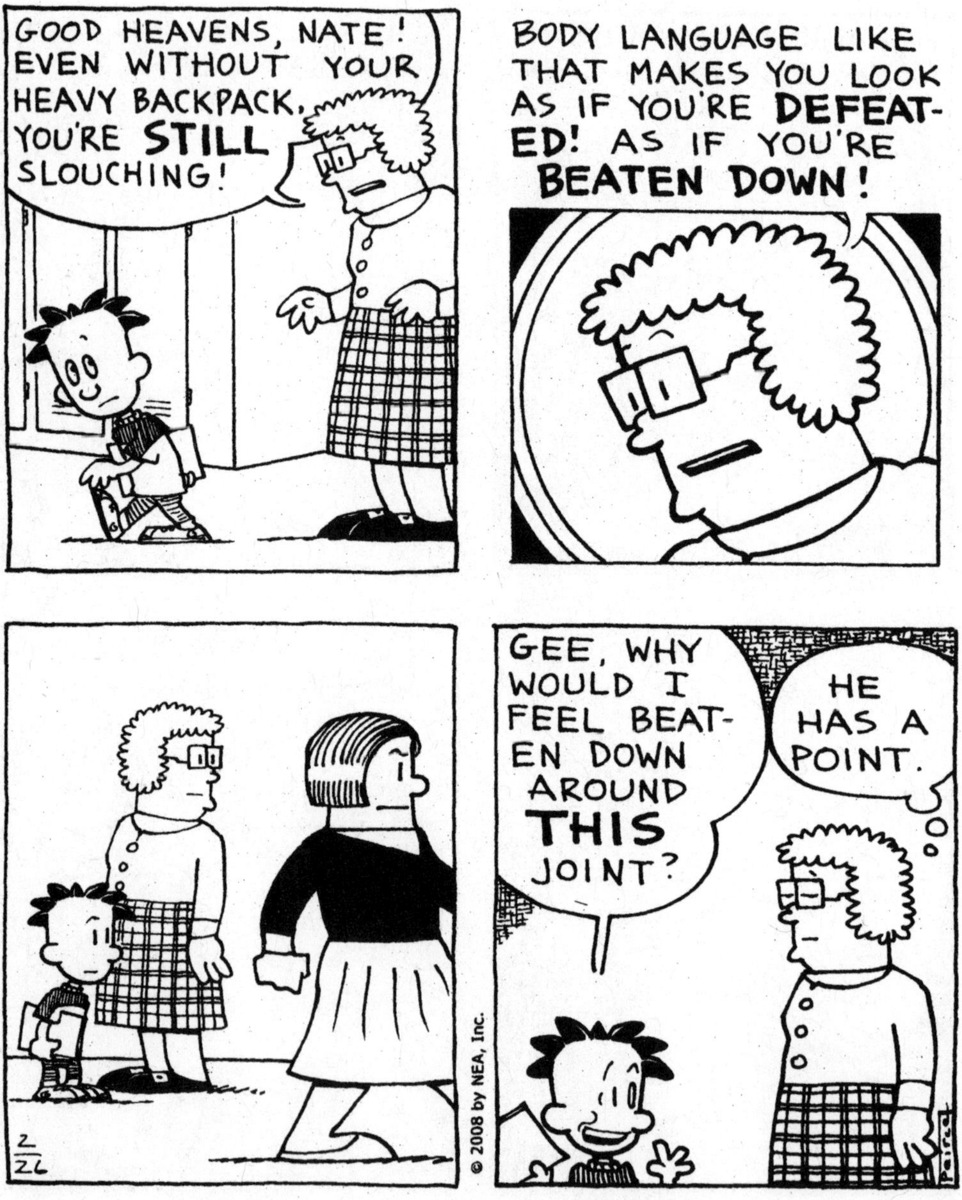
GOOD HEAVENS, NATE! EVEN WITHOUT YOUR HEAVY BACKPACK, YOU'RE STILL SLOUCHING!
BODY LANGUAGE LIKE THAT MAKES YOU LOOK AS IF YOU'RE DEFEAT-ED! AS IF YOU'RE BEATEN DOWN!
2/26
© 2008 by NEA, Inc.
GEE, WHY WOULD I FEEL BEAT-EN DOWN AROUND THIS JOINT?
HE HAS A POINT.
Peirce

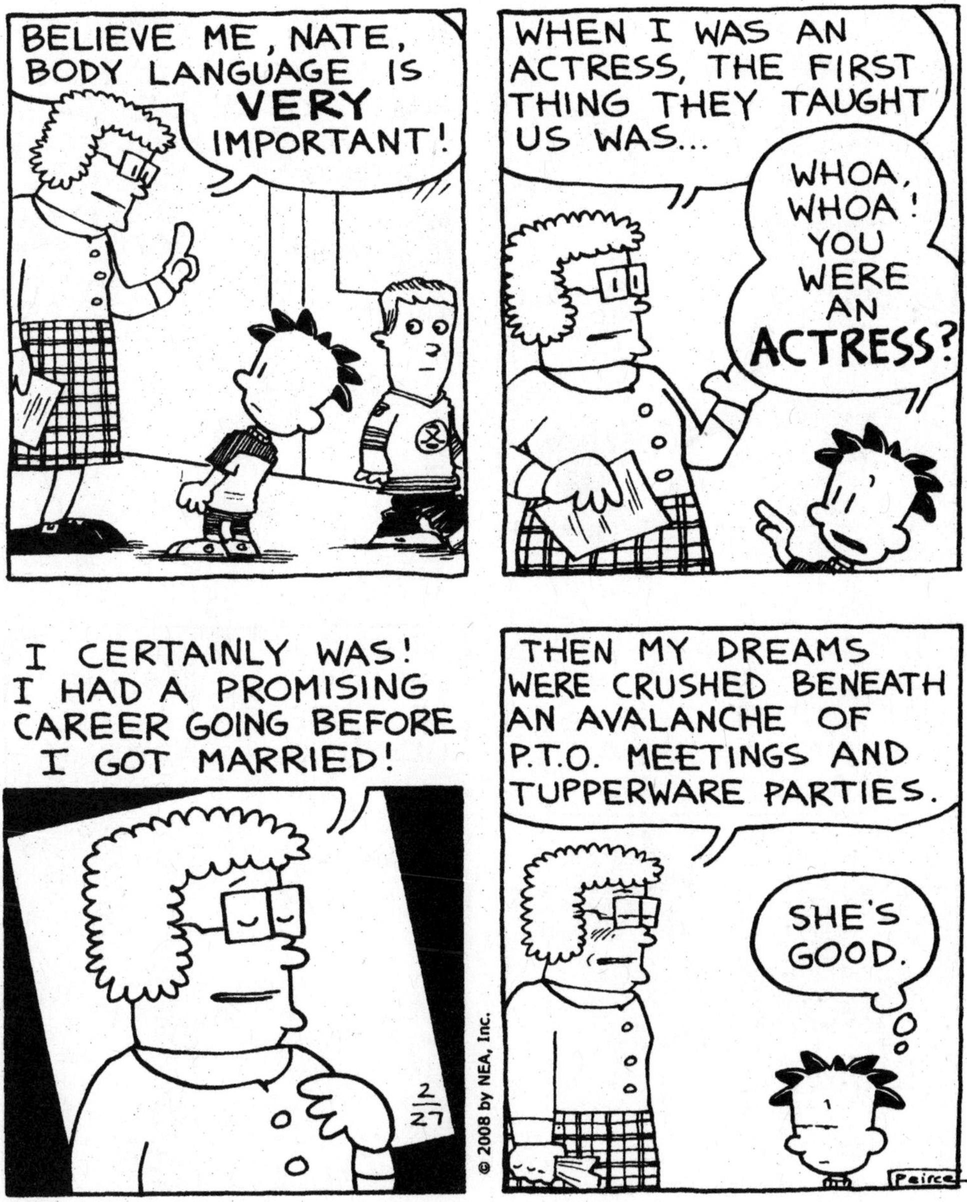
BELIEVE ME, NATE, BODY LANGUAGE IS VERY IMPORTANT!
WHEN I WAS AN ACTRESS, THE FIRST THING THEY TAUGHT US WAS...
WHOA, WHOA! YOU WERE AN ACTRESS?
I CERTAINLY WAS! I HAD A PROMISING CAREER GOING BEFORE I GOT MARRIED!
2/27
© 2008 by NEA, Inc.
THEN MY DREAMS WERE CRUSHED BENEATH AN AVALANCHE OF P.T.O. MEETINGS AND TUPPERWARE PARTIES.
SHE'S GOOD.
Peirce

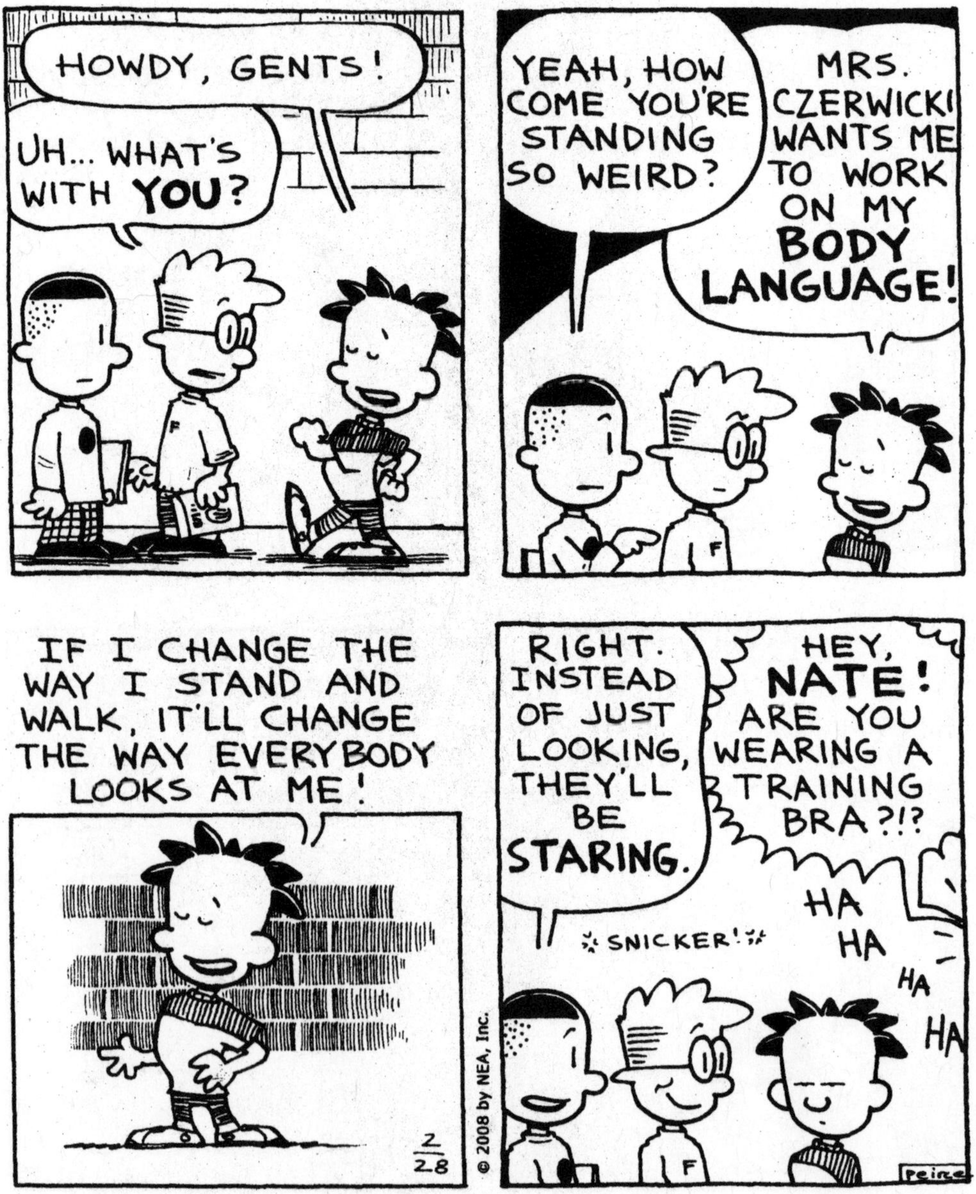
HOWDY, GENTS!
UH... WHAT'S WITH **YOU**?
YEAH, HOW COME YOU'RE STANDING SO WEIRD?
MRS. CZERWICKI WANTS ME TO WORK ON MY **BODY LANGUAGE**!
IF I CHANGE THE WAY I STAND AND WALK, IT'LL CHANGE THE WAY EVERYBODY LOOKS AT ME!
2/28
© 2008 by NEA, Inc.
RIGHT. INSTEAD OF JUST LOOKING, THEY'LL BE **STARING**.
HEY, **NATE**! ARE YOU WEARING A TRAINING BRA?!?
SNICKER!
HA HA HA HA
peirce

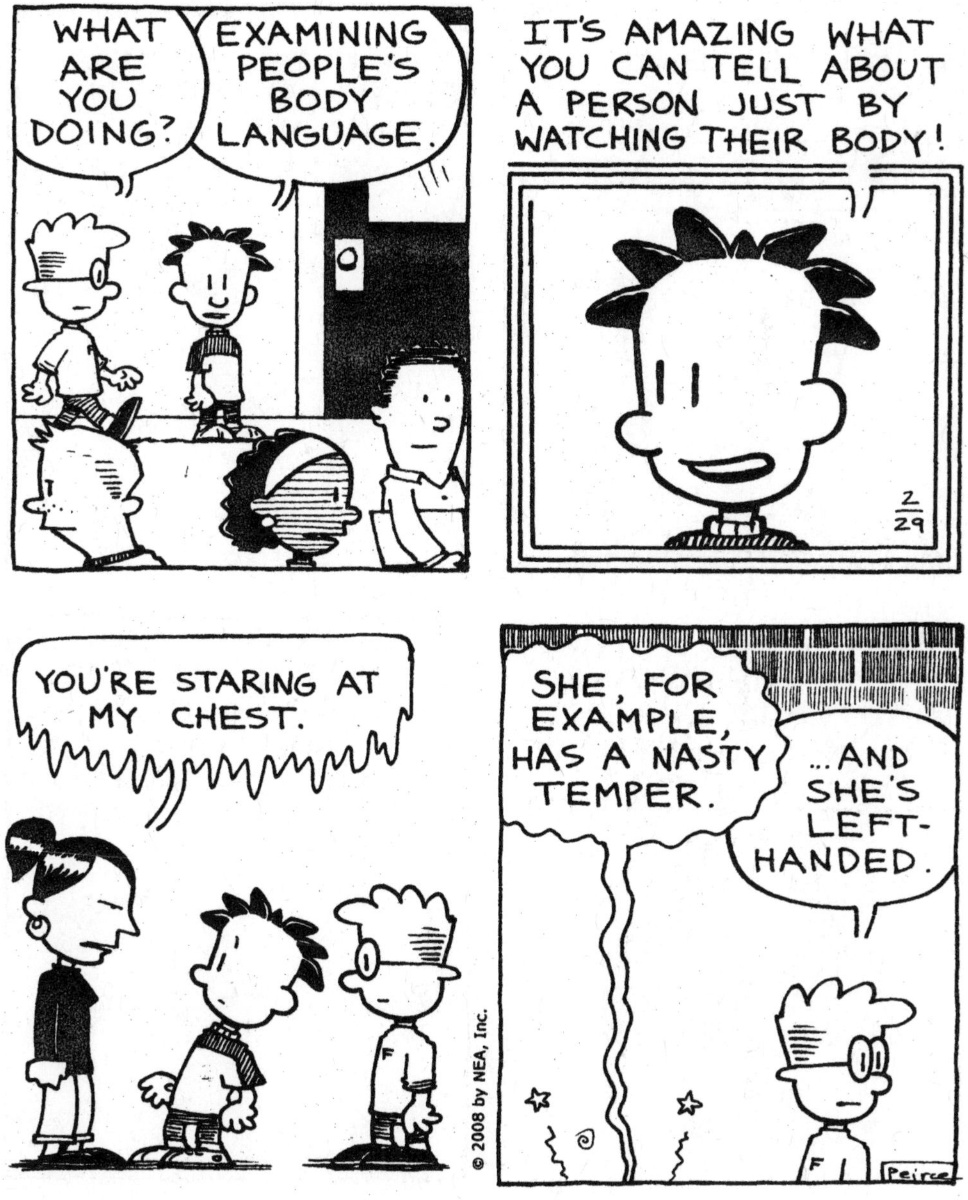
WHAT ARE YOU DOING?
EXAMINING PEOPLE'S BODY LANGUAGE.
IT'S AMAZING WHAT YOU CAN TELL ABOUT A PERSON JUST BY WATCHING THEIR BODY!
2/29
YOU'RE STARING AT MY CHEST.
© 2008 by NEA, Inc.
SHE, FOR EXAMPLE, HAS A NASTY TEMPER.
...AND SHE'S LEFT-HANDED.
Peirce

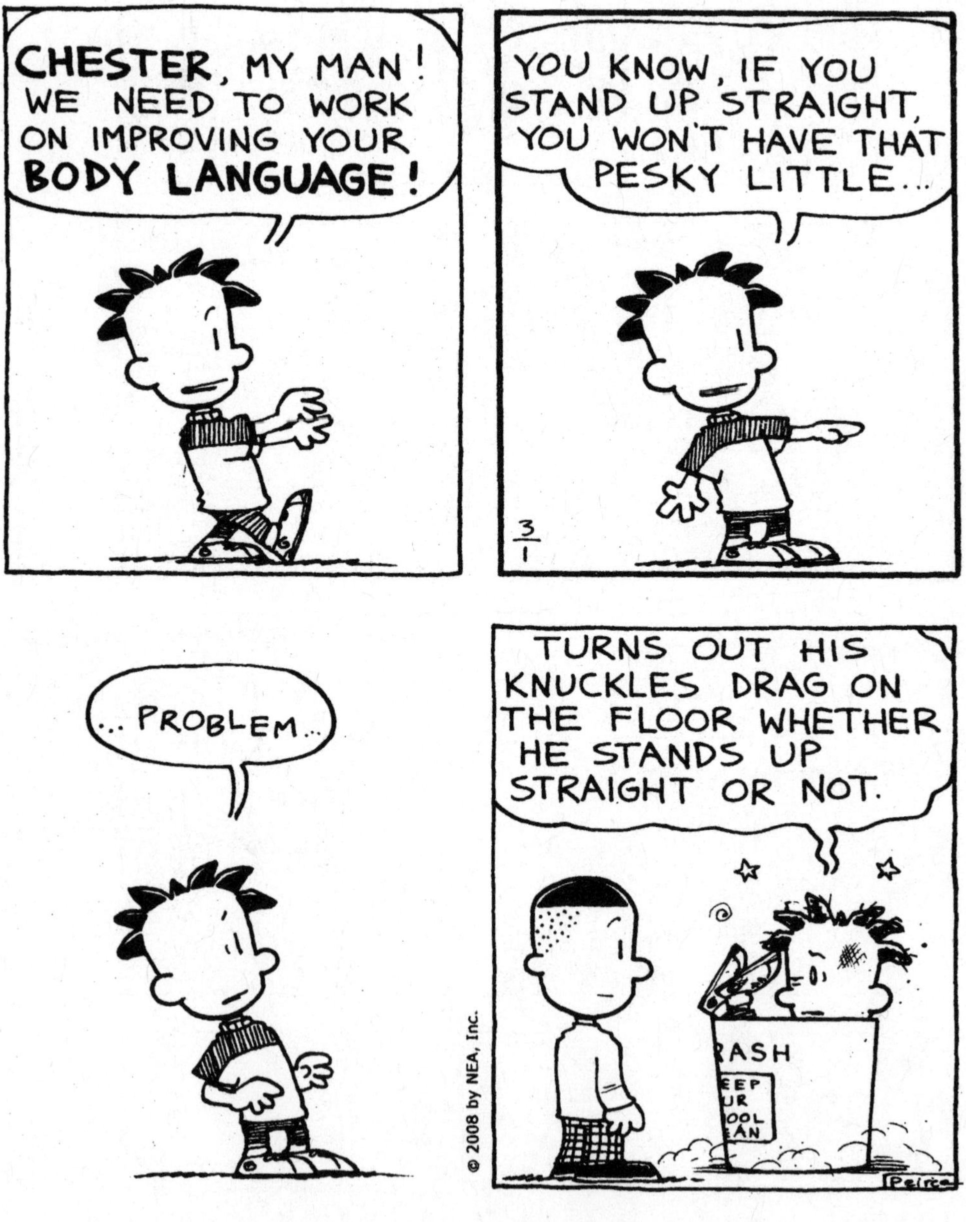
CHESTER, MY MAN! WE NEED TO WORK ON IMPROVING YOUR BODY LANGUAGE!
YOU KNOW, IF YOU STAND UP STRAIGHT, YOU WON'T HAVE THAT PESKY LITTLE...
3/1
... PROBLEM...
© 2008 by NEA, Inc.
TURNS OUT HIS KNUCKLES DRAG ON THE FLOOR WHETHER HE STANDS UP STRAIGHT OR NOT.
Peirce

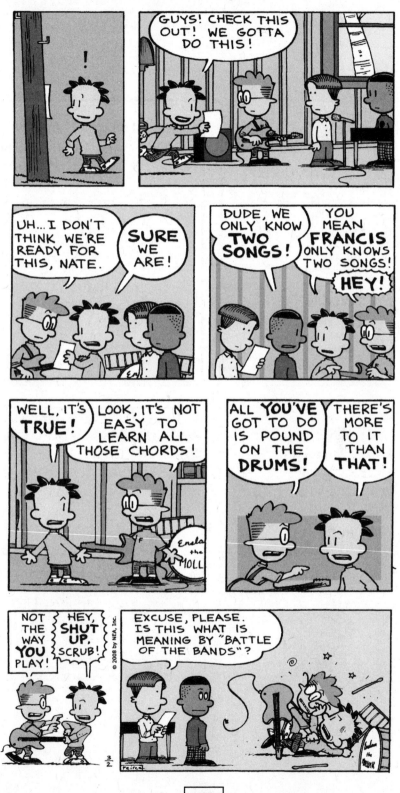

RUBBER BANDS RULE!

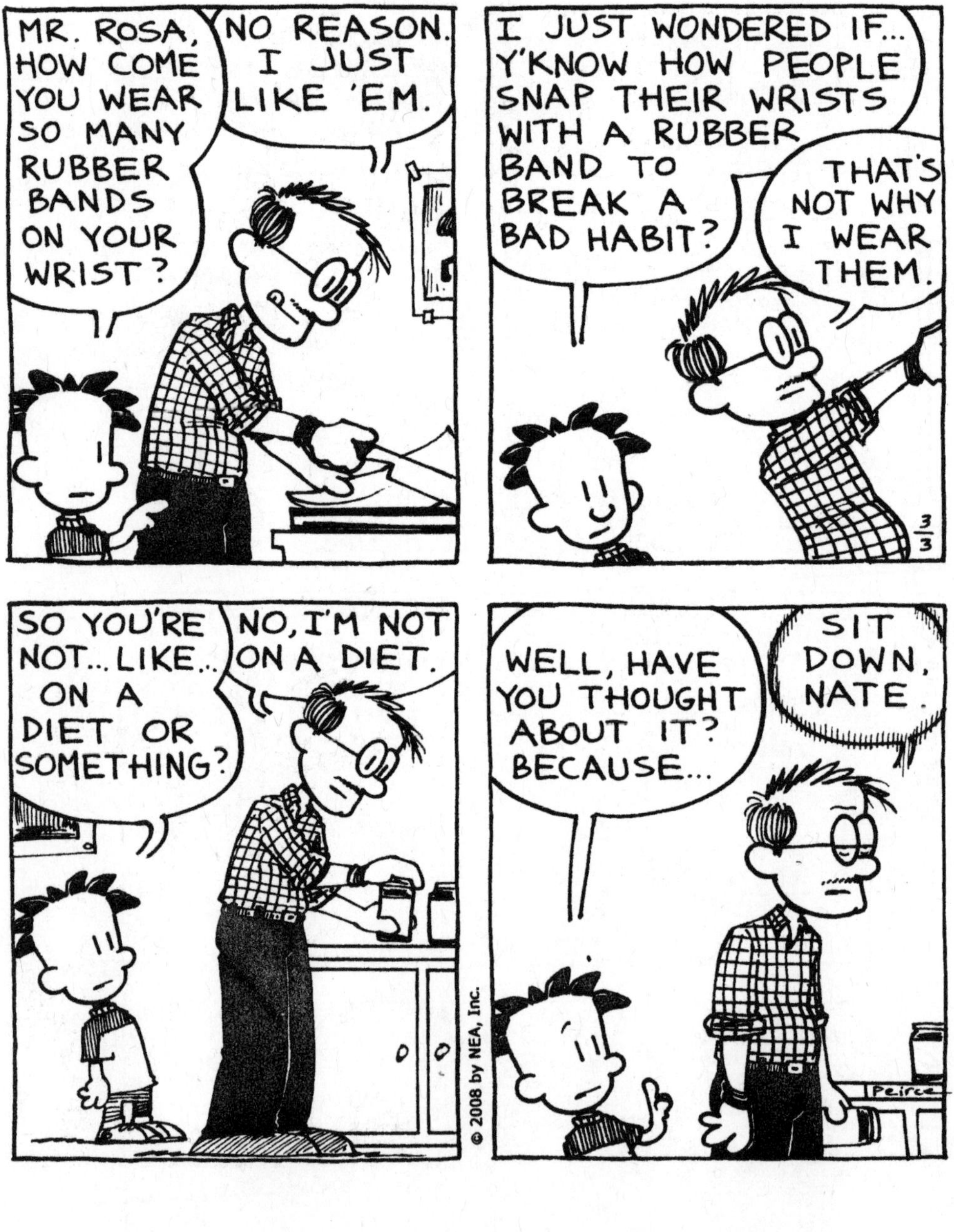
MR. ROSA, HOW COME YOU WEAR SO MANY RUBBER BANDS ON YOUR WRIST?
NO REASON. I JUST LIKE 'EM.
I JUST WONDERED IF... Y'KNOW HOW PEOPLE SNAP THEIR WRISTS WITH A RUBBER BAND TO BREAK A BAD HABIT?
THAT'S NOT WHY I WEAR THEM.
3/3
SO YOU'RE NOT... LIKE... ON A DIET OR SOMETHING?
NO, I'M NOT ON A DIET.
© 2008 by NEA, Inc.
WELL, HAVE YOU THOUGHT ABOUT IT? BECAUSE...
SIT DOWN, NATE.
Peirce

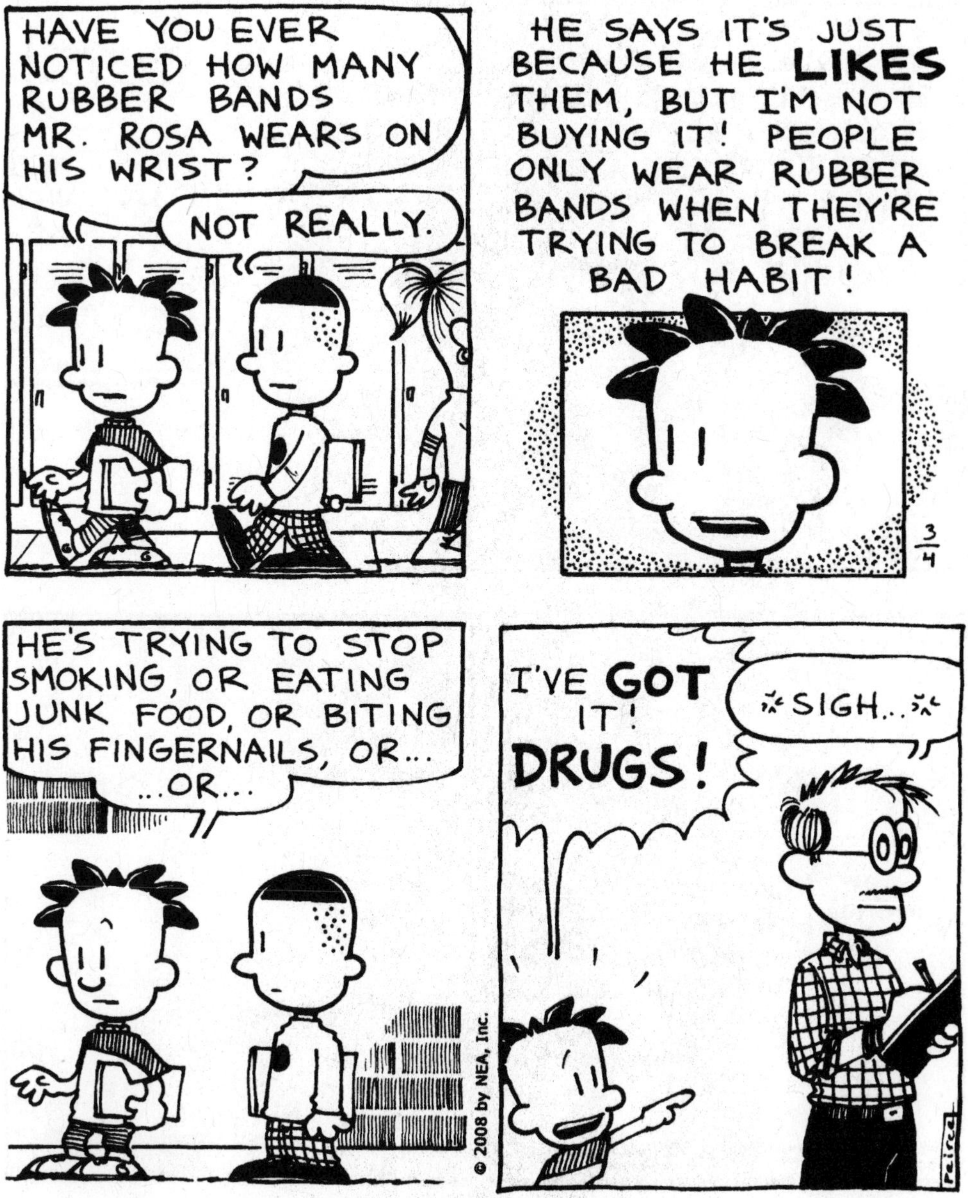
HAVE YOU EVER NOTICED HOW MANY RUBBER BANDS MR. ROSA WEARS ON HIS WRIST?
NOT REALLY.
HE SAYS IT'S JUST BECAUSE HE **LIKES** THEM, BUT I'M NOT BUYING IT! PEOPLE ONLY WEAR RUBBER BANDS WHEN THEY'RE TRYING TO BREAK A BAD HABIT!
HE'S TRYING TO STOP SMOKING, OR EATING JUNK FOOD, OR BITING HIS FINGERNAILS, OR... ...OR...
I'VE **GOT** IT! **DRUGS!**
SIGH...
© 2008 by NEA, Inc.
PEIRCE

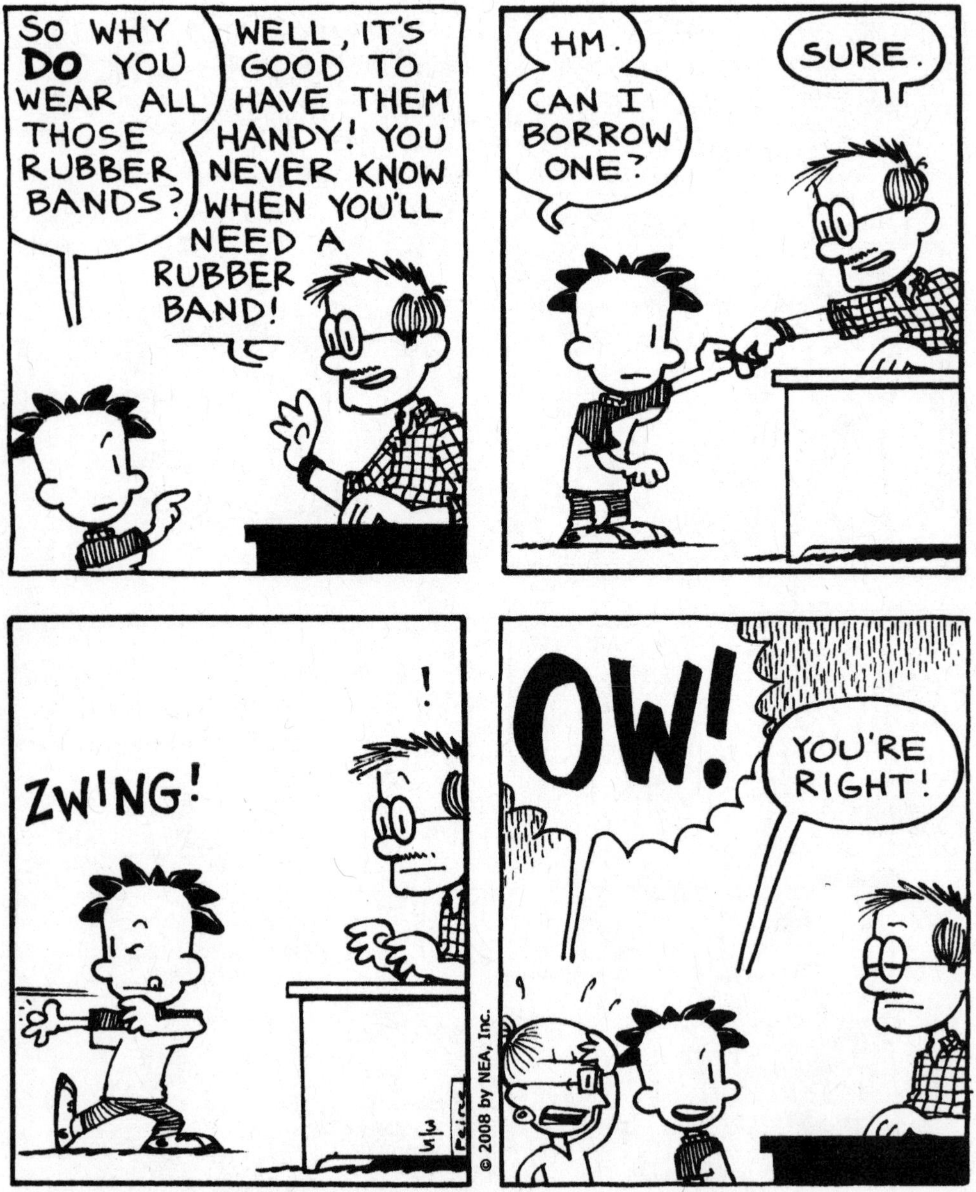
SO WHY **DO** YOU WEAR ALL THOSE RUBBER BANDS?
WELL, IT'S GOOD TO HAVE THEM HANDY! YOU NEVER KNOW WHEN YOU'LL NEED A RUBBER BAND!
HM.
CAN I BORROW ONE?
SURE.
ZWING!
!
© 2008 by NEA, Inc.
OW!
YOU'RE RIGHT!

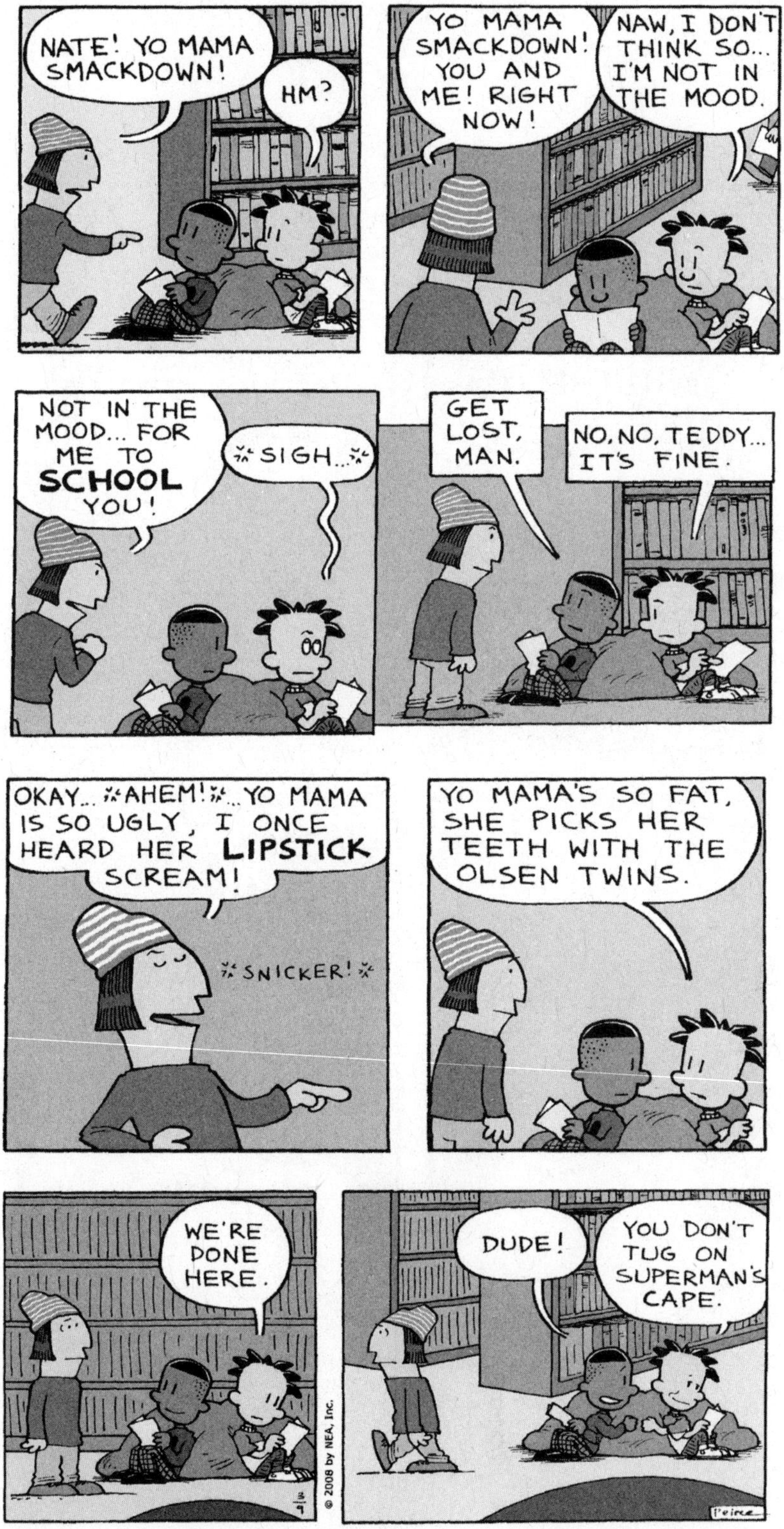
NATE! YO MAMA SMACKDOWN!
HM?
YO MAMA SMACKDOWN! YOU AND ME! RIGHT NOW!
NAW, I DON'T THINK SO... I'M NOT IN THE MOOD.
NOT IN THE MOOD... FOR ME TO **SCHOOL** YOU!
SIGH...
GET LOST, MAN.
NO, NO, TEDDY... IT'S FINE.
OKAY... *AHEM!* ...YO MAMA IS SO UGLY, I ONCE HEARD HER **LIPSTICK** SCREAM!
SNICKER!
YO MAMA'S SO FAT, SHE PICKS HER TEETH WITH THE OLSEN TWINS.
WE'RE DONE HERE.
DUDE!
YOU DON'T TUG ON SUPERMAN'S CAPE.
© 2008 by NEA, Inc.
Peirce

ARE YOU COOL ENOUGH?

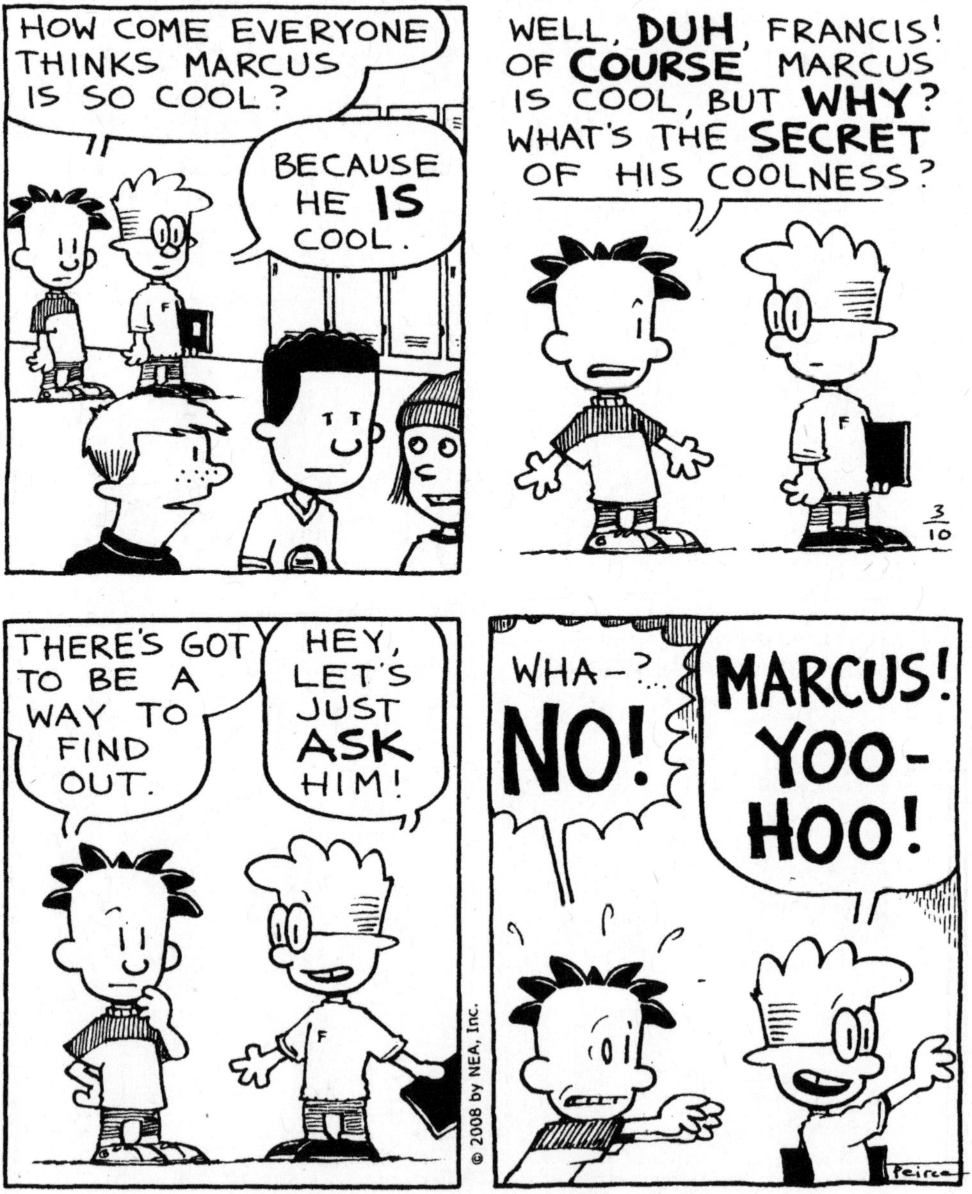

HOW COME EVERYONE THINKS MARCUS IS SO COOL?
BECAUSE HE **IS** COOL.
WELL, **DUH**, FRANCIS! OF **COURSE** MARCUS IS COOL, BUT **WHY**? WHAT'S THE **SECRET** OF HIS COOLNESS?
3/10
THERE'S GOT TO BE A WAY TO FIND OUT.
HEY, LET'S JUST **ASK** HIM!
© 2008 by NEA, Inc.
WHA-?... NO!
MARCUS! YOO-HOO!
Peirce

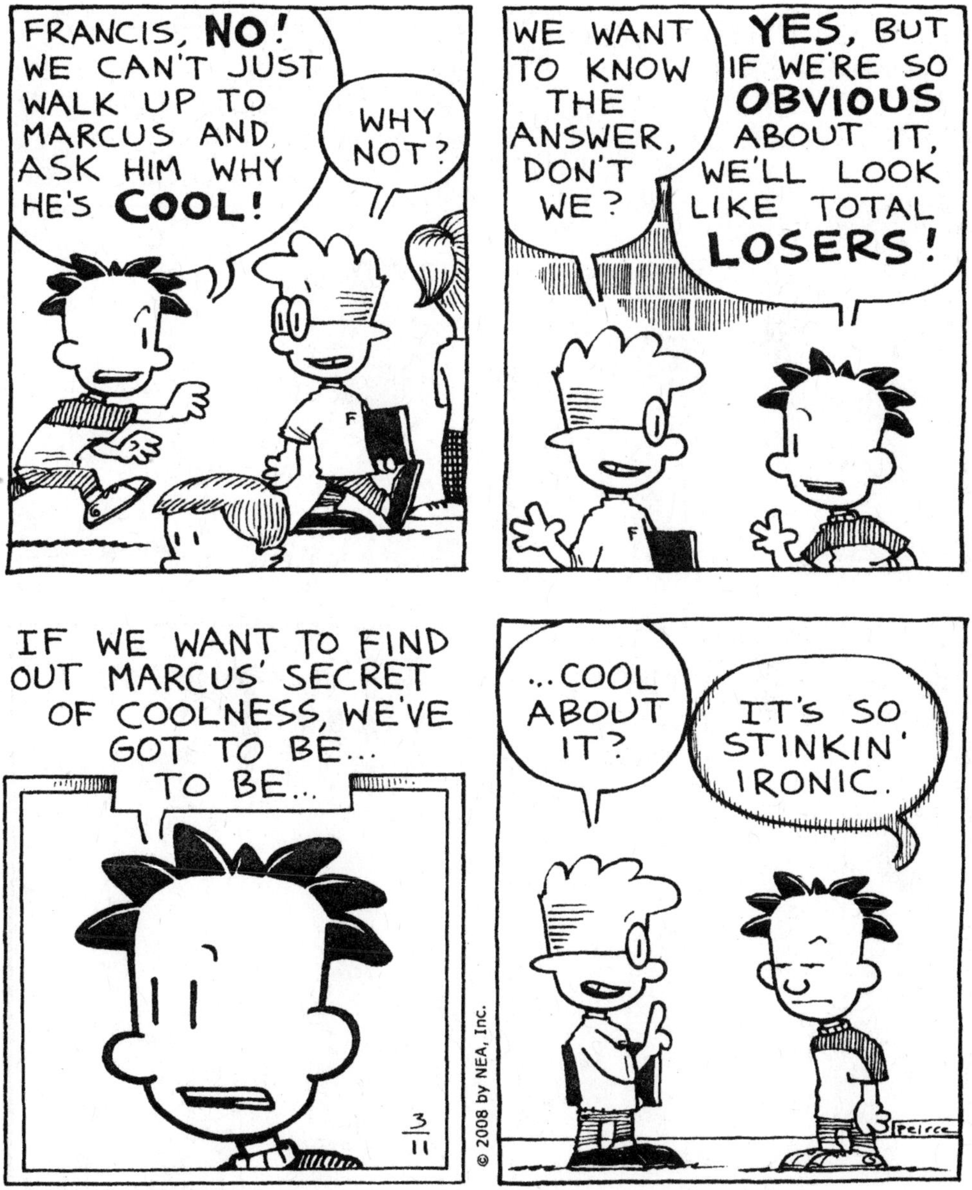
FRANCIS, **NO!** WE CAN'T JUST WALK UP TO MARCUS AND ASK HIM WHY HE'S **COOL!**
WHY NOT?
WE WANT TO KNOW THE ANSWER, DON'T WE?
YES, BUT IF WE'RE SO **OBVIOUS** ABOUT IT, WE'LL LOOK LIKE TOTAL **LOSERS!**
IF WE WANT TO FIND OUT MARCUS' SECRET OF COOLNESS, WE'VE GOT TO BE... TO BE...
3/11
...COOL ABOUT IT?
IT'S SO STINKIN' IRONIC.
PEIRCE

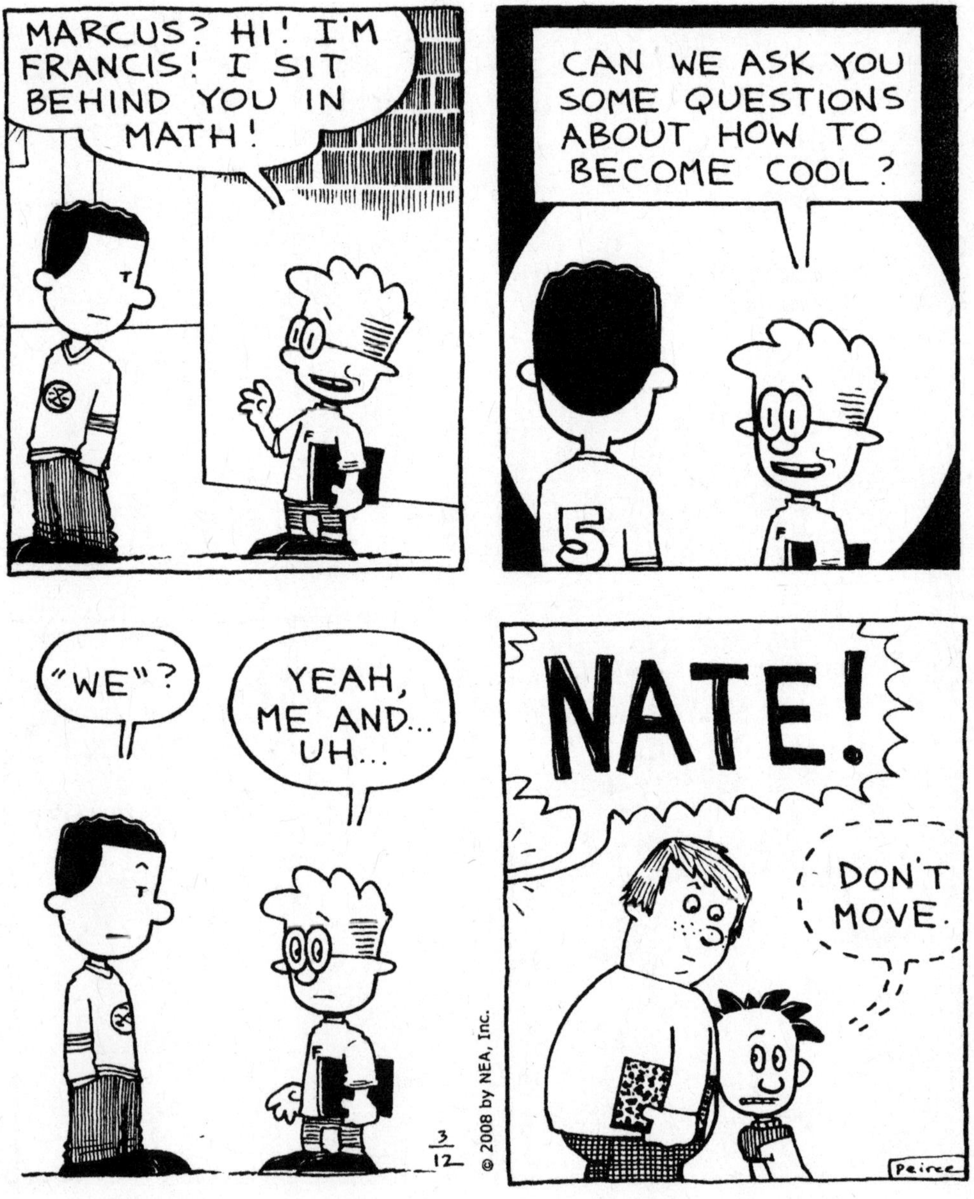
MARCUS? HI! I'M FRANCIS! I SIT BEHIND YOU IN MATH!
CAN WE ASK YOU SOME QUESTIONS ABOUT HOW TO BECOME COOL?
"WE"?
YEAH, ME AND... UH...
3 12
© 2008 by NEA, Inc.
NATE!
DON'T MOVE.
Peirce

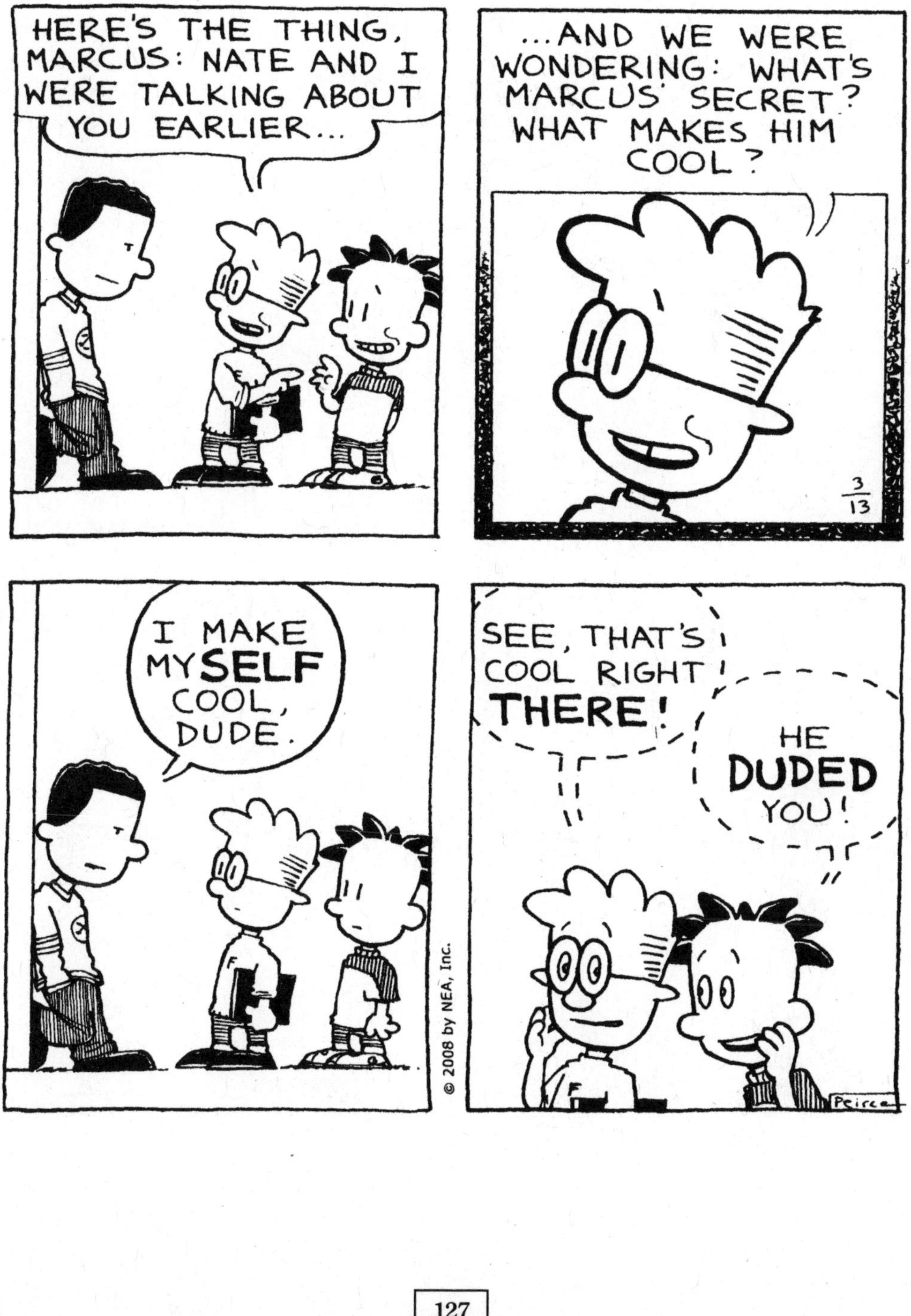
HERE'S THE THING, MARCUS: NATE AND I WERE TALKING ABOUT YOU EARLIER...
...AND WE WERE WONDERING: WHAT'S MARCUS' SECRET? WHAT MAKES HIM COOL?
3/13
I MAKE MY**SELF** COOL, DUDE.
© 2008 by NEA, Inc.
SEE, THAT'S COOL RIGHT **THERE**!
HE **DUDED** YOU!
Peirce

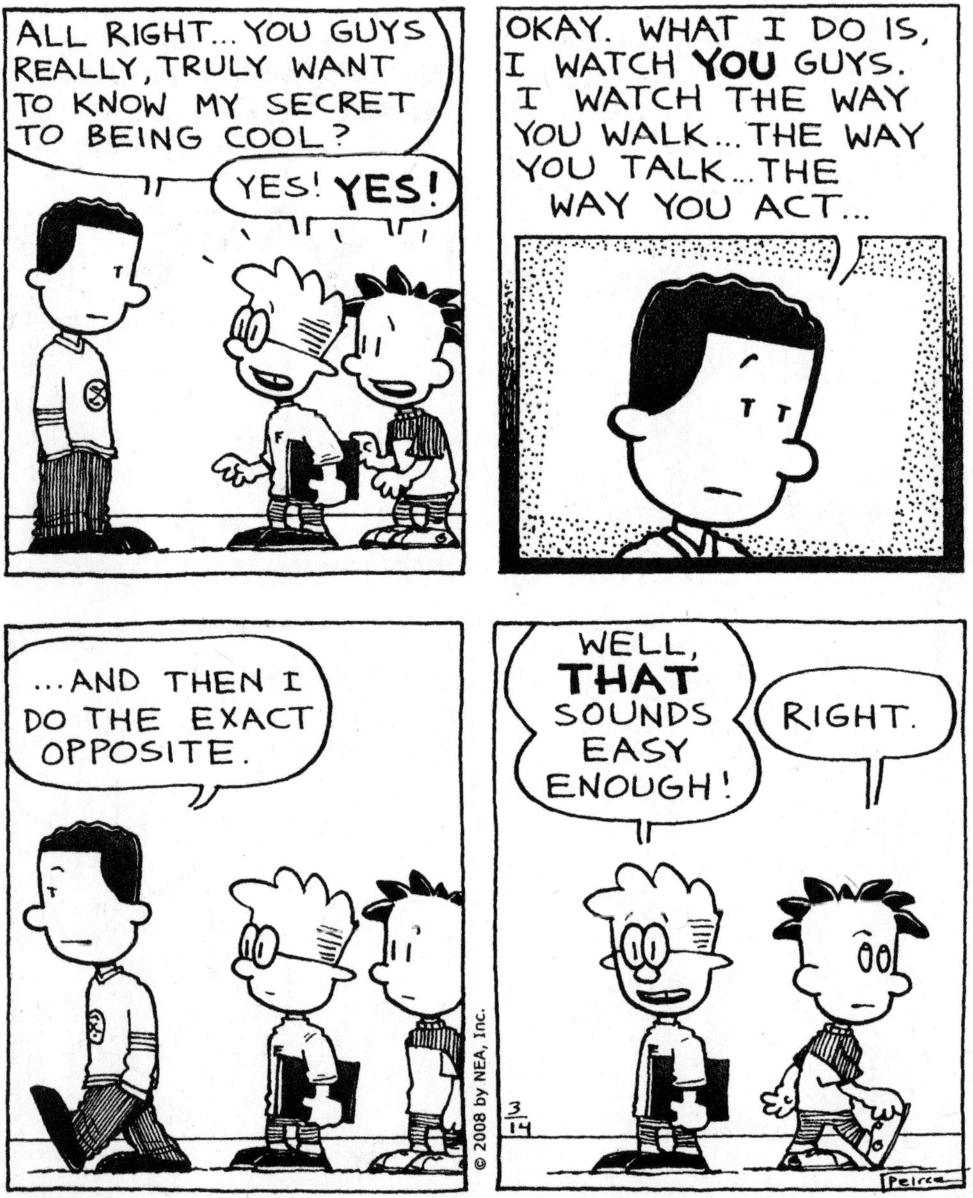
ALL RIGHT... YOU GUYS REALLY, TRULY WANT TO KNOW MY SECRET TO BEING COOL?
YES! YES!
OKAY. WHAT I DO IS, I WATCH YOU GUYS. I WATCH THE WAY YOU WALK... THE WAY YOU TALK... THE WAY YOU ACT...
...AND THEN I DO THE EXACT OPPOSITE.
WELL, THAT SOUNDS EASY ENOUGH!
RIGHT.
© 2008 by NEA, Inc.
3/14
Peirce

THE PERFECT DATE

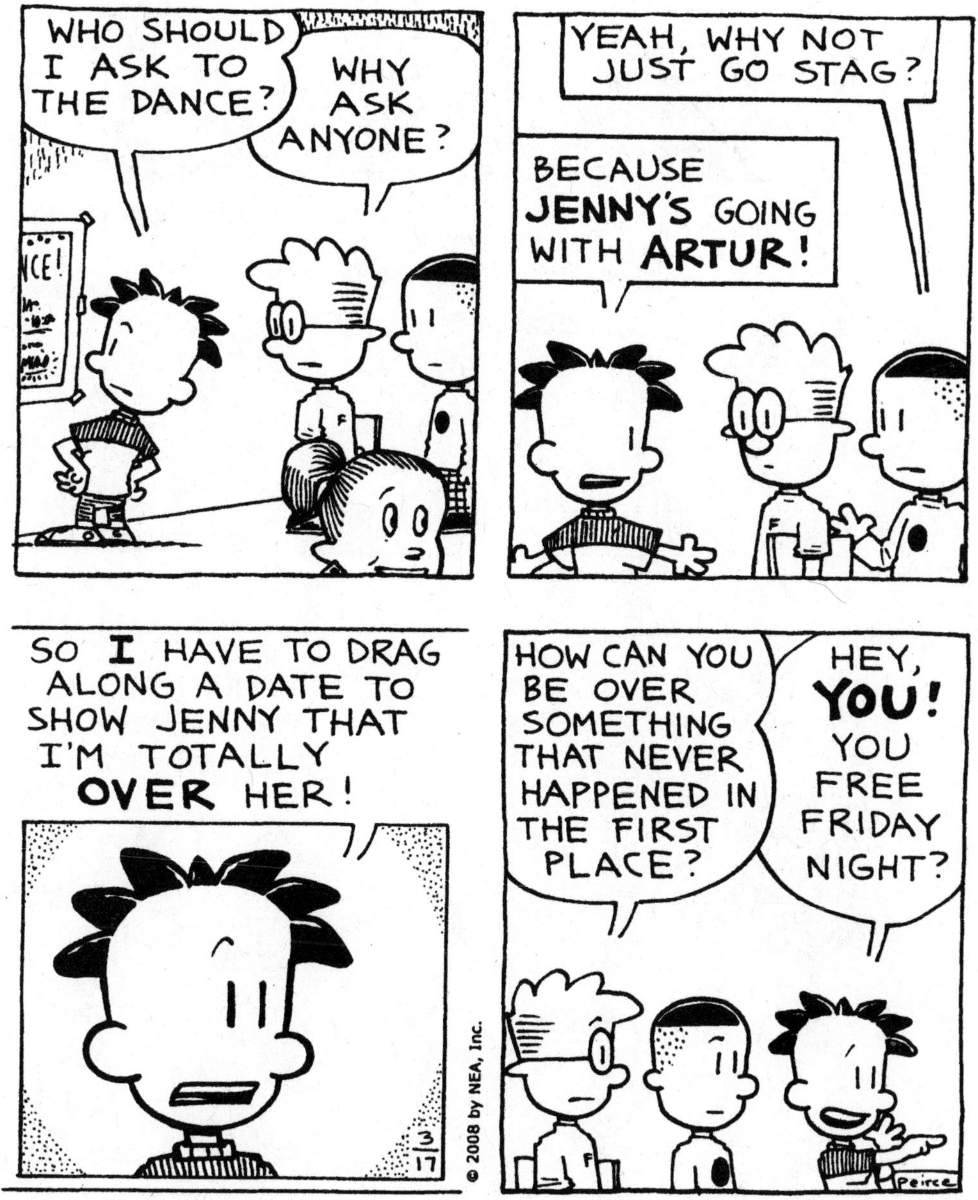
WHO SHOULD I ASK TO THE DANCE?
WHY ASK ANYONE?
YEAH, WHY NOT JUST GO STAG?
BECAUSE JENNY'S GOING WITH ARTUR!
SO I HAVE TO DRAG ALONG A DATE TO SHOW JENNY THAT I'M TOTALLY OVER HER!
3/17
© 2008 by NEA, Inc.
HOW CAN YOU BE OVER SOMETHING THAT NEVER HAPPENED IN THE FIRST PLACE?
HEY, YOU! YOU FREE FRIDAY NIGHT?
Peirce

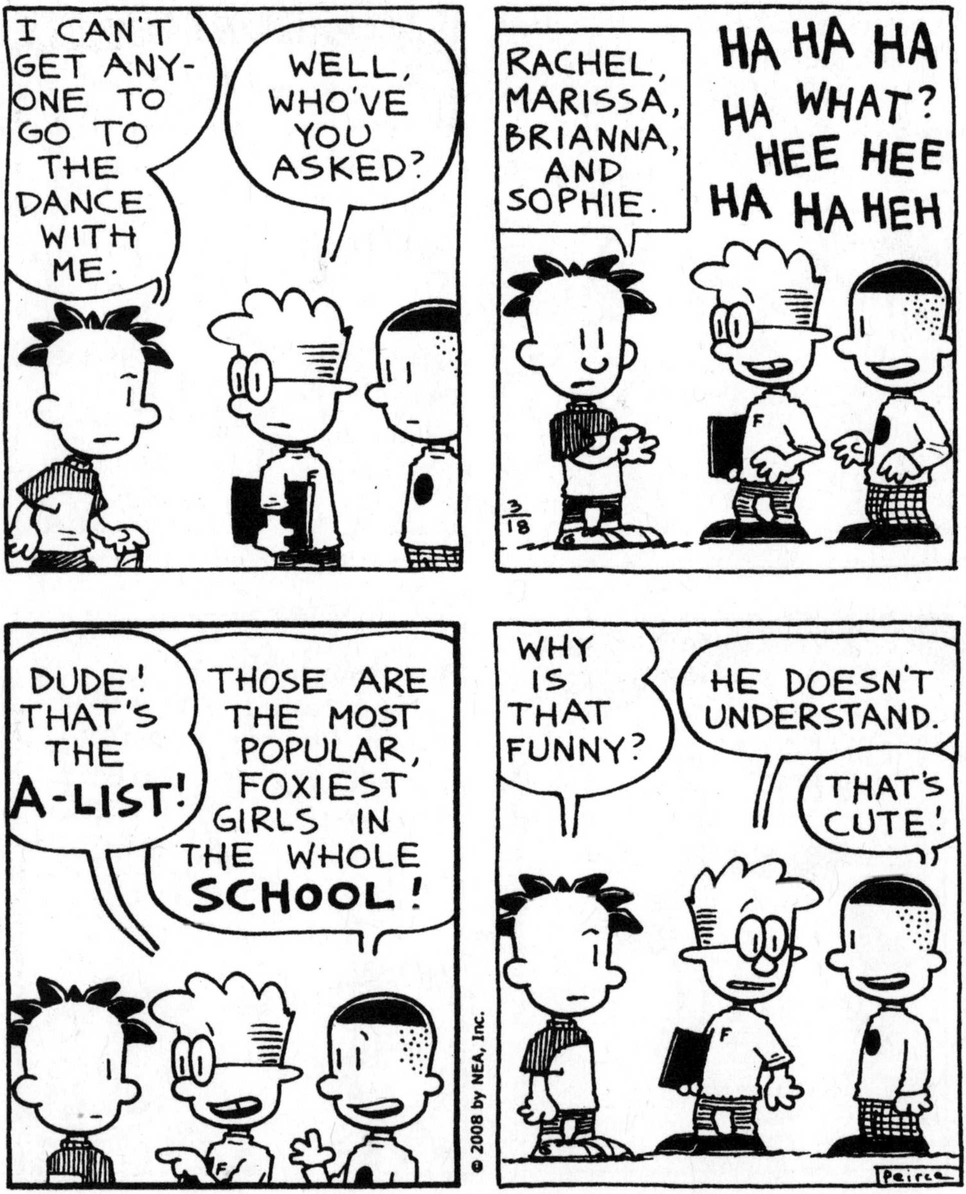
I CAN'T GET ANYONE TO GO TO THE DANCE WITH ME.
WELL, WHO'VE YOU ASKED?
RACHEL, MARISSA, BRIANNA, AND SOPHIE.
HA HA HA HA WHAT? HEE HEE HA HA HEH
3/18
DUDE! THAT'S THE A-LIST!
THOSE ARE THE MOST POPULAR, FOXIEST GIRLS IN THE WHOLE SCHOOL!
© 2008 by NEA, Inc.
WHY IS THAT FUNNY?
HE DOESN'T UNDERSTAND.
THAT'S CUTE!
Peirce

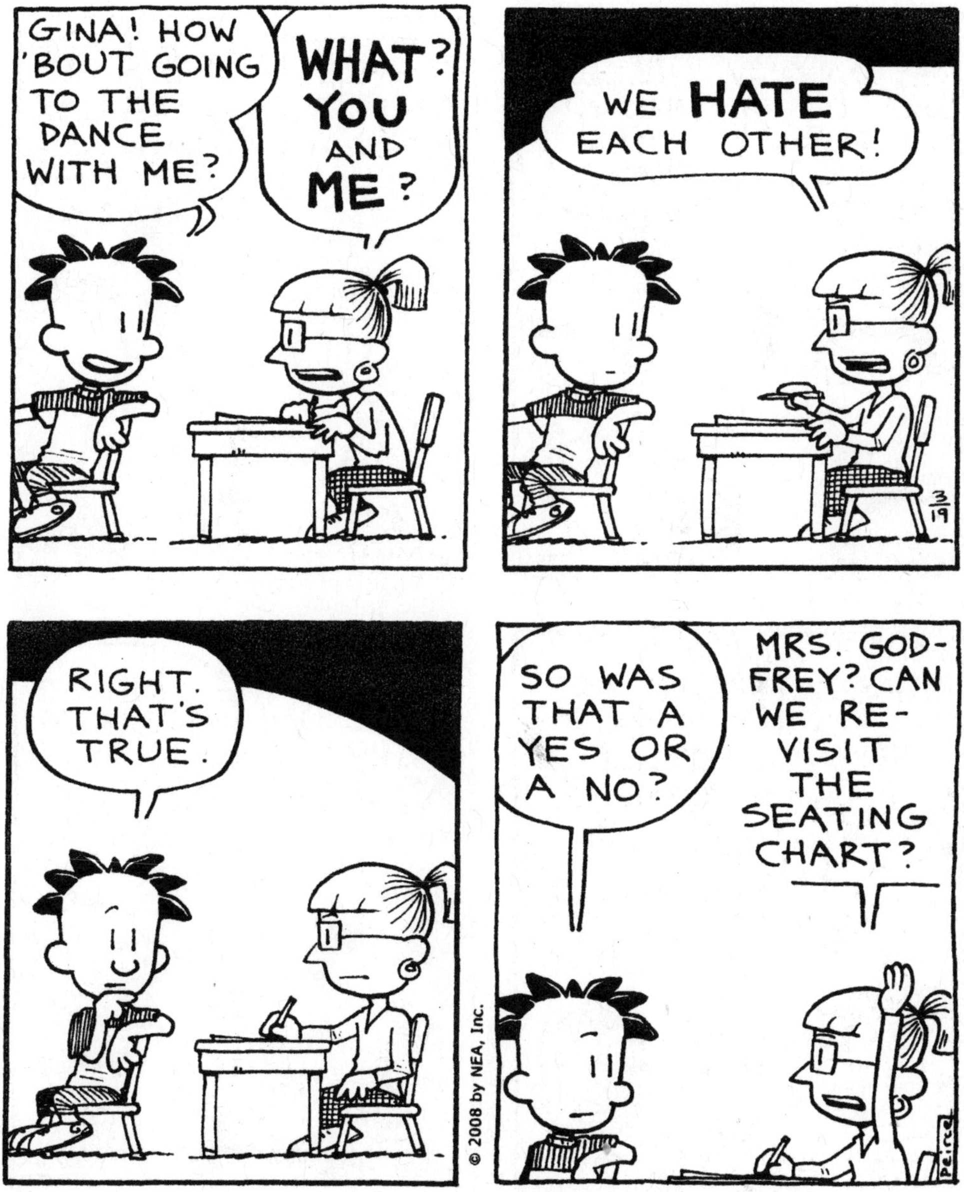
GINA! HOW 'BOUT GOING TO THE DANCE WITH ME?
WHAT? YOU AND ME?
WE HATE EACH OTHER!
3/19
RIGHT. THAT'S TRUE.
SO WAS THAT A YES OR A NO?
MRS. GOD-FREY? CAN WE RE-VISIT THE SEATING CHART?
Peirce

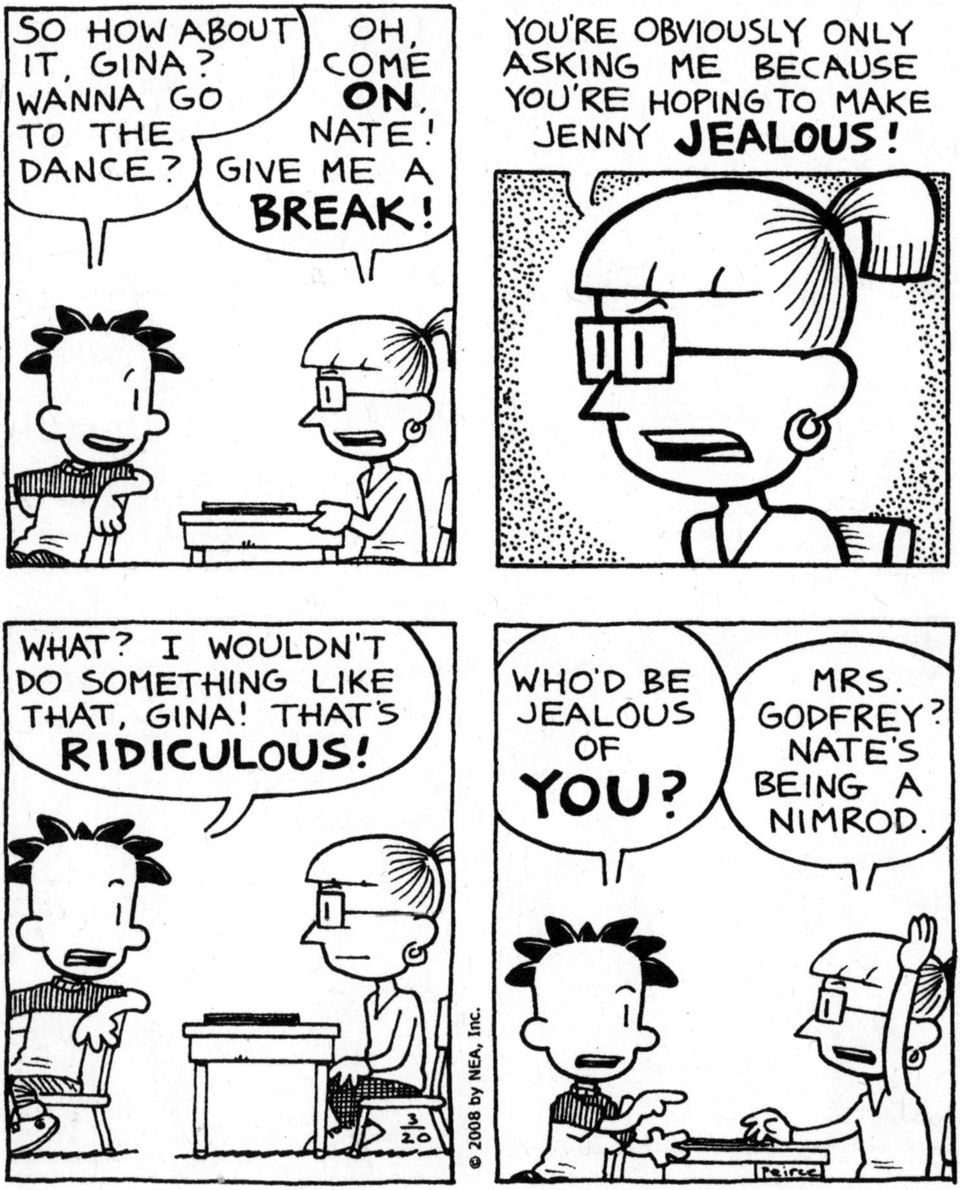
SO HOW ABOUT IT, GINA? WANNA GO TO THE DANCE?
OH, COME ON, NATE! GIVE ME A BREAK!
YOU'RE OBVIOUSLY ONLY ASKING ME BECAUSE YOU'RE HOPING TO MAKE JENNY JEALOUS!
WHAT? I WOULDN'T DO SOMETHING LIKE THAT, GINA! THAT'S RIDICULOUS!
3/20
© 2008 by NEA, Inc.
WHO'D BE JEALOUS OF YOU?
MRS. GODFREY? NATE'S BEING A NIMROD.
Peirce

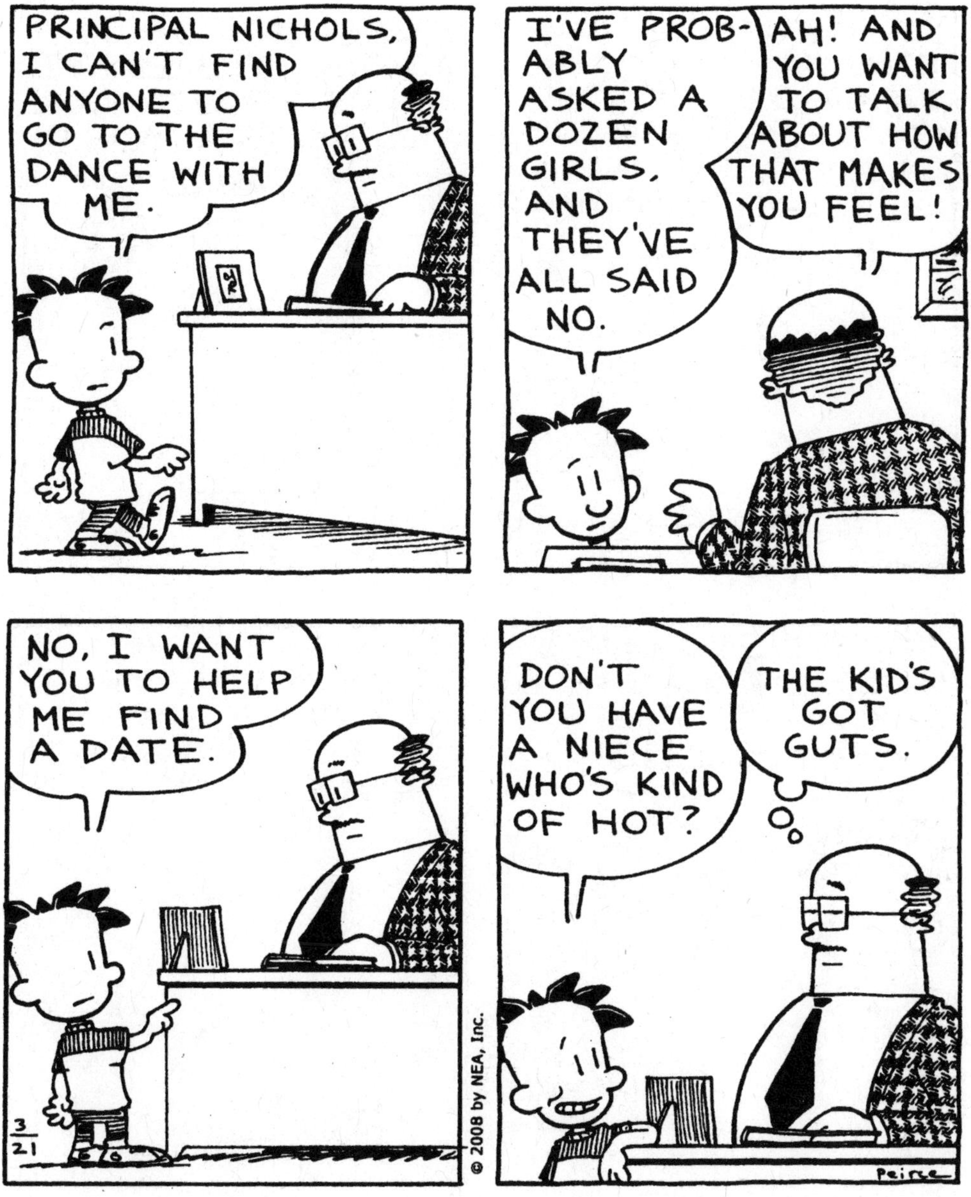
PRINCIPAL NICHOLS, I CAN'T FIND ANYONE TO GO TO THE DANCE WITH ME.
I'VE PROBABLY ASKED A DOZEN GIRLS, AND THEY'VE ALL SAID NO.
AH! AND YOU WANT TO TALK ABOUT HOW THAT MAKES YOU FEEL!
NO, I WANT YOU TO HELP ME FIND A DATE.
DON'T YOU HAVE A NIECE WHO'S KIND OF HOT?
THE KID'S GOT GUTS.
3/21
© 2008 by NEA, Inc.
Peirce

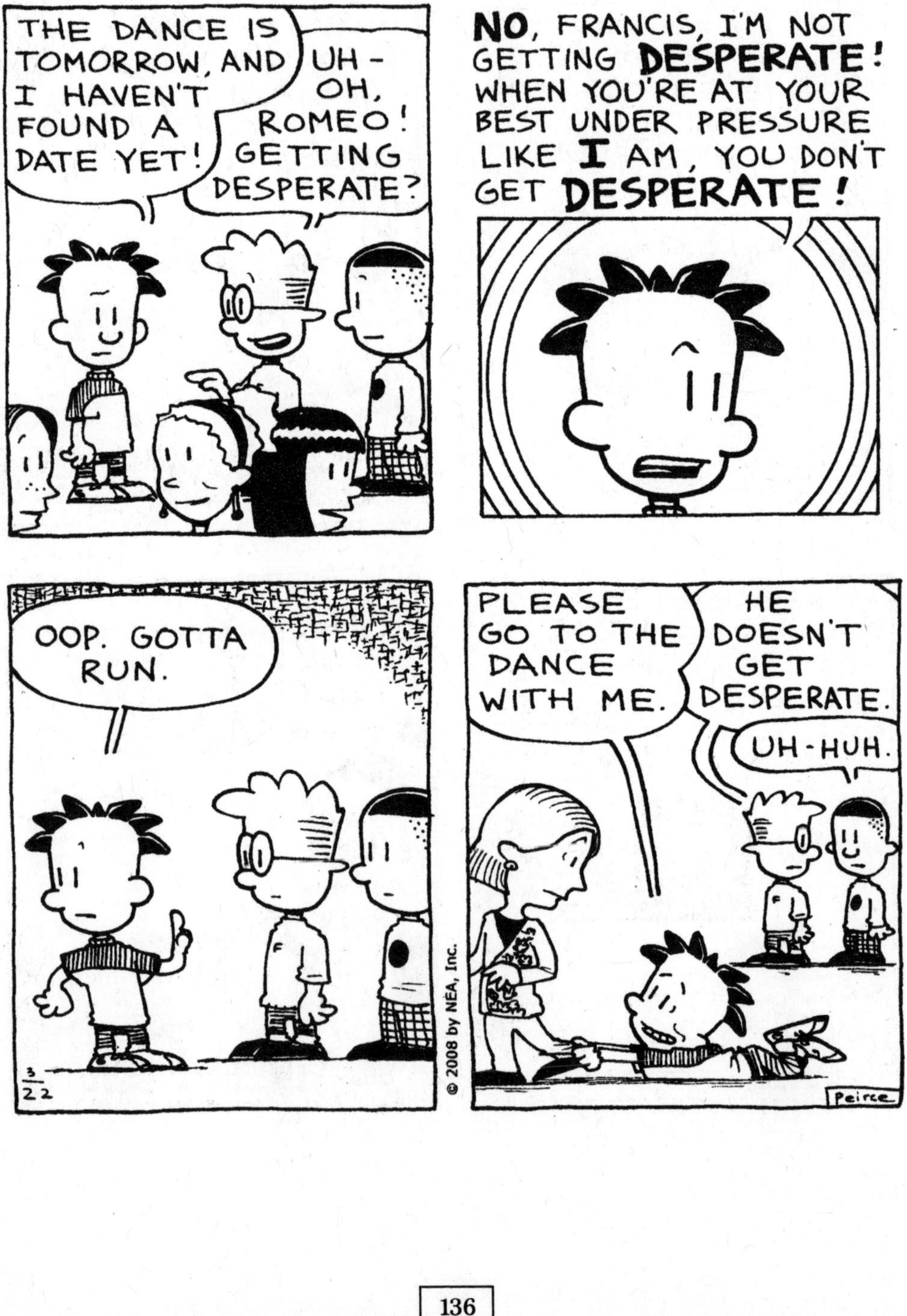
THE DANCE IS TOMORROW, AND I HAVEN'T FOUND A DATE YET!
UH-OH, ROMEO! GETTING DESPERATE?
NO, FRANCIS, I'M NOT GETTING DESPERATE! WHEN YOU'RE AT YOUR BEST UNDER PRESSURE LIKE I AM, YOU DON'T GET DESPERATE!
OOP. GOTTA RUN.
3/22
© 2008 by NEA, Inc.
PLEASE GO TO THE DANCE WITH ME.
HE DOESN'T GET DESPERATE.
UH-HUH.
Peirce

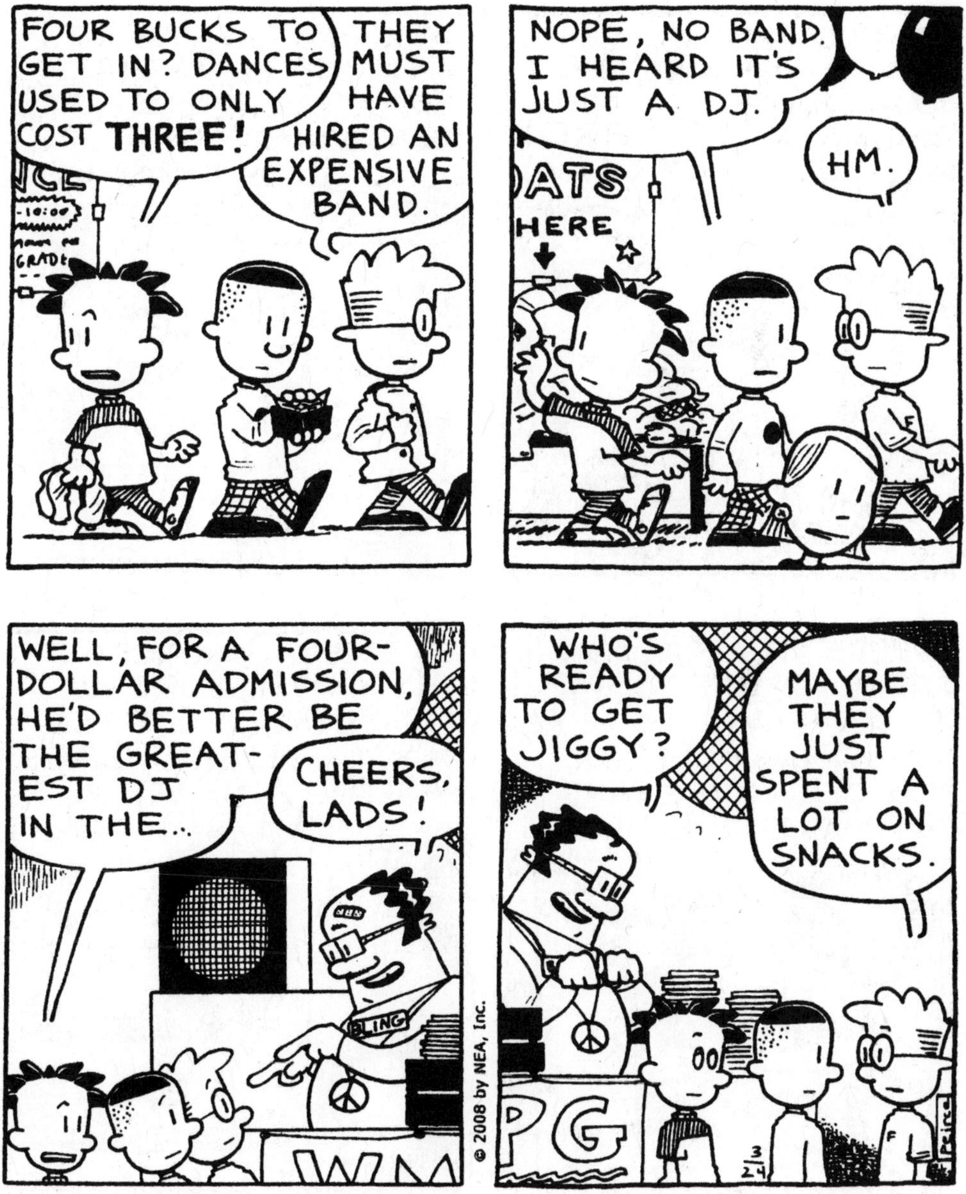
FOUR BUCKS TO GET IN? DANCES USED TO ONLY COST THREE!
THEY MUST HAVE HIRED AN EXPENSIVE BAND.
NOPE, NO BAND. I HEARD IT'S JUST A DJ.
HM.
WELL, FOR A FOUR-DOLLAR ADMISSION, HE'D BETTER BE THE GREATEST DJ IN THE...
CHEERS, LADS!
WHO'S READY TO GET JIGGY?
MAYBE THEY JUST SPENT A LOT ON SNACKS.
BLING
PG
© 2008 by NEA, Inc.

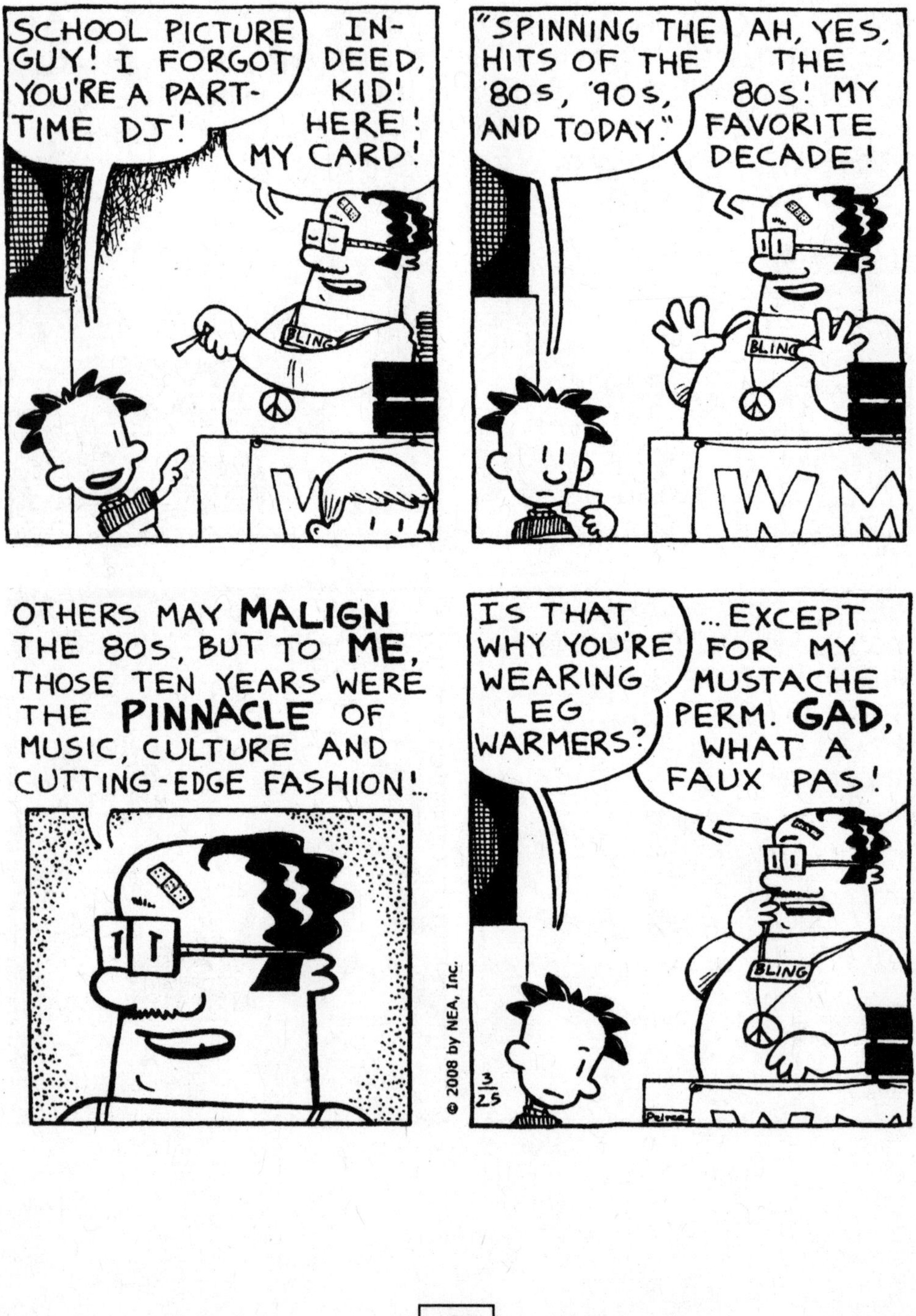
SCHOOL PICTURE GUY! I FORGOT YOU'RE A PART-TIME DJ!
INDEED, KID! HERE! MY CARD!
"SPINNING THE HITS OF THE '80s, '90s, AND TODAY."
AH, YES, THE 80s! MY FAVORITE DECADE!
OTHERS MAY **MALIGN** THE 80s, BUT TO **ME**, THOSE TEN YEARS WERE THE **PINNACLE** OF MUSIC, CULTURE AND CUTTING-EDGE FASHION!...
IS THAT WHY YOU'RE WEARING LEG WARMERS?
...EXCEPT FOR MY MUSTACHE PERM. **GAD**, WHAT A FAUX PAS!
BLING
© 2008 by NEA, Inc.
3/25

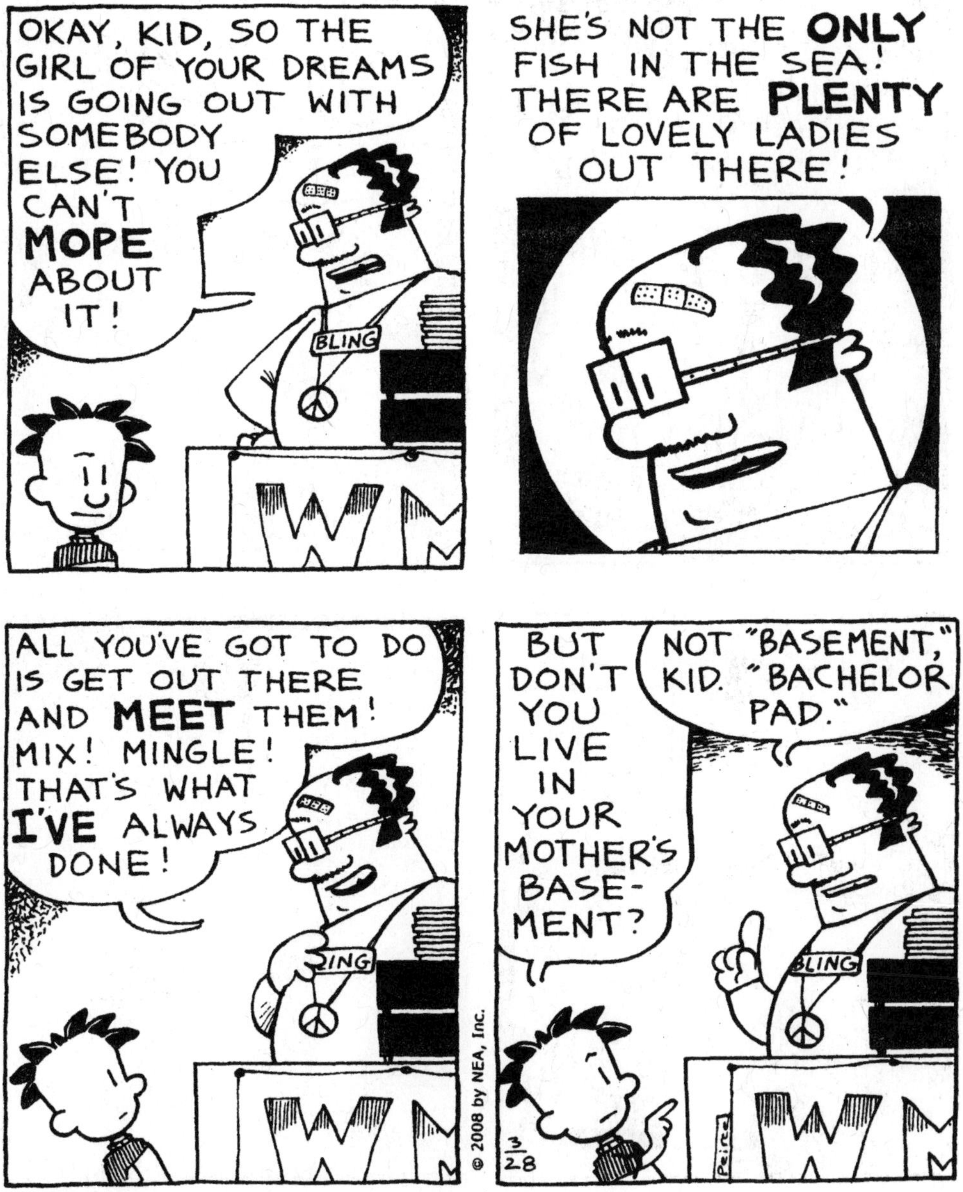
OKAY, KID, SO THE GIRL OF YOUR DREAMS IS GOING OUT WITH SOMEBODY ELSE! YOU CAN'T **MOPE** ABOUT IT!
BLING
SHE'S NOT THE **ONLY** FISH IN THE SEA! THERE ARE **PLENTY** OF LOVELY LADIES OUT THERE!
ALL YOU'VE GOT TO DO IS GET OUT THERE AND **MEET** THEM! MIX! MINGLE! THAT'S WHAT **I'VE** ALWAYS DONE!
BUT DON'T YOU LIVE IN YOUR MOTHER'S BASE-MENT?
NOT "BASEMENT," KID. "BACHELOR PAD."
© 2008 by NEA, Inc.
3/28
Peirce

DETENTION, AGAIN

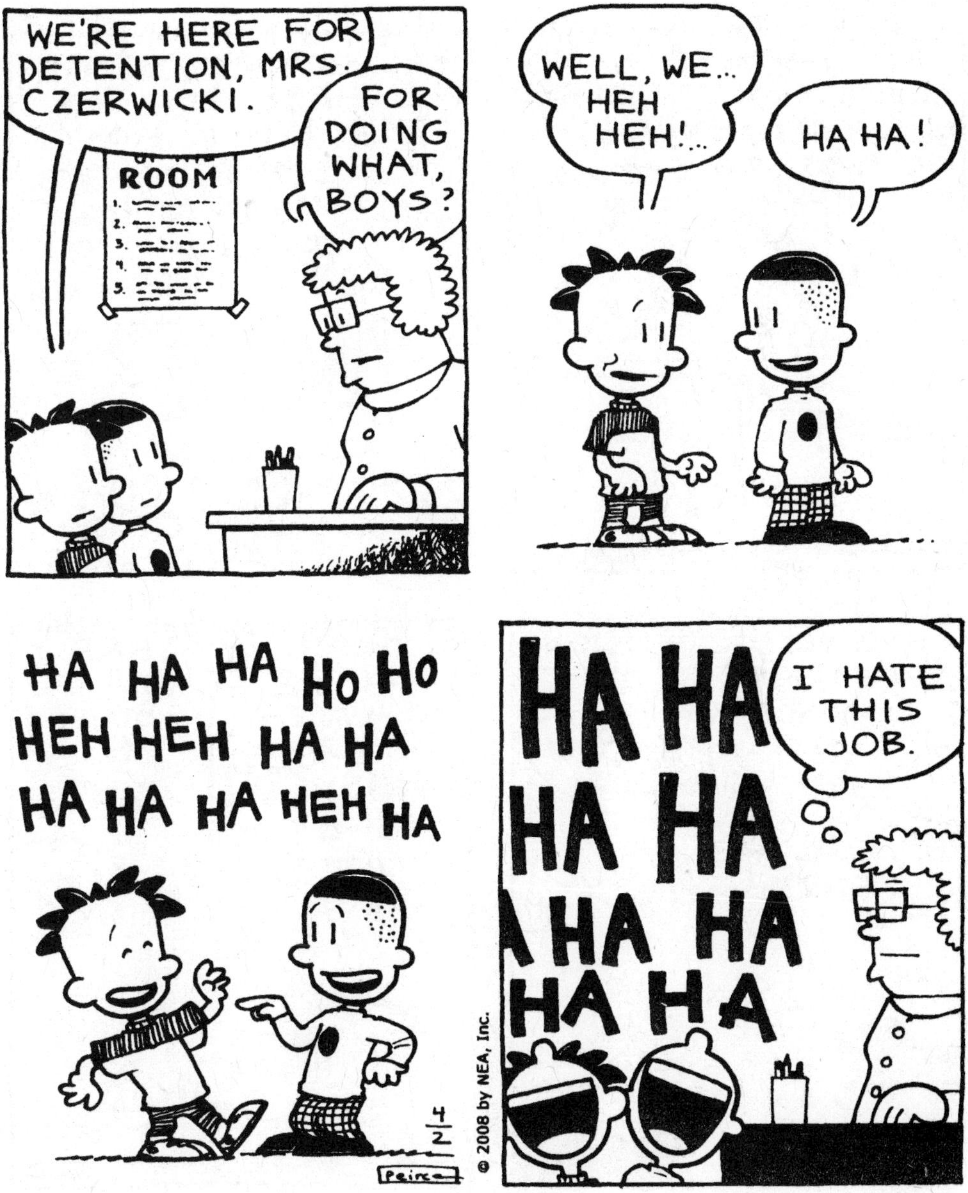
WE'RE HERE FOR DETENTION, MRS. CZERWICKI.
FOR DOING WHAT, BOYS?
ROOM
WELL, WE... HEH HEH!...
HA HA!
HA HA HA HO HO HEH HEH HA HA HA HA HA HEH HA
HA HA HA HA HA HA HA HA HA
I HATE THIS JOB.
4/2
Peirce
© 2008 by NEA, Inc.

CRUSHED

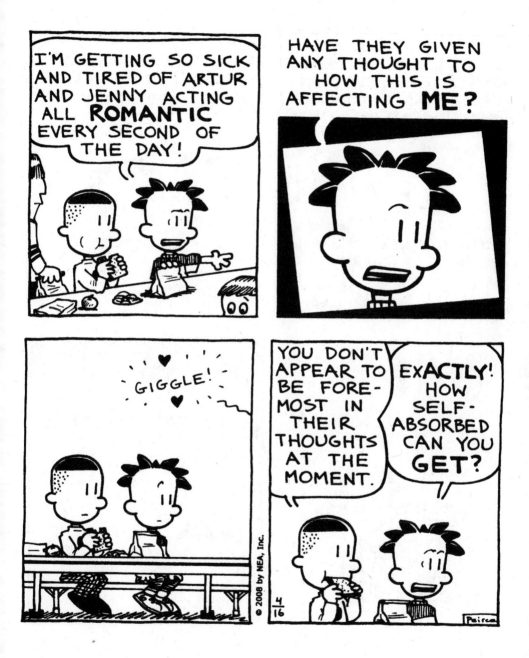

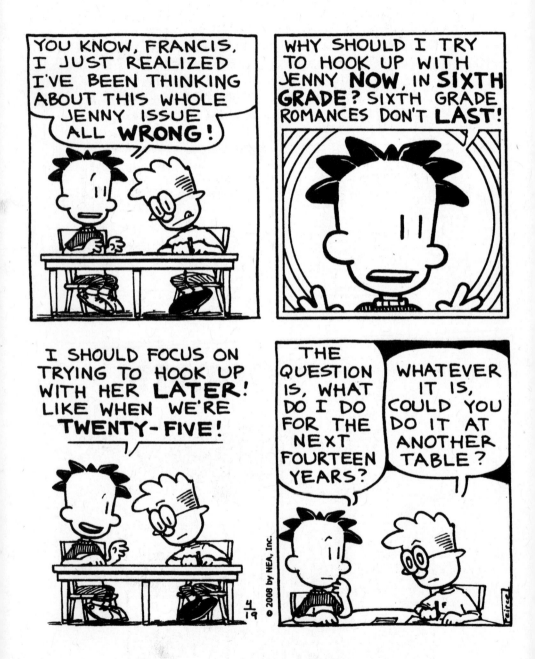

SECRET FAN

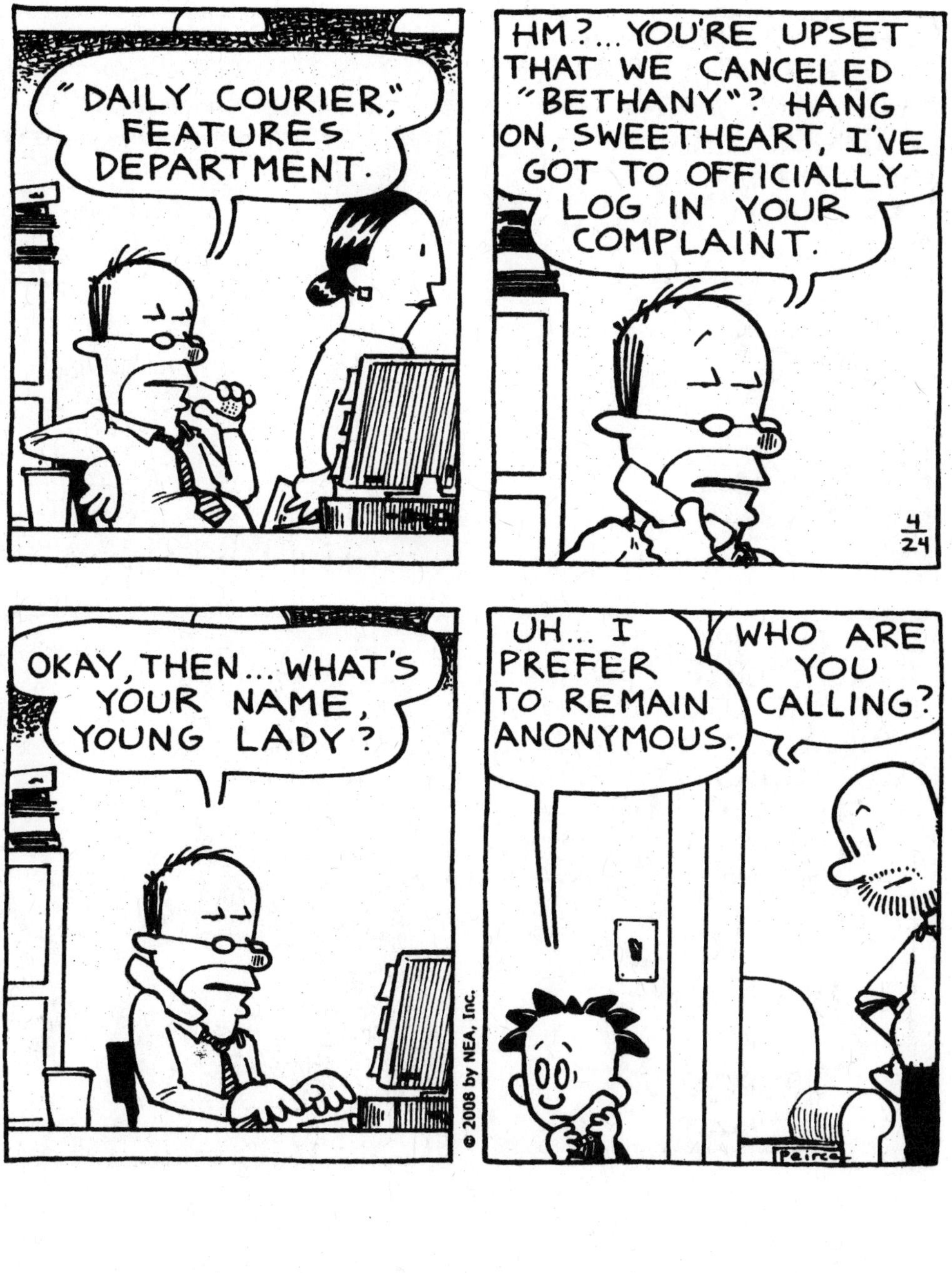
"DAILY COURIER," FEATURES DEPARTMENT.
HM?... YOU'RE UPSET THAT WE CANCELED "BETHANY"? HANG ON, SWEETHEART, I'VE GOT TO OFFICIALLY LOG IN YOUR COMPLAINT.
4/24
OKAY, THEN... WHAT'S YOUR NAME, YOUNG LADY?
© 2008 by NEA, Inc.
UH... I PREFER TO REMAIN ANONYMOUS.
WHO ARE YOU CALLING?
Peirce

WHAT COULD POSSIBLY GO WRONG?

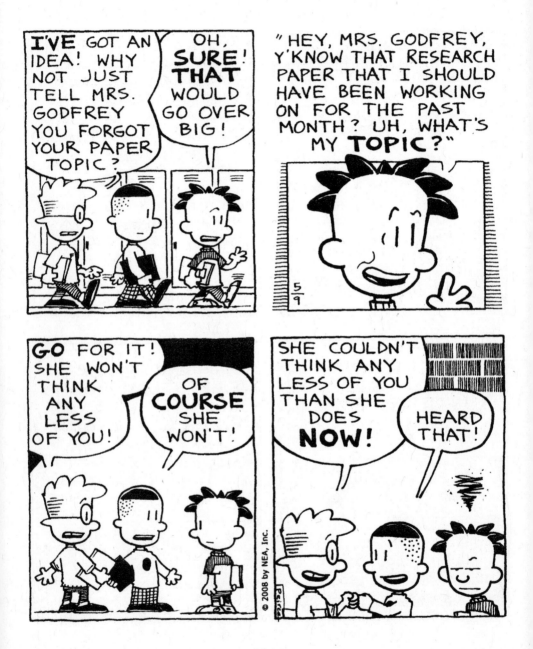

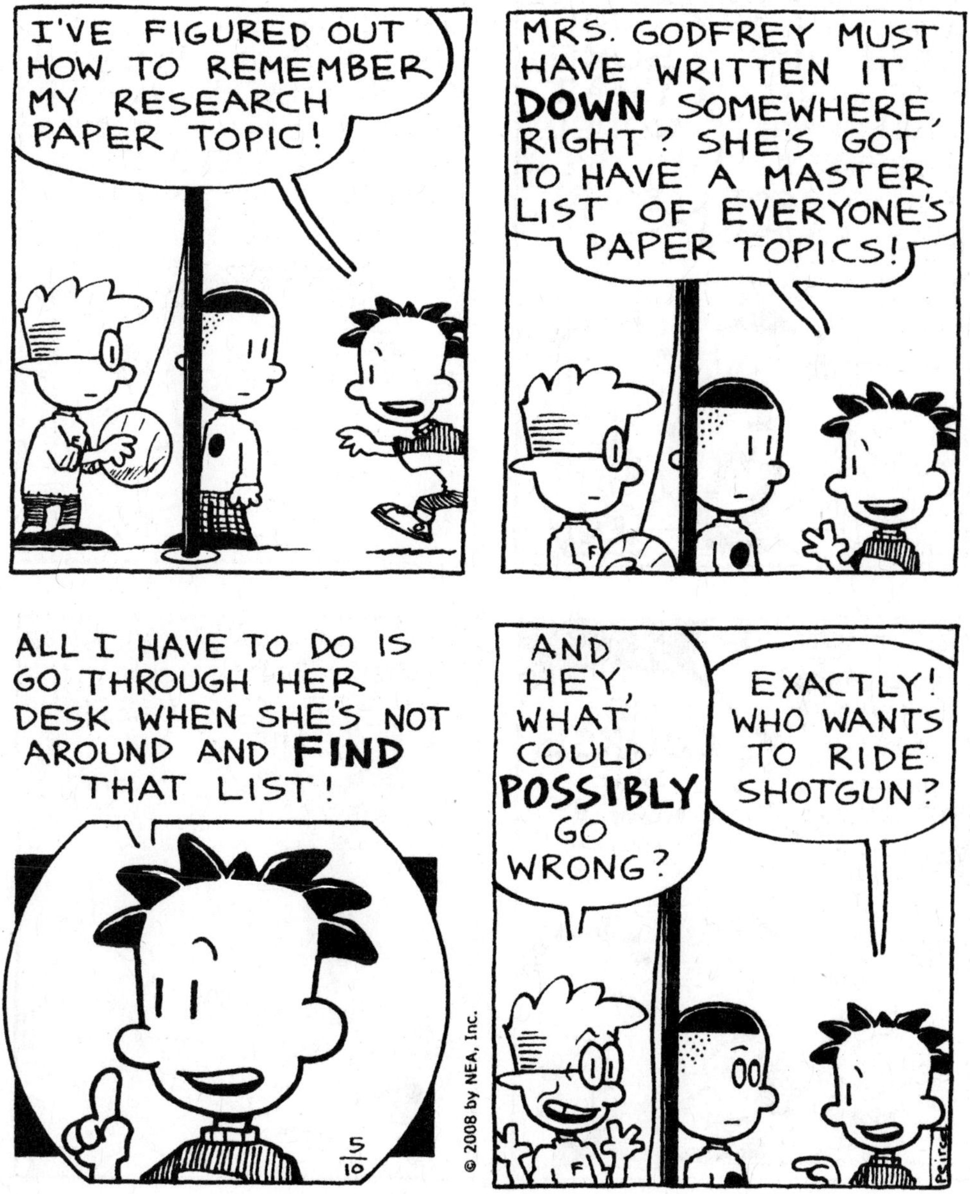
I'VE FIGURED OUT HOW TO REMEMBER MY RESEARCH PAPER TOPIC!
MRS. GODFREY MUST HAVE WRITTEN IT DOWN SOMEWHERE, RIGHT? SHE'S GOT TO HAVE A MASTER LIST OF EVERYONE'S PAPER TOPICS!
ALL I HAVE TO DO IS GO THROUGH HER DESK WHEN SHE'S NOT AROUND AND FIND THAT LIST!
AND HEY, WHAT COULD POSSIBLY GO WRONG?
EXACTLY! WHO WANTS TO RIDE SHOTGUN?
5/10
© 2008 by NEA, Inc.
Peirce

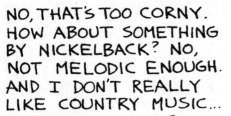

THE LIST

ROCKIN' OUT

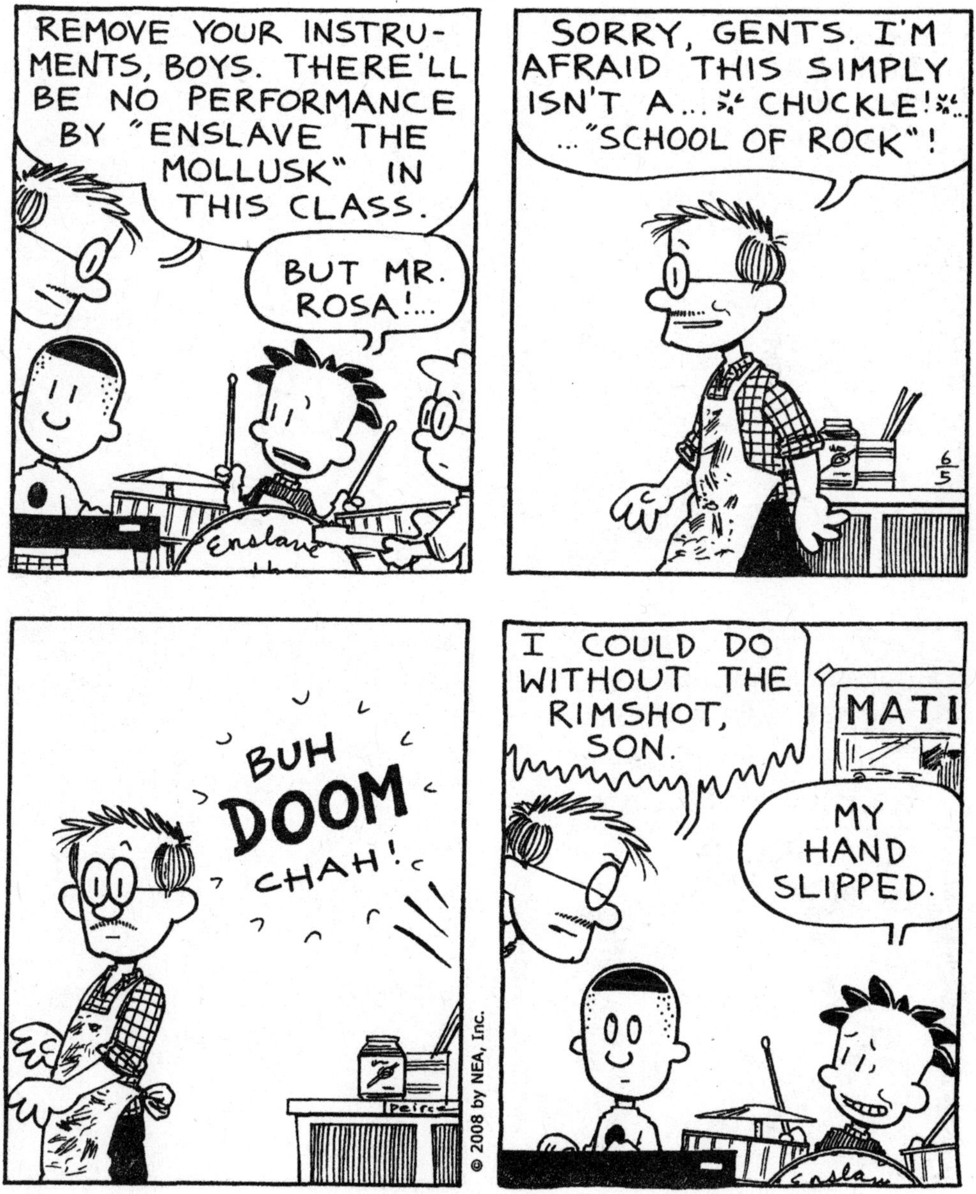
REMOVE YOUR INSTRUMENTS, BOYS. THERE'LL BE NO PERFORMANCE BY "ENSLAVE THE MOLLUSK" IN THIS CLASS.
BUT MR. ROSA!...
SORRY, GENTS. I'M AFRAID THIS SIMPLY ISN'T A... CHUCKLE! ...
..."SCHOOL OF ROCK"!
BUH
DOOM
CHAH!
I COULD DO WITHOUT THE RIMSHOT, SON.
MY HAND SLIPPED.
MATI
6/5
© 2008 by NEA, Inc.

STUCK ON NATE

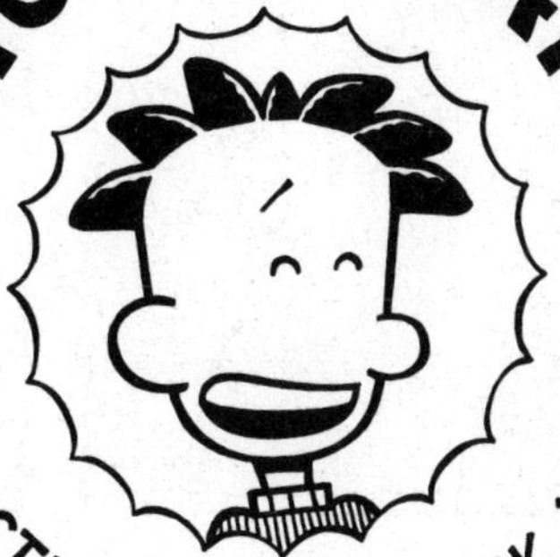

BONUS ACTIVITIES TO CRACK YOU UP!

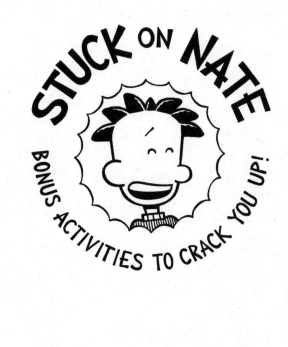

ALL MIXED UP

Can you match each of Nate's sketches to the correct strip?

SUPERCOOL CAPTIONS

Can you come up with captions for Nate's sketches?

SUPER CHALLENGE: Guess which sketch goes with the
Sunday comic strips on pages 49, 59, 112, 151:

Comic A goes on page _____.

Comic B goes on page _____.

Comic C goes on page _____.

Comic D goes on page _____.

NATE ≠ NEAT

Have you ever scrambled the letters in your name to see if they spell anything else? Well, **I** have. And guess what: **MY** letters spell **N·E·A·T!**

Pretty ironic, right? Hey, I realize I'm not exactly Joe Tidy. **EVERYBODY** knows it. But that doesn't stop Francis, who color-codes his underwear, from pointing it out about a jillion times a day.

Your desk is **DISGUSTING**. You have paint on your shirt. Oh, and you have Cheez Doodle stains all over your face. What a SLOB you are!

Francis has been telling me to clean up my act since I poured applesauce down his pants back in kindergarten. Of course, I've always ignored him. But then last week my sloppiness got Francis in trouble... and he **NEVER** gets in trouble!

I felt so bad about it, I decided to actually try to get neater. And thanks to Teddy and his uncle Pedro, the hypnotist, it's working... **TOO** well. All of the sudden, I'm starting to act **JUST LIKE FRANCIS!** Frankly, I think I'm losing my mind.

What a **MESS!**
Read all about it in
BIG NATE FLIPS OUT!!

Big Nate: What Could Possibly Go Wrong?
www.harpercollinschildrens.com
www.bignatebooks.com

Go to www.bignate.com to read the *Big Nate* comic strip.

Library of Congress catalog card number: 2011930716
ISBN 978-0-06-208694-5 (pbk.)

Typography by Andrea Vandergrift
19 20 21 CG/LSCH 20 19 18 17 16 15 14
❖
First Edition

Lincoln Peirce

(pronounced "purse") is a cartoonist/writer and *New York Times* bestselling author of the hilarious Big Nate book series (www.bignatebooks.com), now published in twenty-two countries worldwide. He is also the creator of the comic strip *Big Nate*, which appears in over two hundred and fifty U.S. newspapers and online daily at www.bignate.com. Lincoln's boyhood idol was Charles Schulz of *Peanuts* fame, but his main inspiration for Big Nate has always been his own experience as a sixth grader. Just like Nate, Lincoln loves comics, ice hockey, and Cheez Doodles (and dislikes cats, figure skating, and egg salad). His Big Nate books have been featured on *Good Morning America* and in *USA Today*, the *Washington Post*, and the *Boston Globe*. He has also written for Cartoon Network and Nickelodeon. Lincoln lives with his wife and two children in Portland, Maine.

NATE RATES ALL THE Big NATE BOOKS!

Grade: A+

Comments: I surpass all others!
How could you improve on that?

Grade: A+

Comments: Guess who wins
the face-off with Gina, my
all-time enemy?